Classified

Aella C Grey

The Book:

"You can bite me, Viper, but your venom has only made me crave more than you can give." — Orobas, Prince of Hell

Scarlett Ashford, a half-angel daevari, walks the fine line between light and shadow. As one of the Revenants—a top-secret unit of government assassins—she's dedicated her life to ridding the world of demons. But when she's assigned to infiltrate the home of a prince of hell and gather intel on a mysterious dagger, the predator becomes the hunted.

When her cover's blown, she finds herself at the mercy of Orobas, the crimson-eyed prince of hell himself—renowned for his manipulation magic and powerful political allies.

With a trail of blood and bone left in the Revenant's wake, will she uncover the truth before it's too late, or will her hands be forever stained with as much blood as their enemies?

Find out in Classified, the fifth and final book in the Prince of Hell series.

The Author:

Aella C Grey is an author hailing from Winnipeg, MB, Canada, currently residing in the sunny state of Florida. When she's not immersed in the world of writing, Aella indulges in her other passions, such as playing video games, diving into captivating books, and cherishing quality time with her beloved dog and supportive husband.

With a vivid imagination and a deep appreciation for storytelling, Aella brings her unique perspective to the realm of fiction. Her love for literature and interactive entertainment has fueled her creative endeavors, inspiring her to craft compelling narratives that transport readers to captivating worlds.

Aella's writing draws readers in with dynamic characters, intriguing plots, and a touch of magic. Whether she's exploring mystical realms or delving into the complexities of the human experience, her stories are infused with emotion, suspense, and a dash of the unexpected.

Stay connected with Aella C. Grey through her website to discover more about her upcoming works, behind-the-scenes insights, and to join her on thrilling literary adventures.

Classified

Prince of Hell V

by

Aella C Grey

Aella C Grey - Florida, USA

1. Edition, 2025
© 2025 All rights reserved.

Aella C Grey - Florida, USA

Table of Contents

Trigger warnings:

Anxiety, Alcohol, Battle Scenes, Blood & Injury Depictions, Character Death, Coercion, Cults, Death, Demons, Explosions, Gore, Genocide(mentioned), Gun Violence, Hostages, Hospitalization, Indoctrination, Kidnapping, Murder, Physical Abuse, Poison, Poverty, Post-Traumatic Stress Disorder, Profanity, Religion, Religious Trauma, Sexual Assault(mentioned), Secret Society, Sexually Explicit Scenes, Violence, War Themes

Author's Note

As I'm sure many of you have realized, the Prince of Hell and Unbroken series are linked. These series are part of a multiverse with some aspects oriented in the world we know, but there are many points throughout each of these series that you will be whisked away or that could alter your perception on religion, current events, etc.

The Prince of Hell series is and always was intended to **open the door** for or introduce my future series, Eclipsed Souls. I hope you have enjoyed meeting the princes and learning their stories along the way.

Thank you everyone for joining me on this journey.

Dedication

To everyone who has wondered whether the "good guys" were the true villains, or to those who maybe understood the bad guys perspectives a little too much...

This one is for you.

Glossary

There are multiple pronunciations for these words, especially given different dialects, so please see the phonetic pronunciation below as intended for this series.

Orobas (Oh-roh-bas), Scarlett(Skar-let), Ashford (Ash-for-d)
Maris (Mah-ris), Sylvara (Sill-vah-rah), Sitri (Sih-t-ree)
Caass (Cah-ss), Vassago (Vah-sah-go), Seir (See-er)
Balam (Ba-lahm), Paimon (Pay-mon), Nuiqsut (New-eeks-uh-t)
Thal (Tha-l), Druv (Dr-ew-v), Ishari (Ish-are-ee)
Varkoth (V-are-koth), Azrael (Az-ray-el)
Hylia (Hill-ee-ah), Ilvrost (ill-v-ross-t)
Arkhaios (Are-kay-oh-s), Aetheris (Ay-th-air-is)
Samael (Sam-eye-ell)

Reminder:

Servilia:
A realm that derives from book two of the Unbroken series, Light of Dawn

Servilian:
Non-human being that wields magic originally from the realm of Servilia

Prologue

Scarlett

It's been hours since they separated us from Evelyn.

With each of us bound, and no hope of slipping our restraints, all we can do is wait in this cramped room close to the warehouse we were tasked to infiltrate.

Not a single camera lines the ceiling, and no windows give any hint as to how much time has passed since we've been in here, but I'm certain it's been hours.

I don't know if they realized Eve's our leader, noticed that she's the veteran among us, or if they just got lucky. Either way, since they split us up and brought us to this room, we've been tight-lipped.

This isn't our first rodeo.

Our unit, the Revenants, consists of five assassins with different specializations dedicated to gathering intel, escorting high-profile clients undercover, or taking out opposing factions. For over fifteen years, we brought down countless demons who undermined our government.

And undermine God himself.

Even though we've killed more people in His name than we can count collectively, it's not all we're trained to do. Highly adept at torture, interrogation tactics, and countless other skills make us living, breathing weapons of destruction.

Grizz, nicknamed after the grizzly bear, received her namesake when she popped a man's skull between her thighs during training. That kind of brutal strength is admirable, really.

Messy, but admirable.

Omen got her nickname when we watched her take down an entire operation of fifteen demons by herself without sounding a single alarm. She earned the name because by the time they noticed her masked reflection in the glass; it was far too late and death was upon them.

Mako, named after one of the most aggressive sharks in the ocean, received her nickname when she killed three of the men training us because one got under her skin.

I really thought they'd punish her for it, but, surprisingly, they didn't mind deaths of their own.

If anything, I think it impressed them.

Evelyn, our unit leader and the Harbinger among us, is arguably our strongest fighter, but since we've yet to see her crack, she's kept her name this whole time.

Then there's me, Scarlett Ashford, more widely known as Viper. I'm one of two half-angel hybrids in the Revenants called daevari—the other being Eve. While I excel at striking hard and fast, I'm notorious for my use of poison-coated daggers as my choice of weapon.

Even though various government entities developed our skills from the time they took us off the streets as orphans, the poison training we received intrigued me the most. At first, we'd been simply taught how to spot them, but as with all things in life, I don't stick to the status quo.

I was fascinated and quickly incorporated all kinds into my arsenal. For this reason, I adopted the nickname.

I'd truly earned my namesake when one of the demonic assholes I was authorized to eliminate was beating the shit out of his wife while their child cried in the room down the hall. It was my first solo assignment when I turned seventeen, and I drew on every last ounce of rage in my body to become their embodiment of justice.

To stop the beating, I'd rung the doorbell a few times before finding my way to the kitchen door along the side of the house. The brute of a man had stopped assaulting his wife to check it out, and by the time he was in the doorway, peering outside to look for me, I was already waiting for him.

You see, rich assholes like him always have places to hide, and they think no one else can find them. This hideaway was near the kitchen, and it took nothing for me to keep the pantry door open wide. I'd dropped the ladle on the ceramic floor to make noise, knowing he'd investigate. Embarrassingly enough, the asshole grabbed the ladle rather than a knife in his search through the open hidden entryway.

I guess you can have lots of money, power and still be incredibly stupid. Either way, he didn't stand a chance.

By the time he creeped down the stairs into the hidden room, I'd snuck in behind him, shut the door without a sound, followed him down into the soundproof, insulated and climate controlled space.

I knew that we likely had at least three hours before his wife looked around for him. I spent two and a half bleeding him out while using some of my less common poisons—ones specially made for interrogation that cause unimaginable pain without bringing the target close to death.

What people don't realize is that most poisons that currently exist are in everyday items that all households use. They're just diluted and mixed with other chemicals, or used on our food before we consume it.

But there are some more discrete, top secret, and highly controlled but impossible to track poisons.

Mine is the latter. Specially curated in a lab by scientists who wanted to create the ultimate untraceable weapon of targeted destruction.

Sure, guns, swords, daggers and everything else get the job done, but they're messy and more often than not, innocent civilians are caught in the crossfire.

Not that I mind getting dirty, though. It's one of the many reasons the Revenants are so feared.

Ghosts on the wind. Wraiths and the Harbinger blend with shadows to take out the scores of demons who make this world a scarier place.

It's our sacred duty.

Footsteps fill the air before the heavy metal door creaks open, and a wiry male wearing full black steps inside with his dark irises surveying us. He bends forward, bracing his hands on his knees as he levels Grizz with his stare.

"Tell us what you know, and you'll be set free."

She leans forward slightly before spitting a wad of saliva at the man's feet. Her lip curls with disdain as she inches back, but faster than I can even register, he recoils and slaps her across the face.

Her head snaps to the side, pausing for a moment before she sneers. "You hit like a little bitch."

The male lunges forward just as the door behind him opens, freezing him in place as a tall male stands in the doorway. Glancing between the two, the power dynamic has suddenly shifted to the taller one, and I watch as the demon in front of Grizz straightens awkwardly.

Interesting.

"You think asking them nicely is gonna get you anywhere?" The taller demon says as he steps close to my feet, tilting his head to the side as the shorter male in front of Grizz smirks.

"Giving me the green light, Bash?"

The taller male–**Bash**–chuckles, taking a step closer before reaching behind my head. His fingers tug at the cloth in my mouth as the shorter man to my right slams his fist into Grizz's stomach.

I keep my attention on Bash, but still watch from my peripherals for any opening we might get as their interrogation begins. Though judging by the lack of questions, you could hardly call it that.

Bash tosses the cloth to the ground before bending down to sit on his own heel, resting his forearm on his thigh as he searches my face from a safe distance.

"You're not going to say a word, are you?" He muses, his eyebrows twitching upward as my dry mouth opens.

"Word." I say loudly, and the shorter man to my right freezes as Bash's jaw tenses.

Within seconds, he's laughing, almost too hard, and it takes a conscious effort not to let my guard down as I erect concrete walls in my mind.

They're nearly fully up when Bash surges forward, his fist balling into my hair as he yanks my head back. He's grabbed enough not to tear any out, but pain still radiates from my scalp, and I fight the urge to tilt my head back like he wants me to.

The sound of something hard slamming against Grizz's body rings out to my right repeatedly, but I don't dare to look. It's torture tactics 101 that they'll use the others to get us to crack.

"You think this is a game?" he whispers, glancing to my left where Mako and Omen sit, bound and gagged as they stare at the wall.

I look at him blankly, and a grin creeps across his expression. "John." *Of course his name would be John. **So** fucking basic.* "Bring that one to me and start on the others."

John grunts in response, and I see him haul Grizz's body over, slumping her to the floor alongside us before moving around to Mako.

Bash uses his other hand to force my chin to look at Grizz, giving me a warning glare as if I'll suffer the consequences for not looking.

So I do.

There's a fine line between avoiding their manipulation and buying time to find a way out of this shithole, and I've been taught to toe the line.

God himself knows they put us through enough torture training to identify it.

When my sights land on Grizz, bile rises in my throat. Blood pools around her, and it's obvious he wasn't only punching her earlier by the sheer volume of it.

She'll be lucky to last another five minutes without immediate medical attention, so she's basically as good as dead. The thought sends a wave of rage through me that I try but cannot rein in.

Even though they taught us not to bond too much to one another over the years, we never listened. Whether because of the trauma or the trust required that the others will have your back, I don't know, and don't really care.

We've been like sisters for years.

Bash's arm jerks high before the blade buries into her skull. The sound of metal against bone is one that I've heard far too many times, and the corners of my eyes burn.

"Whoops, sorry. Was she your friend?" Bash asks innocently, and I keep my gaze steady as my eyes find his.

I'm going to enjoy watching this fucking demon die.

He searches my face for any reaction, but I keep my features schooled as Grizz's blood seeps into the material of my pants. Within seconds, he surges to his feet, pacing to the desk against the wall.

I can already tell that whatever he's about to do is more than likely going to hurt, so I reinforce the mental walls of concrete in my mind. Layering brick upon brick, I let my thoughts go distant as John lays into Mako.

Bash turns around, and I see him gripping something in his hand as he grins. My gaze fixates on the wall behind him as he steps closer, and I hear the zap before it hits my abdomen.

My entire body spasms as sharp pain radiates from my core. Bash holds it in place against me as every muscle vibrates with strain. Pain jolts outward from the connection, and my breaths come in shallow as I focus on that.

Torture tactics 101, lesson two: breathing exercises are your friend.

Inhale. Exhale. Inhale. Exhale.

The connection severs, and I choke a ragged breath as John grabs something from the desk behind Bash. My blurred gaze flicks to where he adjusts the bat in his hand before turning to Bash again.

Bash's grin widens as he stares at me. "You sure you aren't ready to talk yet?"

My gaze flicks to Mako as John swings the metal bat full force into her torso, and she sputters blood outward.

I fight the urge to cringe—the crunch sound mixed with the amount of blood tells me she's broken some ribs.

When my eyes find Bash's, I want to rage at the excitement in them—to think I might concede to a fucking demon.

"What do you want to know?" I whisper, hearing John's bat crack against Mako's torso again. There's no way she's going to last much longer. The human body can only take so much.

If it were me or Eve, we'd fair better because we heal faster than the others, but not by much. The biggest difference between us is that daevari are almost immortal in lifespan.

"Tell me who gives your orders." Bash presses, thumbing the edge of the taser.

Mako slumps over in my peripheral, and my teeth clench as Bash sighs. "Suit yourself, then. Maybe another round will convince you."

He jerks his hand forward, this time bringing the taser into contact with the tender area between my neck and skull. Even with my mind walled off, my entire being is alight in the worst way. Electricity radiates down my spine as I'm locked in place, unable to move.

Bash withdraws the taser from my skin as the pain recedes, and I see John repeatedly slamming the bat into Omen's torso, with Mako motionless on the floor a couple of feet away.

Correction. *We're* not going to last much longer.

I'm not expecting Bash's punch as my head snaps to the side, and judging by the force behind it, I'm beginning to understand where he gets his name. Pain blooms in my cheek after the initial shock from the strike, and a metallic taste fills my mouth.

"Well, are you ready to talk, or should I end your misery like John did for your little friends?"

Light from the door brightens for a breath of a moment before disappearing, and when neither Bash nor John turns, a chuckle bubbles out of me.

Bash's eyes narrow, and John stops his assault on Omen to look at me. The nervousness in their expressions only makes me laugh harder, and I'm certain I must seem like I've lost my mind.

"The fuck is so funny?" Bash growls as Eve steps out from the shadows behind them, still fully unnoticed by both men.

She's covered in blood that I'm sure isn't hers, with only the whites of her eyes a contrast to the deep crimson on her skin.

To anyone else, it would be fucking terrifying.

But to me? That's the most beautiful sight I've seen all day.

The blade of her dagger catches the light, and I grin at Bash. "I hope you prayed to whatever god you revere today, demon, because you're about to meet him."

No sooner has the words left my lips when Eve strikes, burying her blade between his ribs to pierce his heart before withdrawing it in one fluid motion. She keeps her eyes on John as she twists and flicks the dagger in his direction, hurtling it through the air.

Faster than the blink of an eye, both men have been struck with critical blows, and Bash falls to the floor as John staggers to the side. A twisted sense of satisfaction comes over me as Eve steps up to John, and yanks the blade from his throat.

He sputters and chokes as blood sprays onto her, but she's hardly phased as she returns it to its sheath at her hip. She turns to me, her eyes traveling the length of my body. "Think you can walk?"

I nod. "Someone has to help you carry Omen out of here."

Eve's jaw tightens, and she glances from Grizz to Mako before moving to check their pulses. I don't have the heart to tell her they're dead, so I stay silent and let her figure it out herself.

We're all bound to die in this line of work, anyway. It's a matter of when, not if.

She falls still as she hovers over Mako with her fingers on the assassin's pulse point, and a long moment passes before she pushes to her feet.

"We'll call for a pickup at the rendezvous." She says as she bends down, and the ropes around my arms tug a couple of times before going slack. "No wonder you couldn't get out of that shit. They quadruple-bound you."

I huff a laugh. "Demonic assholes were too smart for their own good." Pushing to my feet with a wince, I glance at Omen. "Should we finish the mission before transporting her?"

Eve shakes her head in my periphery, and when I lock eyes with her, all I can see is the way her gaze goes distant. "No need. It's handled."

My brows shoot up. "What the hell does that mean?"

Intel said there were nearly a hundred hostiles within the warehouse, which is why we needed *all five* of us. This was a major base of operations for the demons.

She holds my gaze, and even though I know she's capable of destruction, to kill that many...

"All of them?" I ask, my eyes wide as she inclines her head. "Shit, Eve."

She shrugs and moves to kneel next to Omen. "It needed to be done."

I'm no stranger to death, and it's not that she killed people that's shocking to me, but to eliminate *that* many within the time we'd been split up.

Color me impressed. "Can I have your autograph?"

Her bloodied ponytail shifts back and forth as she shakes her head, and hauls Omen's limp body over her shoulder. "I'll sign your tits, but only if you get it tattooed."

"Fuck." I grumble. "You drive a hard bargain, but you have yourself a deal."

She straightens as Omen groans, and I move to the door to open it for her.

"Guess chivalry isn't dead after all."

"Consider it a small token of my appreciation." I chuckle, holding it open as she brushes past me.

"Dinner is on you tonight." She grunts, readjusting Omen atop her shoulder as we walk down the empty hallway toward the rendezvous point.

I offer her a lazy salute, wincing when my bruised face throbs. "Yes, Madame Harbinger."

A small token of appreciation is putting it lightly, if I'm being honest. Eve saved my life, and Omen's. I have no fucking idea how, but she did.

A morsel of guilt rifles through me as I replay the events that led up to this point, and I know I owe her ten times over since it was my fault our mission went sideways.

If she knows, she says nothing else as we continue forward, but I know that today, I found a new level of respect for the leader of the Revenants.

Chapter 1

Scarlett

A week and a half later...

Two minutes and fifty-eight seconds until we're out of here.

Command wasted no time sending us to a new assignment, even given the ongoing investigation into our last one.

I guess most of the demons Eve eliminated in the process of saving me and Omen were possible civilians, but there's no way she could have known that.

After the psych evaluation they'd ordered, I was nearly certain we'd be benched considering the nightmares I've had since it happened. But apparently that's not enough to warrant time off.

"Now," Eve whispers, and I surge from the shadows and around the corner. Seconds pass by before I slip through the open door into the office of some high-ranking demon.

The silver laptop in question sits perched neatly atop the metallic desk, with not a paper or pen out of place. In fact, it's so pristine in this room that if we hadn't been told this was an actively used office, I would have overlooked it.

I quickly unplug it and sling the thin bag over to shove the laptop inside. The charger is a typical nineteen-volt, so I don't bother packing it as I zip the bag closed. Sliding it onto my back again, I ease my way to the door and slip out.

Easiest snatch and grab of my life.

I hurry to the stairwell door around the corner, seeing Eve's tense expression as I grin. "Let's skedaddle."

She doesn't appear to relax any as she turns down the steps, and I follow in close. It's obvious that our last mission shook her, even though we've been taught not to give a fuck.

I don't have to be a rocket scientist to know that Eve takes her leadership seriously, and losing one of her Wraiths is worse than just losing a weapon.

We descend a flight of stairs with two more left, with the quiet sound of our footsteps fills the air.

It's not like our life expectancy is terribly long, but under Eve's leadership, the Revenants have had the best survival rate in the unit's history.

The Harbinger before Eve died after a year of service, and they promoted Eve as the most experienced Revenant. It's how our unit functions. Trainees become Wraiths if they don't die during the shit Command puts us through—and many die. Wraiths maintain their roles, with the most tenured of them taking the place as the new Harbinger.

The reason being that the life expectancy for a Harbinger has historically been less than a year with the missions they're sent on, which is likely why they didn't punish Eve for killing so many alleged civilians.

She did what she had to do to escape and save her unit.

Or at least what remained of us.

Now, they'll have to recruit and train replacements, but that will take time. With Omen in critical care, though, it'll just be Eve and me on group assignments for the foreseeable future.

Not that that's a bad thing.

I've always preferred missions with less noise to complicate matters, so now that the dynamic is just the two of us, I'm not complaining.

At the bottom of the stairwell, Eve opens the door a sliver to glance outside. She's surveys for a moment before she pushes it open, and we file into the brisk fall air.

The rest of the journey to our rendezvous is quiet as I scan for any hostiles apart from those we incapacitated on the way in, but there are none.

Nothing like a good, quick and easy mission to get back in the saddle.

~

By the time we're on base, Eve scans her wrist over a reader, and it chimes once when it registers the chip implanted beneath her skin.

A message flashes on the screen, and she sighs loudly in resignation.

"Guess you won't be bringing the laptop to Grant just yet." I whisper, and she shakes her head.

"It's always something." She retorts, and I stifle a laugh as she leads the way past the main entrance. It's not until we turn down the long hallway toward the administration offices that I notice the way Eve's hand has balled into a fist at her side.

Something in my gut twists at her nerves being so clearly on display.

In the years I've worked with Eve, she's always been a vault, but that's expected considering how they source trainees. I know Eve wasn't recruited as an orphaned child like the rest of us, but she's lived and breathed for command since I'd known her.

She told me once how they'd cleansed her of her sins, and offered to train her to join a special operations team. But it doesn't make sense that they'd punish her now for doing what they taught her to do.

They expunged the record of her killing the assailant who tried to murder her in her own quarters, so why wouldn't they look the other way now?

She comes to a stop in front of a small office, and blows out a breath. "Let me do the talking." She whispers inaudibly, and I glance over at her.

She's staring at the closed door, but the tension in how she holds herself sends a shiver through me as I nod. "Say less. Understood."

Whatever has her shaken, I'll be ready for it. Command might employ me, but this woman saved my life. I'm as indebted—if not more—to her than I am to Command.

Without another word, she knocks twice, waits two seconds and pushes the door open. We stride in and come to a stop in front of a wide desk with a speaker in the center.

My arms clasp behind my back, with my shoulders squared, mirroring Eve's stance, and her voice is steady as it fills the air.

"Revenants stand ready at your request, Commander."

Command consists of at least six high-ranking government officials that we know of. Commanders Vale, Redd, Knox, Holt, Kell, and Ward.

Rumor has it that Commander Vale is the highest ranking and most decorated of them, which is why he gives us our orders, but we've never actually had any face-to-face interaction with them.

My gaze travels the room, and I don't see a single camera in view as the speaker clicks.

"I trust everything went according to plan?" The gravelly voice on the other end fills the air, and I see Eve nod once.

"Yes, sir."

"Good. We received word roughly an hour ago that demon organizations in several states have mobilized. Whether this is due to them realizing they've been infiltrated or another reason, we'll know once we gain access to that laptop. Once Major Allen learns its contents, I expect a full report. Until then, we need eyes on the ground. Harbinger, you're to remain on station and help retrieve information off the tech. Wraith, you've been assigned a new mission."

My stomach twists, and adrenaline pumps hard in my veins. There's a light feeling surging through my body that I always get with a new solo mission, and I nod once.

"Yes sir. I'm ready to go at your command."

The gravelly voice lowers to a chuckle. "Always eager for a fight, aren't you, Viper?"

My lips twitch. "These demons never know what hits them." I see Eve's jaw tense in my periphery to my left, and mentally step back from saying anything more.

"You likely won't be killing anyone on this mission unless it is absolutely necessary, Viper. You're going to be planted undercover as part of a cleaning crew to infiltrate their organization and gather intel. The sooner Major Allen can break into the laptop, the sooner your mission ends."

My brows shoot up, and I'm absolutely certain they have a hidden camera in the room when the commander laughs under his breath. "Not your usual detail, I know, but you've always flown beneath the radar. I assume this will be no different. You'll have an encrypted file sent to you to review in your room, along with a uniform to wear. We specially made it to conceal a single dagger, but nothing more, so don't get ahead of yourself."

He says that like I couldn't kill someone with a paper clip.

"Revenants, you're dismissed."

"Sir." We both say in unison, turning on our heels to file out of the room.

When the door closes behind us, Eve holds her hand out. "I'll bring the laptop to Grant so you can rest and review the file."

"Thanks, Eve." I murmur, already knowing she'd offer like always, so I shrug the pack off and hand it over to her. "This mission will be done in no time. I'm sure of it."

She grabs my wrist gently, and my gaze snaps to hers. "Be careful,

Scarlett." She says, keeping her voice low. "These demons are dangerous. If you get into trouble—"

"I won't." Letting out a sigh, I resign myself to placating her anxiety. "I'll be careful. I promise."

She searches my face with her chestnut-brown eyes and nods. "Be safe, Viper." She says, releasing my arm to slide the bag over her arm.

Tossing her a wink that I'm certain will infuriate her, I grin and walk backward in the opposite direction. "See ya later, alligator." I say loudly, peering over my shoulder at her.

The last thing I see is her shaking her head before she turns to walk toward Grant's office, and I twist to continue to my quarters.

The thought of getting an undercover solo assignment sends a wave of excitement over me, and I feel it echoed in the way my speed picks up.

Secret identities aren't my strongest point unless it's a party or some kind of event where there's a bunch of people. Eve and Mako always took on smaller, more intimate undercover missions because they focused a lot on the details for that type of work.

Still, this is a change, and I welcome the chance to draw demon blood in His honor.

Solo mission, here I come.

Chapter 2

Evelyn

"Knock, knock." I announce loudly and my knuckles rap three times on the door in a pattern only Grant would know.

Seconds pass with no movement, so I key the pin he'd shared with me into the touchpad, and swing the door open, only to find it empty.

The faint smell of fresh coffee and cologne greets me as I scan over the three computer desks covered with paperwork. Tangled and disorganized cords run from the outlets along the baseboards.

Various tools and knick-knacks, coffee mugs, empty paper cups, and other items, spread across the desks, suggest Grant still spends an exorbitant amount of time in here.

I've known the cyber warfare specialist for the entire duration that I've been working for command, and he's always been a quick worker with cracking into devices we find.

I can't imagine it'll take long for him to jailbreak this one, which I couldn't be more grateful for considering Scarlett's solo mission.

A year ago he'd cracked into one and uncovered coordinates for a ritual sacrifice—not that he should have told me about it—but command didn't make any moves on it. Instead, they raided another warehouse of illegal arms being imported.

I'll never forgive them for not choosing to act back then.

Crossing the room to one of the empty chairs, I ease into it, pulling the bag in front of my chest, and exhale a long breath. My mind wanders to Scarlett, and I choke down my building concern for her.

This isn't her first solo mission, but damn if I don't always get heartburn every time command sends her on one. Fortunately, over the years I've been with the Revenants, I've been able to infiltrate most of the solo missions the Wraiths were assigned.

A power outage here, a distraction there. All of it helped keep them safe.

I won't say it's the reason we lasted this long without new recruits, but it certainly has helped.

A tiny screwdriver sits beside me on the desk, and I reach over to pick it up, mindlessly twirling it in my fingers.

It's even harder to keep myself from intervening in Scarlett's mission, considering the fact that Mako and Grizz are dead.

I will atone for their losses for as long as I live.

Because once the demons situated me across the warehouse, it had taken me fifteen minutes to slip my bindings and kill the bastards that had separated me from the others. It took another hour and thirty to clear the mission while searching for the rest of the unit.

I'd foolishly thought they'd torture them for information, and that I'd have more time.

So much for that.

A heavy blanket of guilt twists my gut, and the bloodied image of my Wraiths on the ground sends bile up my throat.

We shouldn't have lost them.

I should have found them first.

The screwdriver slips from my hand and clatters to the floor just as the bathroom door opens, and a towering form appears. Grant's taller than the majority of men by all counts, and his bright blue eyes are so vibrant that most people ask him if he's wearing contacts when they first meet him.

Or maybe that was just me.

Today, his long dark brown hair is thick and lusciously soft looking, not styled with gel like it usually is, and in place of his typical cargo uniform is a white undershirt that's tucked into his pants.

For a computer tech nerd, he's tall, dark and handsome—not to mention surprisingly more muscular than most would expect.

Sure, everyone here works out, so it wasn't hard to tell he was decently fit with his uniform on. I had the biggest crush on him when I first met him when I joined the Revenants... which in all honestly feels like a lifetime ago.

Grant and I have a complicated relationship, to put it mildly.

Our duties demand so much that while we get these moments here and there, there's no way we'd truly be able to commit to each other.

The first time we'd kissed was when he'd helped me with a hand-to-hand combat training technique when I'd joined. Command had sent me to Grant's office to retrieve new gear he'd created for night vision.

I'd been on the verge of being eliminated from the Revenants, because I'd failed every grapple during training. One move always ended up with me on my back.

That week, Grant spent an entire six hours teaching me, and when I finally beat him, with my body on top of his on his office floor, panting triumphantly, I was so excited that I'd kissed him without thinking.

Something with Grant has always been that way. Natural, like breathing.

He's like the deep breath taken after a long rest, which expands your lungs and makes your heart pound.

I have spent years looking forward to that feeling. Yet each time I see his handsome grin and expressive eyes, it's like the first. And if I thought he was attractive every time I'd seen him before this...

Now? Well. Fuck.

His eyes widen until he realizes it's me, and his surprise turns into a broad grin. "Fancy seeing you here, Eve."

The reminder of what this visit cost me and the Revenants suddenly comes rushing back, and I swallow against the lump in my throat.

"Can't seem to stay away." I say dryly. "Command sent this over for you to work your magic. Again."

He raises a thick brow, but I don't miss the way he glances down my body before settling his gaze on the bag. He groans. "Another one?"

"Yep." I say, leaning back and crossing my legs. "This one was fucking expensive, though. So there better be something worthwhile on here, or I'll have half a mind to hunt down every fucking demon in this plane of existence and take them out myself."

He steps closer with his brow furrowed. "Expensive? What do you mean? What happened?"

That's when I regret having said anything.

My gaze drops to the floor, and my pulse picks up. "A week ago we took out a warehouse full of demons to find the fucking coordinates for this laptop. During that mission, Grizz and Mako didn't make it, and Omen is in critical condition."

"Fuck."

My teeth grind together. The admission tightens my throat as tears sting the corners of my eyes.

"I'm sorry, Eve." Grant's voice is agonizingly soft, and I can't stand it. Not when it's my fucking fault they're dead.

Shaking my head, I push to my feet, ready to take the nearest fucking exit and return to my room where I can curl up in the shower and disassociate for the next three hours.

It's only when Grant steps in front of me with his hand curling around my arm that I stop in my tracks.

"Nuh-uh." He tuts, pulling me into his arms. "You're not leaving here like that."

My spine's stiff until he's encircled my shoulders—only then do I return the embrace, burying my head in his collar. The tears burning my eyes finally fall onto Grant's white shirt, and I shudder as the rest pour freely.

It's a selfish feeling to have someone holding me while I mourn the deaths of two incredible human women. Strong, resilient, deadly, but like the rest of us—expendable.

Death will find us eventually in this line of work, but it'd been so long since a Revenant was killed, we'd gotten sloppy. Turnover had been monthly or yearly before the five of us worked together. Now we'll have to bring in two more Wraiths and pray to God we all mesh.

I'd secretly hoped that we'd never see an end to our group. We'd exceeded all expectations between the five of us, but I guess that was our downfall.

All good things must come to an end someday.

He holds me for what feels like an eternity, his arms tightening whenever a tremor works its way through me. By the time I pull back, my tears have all but dried, and he gently wipes them from my cheeks.

"It wasn't your fault, Eve." He whispers, and I shake my head, blinking to fight the tears threatening to return.

"You don't even know what happened."

He gives me a look, as if he doesn't need to know the details to know the risk of our missions. "Do you want to talk about it?"

"Not a chance." I say with a dry laugh. "I'd rather drink myself into a stupor."

"Ah," he says with a sad grin, turning me toward his desk and walking me to it. "Well, lucky for you, I always keep enough liquor for two."

"I should have known you were a sinful influence." I muse, sliding into the chair again, and he cuts me a joking glare.

"That's odd; I seem to remember Jesus turning water to wine." He offers, reaching over to grab his bottle of scotch. "Besides, unless you're planning to tell anyone..."

I laugh under my breath and shake my head as he pulls two glasses out from his desk. "You're impossible."

He tugs the corked cap off and pours us each a generous portion, sliding one to me. "I mean it, though. It wasn't your fault."

Swirling the dark liquid, I release a tense breath. I shouldn't be discussing this with him, but it's not like he isn't already in our business with our missions.

Instinctively, I glance around the ceiling for cameras.

"Swept the room this morning." He says softly, reminding me like he does every time I see him. "You can speak freely here, Eve."

Taking a swig of scotch, the fruity notes and hint of vanilla burst on my tongue before the aftertaste sends a shiver through me. "How do we know what we're doing is making a difference, Grant?"

He leans forward in his chair, resting his forearms against his knees with his glass held in both hands. Bright blue eyes peer at me from beneath thick, dark lashes as he considers my question.

"Do you feel like it is?"

I frown, swallowing another burning sip of scotch. "After two incredibly talented humans just died? No."

He grimaces. "We'll all die someday, Eve. Are you saying their deaths were in vain?"

Swirling the dark liquid in my glass, I feel the lump in my throat grow. "Nothing is changing for the better. If anything, shit has been increasingly worse year over year. The number of demons we see on missions has tripled. They're using civilians as cover. I fear we're losing this battle."

A long moment passes, and when I look at Grant, he's throwing back the rest of his drink. His throat bobs as he swallows, and I track the movement before he sets his glass on the desk.

"I can't tell you whether it's making a difference, Eve. But what I can tell you is that you should trust your instincts. You're the best damn Revenant I've seen, and one hell of a leader to those women. You can't steer yourself or them wrong."

The look on his face is so certain, it's hard not to believe him.

I consider for a moment all the times I infiltrated the others' missions, and how many would have gone sideways had I not been there to nudge them in the right direction.

Guess there's a point to what he's saying after all.

I throw back the small amount of remaining scotch, and set the glass onto the table beside his.

"Thank you for this." I whisper, watching as he slides the laptop in front of him. "I owe you one."

His head tilts to the side, and he grins. "I'll cash in what I'm owed at some point."

That earns him a quiet laugh, and I gesture to the laptop that he inspects and flips open. "Do you enjoy what you do here?"

Grant pauses. He shrugs as he maneuvers it around, plugging in cords and typing every now and again. "Enjoy is a loose term for it. I can see and control more than I would in any other position, without catching too much attention," he looks at me pointedly. "Unlike someone I know."

I roll my eyes. "Yeah, yeah. Sue me."

"Still, what I do might have some small impact now, but someday, I think it will pay off. And I feel every day like that payoff is approaching sooner than the last."

"Do they ever let you out of this room?" I ask, biting back a smile and failing. Considering the state of his office, I'd say no.

Grant, however, just looks at me with a mischievous grin. "Wouldn't matter if they didn't. Nobody *lets* me do anything. I do what I please, Eve. I'd suggest you do the same."

"Then we'll both be in the doghouse together." I toss back, pushing to my feet. He glances over, watching me as I smooth the wrinkle in the thick black Kevlar material of my suit.

"Wouldn't want to be anywhere else."

My brows twitch upward, and I look at him over my shoulder just in time for him to wink. My cheeks burn, but he's right back to work, so I aim for the door.

"Careful, Major Allen." I warn, waving my hand over my head lazily. "The last thing we need is to speak that into existence."

Chapter 3

Scarlett

Carrying the box of clothes left in front of my quarters, I key in the pin to my room, and the door beeps once in acceptance.

Undercover assignments aren't my favorite thing, but if it means I get a solo mission, I'm all in. Anything to dig up information on these demonic assholes and keep myself distracted.

The door clicks shut behind me, and I place the box of clothes on the dresser, seeing the screen above it with the envelope icon flashing.

Here goes nothing.

I scan my fingerprint and input the pin before pulling it up, feeling nervous excitement simmering inside of me.

Cover name: Nora Lynn

Cover job title: Housekeeper/Maid

Cover employer: Glensborough Cleaning Services LLC

My eyes stare at the start date and location as another surge of excitement rifles through me.

I thought I'd have more time to prepare, but I suppose twelve hours is enough since it's local. I can always fake it until I make it. It's just cleaning, right? How hard can it be to seem like I know what the hell I'm doing?

My gaze travels down to the layout of the property—which isn't much, two floors, four towers, twenty-eight rooms on the first floor, twenty on the second—before landing on the persons of interest.

Orobas, Prince of Hell.

The next section outlines the various ways he's undermined the government's efforts politically, even citing that he's used manipulation magic to convince political figures to do his organization's bidding. Various names of senators and other politicians are mentioned before describing how they suddenly changed their political careers into ones radically opposed to the government's decisions.

The description details the shift's negative impact on civilians, leading to riots with deaths and imprisonment as my teeth grind.

What kind of asshole makes other people do their dirty work?

Manipulative coward.

Cover duty: Gather intel to identify the location of government property. The stolen relic in question is a four-pound, five-ounce, solid gold dagger forged by the angel of death, Azrael. The dagger contains a detailed inscription etched into the surface, and two rubies inlaid into the hilt. In the event of recovery of the stolen relic, immediately meet at the rendezvous stated below by any means necessary. All intel must be communicated as quickly as possible to command, with no exceptions and no delay.

Warning: Under no circumstances should this relic be used as a weapon. Recover with utmost caution.

My brow raises, but I reread the duty to memorize the description before turning the page to see a photo labelled as the person of interest.

His deep red eyes, like two molten embers staring into the camera, are the first thing I notice, and a shiver works its way down my spine. Something about them makes the hairs at the back of my neck stand up, like just looking at his photo is enough to tell me he's bad news.

Tattoos peer out from the collar of his black suit, and his dark hair falls on either side of his face, from his cheeks to the base of his neck. Beyond looking like a mafia boss, he's unfortunately conventionally attractive, and the bad guy appearance only adds to that allure.

Leave it to me to have a toxic taste in men, I guess.

Lord, forgive me.

Closing the email, I release a sigh and open the box to prepare for tomorrow with anticipation building in my body. Seeing a slim fit black dress with white ruffling embroidered into it, I blink.

You've got to be kidding me.

The uniform is a *literal* maid outfit?

Rolling my eyes at how cliché it is, I set it aside before rummaging through the rest of the box. The provided dagger is tiny, and clips along my hip under the seam of my dress, but the two-inch heels are narrow enough that I could use them for weapons if needed.

Tugging the outfit on to make sure it fits, I turn to the mirror and smooth it out along the length of my body. The hem sits halfway up my thigh, with the bodice a slim fit.

Tearing the dress off and setting it aside, I move to research the basics about professional housekeeping.

Solo mission, here I come.

~

"Thanks for coming on such short notice, Nora." Linda, the owner of Glensborough Cleaning Services, gives me a tight smile as she passes a bag full of various cleaning items over. "Thank God for your staffing agency reaching out, because I worried I'd have to fill the position myself, and I just don't have the time or energy for that."

I smile sweetly at the older woman. "I'm glad I could help, Ms. Linda. Anything I should know before I head over?"

"They've got security around the front gate that shouldn't give you any problems, but if they do, just call me." I nod as she continues. "We rotate cleaning sections of the house on different days, and the kitchen staff will provide lunch at one o'clock."

I nod again, offering a warm smile as she hands over the key card for the front gate in case the guards aren't there. "That all sounds easy enough."

"We include a fifty-dollar weekly gas rebate in your wage, so if you exceed that, it's at your cost." She grunts, waving me off dismissively. "Now get on the road before you're late."

My lips twitch. "Yes, ma'am. Thank you."

She grumbles about being called 'ma'am' as I stride to the driver's side and climb in, turning the key in the ignition as the compact sedan's engine rumbles to life.

The GPS leads me closer to the large estate on the outskirts of town, and every minute that passes I spend repeating the details of the mission in my head over and over.

Orobas' picture is seared into my mind from how much I reviewed the file. He's the only wildcard of this assignment that makes me on edge. Not because he's the head of this organization, but due to his ability to manipulate people.

I'll have to be very careful if I run into him.

All too soon, I'm pulling off the main road onto a well-paved driveway, coming to a stop in front of the gate where two guards stand. One glances at the cleaning supplies in the car before murmuring into a radio at his shoulder, and the gate slowly swings open inch by inch as I spot two cameras on either side.

Sneaking in and out won't be possible, but I'm sure there must be another side entrance. Worst-case scenario, I can scale the fence that lines the property in a pinch.

Easing on the gas, the estate has a gothic, baroque architectural style with peaks that stretch into the sky. The trees surrounding it obscure it from view from the street, with enormous pines reaching mere feet taller than the towers.

The building is impressive, and I'm certain from the length of the property that it stretches further back than I can imagine.

Knowing the possibility that the relic could be here sends a thrill down my spine, and I follow the doorman's gesture, bringing the car to a stop along the side of the house.

The gate is a seventy-yard stretch to the front entrance, and judging by the cameras above the door, there's a low chance if push comes to shove I'll be able to escape unharmed.

The few windows I can see have ledges I can use if I need to climb up or down, but who knows whether they actually open.

By the looks of it, they don't.

Pretty, but not functional.

I climb out as the guard walks toward the vehicle.

Long dark hair flows past his shoulders, blending into the black t-shirt and cargo pants he wears. His hard gaze lingers on me for a second too long before flicking to the car, and I know he's looking at the supplies jammed into the back seat.

"Good morning." I smile warmly, opening the side door to pull the bag out. Linda said the vacuums and mops stay at the house, so only the provided rags and specialty cleaners are hauled to and from, making this an easier transition.

"Morning." He says as his eyes narrow on me. "You're not the usual girl. What happened to Melanie?"

I blink at him and shrug. "No idea. Linda said I needed to take over for her. You can call her if you want."

The guard's jaw muscle ticks, and he shakes his head. "No, it's fine. Just make sure you're thorough. Melanie did a good job."

I nod, keeping my features warm and inviting. "I'll have to do an even better job than her, I guess." His brows twitch up as I let out a laugh. "A little friendly competition never hurt job security."

He offers his hand between us. "I'll park it in the garage until you're done."

Shit. There goes another escape plan option.

Placing the keys in his palm, his fingers brush mine, and I fight the urge to recoil as he shakes my other hand gently with his.

"My name is Thal. Druv is inside and can show you where Melanie kept everything."

The moment he releases my hand, I clasp mine together. "Thanks. I'm Nora."

I know it's probably all in my head, but I want to tear the skin off my palm. Having spent my entire life killing demons to save humans from their influence, these hands are made to hurt them, not for gentle touches and exchanged pleasantries.

Thal gestures inside, and I breeze past him, eager to put space between us.

I really need to get a grip, and fast.

This shouldn't be an arduous task. If they were human, I wouldn't be having such a problem with showing up on good terms.

A rock the size of a large boulder settles in the pit of my stomach as I think of Mako and Grizz.

For now, until I find this relic, I can pretend they're human.

And then maybe, just maybe, I'll kill them all.

Chapter 4

Scarlett

It's been three days, and there's been no sign of the relic or Orobas.

My nightmares have gotten worse, and I've been running on less than an hour of sleep per night because of it. The lack of rest has stunted my healing too, with the deep incision from Bash's dagger taking longer than expected.

It doesn't help that every night I thrash in my sleep and tear open the wound again.

Pulling up alongside the house as Thal walks over nonchalantly, I climb out and grab my bag from the back before handing him the keys.

"Morning, Nora."

I yawn and give him a lazy wave. "Morning, Thal."

"Stayed up too late partying?" He offers with a raised brow, and I shake my head.

"Afraid not—the partying life is not for me." When both his brows shoot up, he lets out a laugh, and I add. "I don't drink much, and I'm not exactly sociable."

I mostly say it to shut down conversation, and it seems to have the intended effect as he shrugs, positioning himself at the door to the driver's seat. "Could've fooled me."

I roll my eyes and turn to the front door, hearing him laugh as I walk inside. Footsteps carry in the air from both up and downstairs, and I file the increase in activity away for later as Druv grins from the hallway across the room.

"You're late."

"No, I'm just not *early*."

"Exactly. You're late."

My eyes narrow at him, and he laughs. "We have company today. Can you start in the boardrooms and offices first?"

I nod and smile. "Sure. Anything else I should prioritize or be aware of?"

Druv's head shakes, and his long hair shifts from side to side. "Nothing of importance. Let me know if you need me, Nora."

Thal and Druv both seem to be in particularly good spirits today. The suspicion that something big is about to happen hangs over me as I make my way to retrieve the cleaning supplies.

I hear two pairs of footsteps coming down the stairs as I leave the closet with a vacuum in tow. When I finally close the door, I turn, seeing two men standing mere feet before me.

One is tall, with longer, dark hair that's pulled back to keep it from his face and blue eyes like the sky on a clear day. He's dressed in business casual clothes, which is a stark contrast to the suit the man beside him is wearing. I quickly cast my gaze downward as my lungs seize.

Orobas.

The first man was intimidating, but Orobas' presence *suffocates*, like someone had sucked all the oxygen from the air before I could breathe it in.

His deep-crimson eyes are a contrast to the smirk on his face as he looks at the man next to him. My heart thrashes and his expression turns more serious as he follows his companion's gaze, and those blood-red irises land on me.

That's when I stop breathing in earnest.

The picture didn't do him justice, and I glance between the two before realizing my place.

Clearing my throat awkwardly, I tug the vacuum behind me as I step aside. "I'm so sorry, I'm in your way, aren't I?" My gaze remains trained on the opposite wall before it drops.

Shit. Smooth move, Scarlett. Real smooth.

When neither of the men budges, I chance a look at them, only to find Orobas' brows furrowed as he watches me, and my gaze drops once more.

"Where's Melanie?" His deep tenor is smooth, and my heart thunders as I shake my head.

"I'm not sure. Linda said she can answer any questions you might have, though."

Something about his presence has shaken me more than any other mission I've done, and I'm hanging on by a thread not to compromise it before it starts.

"I see. Well, I hope she's okay." He says cautiously, and I nod. "And who might you be?"

My mouth drops open, and I suck in a breath. "Forgive my manners. My name is Nora Lynn."

Orobas' gaze lingers on me for a moment as the man beside him grins. "Fortunately, you're speaking to two people who also know little about manners. My name is Pai, and this is Oro. It's a pleasure to meet you, Nora."

I offer a small smile as my heart thunders. "The pleasure is all mine. I didn't mean to interrupt you both, but I need to return to work."

"Ah, of course. Thank you, Nora." Pai smiles, but the way Orobas is distantly looking at me sends warning signals off in my mind.

What if he knows?

Shit.

Nope, don't even go there.

Orobas snaps out of whatever daze he was in and his brows furrow as he looks at Pai, but I don't linger to eavesdrop as my feet carry me down the long hallway to the boardroom on the first floor.

I'm tempted to simply do my job as the housekeeper, but as I get to dusting and wiping down each surface, I know that I still have an assignment.

My actual job.

Fuck.

I walk into an empty boardroom and shut the door behind me before letting out a tense breath.

Next time we meet will be better, and I'll be more prepared.

My pulse finally calms, and I clean the first room. Each wooden surface and fixture is spotless by the time I'm done, with a bright lemon scent filling the air from the cleansing agent as I haul everything out the door and head to the office three doors down.

It's as empty as the next four before hauling the cleaning supplies into the offices upstairs. Even being in the best shape of my life, I still feel a deep ache in certain parts of my back and shoulders that gives me a newfound respect for people who do this daily.

Melanie had to have been a fit goddess.

Hell, maybe I need to incorporate some of this into my routine to build up the muscles used for it.

Setting my bag aside, I start in the first office on the second floor, dusting and wiping down surfaces that were already arguably clean. It doesn't take long for me to approach the desk, and when I see a gold box sitting atop it, I freeze.

It's big enough to fit a small dagger, and it's intricately made in a way that makes it look like it holds something important. The inscriptions along it aren't anything I've ever seen before, and I step quietly to the center of the desk with a cloth and spray as my heart rate spikes.

Could this be it?

My fingers brush the gold wooden surface, and I tilt the lid with my heart in my throat.

The box is empty with nothing more than a silken lining, and I jolt when the door behind me creaks. My pulse hammers in my chest, and I lightly shut the box, grabbing the cloth beside it and pretending to wipe it down like I didn't hear the door. Setting the box aside to clean beneath it, I pace around to the side of the desk, putting distance between me and the box.

When I see a black suit in my peripherals, my heart thrums loud in my ears, and I offer Orobas a polite smile. "I didn't hear you come in. Apologies if I'm in your way yet again."

Orobas' eyes remain glued to me as his lips twitch. "So you didn't." He strides forward, and I step back to let him pass. "If anyone is in the way, it's me."

He eases into the chair and opens his laptop, typing away as I hesitate.

I don't want him to suspect I'm snooping by being eager to clean behind him, but I also don't want to miss out on the opportunity.

What a fucking conundrum.

He pauses, and his eyes flick to mine. "Is something wrong, Nora?"

Hearing my fake name seems to snap me back into reality, and I huff an awkward laugh. "Ah, I'm sorry. No, I just didn't know if you wanted me to clean around you or return later."

When I gesture to the chair and desk, his lips tug upward, and he leans back as amusement paints his features. "Feel free to clean around me."

Realizing I should have done so to begin with, he watches me intently as I wipe down the top of his desk before repeating the same action along the sides. Whenever I straighten and glance over, his attention remains fixed on me, and by the time I finish the desk, I turn to the chair with my heart in my throat.

When I don't say anything right away, he tilts his head to the side. "Do you need something?"

I feel out of breath, and my gaze drops to the chair. "I need to dust the chair."

The humor hasn't dissipated from his expression, and he gestures openly. "Go ahead."

When my eyes widen, he stifles a laugh and waits, so I swallow my nerves and incline my head. "Suit yourself."

Starting with the top of the chair, I make my way down the left side, and when I get to his arm, I don't hesitate. My fingers slide under his forearm, lifting with one hand while I drag the cloth down the armrest.

Why the hell is his arm so fucking heavy?

His lips twitch as I let it dry off before gently setting his arm back down. The amount of pleasure he's getting from how uncomfortable I am makes me want to rage, and I swallow my nerves.

He's a demon who enjoys cruelty. Don't let him get to you, Scarlett.

I don't bother walking to the other side of his desk, and instead I straighten to my full height, and stretch over where he sits to reach the top of the wooden chair.

I chance a look at him, only to find his crimson eyes already fixed on me, and my chest is mere inches from his face as I drag the cloth along the edge of the chair. Gently raising his other arm, I feel his gaze burning into my skin as I wipe the armrest beneath before easing his arm back down.

Straightening again, he's still watching me but this time with a guarded look.

Shit. Did I blow my cover?

"Did I do something wrong?" I ask, knowing that is what someone would say if they received this kind of look and weren't undercover.

Orobas shakes his head. "Not at all, Nora."

"Great." I breathe, moving to the credenza behind his desk. "I'll be out of your way in a moment, then."

He types away at his laptop as I finish cleaning, and I'm about to walk past his desk when his hand raises, halting me in place.

"All done?"

My eyes meet his, and I nod once. "Yes, sir."

He gestures to the box on his desk, and I feel the blood drain from my face. "Were you looking for something earlier or just curious?"

My mouth drops open, and my heart hammers in my chest. "Curious. My mother always told me I was too nosy for my own good."

It's more of a half-truth since it was Evelyn who said it originally, but it's true, nonetheless.

Pushing off the chair, he walks around to the front of the desk and picks up the golden box. "Would you like to know what this was designed to hold?"

I feel like I'm walking headfirst into a trap, but I already said I'm too curious for my own good, so I nod.

"Two of my brothers created this box, one who specially provided the wood; you see, this is not oak nor spruce, nor any native tree to this land for that matter."

When he sees me frown, he chuckles. "How much do you know of the realm of Servilia?"

More than I'll ever admit. "Not much."

He offers the box between us, and I take it, noting the weight to be lighter than expected, like wood. When my eyes widen, he laughs again.

"Servilia has a tree that grows in their land called hylia ilvrost. There is only one known place on Earth where you can find it, and it sprung up years and years ago, but it's highly guarded, so gathering enough for a box this size was quite the task."

I frown at him. "You mean to tell me that there's a giant golden tree somewhere that no one talks about?"

Realizing I let my persona slip, my mouth snaps shut, and his face lights up as he smiles.

"That is precisely what I'm telling you. Hylia ilvrost are not of this world. Why would the government want to remind everyone that stronger forces exist?"

Feeling a lump in my throat, I nod as I open the box. Orobas steps in close, his suit brushes my arm, and my pulse stutters in response to his proximity.

I really am playing with fire right now.

"Do you see these markings?" He reaches to point to the one under my finger, and the contact makes my stomach flip over itself as I nod.

"Another one of my brothers did these because the item this box is intended to carry is so powerful that it could reap the soul of every living being within five miles."

My eyes widen as my head snaps toward him. "Five miles?"

He laughs under his breath, and I shove my annoyance at it down. "If not, more. You see, having been created by the angel of death himself, it has the ability to end lives at horrifically destructive rates, which is why our enemies seek it out. But thankfully, these markings are there to keep the dagger from getting into the wrong hands."

The dagger.

Shit.

I frown and feign ignorance as I look at the empty box. "If it's so dangerous, where is it?"

He takes the box from me, his expression unreadable as he reaches inside, and when he withdraws his hand, my eyes widen at the golden dagger with rubies inlaid in the hilt.

Oh my god.

"It dis—"

His words all of a sudden make sense, and my gaze flicks to his as I take a cautious step back.

He places the dagger in the box and shuts it, stepping in close as I continue to retreat. "Your name isn't Nora, is it?"

My heart thunders in my chest as he tosses the box with thought-less precision, and it clatters onto the desk.

"Whatever you're thinking, you're—"

"Wrong? Is this the moment you tell me that my assessment that you're not a real housekeeper is incorrect? That you didn't have the box open earlier and that the magic protecting it is a farce?"

"I—"

"No lies." He growls, his crimson irises searching my face as my heel hits the wall. He pauses a mere foot away. "What's your name?"

My chest heaves, and I glance past his shoulder toward the door.

"Even if you try, you won't get far. What is your *real* name?"

He takes another step closer, placing his hands on either side of my head.

"Scarlett." I whisper as I lean back, and my right hand tugs the dagger under my dress free. Within seconds, I've dropped an inch and lashed out with it, but Orobas moves with unexpected speed as he dodges the strike.

Grabbing my wrists, he slams me back into the wall with a thud, using his thigh to block my knees. His crimson gaze searches my face without a hint of anger.

I adjust the dagger in my hand before flicking it at his head, and he dodges that too.

When it slams into the wood loudly, his eyes are wide as they rise to meet mine. "I suppose I should have seen that coming."

He's strong for a demon, and I push against his grip on my wrist, but he doesn't budge no matter how I twist or yank.

"So, you made me. Now what will you do, demon? Slit my throat and be done with it?"

Memories of Bash and John threaten to come flooding back, but I shove them away with force.

No, if I'm going to die, it'll be on my terms.

Orobas tilts his head to study me, and my teeth grind together. "Contrary to popular opinion, I really don't care for needless murder. That said, I can't have you wandering freely and risk the lives of people in my home."

He brings my wrists together and grips them with one large hand, using the other to pull out his phone.

"You're making a phone call?" He shushes me, and I roll my eyes, still trying to free myself from his vice-like grip. "Unbelievable."

"Mind bringing some rope to my office on the second floor?" He glances between my arms and my torso. "About four feet. Thanks." The demon slides his phone back into his pocket and takes one look at my unimpressed expression. "Just remember, you're the one who came into *my* home with ill intentions."

"I didn't have ill intentions." I bite back, even though I know he's right.

I'm not about to admit that to the demonic asshole.

He gives me a deadpan look. "The box doesn't lie, Scarlett. If your intentions were pure, you would have seen the box and wouldn't have looked inside." His eyes narrow on me. "Did you kill Melanie?"

I scoff. "Oh, please. I don't even know who Melanie was."

"Then how did you just so happen to take her place when she mysteriously disappeared after *years* of employment?"

The door opens, and I gape at him. "I don't fucking know, why don't you ask one of your demonic minions if they killed her!"

Pai steps over with a handful of ropes. "Do I even want to know?"

Anger flashes across Orobas' face, and a lick of terror runs down my spine. "No one here would have harmed a hair on Melanie's head. Yours, on the other hand, might be up for grabs."

He spins me around until I'm facing the wall, and he tugs my arms behind my back tightly. "Forgive me, Scarlett."

"A demon asking for forgiveness—that's rich."

"Need me for anything else, Oro?" Pai asks lightheartedly, and I fucking wish I had stabbed them both earlier when I had the chance.

"No," Orobas answers, and Pai whistles as his footsteps retreat to the hallway.

With my arms pulled tight behind my back, the rope cinched at my elbows and wrists. My breathing picks up, and I fight the urge to disassociate, retreating to the safety of my mind. Lack of sleep and my nightmares have made recovery nearly impossible to battle the flashbacks to that night when Grizz and Mako died.

The rope tightens almost painfully, but I hardly register it as he turns me around. "There. Threat somewhat neutralized."

When I don't say anything, he sighs. "Do you have any pets, Scarlett? Any little ones?"

When I stay silent, he searches my face, albeit impatiently. "I need to know if you have a pet or child that requires care in your absence. If you don't answer, I'm going to assume you don't, and you'll remain here for the foreseeable future with no one tending to them."

His words reach my ears, but with my frayed nerves, how hard it is to breathe and the ache in my shoulders, I couldn't respond if I wanted to.

My mouth remains glued shut, and he sighs again with more force this time. "Right. Well, it's nearly lunch. I'll call them to bring food up while I work." He glances around thoughtfully. "And perhaps a second chair."

I frown as he leaves me standing there near the wall and takes a step back. "Right, well. You can't leave the room, but you're free to move around as you wish."

My brow raises, and I lean back against the wall, watching as he retreats to the chair, pulling his phone from his pocket. He dials a number and places the cell to his ear. After a few seconds, he laughs quietly.

God, I fucking hate his stupid fucking smile.

"Yes, but bring a second plate, please, and a spare chair. Thank you."

My eyes travel to the ceiling, and I trace the lines until the door to the room swings open. Druv's hauling a chair in alongside a woman carrying two plates, and when his eyes land on me, they widen.

"Oh, shit." He murmurs. "Don't tell me you killed Melanie."

I sigh. "I didn't fucking touch Melanie."

"Good." He grunts, setting the chair down beside me. "Cause I'd have to kill you if you did."

I scoff and roll my eyes. "Demon and vigilante justice? What a combination!"

"Better than an assassin and a housemaid." Orobas muses from behind his desk, and my teeth grind together.

The more inept they think I am, the more likely they are to let their guard down, so this could work in my favor.

As long as my ego will let their jabs go.

Chapter 5

Scarlett

One of the kitchen staff who brought lunch places the plates on Orobas' desk as Druv sets the chair down beside the demon prince, and I swallow.

I suppose keeping me at arm's length makes sense.

When he saunters over to stand in front of me, he just leans in and grins. "Not so tough now, are ya?"

Tilting my head, I toss him a saccharine smile. "Untie me, and I'll show you."

His eyes narrow as his hand wraps around my bicep, and he pulls me to the chair. "You sure you don't want her locked in one of the offices?" He offers, and I slide into the seat with a huff.

Orobas shakes his head in my peripherals, and my eyes gravitate to him as he pushes his plate closer. "And do exactly what she wants by leaving her alone to find a way to escape—or worse—kill every person in this house? No, she's going to stay here while I figure out who she is, who she works for, and what they want with the dagger."

My mouth goes dry at the thought of him torturing the information out of me. I lean further back in my chair, ignoring the ache that radiates down my arms as Druv walks toward the open door, giving us a shrug.

"Suit yourself. Just don't come whining to me when she drives you crazy."

Orobas laughs under his breath as Druv disappears down the hall, and I stare at the open door as the demon's fork and knife scrape the plate.

As much as this is possibly the worst-case scenario, it's the better end of it. I know where the dagger is, having seen it with my own eyes, and even though Orobas caught me like a fish out of water, I'm not dead yet.

And I still have a job to do.

By the sounds of it, he doesn't have a plan to murder me right away, which I can use to my advantage.

My mind wanders to Eve, and I can't help the wave of shame that washes over me.

She'd beat my ass until next Tuesday if she knew I blew my cover so easily.

Somehow, Orobas knew I'd opened the box, even though I'm certain I'd heard him and closed it in time. Which leaves two scenarios—he must have cameras or an ability that helped him figure me out so easily.

While both are possible, I'd wager it's the latter.

His chair beside me creaks, and I'm dragged to the present as my eyes slide to him. I blink at the sight of him reaching over with a piece of roasted carrot impaled at the end of his fork.

When I don't move, he gestures the utensil closer, pressing the warm carrot against my lips.

"I'm not fond of starving guests nor prisoners. Eat, Scarlett." Our eyes meet, and he raises an eyebrow. "Open your mouth."

Years of training tell me not to accept anything a captor gives you, but at this point I don't think I have much of a choice. If I refuse it, he becomes pissed, and I either starve or he beats me to shit. If I eat it, he feels in control; I maintain my strength and possibly get poisoned.

I can feel his crimson eyes locked onto me as my mind wars with itself, and I start to wonder if he's used his abilities on me.

What if he can hear thoughts? Shit.

All of this considered, I think I established that he doesn't want me dead yet, so my lips part, letting him slide the carrot between my teeth.

His eyes drop to the fork as he pulls it out, and my teeth scrape metal before he jabs a piece of meat.

"If you untie me, I can feed myself, you know."

Orobas raises a brow, but shakes his head as he lifts a slice of meat to my lips. He says nothing, but watches intently as I take the food from the fork and chew slowly.

By the time my plate is clear, he still hasn't said a word, and he returns to finish his own.

I sit in silence, watching as he slides his laptop closer to type on it. His brows furrow as his fingers fly over the keyboard, and my gaze wanders to the rest of him.

Before I'd avoided looking at him too closely so I could focus on the task at hand or not tip him off, but now with nothing better to do, I study the visible part of his inked skin more freely.

The long locks of dark hair that fall to his cheekbones, framing his face almost perfectly, with shorter stubble that lines his jaw. His deep crimson eyes flick to me from beneath dark lashes, and I feel my pulse spike.

Movement in the corner of my eye catches my attention, and I recognize the woman from the kitchen approaches to retrieve the dishes. When she moves to grab the plate closest to me, the fork slides off the edge, clattering to the ground, and it lands against my foot.

She looks down before raising her eyes to mine, and I know she's wondering if I'm too dangerous even when bound like this.

The answer in this situation is yes, but I won't give them that much insight.

After Bash beat me senseless and Omen almost died, I kicked myself for not relying on my legs more when faced with death.

Although, looking back, there's a chance that if I had, I would have been killed by Bash or John before Eve could show up, anyway.

I shudder.

The woman inches forward, but freezes when Orobas pushes his chair out from the desk. "I'd rather not risk death over a fork."

He bends, grasping the utensil between his fingers, and my foot juts out to knock it from his grip as it clatters toward her. He pauses, tilting his head slightly to bring his gaze to mine.

"Oops. Muscle spasm, sorry." I whisper with a suppressed grin, and he sighs as the woman reaches down to grab it.

"We'll be going now." She says, her voice trembling, before she hurries out the door with her two counterparts in tow.

Orobas doesn't look at her as she exits, but instead keeps his burning gaze fixed onto me as if trying to decide whether he should lock me up or beat me.

Honestly, I'd prefer either to this. At least those options would make sense.

His phone rings in his pocket, and he pushes to his feet before answering it. "Sitri, now isn't a good—" He pauses, and my gaze gravitates to the way his jaw feathers. "I'll call you when I know more."

The call ends as he slides his phone into his pocket and slams his laptop shut. He leans back in his chair and goes silent, zoning out for a moment, with his thumb rubbing his jawline.

The longer he sits there, staring into the space in the center of the room, the more I start to wonder if he's lost it.

Whatever that call was, it wasn't good news, but he doesn't seem to be **doing** anything with it.

I swallow, and the sound must have been louder than I thought because his eyes snap to where I sit.

"You doing alright there, demon?" I ask, and his brow just raises in response.

"Are you afraid of heights?"

I blink at him. "Only if you intend to throw me from them."

Stepping over, his large hand encircles my bicep, and he tugs me to my feet. "Don't give me any ideas."

His grip isn't painful on my arm as he leads me from the room, but the bindings have made my fingers numb, so I flex them to get my blood flowing.

We turn left in the hallway, away from the stairs toward the back of the enormous property, passing countless rooms I hadn't gotten to explore yet. His grip on me becomes more firm as he slows to a stop, and I follow suit as he opens a door to a stairwell.

The dual towers I saw from the front of the building come to mind, and I can't help but wonder if he plans to lock me in them.

It would be one of his less intelligent decisions, but better for me in the long run.

"Planning to turn me into a princess and lock me away?" I ask, glancing to my right as we scale the steep staircase.

His crimson irises catch the light, but he says nothing as we venture higher. By the time we're in the doorway at the top, I know if I try to climb my way down from here, it'd take me a while.

The small room at the top holds only a desk, and I turn to look at Orobas with furrowed brows. "I didn't seriously want you to throw me from the towers."

His lips twitch. "I did not come here for that."

I watch as he grasps two pillows from beside the desk and places them on the ground.

"Sit."

Glancing hesitantly between him and the pillows, I obey, swallowing my nerves at the still-fresh memory of sitting before Bash and John.

Orobas moves to sit beside me, leaning back against the wall to my right. I mirror his actions, and my forearms brush the surface behind me.

The wind howls all around, and every so often a creak in the wall breaks the silence. My gaze gravitates to where Orobas is, his head tilted to the ceiling with his lids closed.

If he weren't a demon and a prince of hell, he might actually look peaceful.

My attention drops to where his chest peeks out from the open collar of his shirt, and I watch his inked skin rise and fall. Soon, it moves in time with the gales of wind, and I find myself entranced as I anticipate each inhale and exhale.

I'm not sure how much time has passed when he sucks in a breath. "Is the word relaxation foreign to you?"

"Relaxation and being tightly bound are not two things I'd imagine go together."

His crimson eyes crack open at my sarcasm, focusing on my arms before they meet mine. "They go together."

It takes a long moment to realize what he's insinuating, and my cheeks warm. "Why are we up here, anyway?"

He turns his gaze to the ceiling. "It's the only place I can think properly without distractions."

When his eyes flutter shut, I last all of twenty seconds before I break the silence between us.

"What's so important that you need to hide away in a dark corner of this enormous property to think?"

Orobas' crimson eyes peer out from beneath his dark lashes. "If this is your attempt at prying, you're not very sneaky."

I huff a laugh. "Shucks. And here I thought I was going to acquire damning information from such a deeply personal question."

Being honest with myself, I'm not sure why I even asked considering that I know he won't willfully give away anything of use, but it's better than nothing, I guess.

When he stays quiet, my eyes slide shut, and I release a tense breath.

"How much did they tell you?"

My eyes snap open to where he sits with his head still upturned to the ceiling. "I don't know who you're referring to."

He grins, and his tongue grazes the sharp end of his canine. "Whoever hired you to steal the dagger."

My brow raises. "Who said anyone hired me? For all you know, I could be a crazy stalker."

He laughs—actually laughs—and I stare at him with wide eyes.

"Why don't you tell me what you know about me thus far?"

An unexpected scoff escapes me that nearly comes out as a snort. "Assume I know nothing."

"Clearly, you knew enough to be afraid of me when you first saw me."

My eyes widen, and the smirk on his face only hits my ego even harder. "I was *not* afraid."

"If you knew who I was, you should have been."

"Why? Because you're a big bad demon who will kill me without a second thought?"

His crimson gaze burns into mine. "Perhaps, but I don't believe it was fear of death I saw in your eyes."

My teeth grind together, and as much as I want to deny it, sometimes you can gain truth by offering some. Telling him the nugget of what I know without divulging everything can't be that bad.

"The moment I saw you, I–" I hesitate, feeling slightly insane that I'm about to say this out loud. "I was worried that you'd manipulate me."

His brows shoot up, but to my surprise, he nods thoughtfully. "I guess you wouldn't believe me if I told you that my powers are not ones of manipulation, would you?"

There's no way that command would have lied to me about his abilities. "You'd expect me to believe that?"

Orobas shrugs. "Believe what you wish, doesn't change the fact that I loathe those who take free will away from people."

The look I give him says I'm entirely unconvinced, and he just laughs as he shakes his head. He tilts his chin to the ceiling before releasing a sigh. "Father forbid you make your own mistakes instead of blaming Samael for them, right?"

"Great. I give you truth, and you mock me for it." His eyes remain glued to the ceiling as his gaze becomes distant. "I guess that shouldn't surprise me." I murmur, but he doesn't seem to hear me.

One long moment turns into two, then four, and by the time half a minute has passed, he blinks, straightening as something flashes across his face.

When he looks at me, there's a hint of urgency in his crimson irises that I don't miss. "We need to leave."

Chapter 6

Scarlett

With my arm firmly in his grip, Orobas leads us to the other side of the building at a quick pace. After he jerks me to the right and into an empty room, I can't stop the huff that escapes me.

"What the hell are we rushing for?"

He walks over to the counter and grasps a small amulet from the table to his right. "It's about to be even more empty."

Murmuring as his tightened fist, something in the center of the room catches my eye. A shimmering portal appears, it's sheer before solidifying into a holographic visage of an office.

Rippling from top to bottom, I swallow against the lump forming in my throat. "What the hell is this?"

When my gaze flicks to his, I see a hint of amusement in his expression before he gestures to it. "What does it look like?" His voice is thick with sarcasm, and I just blink at him.

"Uh, I have no clue."

"It's a portal." He says, and my jaw slackens, which only makes him grin more. "I don't know about you, but I'd rather not fly six hours to handle something small."

"And I need to join you through said portal?" My voice comes out more shrill than intended, but I can't move past the fact that he just summoned a freaking *portal*.

It's cool and horrifying at the same time.

Glancing around the room, he raises a brow. "Well, I'm not about to leave you here, so yes."

Before I can respond, his grip tightens on my arm, and he pulls me forward. With my eyes squeezed shut, it feels like a layer of silk against my skin. It's not dissimilar to walking through a doorway of water.

When it disappears from my back, my eyes snap open to what must be a private office. The oak desk in the center has papers strewn across the top, with tall shelving units crowded with various books.

Orobas' tall form breezes past me to the desk, picking up a folder and shoving the amulet in his internal coat pocket.

He turns to me, placing his hand on my chest as a wave of warmth ripples over my skin. "You won't be seen or heard when we leave this room, so don't bother trying."

A shiver runs down my spine, and my teeth grind together. "Why keep me bound then?"

He raises a brow at me like I should know the answer before his eyes flick down my body. "I rather prefer you like this." He murmurs, and when his gaze meets mine once more, he shrugs. "That, and I know you'd try to murder me the moment I unbind you. Now, come."

He strides past me to the door and gestures for me to follow as I roll my eyes. The action is mostly performative, and a stark contrast to the surprise I choked down at his words.

Since meeting him, he has yet to torture or bribe me, which is exactly what I expected him to do. He hasn't even done so much as threaten me to get information.

All the threats made have been me taunting him.

Obediently, I follow him to the door, and he swings it open, taking long strides into a short hallway. The glass walls on either side of me stretch to the end, and I survey the two large offices to my right before turning to the boardroom.

When Dennis Tildman, one of the best-known and most progressive politicians in the country, comes into my field of view, excitement makes my stomach do somersaults.

Little does Orobas know, silent observation is my favorite.

Even more when it's with high-profile targets.

Orobas strides past me with confidence, walking through the open doorway as Dennis pushes to his feet, fixing his suit jacket as he straightens.

"Ah, Oro. You're just in time." Dennis's face is flushed as he steps around the corner of the table to shake Orobas's hand.

"That seems to be a recurring theme, doesn't it?" Orobas' voice drops another octave, and I suppress a shiver as I watch both men shake hands.

Stepping around to the other side of the table from where Orobas stands, I get a good look at the two men greeting one another. The way Orobas holds himself makes him seem impossibly taller than he already is as he gives Dennis a small smile.

"I'm certain at this point you're the only thing preventing me from going fully grey."

Orobas laughs under his breath. "True, but the bald spot at the top of your head even I couldn't prevent."

Dennis blows out a breath, feigning exasperation as he tilts his head down, his fingertips gingerly touching his full crown of brunette hair speckled with grey. "Balding my ass." He breathes as he straightens once more.

They both laugh, and Orobas places his hands inside his pockets. "Care to explain what wolves are at your door now?"

The humor on Dennis' face falls, and he leans over to his laptop. He clicks around a couple of times before turning it toward us. "See for yourself."

On the screen, an article with the header "Dennis Tildman; The Real National Threat" reads in extra large, bold letters. Dennis's eyes linger on it for a moment before they return to the demon as if waiting for a reaction.

When Orobas doesn't show any, I see Dennis' jaw clench, and the perspiration on his temple tells me he's clearly nervous, so it must hold some kind of truth.

"You're worried about that? It's just an article written by some low-grade press." Orobas tilts his head as he speaks, and I note the ease in his body language, which is such a stark contrast to the tension of the politician in front of him.

Dennis scoffs. "Yeah, except that some of my emails were leaked, and now the press is yelling that I'm corrupt. They're trying to say that I'm working with and being funded by terrorists. Protestors were outside my daughter's school, Orobas. *My daughter*."

Orobas pulls one hand from his pocket to rub his jaw thoughtfully. "I see."

"Someone who works for me has betrayed me, Oro, and my family is being targeted—" Dennis cuts off abruptly as Orobas puts his palm out to interrupt him.

"Your daughter will be fine, but we will need to draw out and expose the rat." His crimson eyes drift to where I stand. "It seems our enemies are becoming more bold and the sooner we can drive them out of their nest, the better."

Is he talking about me? I'm the rat?

I should have killed him when I had the chance.

Dennis sighs. "And how do you suggest we drive the rats out? I don't have time for an investigation."

"We don't need one." Orobas says with a grin. "You have that fundraising event tomorrow night, right?"

My gaze lingers on Dennis as his brows pull together. "Yeah, what about it?"

"You'll have most of your team there. I'm going to attend. With each person you introduce me to, we'll tell them something different.

To one, I'll be a member of foreign interest, or an advisor for your offshore accounts."

Before Orobas can continue, Dennis' eyes widen, and he lets out a dry laugh. "You think my old mind can remember all of your fake career choices?"

Orobas grins. "Write them down then, either way; by the end of the week we'll uncover who your rat is."

Dennis blows out a breath and throws himself into his chair. "And my daughter?" The weariness in his eyes is a clear sign that this has been the major stress of the whole situation, and Orobas must know it as he nods his head.

"I can send some of my men to monitor the school, or she can stay on my property, which would be infinitely much more secure."

My brows shoot up, and my head snaps toward him. Did he really just offer to have his demons watch a child?

No fucking way.

I can tell Orobas noticed my reaction with the way his eyes nearly flicked to where I stand, but he keeps his focus on the politician in front of him.

"She's already missed so much school because of me, I don't think she can afford to be pulled out without being held back a year." Dennis murmurs, but I didn't miss the way his voice cracked.

"Then I will plant my men around the school for protection, have her picked up and dropped off, as well as a teacher's aid in her classes."

He would do that for a single child? What about all the others that die all the time?

Selfish asshole, wanting to do something that'll benefit him.

Dennis nods, and the pained look dissipates from his expression. "Alright. But if **anything** happens to her—"

"Nothing will."

"But if something does, I'll kill you and every damn demon who let her get hurt."

Orobas inclines his head. "I wouldn't respect you if you said anything different." He says and clicks his tongue. "Is that all you needed from me?"

My eyes narrow at the prince of hell.

Dennis looks hesitant but nods. "The supplemental legislation we introduced to require religious organizations to have oversight into their operations; it's at risk of being held up in the Senate. We need five more votes."

Orobas rubs his jaw, and I notice his gaze becomes distant for a moment before he nods. "We'll get them." He murmurs, leaning down to type into the laptop.

The keys clatter as his fingers fly across them, and a minute later he leans back, giving me a sidelong glance. His expression is guarded, and he fixes his attention on Dennis.

"Here's how. Expose it in the next week and a half." He turns the laptop toward Dennis, and I watch the politician pale.

"This is—"

"I know." Orobas says, his voice hardly more than a whisper. "There's a chance they'll lose re-election, but this is how it must be."

A long moment passes as Dennis stares at the screen, blowing out a breath when he looks away.

"Alright then." Dennis whispers, pushing to his feet and offering his hand to Orobas. "I'll see you tomorrow night. Will you be bringing anyone with you?"

Orobas nods, and a hint of amusement graces his features. "Possibly. It'll have to be a surprise."

The politician's brows shoot up, but he doesn't ask as the prince of hell takes slow steps toward the open door.

"I'll see you tomorrow, Dennis. Get some sleep."

I follow the prince of hell down the hallway, and he holds the door to the private office open. Each step I take past his tall form sends a nervous shiver through me until I'm in the center of the room.

The door clicks shut, and I feel the material of his suit against my arm as he moves to stand beside me.

"So he knows you're a demon?"

Orobas' holds the amulet up, murmuring into it as the shimmering portal appears before us. His fingers curl around my arm, and he leads me through it as the silken barrier washes over me.

When the empty room of Orobas' property comes into view, he places the amulet on the table and turns to face me.

"He does."

My eyes narrow at his minimal response. "And he's just okay with that?"

The prince gestures for me to follow and walks away. "Originally he was upset as most humans are, but with his position he's seen enough that it didn't take long for him to come around."

"So you manipulated him."

Orobas shakes his head. "Believe it or not, there are worse beings than me that walk this earth, Scarlett."

I nearly scoff. "Or not."

He stops, turning to look at me with his eyes burning bright. "Tell me, Scarlett, are you so blind to ignore your own actions and *your* part in the death of what, hundreds? Thousands? How many have you killed in your profession, *Scarlett*?"

My eyes widen, and even though his presence is intimidating, his prodding hits a nerve I didn't know existed. It's not the number of lives I've taken that bothers me by any means, but how *dare* he compare us.

"We are not the same." I chew out, and he laughs.

I want nothing more than to beat the humor out of him.

"No, no. You're right; we aren't. I am not disillusioned about the strife I cause and the choices I make, but you? You willingly take lives for what? Honor and glory?" He drawls.

Something in me snaps, and I know he's got me.

I know it, but I can't stop myself.

"Honor and glory? How about survival?" I snarl. "Every single one of the lives I've taken, the assholes command assigned me to, were pieces of shit. I saw their files and witnessed the greed, the abuse, the terror they caused. I am not blinded by honor or glory but bound by my sacred duty to do the right thing!"

He searches my face, and his eyes narrow. "You know nothing. You've **seen** nothing."

"Bullshit." I growl, stepping in close as my arms flex against my restraints. "I've seen some of the best people I know lose their lives to your kind, and I vowed I would kill every last one of you. I've been so close to death I could see it clawing at the corners of my vision, all because of demons like you."

He tilts his head, and a flash of understanding crosses his features. "You're being manipulated, Scarlett, whether you know it or not, and I can help you, but you have to be willing to see what is right in front of you."

I scoff. "You can't fake what I've seen with my own eyes."

"Give me one example."

"Why, so you can—"

"Now."

The commanding tenor in his voice sends a shiver down my spine, and he steps in close until we're chest to chest. "You want truth? You want honesty about what I'm doing? What I'm planning and plotting? You tell me an example of something irrefutable, Scarlett, and I will tell you **anything** you want to know."

He's lying. This is just another trick to convince me to talk, but I'm so worked up that purely out of frustration, I bite.

"Henley Corporation had a series of warehouses where demons were importing illegal arms, funneling them through the southern border. My team was to investigate and take out hostiles, while finding the location of an item of interest, but we were caught. They killed half of our team, but we still finished the job. Ten million in imported weapons was impounded and taken out of street distribution."

He laughs under his breath. "Henley Corporation. I'm damned."

"You think this is a joke?" I chew out, and his crimson gaze burns into mine.

"The joke is that you believed that outcome. Have you looked into Henley since?"

He can't be saying what I think he is, can he...?

Orobas must see the answer written on my face as he holds the amulet up once more. "I'll show you then."

The portal reappears with a murmur, and Orobas pulls me through it before I can object.

The dim light brightens the main area of a warehouse full of boxes and crates. Stairs at the back of the large room lead to a hallway with doors at the end. The space is not dissimilar to the one Grizz and Mako died in, and my heart thunders in my ears.

Too soon. It's way too soon for me to be back here.

With blood raging in my ears, my stiff legs feel like they're on autopilot as I turn in a circle. Movement catches my attention, and I see someone loading a crate thirty feet away. A bang to my left makes me jolt and whirl to see another worker shoving a crate into a truck bed.

"Relax, Scarlett. They can't see us."

His words reach my ears, but I'm still staring at the fully functional smuggling operation that should have been cleared out and wiped off the map.

That's when I see an open crate a few feet away filled with the same vials that they used to store the daevari blood they harvest from us every other week.

"Why are those here?" I ask, my voice hardly audible.

"They're used to establish control over others." Orobas says cautiously, and I shake my head.

"This isn't real." I whisper, turning until Orobas comes into view again. "You fabricated this."

"As much as I'd like to take credit for such an intricate illusion, I don't have those capabilities." He muses, his piercing gaze lingering on me.

"Command would never—" My mouth snaps shut as a door rolls closed behind us, clattering loudly.

"An assassin, undercover as a housekeeper, given assignments by 'command' to take out smuggling operations that were never actually shut down." He tilts his head to the side, and a worker walks past us without so much as a second glance. "You're not DEA, not CIA or FBI... Possible branch of the DOD..."

My pulse hikes, and he must notice as his gaze drops to my throat.

"Latest intel says that the Revenants suffered a major loss, but knowing the government, that wouldn't stop them from stepping up their game..." When his attention returns to my face, I feel exposed, vulnerable, naked.

"Judging by what I've seen thus far, you're either the head of the Revenants who has flown under the radar, or—" He clicks his tongue. "—you're the legendary Viper."

Either I've stopped breathing, or the air was sucked out of the room, and with the way his crimson ember eyes are burning into mine, I know he knows.

"I'm not—"

"Do me a favor, Scarlett, and don't lie to me. I'm hundreds of years old, and I've seen far more than you could ever imagine in your wildest dreams."

My brow twitches upward. "A demon asking me not to lie? That's rich."

He brings his palm up, and murmurs, holding my gaze as the portal appears. "Lie, then. Not that it will matter in the long run."

Chapter 7

Scarlett

"Fine. You're right. Now what? Are you going to take the legendary Viper out of the picture for good?"

Orobas leads me through the portal, and back into the center of the room. "It's time for you to see clearly, Scarlett, and that starts with you coming to terms with the truth of Henley."

He turns to me and crowds my space, forcing me back a few paces as he continues to advance.

"What the hell does that mean?" My heels hit the wall, and I tug hard at the bindings around my arms, feeling the rope bite deeper into my skin.

"It means that you might hate me for what I'm about to do, but I'd rather you despise me than stay under their influence."

I scoff. "A demon talking about infl—"

Orobas' hand wraps around the base of my neck, with his palm over my collarbone. His fingers flex on my pulse points, and I tug harder at the ropes.

I stare into crimson embers with wide eyes, yanking at my restraints. His free hand flattens against my temple as another wave of warmth washes over me, rising to my cheeks, and I shudder.

He used his power on me? Was that what that was?

A long moment passes before he backs off, releasing my neck as I feel the tension slowly leave my body.

"What did you just do to me?"

He watches me cautiously. "Against my better judgement, I freed the Viper."

A genuine huff of dry laughter escapes me. "Release me from these bindings, and I'll be free."

"Nice try. You can get your fangs back when you learn to play with others."

He gestures to the open doorway, and my teeth grind together as I follow his instruction.

Whatever he did, it didn't really *do* much, but if he wants me to play nice to be given some freedom, I can do that.

Hell, I posed as a damn housekeeper and wore this dumb ass out-fit. I can pretend to be sweet as pie long enough to kill him.

Walking down the winding hallways, it takes some time to get back to Orobas' office, and he gestures to the chair as he moves to sit behind his desk.

"I have an appointment scheduled—"

"Let me guess, they won't be able to see or hear me?"

His eyes flash, and he leans back with a grin. "So the infamous Viper is a quick learner. Impressive."

I walk over to the chair beside his and slump into it with a resigned sigh. "You haven't seen anything yet, demon."

He just chuckles, and I fall silent as he flips open his laptop. His fingers fly across the keyboard.

Whatever secrets he's hiding, I'll uncover them, steal the dagger, eliminate him and return to command with the accolades of being one of the few to kill a prince of hell.

That's if he doesn't kill me first.

~

A loud knock raps on the door three times before it opens.

"Ah, look who the devil dragged in." An older man grins from the doorway, taking strides to the chair in front Orobas. His grey, wiry hair is pulled into a bun, and a broad smile stretches across his wrinkled face.

"Still young as ever, Varkoth."

Varkoth steps up to the desk and slumps into the chair. "Well... everything went as expected."

"Everything?" Orobas raises his brow with a knowing look as Varkoth scoffs.

"By that, I mean absolutely nothing." The demon laughs dryly and shakes his head. "I hung around for days, and the branch is in organized chaos. The General has the commanders busy; none of them are aware that we have the third yet."

Orobas inclines his head. "Good. I need you to return, and I tell me every move the General makes."

Varkoth's expression turns serious. "You think they'll send one after their own?"

The prince of hell rubs the stubble along his jaw. His gaze flicks to me for a breath of a moment before returning to the demon in front of him.

"I wouldn't put it past them. Either way, I want to know the moment they make any decision." Orobas murmurs, and I swallow.

I'm not enough of an idiot to think command would allow a weapon they've invested years and hundreds of thousands, if not millions of dollars into, to just roam free.

Varkoth sighs, pushing to his feet. "You've got it." He walks to the doorway and turns to glance at Orobas. "Are you sure about this? Is all of this really worth it, Oro?"

My gaze slides over to the prince of hell as his lips twitch. "We won't win this war if we don't take chances, and playing it safe just isn't doing it anymore."

Varkoth grunts and waves him off. "Alright, alright. I'll check in."

He disappears through the doorway, and Orobas' eyes find mine as my heart thrums in my chest.

"Not playing it safe anymore, huh?"

Crimson irises travel along the length of my body, and my cheeks warm.

"If we were, Viper, you wouldn't be sitting here."

Chapter 8

Scarlett

"You have to be kidding me."

Orobas' deep chuckle sounds out behind me as the door clicks shut. "I appreciate a joke as much as the next demon, but no."

I take two steps into the enormous bedroom, and a pit forms in my stomach. A king-size bed dominates the center of the room, with a large oak dresser to my left, lining the wall.

If I hadn't seen the suit hanging in the closet doorway to my right or the cologne and loose tie atop the dresser to my left, I'd have assumed this was a regular room.

Not *his* room.

"I'm not sleeping here."

I turn to look at him, but his crimson gaze is already locked onto me.

"You're not sleeping anywhere else, little Viper."

Swallowing hard, I take confident strides to the corner by the closet, and slide down the wall until I'm seated on the floor. "This will be just fine."

Orobas grins and walks to the dresser. "Suit yourself."

He stands tall across the room, unbuttoning his suit from his chest to his navel, and I watch as inch by inch, more of his chest peers out from beneath his shirt. Removing his belt with one hand, I avert my gaze to stare at the door as he continues to undress.

Is it a demon thing for indecency to be normalized?

He tugs off his shirt in my peripherals, and even though I'm fighting to keep my gaze on the door, I still see ink sprawled over his bare shoulders.

Curiosity gets the better of me, and I glance over to where he stands.

Various tattoos stretch from his neck and along his shoulders. The ink covers his arms and back, a broad canvas of swirling black flames surrounding a silver and brown horse. Enormous wings spread to each shoulder as it rears back. Muscles lining his back ripple as he sets the shirt aside and kicks off his shoes.

I could tell he was muscular, but—

He tugs his pants down, turning slightly. The deep line along his hip comes into view, and my gaze drops.

It's bad enough he had to be attractive, but of course he had to have the *entire* bad-boy look. Ugh.

Orobas tosses his pants on top of the rest of his clothes on the dresser and flops into the bed. "Sleep well, Viper." He sighs, and my teeth grind together.

"I'd sleep better if you stopped breathing. Permanently."

The resulting chuckle is all I hear, and I roll my eyes, leaning further into the wall.

My mind wanders to Eve and Omen as my gaze traces the shadowed lines on the ceiling.

If what Varkoth said was true, command has kept them busy. Orobas is right to be cautious about whether they'd come after me, though. They would most definitely wipe my ass off the face of the planet the moment command said so.

At least death at their hands would be swift.

My eyes slide shut, and I fight a yawn.

Swift is better than slow and tedious like this.

Sweeping the dark room, there's nothing I'd be able to get hold of and dispatch him with, so I resign myself to taking the time to rest.

Even if I got to his clothes, based on his strength earlier, I'd need both hands to take him out with them.

My feet just won't do with what's in here.

Orobas' breathing evens out as the minutes pass by, and though I despise the demon, I have to commend him for having the balls to sleep in the same room as me.

Minutes pass, and my chest rises and falls in time with his deep breaths, with the world fading away around me.

~

My eyes snap open at the sound of something heavy hitting flesh.

John recoils the metal bat and slams it into Omen's side as she collapses.

Glaring at Bash, his lip curls. "Your friends won't last much longer. If you have any final words, I'd recommend saying them now." With a single jerk, he backhands me as pain blooms across my cheek.

"Fuck you." I murmur, my actions are lagged as I spit blood in his face.

John slams the bat into the side of Omen's head, and she grunts as the crunch of metal against bone fills the air. My heart stutters as I look toward the door behind Bash.

But it doesn't open.

Something's wrong.

Eve should have been here by now.

Omen won't last much longer.

Tears sting my eyes as they turn to Bash, and he just grins. "Say goodbye." He snatches the hair at the back of my head, recoils his fist and slams his knuckles into my face. I thrash in his grip, but hardly get a moment to breathe when he repeats the action, and pain ricochets through my skull.

Even with Bash's assault, I'm vaguely aware of Omen's prone form, still as death as he swings the bat overhead, slamming it into her limp body.

We're going to die.

Eve isn't coming.

Omen. I need to save Omen.

My legs jerk beneath Bash as all my training goes out the window, making my already lagged movements unpracticed and desperate. Bash brings his heavy fist into contact with my ribs, and I gasp as pressure on my shoulders jolts me.

"Scarlett—"

I hardly recognize the voice as Bash slams his fist into my stomach again, knocking the wind out of me. Pain coats every inch of my body, and I thrash against his grip once more, but my arms stay bound at my back as I shake uncontrollably.

"Scarlett—" The voice is clearer and more urgent as my eyes snap open, and I suck in a greedy breath. Wide crimson irises stare back at me, and a lick of terror slides down my spine before I glance on either side of him.

The darkness of his room is dimly lit by the lamp on the table at the far side of the bed.

Dream. It was a dream.

Eve saved us. Omen is still alive.

My chest heaves as I look up at Orobas' hard gaze, and a mixture of embarrassment and wounded pride creates a noxious dose of anger that roils in my veins.

"If you knew what was good for you, demon, you'd back up." I growl, my lip curling into a sneer.

He chuckles, the sound only pissing me off more. "Such enormous threats from a fangless Viper." He muses, lifting my torso from the floor to sit upright. His bare tattooed arms flex as he positions me with ease, and he rests his arm on his knee.

Fuck this. The rage in my body comes to a peak. Residual frustration from my inability to fight back snaps my restraint.

My leg swings high with lightning speed to hook around Orobas' head. The tight hem of my housekeeping dress tears loudly, and his eyes widen in the split second it's taken to make my move.

Before he knows what's happening, I've wrapped my thighs around his head and thrown my weight into the shift in momentum. He lurches in the opposite direction and we both land with a thud, but with my arms still firmly bound behind my back, I'm a sitting fucking duck.

My thighs squeeze his neck, but when his fingers wrap around the back of my legs, just under my ass, I know I've made a mistake.

He shifts his weight onto one leg and stands with frustrating ease as I dangle forward, my nose brushing the bare skin of his waist. His deep-set V-line stares me in the face from where I hang upside down, and I grind my molars.

"It will take much more than that, little Viper." He taunts, and my head swims as he reaches down to hook his arm under my back. Using all my strength, I thrust my legs off his shoulders before he can grab hold of me.

Gravity works faster than I want as my leg slips from his palm, and I fall to the floor. But I react just in time—my chin tucks to my chest, and I roll onto my back, using my momentum to surge to my feet.

Crimson eyes fixate on mine, and he grins. "Looks like I still have my head." He goads, stepping closer, and I mirror him, retreating until my back hits the wall.

"Untie me if you want an actual fight, demon."

He just laughs, and damn if it doesn't piss me off more. "We tried that earlier, remember?" When his bare tattooed chest is inches from mine, with nowhere left for me to go, he tilts his head slightly. "Is Omen a Revenant who survived?"

Anger flares through me, and I bring my knee up toward his groin, but he's fast to catch it with his hand.

"Is that what you want? To fight? Will that make you feel better?" He searches my face for a long moment. "Because it won't bring anyone you lost back. Or perhaps the only pleasure you find in life is drawing blood."

The thought sends adrenaline pumping through my veins, and he must notice the change as he laughs under his breath.

"Bloodthirsty Viper." He tuts, and before I know what's happening, he twists and scoops me into his chest. His grip becomes a vice, holding me tight as I squirm, and he crosses the room only to toss me into the air.

A choked sound escapes my throat as I'm airborne, but when I land onto the plush surface of his bed, I freeze.

"Absolutely not. I'm not sleeping here, demon."

He chuckles and snags his tie off the dresser, wordlessly leaning over and securing it around my ankles. I contemplate struggling against it for a heartbeat, but between the dream, lack of sleep, and my meager attempts to fight him without my arms, I'm drained.

My molars grind as he fastens the tie, effectively binding each of my ankles together as I lie there prone in the bed.

"I fucking hate you." I grumble as he flops into the bed beside me.

The sound of his laughter fills the room, but he says nothing as he turns off the lamp next to the bed. Silence extends, and he sighs deeply, tucking his arms under the back of his head.

A long moment passes, and I don't know if he's still awake, but his question about who Omen is swirls in my mind, flashing between mental images of the bat breaking her bones.

"It was my fault." I whisper into the silence, but I might as well have yelled it with how invasive it feels in the stillness surrounding us. "The night Mako and Grizz died, it was because I was cocky, and when push came to shove, I couldn't save us."

The admission makes my chest tighten almost to the point of pain, and I swallow against the lump in my throat.

"How?" His single whispered word sends a wave of guilt through me, and my eyes slide shut.

"We had clear orders to locate the coordinates of a laptop from an office in the warehouse, but when I saw a group of demons drinking in a room together, I'd snuck away to poison them. I was successful, but when I'd caught up to the others, my guard was down and I compromised our position."

Silence extends between us, and I take a deep breath with a shudder working its way through my body. I still don't know why telling him this mattered, or what purpose it's going to serve other than to gain his trust, maybe, but some piece of me feels lighter because of it.

"Four hundred and twenty-three successful missions over fifteen years almost went down the drain because of my ego."

"So your nightmare was of them dying?"

My eyes open when the bed shifts, and Orobas crosses his ankles comfortably. The limited light in the room just barely illuminates the corded muscles along his abdomen, and my gaze slides up his inked chest before settling on his face.

When I see his shadowed crimson eyes already on me, I flush, but nod. "Ever since that night, I've dreamt of Mako and Grizz dying, Omen being beaten to death and Eve rescuing us. But tonight Eve didn't come."

A long moment passes between us, and I trace the shadows on the ceiling, convinced that I've gone insane for admitting such a vulnerable mistake to the demon holding me captive.

"A wise person once told me that all outcomes serve a greater purpose, regardless of how we favor them in the moment."

I snort and roll onto my side, bending my knees slightly. "Was your friend a theologian? Because that sounds like something a theologian would say."

He chuckles. "Something like that... either way, there's nothing to say that you wouldn't have gotten caught had you stayed with them. It's odd that you'd take the blame for those who actually killed or harmed the people you care about."

His shadowed crimson eyes slide shut, and I suck in a deep breath, letting his words sink in.

As much as I want to disagree vehemently with Orobas and riot against him because of what he is, I can't deny the truth. But I'll never know what could have been, which is truly what will drive me more insane than anything else.

The what-ifs have kept me awake every night in their own way, and I don't know if I'll ever truly come to terms with what happened.

"Thank you, demon." I whisper, my attention returning to his face, which seems oddly peaceful for a prince of hell that wreaks havoc on humanity.

His lips twitch, but his eyes remain shut. "Get some sleep, Viper."

Chapter 9

Evelyn

"You'll just feel a pinch." The nurse slides the point of the needle into the crook of my elbow, the sharp sting quickly fading as she draws blood.

I'm no stranger to this process as one of the two daevari in the Revenants. Command frequently harvests blood from us, sometimes as often as twice weekly when we aren't on missions.

It doesn't matter if we're healing or broken, we never complain since we heal slightly faster than the others. It's just those same healing properties that command was determined would help the others get on with their next mission faster.

With all of that in mind, it makes sense why they'd want to draw blood from me right now considering the battered state Omen is in. She'd gotten multiple transfusions and wasn't even awake when I'd gone to see her earlier.

The swollen, discolored bruises covering her skin would be enough to make anyone uncomfortable.

They're oddly normalized to us, though. Between training and missions, I can't remember a time when we'd gone a month without an injury of some sort. That's not to mention internal affairs.

I don't think I'll ever forget my last resistance training instructor, Gunner, for as long as I live.

Considering the content of the class is withstanding torture tactics, it wasn't the first time I'd wondered if I was going to die, but it was the first time someone had truly attempted to end my life.

After all, it's not every day that your instructor breaks into your personal quarters. The incident was eight months ago, but I still remember waking up with his hands wrapped around my neck like it was yesterday.

The nurse removes the needle from my arm, keeping pressure on it for a moment. Seconds later, I've got a bandage holding a cotton ball on it, and she's cleaning up.

Ever since that incident, command has treaded lighter around me in some senses. Whether the space they give me is because I severed his trachea with my bare hands or because I killed one of our own, I'll probably never know.

"Right. Here is a soda in case you get light-headed." The nurse hands it to me with a grin. "But I doubt you'll need it."

"Like the million other times." I toss back and slide off the chair toward the door.

"Pleasure as always, Eve."

I don't bother looking back, passing by the lab on my way to the main administration hall. My gaze lingers on the workers inside, busy concocting some new poison for Scarlett or testing some kind of chemical.

They're always wearing heavy-duty hazmat suits when they deal with any kind of substance, so I hardly want to know what shit they used to make Scarlett's weapons.

My phone vibrates as I pass by the main administrative office, and my steps slow to a stop.

Grant: Got a damn good hot dog at the cafeteria today.

I don't bother responding and slide my phone into my pocket. On my first day meeting Grant, he made it clear that he'd never text anything important to me.

Since then, everything we've put in writing has been code. At first, it was odd—keeping a secret from command and the others, or acting like double agents—but like most things with us, it just became second nature.

Knowing Grant, though, he could have an update on the laptop or something moderately less useful to me. I'll never forget the nights after that asshole instructor nearly choked me to death. Grant dragged me into his office every evening for some random reason.

Every coded text ended up being for as little as grabbing a bite to eat, or as big as helping him decode some cryptic message he had intercepted.

Even though I never told him what happened, and if he knew, he said nothing. But what would there have been to say?

Pissing people off in this profession is second nature. Hit someone the wrong way? Enemy. Win too many times in combat training? Enemy.

When I get to the door of his office, I knock three times and wait. The walls and door are soundproof, so I don't hear a peep before it swings open.

"That excited to hear more about a hot dog?" Grant grins broadly, propping the heavy door open with his foot. He gestures inside with one hand, rolling up the long sleeve of his shirt with the other.

My lips twitch, and I breeze past him, hearing the door swing shut with a click behind me. "I did win that hot dog eating contest once, you know. I consider myself quite the connoisseur."

"I still don't think that was a fair contest." He grumbles, but the hint of amusement in his voice betrays him. "Who puts a daevari in a competition with humans?"

I laugh under my breath and shake my head. "There's been no evidence that my genetics make me more successful at eating, of all things." Crossing my arms, I gesture to his desk. "Now, care to tell me the real reason you texted me?"

"Do I need to have an actual reason?" He tosses back. His gaze burns into mine, and even though he asked in such a benign way, my heart stutters all the same.

My lips twitch. "If command ever deciphers your texts, you will."

His eyes flash before he takes long strides to his chair. The springs creak as he eases into it and leans back. "Bold of you to assume they'd ever stoop that low. I'm an upstanding cyber warfare specialist."

I nearly snort. "And I'm a monkey's uncle."

Laughing under his breath, he turns the laptop on his desk toward me. "I suppose you wouldn't want to know what was in this handy-dandy device you brought to me?"

My eyes narrow on him. "You say that as if you could ever keep the information from me."

He just shrugs and hits the spacebar, lighting the screen up to display an email thread. I feel his eyes burning into the side of my head as I lean forward to read through.

At first, the back and forth doesn't seem like much—just some discussion about supplies and shipment timings. Most of it looks trivial and not worth a fraction of our time.

But that's when I see it.

Just after a message confirms a future arrival of goods, the one after makes my blood run cold.

Leo: Bring goods to ritual site on the 30th. Female only.

This was sent two days before we'd acquired it, which means we still have time to save whoever these demons are planning to sacrifice.

My eyes snap to Grant's as his jaw feathers. "We have a date; do they give an address?"

He nods and reaches over to his notepad, where he's elegantly written an address is what looks like damn calligraphy.

"One month to prepare. I've had worse." I breathe, memorizing the location on the pad of paper before straightening. "Good work, upstanding cyber warfare specialist. We can't let command know yet, or they're liable to give us five missions that have nothing to do with the ritual."

"Eve." He says in a low tone and pushes to his feet. "Let me come with you."

I just shake my head. "Not a chance. With all the time you spend holed up in this office, I'm not risking you being rusty and sending this mission sideways."

Not to mention, the last thing I want to do is lose him.

His mouth drops open to argue, so the words rush out of me without a second thought. "Besides, this isn't like some mission that command is sending us on that's fully vetted. This is the second time we've gotten a lead on these ritual sites, and I'm not letting them ignore this one. The Revenants are doing this, and we're doing it alone."

I realize that Scarlett and I would be severely outnumbered if we went to a ritual site alone without backup—but it wouldn't be the first time we've managed something so ballsy.

I won't make the same mistakes, though.

Losing Mako and Grizz still leaves a bitter aftertaste in my mouth. I'll do whatever it takes to keep Scarlett from the same fate as them.

Even though the demons weren't able to stand against me in combat once I got free, they somehow had gotten the best of the others, and that's on me.

I fucked up, and I won't let it happen again.

His fist tightens around the pen. "Scarlett is already on a solo mission, Omen is still in critical condition, even with daevari infusions, and Grizz and Mako are dead. You can't do this alone, Eve."

"Then I won't do it alone." I snap. "Me and Scarlett can handle a handful of demons doing some sick sacrificial ritual. It's child's play, Grant."

"This isn't the same—"

"I'm the Harbinger for a reason." I growl, stepping closer to Grant until we're chest to chest, and I'm glaring up at him. "The world is a scary place from inside a room full of tech, Major Allen. But that's why the Revenants exist. I'm the strongest fucking weapon command has against these demons."

"Eve," Grant says in a low tone, but I don't miss the flicker of concern in his gaze. He hesitates for a moment, and whatever argument he had must have had dies before reaching his lips as he sighs. "Just be careful. Be more careful than ever before."

I can tell there's more he's not saying as I search his face, but I can't bring myself to demand it from him. Grant already shares more with me than he ever should. He shares enough to get us both executed.

But what command is doing to rid this world of demons isn't enough. Their delay of the inevitable is partially what cost us the lives of two of the best human Wraiths to exist.

What fault doesn't remain with me will always lie with them for not acting sooner. It feels treasonous to blame them and their inaction, but more and more I've taken more control over these missions and take things into my own hands.

Many times, that's been what has saved us or made our missions successful.

Grant's tongue glides along his sharp canine before he shakes his head. "You're the most stubborn woman I've ever met."

"You say that like it's a bad thing." I muse, my gaze lingering on his mouth as his lips pull into a grin.

Something in my chest flutters, suddenly very conscious of the lack of distance between us, and when my eyes meet his, the knowing look he gives me makes my cheeks burn.

"Eve." The deep tenor in his voice reaches my ears, but I can't think through the way his voice makes me feel.

I've done all I can to keep the relationship between us as platonic as possible, but I lose that fight time and time again. Just like the first time we'd kissed in this very office years ago, to every stolen moment we'd shared since, Grant's been steadfast through it all.

"Tell me what you're thinking, Eve." He says, brushing my hair aside to caress my jaw with his thumb.

Grant's touch has always been a stark contrast to this place. Gentle amidst a world of aggression and pain. A safe alcove hidden within a battlefield of terror.

At first, it scared me. I didn't know what to do with it.

Then, late at night, long before our first kiss, I craved it when I had no right to.

There are no rules against a daevari and a human having a relationship that I'm aware of, but I'm pretty sure that's because they never considered the possibility.

They make it clear that we're nothing more than weapons.

Their training aimed to prevent us from forming bonds, emphasizing loyalty to command above all else. It worked for a time.

Three months after our group formed, we had one of our biggest fights over one of my decisions that went against command, but it strengthened us for it.

Just like my wariness of Grant's secrecy became one of my favorite things about him.

"Eve." Grant's voice pulls me from my thoughts, his bright gaze burning into mine.

"I'm thinking that I should go call Scarlett, and give her the good news."

His lips curl upward, and his other hand cups the back of my neck. "Scarlett can wait a few more minutes." He says, leaning in to press his lips to mine, and the world suddenly fades away.

Chapter 10

Scarlett

My arms ache, tingling with pins and needles as I slowly rouse from my sleep.

Even with the raw pain rippling from my shoulders to my wrists, there's a warmth surrounding me that keeps it at bay. When a tattooed chest fills my vision, my eyes widen, and I track the inked skin that disappears under my cheek with a mixture of surprise and denial.

Of course a **demon** would try something like this.

"Sleep well?" Orobas' voice is thick, and he yawns.

My arms throb with electrical bolts of pain traveling through them as I wince. "Oh yeah, peachy."

He chuckles, and I roll to the side, away from him while inadvertently taking the duvet with me. The blanket's plush, and I don't notice the edge of the bed until it's too late.

A shrill sound escapes me as the mattress disappears.

My body drops like a stone, and even though I'm effectively burrito'd, I land on my arms restrained at my back with a loud thud. I gasp and roll onto my stomach as tears sting my eyes.

Normally, I can handle inescapable pain, but waking up to it like this…

Footsteps grow closer, and Orobas gently rolls me onto my side. His hand encircles my bicep, and he tugs to help me up, but the moment a strangled cry catches in my throat, he freezes.

I can feel his crimson eyes on me, even with my forehead tilted to the ground. There's not a chance in God's green earth that I'm about to ask him for help.

His arm slides under my back, and he eases me upright as pins and needles travel from my shoulders to my fingertips. My hair falls forward, obscuring some of my vision as I keep my focus on breathing.

"What's wrong?" Orobas murmurs, but when I don't respond, he moves to grab my arm again and tugs on it.

My head snaps toward his, the pain sending me into a rage as electrical jolts travel throughout my arms. "Don't fucking touch me." I snarl, my shoulders throbbing as my chest heaves.

Orobas kneels before me, his sculpted tattooed body on full display. He doesn't flinch or back down as his gaze tracks to the wet stains on my cheeks. When his crimson orbs drop to my arms, he leans behind me and curses.

Within a second he's over my shoulder, and my bindings move, the pressure getting worse and better in waves before the ropes finally fall free.

My hands drop limp to my sides, and I bring them forward as my stiff joints crack loudly. My eyes widen at the way they've swollen, turning an unnatural hue of black and purple. The ache in my shoulders hasn't gotten better, but it's all I can do to pull my knees up, and press my forehead to them.

Inhale. Exhale.

Just breathe through it, Scarlett.

Inhale. Exhale.

The pins and needles have gotten worse by the second, and even though it's not the worst pain I've felt, somehow it sure comes close.

As the throbbing subsides, I pull my head from my legs and blow out a breath, my fingers wiggling despite the nerve pain running rampant through them.

Note to self, use that as a torture technique.

Orobas gently takes both my hands in his, and he makes quick work of binding them in front of my body. He ravels rope around my arms, the corded muscles in his shoulders tense with his movements. When my gaze flicks to his, he tosses me an apologetic look.

"I do need to keep my staff alive. Surely you understand."

I release a breath. "You'd be an idiot not to."

The ropes tighten around my wrists as he moves to secure my forearms and my biceps. The knots are complicated and reinforced in multiple places, which will prove to be an issue if I want to slip out of them.

Even more so since my arms are in front of me, any movement will catch his attention.

He pauses once they're secured, all the humor having drained from his face as his crimson irises hold mine. "I mean it, Viper. If you lay a hand on any of my staff—harm them in any way—you will regret it."

A lick of fear travels down my spine, and I suppress a shudder. "It's a good thing you triple-tied me then, demon. You might as well hog-tie me at this point. Maybe you'll really fuck up my plans to murder at least half as many demons as you have humans." I say sweetly, but the malice in my words is clear.

His eyes flash in warning, and I know I'm pushing my luck, but it's not like I'm here to befriend the demon prince. I'd much rather see his head on a pike.

Along with all his little minions.

He straightens, tugging me to my feet in front of him. I'd always been shorter than the other Revenants, especially Grizz, but next to Orobas' height, it's like I'm standing beside a damn giant.

I shoot a glare in his direction. "So, what's the plan now? Lock me up in the tower all day?"

He raises an eyebrow. "Tempting, but no. We have a banquet to attend tonight." His gaze trails down the length of my body critically. "And you can't wear that—not to mention you smell."

I rear back and stare at him with wide eyes. "I do ***not***!"

He turns to the bed with a chuckle as he grabs his phone, his fingers flying over the screen.

"The disgusting demon standing there in his underwear has the gall to tell me *I* smell? That's rich." I scoff, which only makes him laugh infuriatingly harder.

It's like the more he pisses me off, the more he enjoys it, and I'm done playing his games.

"That I am." He muses, and the door to the room opens. When I turn to see Druv and Thal, my heart sinks. "These two will get you cleaned up and ready."

I want to ask how the hell he's planning to explain bringing a bound woman to a banquet, but since he can just hide me from view whenever he wants, I doubt he's overly concerned about it.

My gaze slides to his demonic little minions as they grin, and I want nothing more than to smack the smug look off their faces.

"Well," I breathe, stalking toward both men. The subtle way they adjust their footing as I approach them sends a sliver of satisfaction through me. "Let's get this over with then, demons."

Thal's first out the door, with Druv close behind me. Walking with them is like being sandwiched between two unholy sentinels, their footsteps thundering compared to mine.

A week ago, I would have said I wasn't afraid to die in my line of work, and that if captured, I would be the first to take down as many demons as possible.

From the last two times I've been compromised, it's obvious that my ego is the one talking.

Ever since the demon prince figured out what I was, all I've done is consider my options on how to escape.

"I think I could take her." Druv offers, quickening his step to my left and shoving his hands in his pockets.

Thal huffs a dry laugh, his gaze sliding to my arms. "Without her hands, maybe."

I glance between them, feeling the tentative excitement that I'm certain is showing on my face. "Want to give it a try? I'll promise to let you tie me up again after." Holding my bound arms out in offering, both demons look at them before exchanging a glance, and I shrug. "Can't blame a girl for trying." I sigh, following close behind as they lead me down a flight of stairs.

Surprisingly enough, there are more demons roaming the halls than usual, and by the time we come to a stop in front of a closed door, I've counted twelve excluding Orobas, Thal and Druv.

Thal twists the knob before he gestures inside, and my pace slows as I wonder why the number has doubled overnight.

Either they're preparing for something, or they're just more active now that they have a captured assassin in their midst. My mind wanders back to the dagger with a note of uncertainty, twisting my stomach into knots.

There's no way they'd be preparing to use it so soon... right?

The thought that they could be planning to use the dagger at the banquet crosses my mind, and a heavy note of dread settles in my gut. My gaze bounces between Thal and Druv when I pass by them, as if I'd be able to see they're plans written on their faces.

The dark hardwood floor creaks quietly with each step until I've stopped next to the queen-sized bed that dominates the wall opposite the door.

Thal walks through the illuminated hallway to the right of the bed, and Druv shoves me forward. "We're not getting any younger."

I roll my eyes. "Push me again, demon, and I'll make sure you don't get any **older** either."

Druv lets out a hearty laugh that makes me want to find the nearest sharp object to stab him in the jugular. "You'd really kill me? After I was so nice to you, *Nora*?"

I snort, following Thal into a long bathroom. A middle-aged woman with curls of brown hair stands near the tub. She gives both demons a warm smile, but when her attention lands on me, the warmth disappears as quickly as it came.

Can't say the feeling isn't mutual.

Her gaze travels the length of my body as Thal walks over to plant a kiss on her forehead. "*This* is who he's bringing to the banquet?"

The malice and disgust in her voice itches a nerve that tempts me to lash out until Druv steps more into view, and I remember just how outnumbered I am.

"He's officially lost his mind." Thal grumbles, grabbing a towel off the door.

Is this banquet really *that* big of a deal?

"Think you can make her at least smell a little better, Ishari?" Druv taunts, his gaze sliding to me, and I stick my tongue out in his direction.

When my attention turns to Ishari, she just blinks before nodding at him. "Should be easy enough."

She crosses the distance between us, towering over me by at least two and a half inches as she thumbs the thin straps at my shoulders.

"We'll have to cut the clothes off her, but we won't need to worry about her bindings since the dress is strapless."

My jaws clench at the thought of them cutting clothes off me, but I let it go. It's not like I can control this.

Ishari steps closer, grasping a pair of scissors in her slender hands. When I notice the tremble in her fingers, my gaze flicks to hers. Her jaw's as tense as the rest of her features, like she's caught a wild animal that will strike the moment she slips up. The look in her eyes tells me everything I need to know.

It doesn't take a rocket scientist to see she's terrified.

Thal hovers closer, and even though I'm confident I could kill her relatively easily, it would be a death sentence in front of the other two.

So I stay still, feeling the cool edge of the scissors against the skin on my shoulder. The chill sends a shiver down my spine, and I stare at Ishari as the sound of my outfit being cut fills the air.

The air's charged around us, like a tense undercurrent threatens to suddenly zap us at any moment, and I know it's because all three of them expect me to lash out.

I'd be lying if I said the thought hadn't crossed my mind, but I *am* bound, after all.

I might be an assassin, but I'm not Eve.

The first strap falls loose, with the front of it hanging over my chest, and Ishari moves around Thal to my other side. She repeats the action; her coiled muscles are tense—ready to jerk away from me at any moment.

Setting my gaze on the mirror across the room, watching Druv's reflection, my thoughts wander away from the immediate threat of a flighty demon with scissors close enough to kill me. The still-healing incisions above my breast will soon be exposed for all to see, bringing me back to the night Grizz and Mako died with a bitter taste on my tongue.

Logically, I know why the wound hasn't fully healed yet, but I'd be lying if I said I didn't think it was God's way of punishing me. As if my negligence that got them killed has come back to me in some karmic way.

When the material at my shoulder falls away, Ishari's eyes widen in my peripherals, and she turns to look at Thal.

I yawn deeply, trying to force the memories out. "Have you never seen a woman's body before?" I taunt, my gaze flicking to meet hers.

When her cheeks flush, I toss her a wink. "I can bathe myself if it makes you uncomfortable." I offer, holding my arms out, and letting them fall limp against my stomach again.

Can't say I didn't try.

Druv chuckles behind them, and Ishari finally moves in close to tug the dress down my torso. Inch by inch, more of my scarred skin is exposed.

When the outfit pulls past the edge of my bra, Thal and Druv both avert their eyes, and I file that information away. It doesn't make sense for two demons to care about indecency, especially after Orobas stripped down to his boxers last night as if it were nothing.

When Ishari tugs the dress to my hips, she bends lower until it drops to the floor, and cool air licks my newly exposed skin. When she moves to straighten, and her eyes land on the rest of my stomach, she gasps.

The scissors fall to the ground, and I jump back to keep my feet from being impaled, drawing both demon's attention.

Druv's taken a heavy step forward, and Thal's jerked his arm between me and Ishari as she stares wide-eyed at my torso.

"Watch what you're doing, demon." I growl, kicking away the scissors as they clatter against the tile floor.

The various scars that litter my body must be a shock, considering the way Ishari's turned to Thal—as if looking for him to reaffirm she's not imagining what she's seeing.

He says nothing, though, and I yawn deeply. "Are you done staring, or do you have something you want to say?" I grumble and turn away from them, making my way to the shower.

Tears formed at the corners of my eyes from my yawn, and I blink them away. When my attention settles on Druv, the shadowed look on his face has me frowning.

"The hell is your problem all of a sudden?" I growl, but infuriatingly he says nothing.

How dare they act like I'm the freak here? They're **demons**, for fuck's sake.

I turn to Ishari and Thal again with a huff, my bare feet making a soft smacking sound against the tile. Her eyes are still wide, but she steps into the shower to turn it on.

It's not until she tugs her shirt overhead and hands it to Thal that I understand her reaction. Her tanned, creamy skin is unmarred except for the single deep scar on her abdomen.

Her one that matches several of my own; the number over the years has grown too numerous to count between training and my missions. The scars I didn't acquire from the intensive torture exposure therapy were accolades from my achievements and successful assignments.

Evidence of my survival, and a bitter reminder of my mortality.

My gaze flicks to hers, and for a moment, I almost feel a flicker of understanding. A hint of empathy for a singular shared experience between us, but it's fleeting, gone as soon as I step into the cool water.

Chapter 11

Scarlett

Liquid sluices along my skin, weighing down my hair as I submerge my head beneath the onslaught, letting it saturate the lengths before stepping out once more. Long, dark locks stick to my face, and I blink away the water in my eyes, my attention on the motion behind Ishari.

Thal adjusts his grip as he holds the door open, keeping us in view, but his head turns to Druv as Ishari pumps shampoo into her hands. Druv, however, has no issue with his eyes glued to me as Ishari's fingers massage the suds into my hair.

I half expect her to dig her nails in, and I feel myself tense subconsciously with each move she makes. One long minute turns into two, and by the time she retracts her arms, I'm fully coiled, ready for some kind of strike.

I've had people tend to my wounds before, but she's being more gentle than even they had been.

It's uncomfortable.

I wish she'd just fucking hit me already instead of beating around the bush.

She pauses for a moment and gestures to the water. "Rinse, please."

I say nothing, and step beneath the shower once more, letting the shampoo drain from my hair. My eyes squeeze shut as the suds trail down my face, and with each second under the water, my arms twitch with the need to wipe it away.

It's an odd feeling to be trained to assassinate someone with minimal weapons, and be completely at the mercy of that which you've been taught to destroy.

Ishari pulls my hair from my face as I step out of the water once more, but when our eyes meet, I don't feel so aggravated.

Confused maybe, but not aggravated.

"I'll have to wash your wounds." She whispers, and I just nod.

After removing my undergarments, she gets to work lathering soap over my skin, moving my arms and turning me before guiding me under the water once more. Thal and Druv are uncharacteristically quiet as she rinses the soap and shuts the faucet off.

"Right, well, all that's left is to get you dressed, do up your hair, and you should be all ready to go." She murmurs, grabbing a towel to swipe the water from my skin.

Druv walks over to stand alongside Thal in the corner of my eye. "Should we make bets on how long it'll take for her to go for Oro's throat?" He asks gruffly, and Thal releases a heartfelt laugh.

"My money's on less than one minute."

I raise an eyebrow. "You think I'd be capable of it like this?" I ask, lifting my elbows and forearms into the air suggestively.

Ishari snorts, but Thal's voice fills the air as he shakes his head. "Oro won't make you attend the banquet like that."

My eyes widen, and even though I don't believe a word he says, a small piece of me wants to. "He'd be an idiot to let me attend without binding me." I whisper, and all three of them nod their heads in agreement.

"Maybe he *has* lost it." Druv muses, handing Ishari another towel for my hair.

Thal shrugs. "That or he knows that the only way for her to see the truth is with a little trust."

I huff a sarcastic laugh, and Ishari flinches at my sudden movement. "The truth—what in the world could *he* show to *me* that could be the truth?"

The three exchange a glance, looking more hesitant than ever, and Ishari scrunches the towel into the ends of my hair.

"Have you ever considered why they made you into an assassin?" She asks cautiously, keeping her eyes on the towel in her hands.

"To send demons back to hell." I respond without missing a beat, but to her credit she doesn't balk as she nods thoughtfully.

"Did you always think your orders were right?" She whispers, tossing the towel aside, and a chill works its way down my spine.

She moves to the door to grab a robe and pulls it over my shoulders.

Truth be told, I doubted everything when I was first recruited. I spent days being broken down to the fabric of who I am, just for them to build me up once more as the machine they needed.

Someone who questions orders, undermines their missions and becomes a liability. Where demons are involved, loyalty isn't requested; it's required.

"It doesn't matter." I grumble.

"Oro's going to have his hands full with this one." Druv mutters, and my eyes narrow on him.

"He'll take his last breath soon if he's lucky enough." I bite back as the three demons laugh.

There's a moment of silence as Ishari tugs her shirt overhead once more, the damp lengths of her hair still dripping. "Judging by the guest list of this banquet and tomorrow's fundraiser, you might be fighting for a place in line to take him out, anyway."

"What do you mean?" I ask, and the three exchange a look.

Ishari guides me to the bedroom, and I watch her disappear into the closet as Druv and Thal both sit at the edge of the bed.

Thal grins. "Oro rarely goes out into the open like this, and especially not something this public—never mind two outings in a row."

Druv nods beside him as Ishari comes out of the closet with a dress. "That's not even mentioning the fact that a third of the fundraiser guest list wants Oro dead, even if most of them have no idea what he looks like."

"Do you blame them? He's a demon prince who has murdered countless people."

Thal's gaze darkens. "Like you have any room to talk, demon killer?"

I snort. "Apples to oranges, demon. Mine was the work of God, doubt he can say the same."

In an instant, Druv surges to his feet, his eyes wild. "That's what you think **God** would want you to do? You don't know shit. You're a delusional idiot."

My brow quirks at his outburst, but Ishari clears her throat, dragging our attention to her. "Not to interrupt, but I have to dress her, regardless of how misinformed she is."

Druv's lip curls in disgust as he whirls in the opposite direction, stalking to take his place at the end of the bed. When I turn to Ishari, she hardly gives me more than a glance before she gets to work fitting the dress and pulling it up the length of my body.

It's obvious we won't agree. I don't know why they're trying. As if they don't kill innocent humans, perform sacrifices to fuel their dark magic and influence people to sin.

They're not commendable in this, no matter how they try to spin it.

I fall silent listening to the three demons make jabs at one another, reminding me of my time with the Revenants when things weren't so dire.

Grizz and Omen would always go head-to-head with sarcastic comments. Mako would interject at just the right time to spur them on some more. Evelyn would wait until we got a little too rowdy before stepping in, but we all knew she'd do it before we took things too far.

By the time Ishari's pulled the dress up the length of my body and secured it, I feel a little less like a failed housemaid and more myself.

Well... myself if I were undercover, maybe. Minus being bound like a criminal.

Ishari lifts my arms to tug the top over my breasts, and I exhale a breath to squeeze into it. The bust is a tight fit, but at least I won't have to worry about the girls moving.

"I still don't get why he's bringing her." Ishari mumbles, leaning back to get a good look at me. "Having countless enemies who aren't professionally trained killers around him is bad enough—why would he decide to **bring** the assassin with him?"

Druv chuckles as the door from the hallway creaks open. "Speak of the prince, and he shall appear."

"Were your ears burning, Oro?" Thal taunts, a broad grin spreading across his face.

Footsteps come to a stop behind me, and I turn to look over my shoulder at the demon. His suit is tailored to perfection, the dark material making the deep red in his irises more prominent. His tattoos are still visible around his neck, with his hair styled in a way that seems effortless.

I'm half convinced that the man could have gone in a t-shirt and jeans and no one would have batted an eye simply because attractive men with power can get away with anything.

Nothing pisses me off more.

Orobas glances between the three demons, a smile tugging at his lips. "Should they have been?"

God, I fucking hate his stupid grin.

Druv pushes to his feet and walks over to the prince of hell. "You sure you want to bring her with you?"

He ignores the question, and I get the urge to break free from these bindings the moment his crimson eyes settle on me. "I'd like to make a deal, Viper."

My eyes widen, and I nearly laugh. "A *deal*? With a prince of hell? I can't wait to hear this proposition." Clearing my throat, I drop my voice an octave to do my best impersonation of him. "Don't murder me, and I will think twice about sucking the soul from your body to burn in the pits of hell for all eternity."

The room falls silent for a long moment before raucous laughter fills the space, with each of the demons either doubling over or throwing their heads back.

Orobas is the first to collect himself, his obnoxious smirk making my blood boil. "I'm not *that* adept at effective deals, evidently. I'd like to barter for your release—accompany me to this banquet, and subsequently the political fundraiser I'm attending tomorrow night, and I will let you go free."

My eyes narrow on him. "What's the catch?"

"To uphold your end, you must accompany me with no attempt to escape nor to murder me."

Noticing several entrapping ways he could find gaps in the deal, I shake my head. "That's not specific enough—I don't want loopholes, demon."

His lips twitch. "Fine. Effective immediately, you will not make any attempt to murder me, and in return, I'll let you go free in two days' time. This means that in two days, after the fundraiser is over, I will not make any attempt to stop you, and you will be free to leave of your own will."

I wait for a moment for him to continue, frowning when he doesn't. "Or else?"

His brow raises. "Or else what?"

"I get dragged to hell? Your magic shreds me to pieces? What's the repercussions?"

He laughs harder, making my molars grind. "Where's the fun in telling you that?"

It's smart of him not to.

I've always been one to push limits or boundaries to test their elasticity. Magical backlash is not an exception to that rule. I'll have to assume I'll be subjected to an instant death if I breach our agreement.

"And what about after I'm free?" I ask, though the prospect of being released in two days is deliciously tempting on its own.

Orobas' crimson gaze flicks to the others for a moment. "I will not send anyone after you, if that's what you're worried about."

All I need to do is accompany him and not try to kill him for two days?

"This doesn't add up." A ghost of a smile graces his features, so I double down. "What's the catch?" I ask again firmly, knowing there's still more he's keeping under wraps.

"You heard my conversation with Dennis. We're going to be knowingly giving false information to uncover the mole, but I'd like a fresh set of eyes observing the other guests. None of them will recognize either of us, so you'll have the advantage of anonymity."

"You want me to become a double agent?"

Orobas shrugs. "You never know… you could learn something new. After all, this is some of the country's most powerful people gathered in one place." He pauses and raises a brow. "Would you rather remain bound here with Druv and Thal?"

Thal shakes his head vehemently as if making my decision for me, and Ishari snorts.

Orobas must know to some extent that his proposition tugs at my curiosity, because he hardly seems surprised when I raise my arms slightly.

"Fine. You have yourself a deal, demon." I murmur, waiting to feel some sort of zap or change from the pact, but there is none.

Orobas' lips twitch, and he inclines his head, stepping in close. My eyes don't leave him as he focuses on removing the bindings from my arms. "So we do."

The ropes drop to the ground, and the three demons behind Orobas fall still.

"For the banquet tonight, you'll come as my plus one, but I'd like you to mostly observe."

My hands rub where the rope had dug into my skin, though none of the marks are painful. "Sounds easy enough."

Orobas seems to be the only relaxed person in the room besides me, and I'm fairly certain the others haven't taken a breath since the rope fell to the floor. It's not until I turn them that they finally snap out of whatever tense daze they're in.

"You sure about this, Oro?" Druv glances between us, as if I'm not a woman of my word.

Well, I'm not. But that's not the point.

I'm viciously curious about what will come of this banquet, and I knew the moment he said he was bringing me I'd do what I need to in order to attend.

Politicians have some of the loosest lips in the world, especially when someone presses the right buttons. And by the sounds of it, Orobas is planning to push all the buttons he can.

Orobas reaches over to lift my still-damp hair from my shoulders as he ignores Druv's question. "She'll need her hair done, Ishari. Once you're finished, bring her to my office."

The action feels too familiar for my taste—too nonchalant—and I grit my teeth.

Ishari nods in response, and I watch as the demon prince disappears into the hallway without another word.

If I'm lucky, his enemies at this banquet will kill him, so I don't have to. Then, I'll waltz back here and retrieve the dagger myself.

Something tells me it won't be that easy, and that if anything is bound to go wrong, it'll be something to do with taking that damn blade from them.

Ishari steps over to me with a deep inhale. "Well." She breathes. "I guess this means we're temporary allies for now."

Druv and Thal look tense enough that I have to consciously bite back my laughter.

"I said I wouldn't kill him," I say plainly, glancing between Thal and Druv. "I never said *anything* about his minions."

Ishari freezes in front of me, and my eyes lock onto hers as I shrug. "But you're safe for now, I guess."

She laughs quietly under her breath, but I know the laughter is more stress related than humor as she grabs hold of my hand and tugs me toward the bathroom.

"You can murder me *after* I do your hair, or else we'll both have Oro to deal with." She says, grabbing the blow-dryer from the cabinet.

Chapter 12

Scarlett

By the time Ishari's done my hair, I've listened to Druv and Thal banter back and forth on several topics, none of which are important in any sense of the word.

Ishari's been quiet, laughing here or there at something they said, but for the entire hour and a half it took, I mostly observed their interactions.

Druv is definitely the strategist of them, which makes sense considering his doubt of Orobas' decision to let me have freedom. Thal is more happy-go-lucky wherever Ishari is involved, and she's somewhere in between the two.

And while I can easily see Druv and Thal murdering innocent humans that give them a wrong look, I can't seem to bring myself to feel the same way toward Ishari.

It's making me uncomfortable.

She sprays some kind of perfume into my hair and appraises her handiwork. "You need a little liner and mascara to finish it all off, but I'd say you are banquet-ready." She reaches over into one of the cabinet drawers, pulling out two black tubes.

When she turns to position herself in front of me with her face an inch from mine, she grins.

"Now close your eyes and don't move a muscle." She whispers, and I fail to suppress a grin as hers widen. "Ah! What did I say?!"

Thal and Druv are tense on either side of me, and if I wasn't trying hard to really listen to Ishari, I'd have rolled my eyes. Instead, going against all instinct in a room filled with demons, I slide them shut.

At this point, she's probably the safest person in this room with me.

The felt-tip liner glides along my closed lid in one long motion before moving to the other side.

"Okay, let's see those beauties." She chimes, and I peel them open slowly, careful not to widen them too much.

No one likes eyeliner on their upper lids.

Her brown eyes search mine, and she gives me such a genuine smile that something in my chest tightens. "Great. Now, I promise not to stab you in the eye."

I snort a laugh, and she grins wider. "Look down for me."

She works on my left eyelashes, and I stare at our feet. Never in a million years did I think I'd be sitting in a room surrounded by demons and letting my guard down this much.

Hell, I never thought I'd be standing in a room of demons and not about to kill them. I'm sure they didn't expect to be in a room with a Wraith and not be locked into some kind of fight.

Things change, I guess.

She finishes putting mascara on my lashes and takes a step back. The satisfaction in her expression is contagious, and I can't fight the smile creeping across my face.

"Good God, that's terrifying." Druv grumbles, moving over to stand beside Thal.

Thal nods. "We need to get them away from each other."

When I raise an eyebrow at both of them, they put their hands up in surrender. "Not that we will."

"No, no. We *should,* but we won't."

"I mean, we're just joking, anyway."

"Yeah, definitely not serious," Druv mutters. "At all."

Ishari shakes her head. "Well, we're not getting any younger. Time for you to find Oro and hit the town."

My stomach grumbles, and she laughs. "Don't worry. There will be plenty of food there."

"I sure hope so," I sigh, following her to the door. "I'm liable to break oaths when I'm hangry."

Ishari laughs, and I hear Thal curse behind us. Their displeasure at Ishari and me getting along only makes me more inclined to enjoy my time around her.

So I do.

"Do you ever get hangry?" I ask, and she just nods solemnly.

"I locked Thal out of the house once and wouldn't let him in until he brought me chicken wings and fries."

My eyes widen, and I turn to stare at Thal. "And did he?!"

"This is unbelievable." He mutters, looking at Druv helplessly. "Any backup here, man?"

Druv shakes his head, and Ishari grins triumphantly. "He did, but he didn't get the flavor wings I wanted."

My eyes narrow at him before I turn my attention to her. "Garlic Parmesan?"

Her eyes flutter, and she smiles. "Hot honey. Garlic Parmesan is wonderful, though." She sighs wistfully and leads the way to Orobas' office. "After he finally brought me my wings, I avoided talking to him until I was done, because I was afraid I'd say something I'd regret."

I chuckle, and she grins in response, her body's relaxed compared to the stiff movements of both men. As if noticing, Thal steps closer on her other side as Druv paces faster to my left, but still giving me enough space not to be crowding.

It's easy for me to see the three of them are close—closer than expected for carefree demons with no morals. That doesn't explain how they came to work under Orobas, though.

"So, you all... work for the demon prince?" *Is work even the right word?*

Druv huffs a quiet laugh, drawing my attention as he catches himself. "I mean, he pays us, but this is the most work we've done in years."

My brow twitches. "I'm **work**?" I ask incredulously, and Thal snickers.

Druv gives me a deadpan stare. "You are."

"Oh, she's not that bad," Ishari chimes, and much to my surprise, she hooks her arm in mine. "She's just... a little different."

Thal, however, stares at her like she's grown a second head. "Ari, **do** you realize they conditioned her to want to murder us in our sleep?"

She shrugs. "Don't judge a book by its cover. Besides, I've been needing some more femininity around here."

We climb the steps to Orobas' office, and I see Thal shake his head. He says nothing though, and by the time we're at the door, I've resigned myself to not getting an answer.

Druv swings the door open to the room where Orobas sits at his desk, his brows pinched together as he stares at his laptop screen. But when we file inside, moving to stand in the center of the room, his crimson eyes are like laser pointers as they fixate on me.

My pulse picks up, and the cool air suddenly becomes stifling. If someone had told me he could summon fire or heat, I'd have fully believed them with how the room warms by a few degrees whenever he's in it.

"Well..." Ishari grins. "She's all done."

Blood-red irises travel the length of my body before a smile graces his features. "Who knew the infamous Viper could clean up so well?" He closes his laptop and pushes to his feet as he smooths out his cuffs. His long strides around the desk suck the air from the room one at a time until he's beside Thal.

Ishari clasps her hands in front of her body. "Remember to be back before bedtime." She teases, and the demon prince chuckles.

The deep chest-rumbled response from him has me swallowing, and he shoves his hands into his pockets, his eyes flicking to each of the demons.

"You can leave us."

Druv pauses, his gaze bouncing back and forth between us, as if he's about to say something. He must decide against it because he turns away, and follows the others out the door.

Definitely the smarter one.

Without the tentative peace I'd made with Ishari, being alone in a room with the prince of hell responsible for sowing so much chaos and division makes me more uncomfortable than I care to admit.

"So," I exhale and rest my hand on my hip. "Anything I should know before we enter the lion's den?"

He considers me for a moment. "When we arrive, Dennis has narrowed his suspicions down to four people. You will meet the others as my threat analyst, my financial interpreter, my cultural liaison or my logistics aide."

I raise an eyebrow at him. "At least I won't have to pretend to like you."

His lips twitch as crimson eyes pin me in place. "Would you prefer to be introduced as my wife?"

The blood drains from my face, and I shake my head. "Absolutely not. Do you *want* me to stab you in front of everyone?"

He chuckles, and I have to resist the urge to glare at him as he tilts his head teasingly. "Now, now, darling. We stab in private, not in front of company."

The taunt in his eyes is infuriating, and I cross my arms. "What's so important about going to this banquet and rooting out this mole? People leak politician's dirty laundry all the time."

He searches my face for a long moment. "Believe it or not, Viper, some people care about their image for more reasons than vanity.

Besides, it's an election year and with the global state of unrest, it's even more important for him to win."

I roll my eyes. "You say that as if he could actually make a difference."

"You clearly disagree." He walks to the door, and I follow close behind.

"Politicians are just a bunch of sleazy dudes all cut from the same cloth. All of it is for show."

He hums in agreement, and I choke down the surprise at how easily he conceded my statement. But I should have known better than to think he'd give up on the topic easily.

"So what should **good** politicians do then, Scarlett? Sit back and let the corrupt run everything?"

The sarcasm in his voice grates on my nerves, and my molars grind together. "That's clearly all they do now, hence why they're all cut from the same cloth."

We approach the front doors, and Orobas moves to hold it open. The bulging veins in his forearms tell me I've clearly gotten under his skin enough to raise his blood pressure.

"Tell me something, Viper." I breeze past him to the car that's parked in front of the steps. "Have you ever actually fought for what you believe in?"

What a ridiculous question.

I snort a laugh. "You're asking a trained assassin this? I knew you were dangerous, demon, but I didn't think you were an idiot."

"So, the answer is no, then?" He reaches past me to open the door as I raise a brow at his response.

Sliding into the passenger seat, it takes everything in me not to jab at what he is. "I've fought for what I believe in every damn day since they pulled me off the streets, demon. Some of us weren't born into our positions and had to claw our way to a life worth living."

His crimson eyes linger on me for a long moment, but he closes the door without a word. It's not until he's walked around the front of the vehicle and slid into the driver's seat that I can tell my response struck a nerve.

"So you believe in killing demons?" He asks, seemingly more cautious than before.

I don't know what his angle is, but this line of questioning makes me uncomfortable. Perhaps because it's like he's trying to undermine everything I've known to prove some point.

"I believe that ridding the world of evil is my duty."

He frustratingly nods, like it's the first sensible thing I've said to him. "Perhaps it is, but have you ever wondered if what you're doing is the right thing to do?"

A dry laugh escapes me, and I shake my head as he puts the car into drive. "I'm a weapon. I don't question where they aim me, but I've seen enough to know that I've killed some truly terrible assholes."

"I don't doubt that, but I do wonder about the circumstances of it all."

Heat rises to my cheeks. "What's that supposed to mean? You think you can just start asking questions about my orders and think I'll change sides?" My sharp tone is more shrill than I expect it to be, but I'm too annoyed by his interrogation to stop. "You're a manipulative bastard. Do you know that?"

There's a long moment of silence that stretches between us, and I don't know whether I'm thankful or frustrated by it.

His hands tighten on the wheel, and I glance over to see the muscle in jaw feathering. "You think me to be your enemy, Viper, yet you've been raised by the very wolves you were taught to kill. I'm not expecting you to switch sides, but I believe you're capable of seeing the contradictions laid out before you. You just have to want to see them."

I stay quiet beside him, if only to avoid lashing out on instinct. Something about Orobas makes me want to rage, to riot against everything he says, and does.

Because how dare he try to undermine my lived experiences that prove there's true evil in this world?

I can immediately recall a handful of times when I witnessed the abuse and greed of the targets I was assigned to. With every single one, if I hadn't been there at that exact moment, innocent people could have died.

And yet, the warehouse and how Henley Corporation is still functional threatens to unravel every confident bone in my body.

If I hadn't seen it with my own eyes, calling Orobas a manipulative demon would be much easier. Still, it begs the question—if I were to return to each target, every location... what would I find?

Denial and anger vie for dominance as I turn my attention out the window, watching trees and houses pass by.

Regardless of what Orobas' angle is, in two more days, I'll be free from his company and I can return to normal.

Whatever that looks like after this.

Chapter 13

Evelyn

With the med-bay door sliding shut behind me, my heels click against the laminate floor.

Omen's condition has only improved slightly since the last time I'd seen her. The medically induced coma they've kept her in hasn't helped my perception either.

They suspect she'd be in too much pain if they were to wake her now, but were hopeful with the infusion of my blood they'd extracted recently, she'd be awake before nightfall.

Soldiers pass by me through the long hallways, giving me plenty of space, most of which I don't recognize. Not that I mind anyway.

The less I know of these militants, the less I will care when they all inevitably pass on. Daevari live almost fully immortal lives, according to command, so most of these humans will be long gone like a drop in the ocean of my life.

If I don't get myself killed before then.

The door to Scarlett's room comes into view, and I exhale a long breath, punching in her pin as a mechanical whirring fills the air. The door opens, and I step inside with my heart in my throat.

With her being on a solo mission, there's only one way to contact her that's low risk.

It takes all of three steps to approach the closet, and I drop to my knees, rummaging through a metal box on the ground.

I know there are cameras in our rooms, but according to Grant, who apparently hacked into the feeds a few times before, they only cover the entrances.

Despite that, I'm cautious, feeling around various bottles of poison and sheathed daggers until my fingers find contact with the familiar smooth edges of Scarlett's burner phone.

When we had first truly bonded as a group, we'd each gotten one. Each one has five pins that allow access, and we add our personal burner to our phone contacts while on missions as a mom, sister, cousin, or best friend.

It's the only number that isn't blocked and deleted when we are on an undercover mission.

Turning the phone over, I press the power button, and the logo flashes bright against the shadows of the closet. The lock screen disappears when I put my pin in, and I quickly pull up the messages with Scarlett's cell.

My fingers fly over the digital keyboard, typing out a cryptic text before hitting send. I wouldn't have to give much detail for her to know it's me. That she's receiving a message from this phone should tell her enough considering only the two of us are in any condition to function.

The message shows sent, and I stare at the screen for what feels like an eternity.

My attention turns to the time, and a pit of dread forms in my gut.

There's no way she'd still be undercover at seven o'clock in the evening.

So I sit there, chewing the side of my thumbnail as I wait impatiently, staring at the checkmark next to the message like that would make her read it faster.

Best-case scenario, she's showering after a long day, and she'll see my message within the hour. Worst-case scenario, she's dead.

Bile rises in my throat, and I shut that train of thought down.

Knowing Scarlett, even if she was caught, she's likely carving someone up into tiny pieces and making them regret their existence.

The checkmarks under the message haven't budged, and I set the phone down, looking around her room thoughtfully. When my attention lands on the touchscreen above her dresser, quickly push to my feet and cross the room.

If I can find out where she was assigned, I can track her down without command knowing that Grant cracked into the laptop's contents.

Keying in Scarlett's pin, the screen flickers and opens to her inbox. Her four new emails are standard news/announcements for the entire base that we all receive, but I spot the most recently read email flagged as top secret and bring it up.

There's a fine line between treason and leadership as the Harbinger, but I like to think I walk it well.

It's not until I read through who her target is that the dread coiled in my gut finally makes a lot more sense.

A prince of fucking hell?

I would understand her infiltrating a demon operation, but the home of a prince of hell?!

She better be safe, or I'm going to kill each member of command myself, and whoever assigned this solo mission to her will receive a very special session.

Surveying the room again, I grow increasingly aware of what a fucking abomination of a mission she's been sent headfirst into. Dust lines her dresser, fingerprints stare at me from the mirror, and the overflowing trash next to her bed brings my horror to a whole new level.

Scarlett isn't even a good housekeeper. She wouldn't last more than a day, and it's been a fucking week.

Shit.

My phone vibrates in my pocket, and I fumble pulling it out of my suit, noticing a notification from the nurse in med-bay that Omen is awake and has been released.

The knowledge is a little reassuring, and I memorize the prince's address before returning to the closet. To no one's surprise, Scarlett hasn't read my messages, but I've already decided the Revenant's next steps to secure Scarlett's safety.

Turning the phone off and placing it in the box, I move everything where it was before I came in.

My feet carry me out the door in record time, and I'm near jogging down the hallway to Omen's room. Hers is only a minute away, but every second that passes until I get there, and each one that follows as I wait for her, feels like an eternity.

When Omen's tall form turns the corner, her steps are slow and ginger. But at least she's alive.

"You look like shit, Omen." I muse, and she stares at me with glassy eyes.

"I feel like it." She croaks, keying in her pin.

The door slides open, and we walk inside. I move to stand outside the view of the camera, and she does the same, slowly heading for the washroom.

"I take it Grizz and Mako didn't make it?"

My head snaps in her direction as she shoulders out of the gown they'd given her. I don't need to answer as she returns my gaze.

"Fuck." She whispers, turning the shower on with a wince.

Grabbing the pen and notepad beside her bed, she watches me silently and peels her underwear off. She says nothing as she gets under the water, keeping the curtain open as I approach, holding the paper in my palm for her to read.

Grant told us the cameras in the rooms didn't have microphones, but warned us never to verbally discuss matters we wouldn't want command to know of.

We learned our lesson the first time we'd disobeyed command's orders during an assignment. I'd pulled the team together, and worked through a plan B, since our mission was sure to go sideways.

We were in line of sight of the cameras by the door, and evidently they'd discovered some of what we'd discussed. It's not enough to say definitively that they can hear us, but better safe than sorry.

Her gaze doesn't seem as sharp as usual, but she reads the note and curses under her breath before giving me a nod in acknowledgement.

I knew she wouldn't argue, considering the note states that Scarlett is MIA on a solo mission undercover, the target is a prince of hell, and that we're going to find her.

After losing Mako and Grizz, I'm certain she'd want to save Scarlett from the same fate as much as I do.

"How are you feeling?" I ask, scribbling down onto the paper for her to meet me at my quarters tomorrow morning.

When I hold it out for her to see, she leans over to it with a wince. Her eyes move from side to side as she reads it and nods.

"Feeling better than Mako and Grizz. I'll be right as rain before tomorrow, though."

My lips twitch, and I nod. "Take it easy tonight, Omen."

"Yes, Madam Harbinger." She says with a hint of amusement, and I glare at her formality, even if it's a joke.

Leaving her to her shower, I return to my own quarters with a heavy mind.

If we're going to have any hope of retrieving Scarlett, we'll have to do so with surgical precision. This means finding as much information as possible about the prince of hell and his organization.

I come to a stop in front of my room and sigh.

Which means a visit to see Grant.

I can't say I'm not excited to see him, but it means bringing another person into my plan, which is another opportunity for command to find out.

~

By the time I've knocked in the familiar rhythm only we would know, my anxiety about Scarlett being on a death-mission has reached its height.

My heart is a war drum in my chest, and a long moment passes when the door swings open.

"Eve?" he says with wide eyes, glancing around before gesturing inside.

The door slides shut behind me, and I walk as far away from it as possible to where his laptop sits. My eyes roam the walls and ceiling as he laughs quietly.

"I did a full sweep this morning, Eve," he says cautiously. "What's going on?"

"Scarlett was given that solo mission and isn't responding." I whisper, tears stinging the corners of my eyes and his brows pull together. "She was assigned to Orobas, Grant."

"Shit." He says, pressing his palms to his eyes and rubbing them. "A prince of hell? What the fuck is command thinking?"

"I don't know, but we have to do something." Am I doing the wrong thing by telling him?

"Whoa, whoa, whoa." He rears back, his expression stern. "You're not seriously thinking about running in there, guns blazing."

"Of course not; I'm not an idiot." I deadpan, pacing back and forth. "But I need all the information I can get. Where he's going to be, what his property looks like, how many demons he has working for him."

Grant releases a dry laugh. "He's a prince of hell, Eve. He has *legions* at his disposal."

"Please, Grant." I whisper, holding his gaze as my eyes burn. "I can't lose anyone else."

A long moment passes, and the muscle in his jaw ticks, but he nods. "Alright. Take a seat. I'll find what I can."

I step over and slide into the chair beside his as he opens a window of some search engine I'd never seen before, and his fingers fly over the keyboard.

The research he does passes by fast, and he seemingly only looks over a page before moving to the next. The first window he sets aside is for some banquet the demon is going to be attending, and the other is a fundraiser, but it's the registered name next to his that has my blood running cold.

Scarlett Ashford.

The fucker used her entire government name to register her in these events, like waving a giant fucking flag, screaming that she's compromised.

"I'm going to kill them." I whisper, and Grant uses his hand on my chin to turn my head away from the screen toward him.

"No guns blazing." He reiterates firmly, and even though I'd always seen him in his cyber warfare persona, for a glimmer of a moment, I see the militant come to the surface.

But the soldier in Grant doesn't feel the same, maybe because he has a vested interest in my life, but I can't let this sudden order make me change my mind.

"I never said we were going to run in guns blazing." I reiterate, because it's the truth. "Recon only. I need to make sure she's alive and figure out a way to retrieve her."

If they have harmed so much as a hair on her head, though, they'll all die. I will tear them to pieces in front of the prince of hell and save him for last.

"Have I ever told you how sexy you are when you're pissed?"

That snaps me out of my vengeful thoughts, and I blink at him. "Now is *so* not the time, Grant."

He laughs under his breath. "Now is most definitely the best time."

I snort. "I'm more likely to hurt you right now than fuck you."

His lips twitch, and he shuts his laptop to yank my chair closer. I lift my legs to keep our knees from smashing together, and he pulls them on either side of his body before hauling me into his lap.

"What is pleasure without a little pain, Eve."

My heart stutters, and I grip his biceps to steady myself, digging my nails in as he winces slightly.

But it's the way he groans and slams his lips to mine that sends all rational thought from my mind.

Chapter 14

Evelyn

Three hours of sitting in this tree, and I've yet to see any sign of Scarlett or the prince of hell.

Omen's assignment should be moderately more safe than this, considering the prince's property is teeming with demons. At any given moment there are several surrounding the building, two watching the gates, one to two by the door, and God himself only knows how many are inside.

When the garage door opened, I saw Scarlett's vehicle, so I know she's either in there or dead.

I really hope it's not the latter for everyone's sake.

As much as I'm an assassin by necessity, it doesn't mean I enjoy killing people. Demons or otherwise.

But evil is as evil does.

Resting my head against a thick branch, I release a long sigh.

By all counts, I've estimated roughly a hundred demons have either guarded the property or come and gone since I climbed into this tree.

A hundred is more than I originally expected, but less than what I suspect the actual number is. It's not outside the realm of possibility for me to take out so many, but judging by their patterns, there's no consistency to when they move around.

Which means they're a chaotic operation at best.

Still, I recognize some faces as I bring the binoculars to my eyes. Four guards rotate every couple of hours at the gates, with two demon males seemingly in command.

The two do rounds of the property, checking in with the guards before disappearing inside for a couple of hours.

Still, it's the closest thing to a pattern I've been able to establish, even if it's not a routine that reduces the number of demons on the property.

They, in all likelihood, are closer to Orobas than the others in rank. Perhaps part of his circle and responsible for maintaining order while he's busy or absent.

The wind howls through the tops of the trees, rustling the branches that sway along with it, and I shiver. After a few more hours of this, I'll hopefully have enough intel to figure out the best time to make a move to look for Scarlett.

Or the dagger.

Motion near the front of the property has me bringing the binoculars up once more, but I already know it's time for the two demons to make their rounds.

I watch as they stop to talk to the guard outside the front door, but it's not the two male demons that have my attention. It's the shorter female with her arm hooked around the waist of one of them that has my eyes widening.

I suppose it's not surprising that demons seek companionship. It's an instinct for all species, regardless of where they come from. Procreation is the king of all.

The trio does their rounds slower than the two would have alone, seemingly more focused on conversation than their job.

Which means the other two likely hurries through it so that one of them can return to her.

Sweet... in some demonic kind of way.

It'll be unfortunate when I have to kill them.

The trio disappear inside shortly after, and I release a long sigh.

I know there are various ways I could recover Scarlett unharmed, with a few more bloody than others, but most will require me to take out countless demons to retrieve her.

But for now, as much as I itch to run in Rambo-style, I will wait.

Grant's order in the back of my mind echoes within every part of my skull, and I swallow the urge to go against him.

I'm not sure what the hell command was thinking when they assigned Scarlett to this fucking prince, but once she's safe and sound, I'll tear into them as much as I will these demons.

They're risking everything for what?

A stupid fucking dagger?

Unbelievable.

Chapter 15

Scarlett

It's not long before the rural streets we pass through melt into immaculately landscaped properties far too expensive for most people in this city.

Having lived here for a short time, it's not surprising that I haven't explored enough of it to recognize where we are, but judging by the look of these buildings, I assume we're in the south end of the city.

Impressively shaped bushes and trees line the street, with vibrant green grass stretching hundreds of yards back to where various mansions sit. Fountains and statues worth more than my weight in gold accent each one, the intricate details etched into them hardly worn from weather.

The further we drive, the greater the distance between the properties, and I know we're getting close.

If the handful of Rolls-Royce and Bugattis were any indication. Orobas skillfully maneuvers the vehicle to the front of an enormous house that's large enough to be a mall. My gaze sweeps over countless people dressed to the nines as they make their way into the entrance, leaving their vehicles to be parked by an impressive number of valet staff out front.

"Look alive, Viper." Orobas grins, his crimson eyes pale in the low light of dusk. "This is your chance to prove me wrong."

Our doors open as the staff wait for us to climb out, and I shove my uncertainty about Orobas' intent aside. He might be here to help Dennis expose a rat in the nest, but this banquet could bring so much more than that to light.

Climbing out of the car, Orobas takes the lead, and we merge with the crowd filing inside. We hardly make it more than a few feet past the front doors when Dennis appears from nowhere.

"Good to see you could make it." He murmurs, his attention sweeping around us until it lands on me. "Is she going to complicate things?"

Orobas' mouth drops open to answer, but I beat him to it. "You have nothing to worry about."

The politician's brown eyes bounce between us warily, but he just gestures toward the doors. "I've seated everyone far enough apart that we won't have to worry about any mishaps or eavesdropping if I can help it."

Orobas grins. "It will be fine, Dennis. Everything will be fine. Just remember what I told you."

Dennis swallows, glancing around with a nod. "Right. Well, here goes nothing."

We're hardly over ten feet into the main hallway when he grabs a glass of champagne from a server and throws it back. He returns the empty cup just to grab another one. The tension in the way he walks is palpable, like he's coiled to run.

If this is how he's going to act the entire night, we're in trouble. Even without training, any normal person would instinctively know he's hiding something.

The long hall is crowded as most people head toward the enormous room up ahead. Extravagant curtains drape from the ceiling to the floor at the mouth where the hallway ends, giving way to countless decorated tables with a stage near the front. There's enough people here to fill a stadium; with half of the crowd chattering lively, the rest focused on locating their seats.

With how many people there are, it'd be a surprise to find anyone you know in this sea of bodies. But I'm sure if you were a mole keeping an eye out for someone, especially one who looks as stand-out as Orobas—it wouldn't be that hard to find him.

The crimson eyes alone are a dead giveaway.

But if they don't know what Orobas looks like, then they'd be watching for Dennis…

My gaze sweeps over the attendees, most too lost in their own world to pay any attention to us. Here or there, someone glances in Dennis' direction, but recognition never reaches their eyes.

With Orobas to my right, his arm brushing against my shoulder, I continue to survey the people to our left as they find their seats. Name cards line each table, clearly showing who's sitting where, but over here everyone seems to know which table belongs to them at least.

"Tildman!" A voice booms, and I slow my steps almost to a halt, slowly turning my attention toward the newcomer without moving my head. A middle-aged Caucasian man grins broadly as Dennis chuckles under his breath. "Here I thought they said they were going to remove you from the guest list."

They clasp hands, and I watch the two men of similar stature grin from ear to ear. "Luckily for you, they'd have to handcuff me to the gates outside to keep me away." Their hands shake, and Dennis is first to pull back, gesturing to Orobas and me.

"Ah, how rude of me; allow me to introduce you to Nathan Cole, my private security advisor." The vein in Dennis' neck looks like it might burst—a stark contrast to the ease in his expression.

Orobas nods curtly and reaches over to shake the man's hand.

"Nathan, this is Tyler Hall, my legal director and royal pain in my ass."

Tyler huffs a laugh as he shakes Orobas' hand. "Dennis never mentioned hiring a security advisor." He says with a smile, but something about him makes my skin crawl. "But I can't deny we need one, considering the recent fire Dennis has been under."

Dennis chuckles as the two men release one another's hands. "Nathan will do just fine, I'm sure. He's spent time in conflict zones and been successful with his assignments in those endeavors, so this should be a cakewalk."

Tyler's eyes shoot up. "Conflict zones, as in—"

"Kharidia." Orobas interjects quickly just as Dennis' mouth opens, and Nathan turns a shade more pale.

When the man's attention leaves Orobas and lands on me, I feel myself tense ever so slightly—an odd feeling considering how accustomed I am to functioning under duress.

"And this is?" He asks, his eyes flicking to Dennis.

"I'm Nathan's logistics aide." I say, my voice coming out steady, but Tyler doesn't seem too interested in my presence anymore. His attention's focused on Orobas and Dennis, letting me do one of the many things I love.

Observe.

Dennis murmurs something that I don't quite catch, but both the others laugh in response, and I count the seconds between his intakes of breath. The two chatter away about who is in attendance, with Orobas contributing to the conversation in minimalistic ways.

As much as I want to uncover who the mole is, half my attention stays on Orobas, knowing at any point I could finally catch him in the act. He might claim innocence to manipulating people, but demons have been known to lie a time or two.

Tyler holds Orobas' gaze as he asks him a question, and his pupils dilate as he finishes his sentence. When the vein in his forehead slightly bulges, I file that information away for later.

"Well, this has been fun, Tyler, but I'm afraid we have a table with our names on it," Dennis says wistfully, and Tyler nods with a broad smile.

"You know where I'll be." His shoulders drop, and he shakes their hands. "Try to keep Tildman out of trouble, will ya?"

Orobas' lips twitch. "He seems to be a magnet for it."

Tyler nods in agreement and waves once before he strides toward his table. Each step seems practiced but tense until he pulls his chair back, and I tear my gaze from him.

With only minor flags of any anxiety or agitation, it's hard to say if Tyler's reaction was due to any number of things. With such a large setting and countless factors, it'll be impossible to know for certain.

For now, anyway.

Dennis leads us to the right, weaving through bodies until we get to an empty table with three names on cards propped up on each.

Dennis, James, Scarlett.

The sight of my real name sends a cold note of dread down my spine.

I might not have slit his throat the moment he removed my bindings, but this puts everything I've worked so hard for at risk.

Orobas slides my chair out, and I grit my teeth as I ease into it.

The tables are far enough apart that I wouldn't need to whisper to tear into him, but it's the fact that something doesn't add up that's holding me back.

Clearly, it's not the end of the world if someone knows my name, given that the Revenants aren't famous enough for that to be my downfall, but it's more than that.

It's the fact that he's put an enormous sign up for command to see that I'm compromised.

And It's the fact that he's hidden his name and exposed mine that's really stirred something in me.

Whether he did it as a slight or to taunt me, I have no idea, but I assume it's the latter.

Typical demons and their attitudes.

"Excuse me, Mr. Tildman." A young woman approaches Dennis' left, her red lips pulled into a smile that reaches her eyes. Her sleek, form-fitting cocktail dress hugs her body in all the right places, with the verdant green making her hazel eyes and long brunette hair stand out even more.

"Ah, Ms. Loren, so good to see you," Dennis says with a grin. By the time he's on his feet, they're embracing, and she lets out a chuckle.

"Remind me next time you send out invites to a fundraiser to request a closer table." She murmurs, glancing the way she came. "I'm next to Glen and Lisa." She adds, veiling none of her exasperation.

Dennis bites back a laugh. "Sounds like you're in a perfect position to understand some of our greatest opposition." He muses and gestures toward the open bar to his left. "Maybe bringing back a drink or two could help?"

She rolls her eyes. "Yeah, help me not throw myself off a ledge, maybe."

My lips twitch, and Orobas' crimson eyes flick to mine, and for once I see a hint of uncertainty behind them. It's gone as quickly as it came, leaving me to wonder if I'd imagined it all along.

Could it be the woman or something else causing it?

He leans to his right slightly, keeping his attention forward even as his head turns to me. "Are you enjoying yourself yet, viper?"

With Dennis and Loren still quietly talking amongst themselves, my gaze sweeps the area for any lingering eyes in our direction. "If this is what you consider fun, demon, I fear you have wasted an eternity."

I don't bother watching his reaction, but hear his answering chuckle. "I'd much prefer to be somewhere relaxing—on a beach, maybe."

The snort that escapes me is unexpected, and it takes a millisecond to compose myself.

Who knew the demon could joke? "That's the last thing I thought you'd ever **choose** to do for relaxation."

"I'm full of surprises, it seems." He muses as a handful of servers bring small plates of appetizers. When I pick up the knife from the table and twirl it in my fingers, his crimson gaze tracks the movement. "I suppose since you've yet to bury that in my throat, you're full of them too."

The giggle that escapes me is genuine, and I shrug. "The night is still young, demon prince."

"So it is." He hums in agreement, but something about his response only makes my temptation to stab him greater, so I take a bite of some kind of quiche that the servers dispersed to each table.

An older man steps up to the lectern in the middle of the stage, and I keep my eyes on him, while watching the surrounding guests in my peripherals.

As his speech starts, heads at tables turn toward him, smiling and laughing as he makes comments that feel more like inside jokes to the powerful few in attendance.

The man drones on and on, talking about Dennis' accomplishments and his team's hard work—all things I'm near certain were part of Orobas' manipulations.

Earning the votes of so many in towns with low voter turnout screams cheating the system.

Pushing for higher spending budgets that I'm sure just line his pockets more than give back to the civilians.

Adding amendments to bills that somehow miraculously pass.

My gaze absently slides to Orobas, from his defined jawline to the tattoos peering from the collar of his shirt.

There's no way Dennis is a straight shooter with that track record.

No wonder he's worried about things leaking.

And our little experiment is going to harm him more than help him when word gets out regarding all the different foreign entities he's involved with.

Motion to my right catches my eye, but I don't directly look at the out-of-place shadow across the room behind the furthest tables. Keeping my attention forward, waiting for it to move again, the dark remains still, frustratingly so.

My eyes water, and I half-blink to clear them, only for the shadow to disappear. My gaze flicks over to see three men sitting at a table, their eyes trained on the speaker.

One brunette, hair coated in gel, the other bald with a deep crease in his forehead and the third—a younger man with longer hair streaked with blonde. All unassuming, but the goosebumps on the back of my neck make my hair stand on end, and I have to force my attention off them.

Lesson number one in the demon-assassin handbook: Always trust your instincts.

And right now, my instinct is telling me that something is off.

"Should I be concerned, Viper?"

I jolt at the sound of Orobas' voice, my heart thundering as I turn my attention to where he's leaned over, his crimson irises trained on me.

When they flick to the table, I follow to the whites of my knuckles from how tightly I hold the knife. Setting it beside my plate and retracting my hands to my lap, I shake my head.

"It's fine."

Orobas' gaze lingers on me for a moment, and I want to crawl out of my skin until he finally turns forward. Surprisingly, he doesn't press more, but I don't miss the way his eyes wander the room.

Could it be that another demon is here? Hiding in the shadows?

Does he know about it, or could there be fighting between demonic factions?

I've felt a general sense of unease the entire time I've been by Orobas' side, but this was different.

Suppressing a shudder, my eyes find the man in the middle of the room as he grins, still prattling on about various things Dennis has achieved.

Two days. I just have to put up with this for two days.

Chapter 16

Scarlett

"Dennis, it's so good to see you."

Ugh.

I suppress an eye roll as the politician leans in to shake Dennis' hand.

"Griffin," Dennis grins broadly. "I was wondering when you'd show your ugly mug."

Griffin bellows a hearty laugh, oblivious to the undercurrent of tension Dennis carries in his shoulders. It's clear that this is another person he worries is the mole—considering the vein on the side of his neck looking like it might burst.

The two exchange a moment of pleasantries, and it's clear Dennis wants to trust him in the way his genuine smile creeps up into his expression when he lowers his guard.

"Ah, I almost forgot—" Dennis gestures toward Orobas. "Allow me to introduce you to James Rourke, my security consultant."

Griffin's eyebrows shoot up, but he reaches over to shake Orobas' hand. "I didn't know we needed one! Are you a contractor or...?"

Orobas doesn't miss a beat as his lips twitch. "Of sorts. Private syndicate on a need to know basis."

The curiosity in Griffin's expression is clear, and when his attention turns to me, my heart skips a beat.

"And you're the hired muscle?"

Orobas lets out a genuine laugh, and part of me wishes I'd held onto the knife from dinner just to stab him with it. "She is my threat analyst."

The way he says the word 'my' makes my molars grind together.

Griffin's eyebrows stay halfway up his forehead. "Huh, I'll be damned. Is there any threat here?"

Dennis smiles, but the way his eyes shift tells me he's worried about us all being seen together, so I decide to do him a favor.

"The only threat in this room is me if I don't get to find a restroom." Clasping my hands in front of me, I give Dennis a saccharine smile. "Would you be so kind as to show this gal to the ladies' room?"

Dennis holds his palms out. "Of course. If you would excuse us, Griffin."

I turn away, my shoulder brushing Orobas' arm as we pace in the opposite direction slowly.

"Smooth exit, Viper."

A mixture of annoyance and satisfaction rifles through me at his words, and my gaze sweeps around us cautiously.

"It was that, or I ask him to show me to the ladies' room, and he seemed like the type to follow me inside."

Orobas clicks his tongue. "I'd rather not have dead bodies lying around a fundraiser that, for all intents and purposes, is otherwise going well."

I snort. "I never said I'd kill him."

Dennis approaches on my left as Orobas leans in, his breath cascading over the shell of my ear.

"Neither did I."

My heart stutters, but I don't have time to respond when Dennis crosses his arms over his chest.

"Two down, one to go." He murmurs, his eyes are fixed on the crowd ahead, so I aim straight in that direction.

I want tonight to be over with. It's bad enough I have to play pretend like I don't want to find the nearest sharp object and ram it into Orobas' throat.

What's worse is that I haven't seen the demon try to manipulate a single damn person—I have half a mind to think he's holding himself back.

Slowing my pace, I let Orobas and Dennis take the lead, weaving through the crowd, eyes lingering as they follow us.

A shadow in the corner of my eye darts out of my peripheral vision, and the hairs on the back of my neck stand on end.

"Dennis!" A man bellows up ahead, and I slow my pace even further, allowing space to grow between me and the others.

From here I can still hear as Dennis introduces Orobas to the two newcomers, but thankfully I'm able to get a better view of the full interaction while keeping an eye out for whatever shadow is following us.

"Jordan, Thomas, this is Elliot Grant, a private energy investor."

Orobas shakes hands with Jordan first, before doing the same with Thomas. "Pleasure to meet you both."

It takes a serious effort not to roll my eyes at how much detail he puts into adjusting his demeanor to match his job title.

Judging by their body language as they talk with Dennis and Orobas, I can confidently say these two aren't the moles. With that knowledge in mind, I let my eyes wander, surveying the crowd as various investors chatter away with others.

The number of people with puffed-up chests, rich laughs and expensive clothes makes me want to gag.

"Ready to leave?" Orobas' voice to my right jolts me, and I blink away my surprise as I nod.

"Lead the way, demon."

Orobas chuckles, and I grind my teeth as he heads toward the front entrance. When I realize it's just the two of us, I glance around before leaning in.

"Is it smart to leave him here alone?"

Orobas' crimson gaze turns on me for a moment. "Are you expecting trouble?"

"Of course not." I murmur, side-stepping a server. "You'd think if he's such a target, though, he'd need extra security."

That earns me another chuckle, and I regret saying anything. "Dennis will be fine."

We slow to a stop in the main hallway that's so overcrowded that even the servers offering refreshments have little room to move with their handfuls of drinks.

Orobas gestures to the door on our left. "We can take that and get around this mess."

The distance to it is a fraction of the length of the hallway to the main entrance, but with everyone being shoulder to shoulder, it's only mere feet before I'm having to squeeze my way between various guests.

Each step to the door only becomes more crowded, with three taller, overweight men constricting my space.

"Excuse me." I chew out as the man in front of me presses forward, his round gut squishing me into the shoulder of the man at my back.

I'm not usually one to shy away from small spaces, but the bodies surrounding me are suffocating—to where I'm beginning to question if I might actually have some form of claustrophobia.

A hand encircles my bicep, turning me sideways as Orobas steps between me and the distended belly, his solid form an odd relief as the shoulder at my back presses in harder.

The length of my body lies flush with Orobas' side, his hip digging into my navel, but somehow it's arguably better than having some man's gut squeezing me to death.

"She was being polite," Orobas says in a low voice to the man. "I do not have such manners."

Brown irises meet crimson, and I suppress a laugh as the man's face turns a shade more pale. He says nothing but adjusts his feet, shifting to the side and out of the way inch by inch.

Orobas doesn't release my arm, but his hand slides down to grasp mine, and he shoulders his way past people in the crowd. My skin crawls with the contact between us, and it takes a conscious effort not to cringe away from him as his fingers intertwine with mine.

Oblivious to the rising urge to find the nearest sharp object to stab him, Orobas gently guides me forward, his imposing form making it much easier to intimidate guests out of the way.

By the time we arrive at the door, a bead of sweat rolls down the back of my neck, and I suppress a shiver. The number of bodies surrounding us has made the room exponentially warmer, and I can't be more excited to see our escape route mere inches away.

Orobas eases the door open with one hand, releasing me as I slip past him into the empty corridor. White and grey marble pillars mark the space at regular intervals before the hallway curves to the right.

I exhale a long breath as my heels click against the porcelain tiles, echoing off the walls of the empty hall.

"Tell me something, Viper," Orobas murmurs as the door slides shut behind him. "How close were you to gutting someone back there?"

I nearly huff a quiet laugh. "Closer than you think."

"Impressive restraint." He says sarcastically.

"Contrary to popular opinion, Prince, I kill demons, not human politicians and wealthy investors."

"Some might argue that those things are one and the same, usually."

Our footsteps shatter the silence, with the distant murmuring beyond the door growing more faint with each passing second.

"So," he says, his crimson gaze sliding to me. "Who do you suspect is leaking sensitive information?"

Crossing my arms over my chest, I tilt my head thoughtfully. "It's definitely not Griffin. The guy is sleazy, but he appeared to be genuine."

"Which would leave Tyler, Jordan or Thomas."

I nod, hearing the chatter behind us grow louder for a breath of a moment.

"Do I need to pry the suspicions from your lips or are you going to take a stab at it?" I hear the pun with his taunt, but I'm still focused on the way the murmuring behind us has quieted down again.

"Stabbing *is* my preferred method." I say in a low tone, my gaze sliding over to Orobas, but I don't see anyone in my peripherals. "Thomas and Jordan appeared mostly disinterested, but Tyler seemed like he had something to lose, but everything to gain. If I were a wagering woman, my money would be on him."

I don't hear footsteps behind us, but that doesn't help me relax at all as we get to another set of doors.

"Unfortunately, most in Dennis' line of work have everything to gain." Orobas opens the door for me, but I gesture for him to go.

"Ladies first." I say with a grin, keeping my attention on my peripherals.

He steps forward just as motion past the door catches my eye, and I don't think, I act.

One second my hands are lowered at my sides, and the next I've yanked him back behind me, knees bent and fists raised, only to find the source of my sudden defensiveness.

Guests stroll past the open doorway tucked into an alcove, and I feel Orobas at my back as my brows pull together.

"Is my threat analyst going senile?"

Ignoring his jab and failing, a modicum of doubt settles deep into my bones when no one pays attention to our small recessed space. Not a single red flag shows in any part of my vision, and I shake my head.

I don't even want to know why the fuck I just protected him.

"Hard to identify threats with a demon prince glued to my side." I grind out as he chuckles.

"Truly a hardship for the legendary Viper, I'm sure." Orobas taunts, and I cut him a glare as he steps alongside me. "So much of a hardship that the demon prince would have had an assassin as a *defender*, it seems."

Heat surges through my body. "Don't push it, demon."

He infuriatingly laughs harder, and I blow out a breath, if only to not snap at him.

I've never been this thrown off in my life, and the only person I can blame is myself.

It's entirely my fault for agreeing to this stupid pact.

Hell, it's my fault for getting caught to begin with.

My feet are on autopilot as I exit the alcove and join the flow of guests, with Orobas at my side moments later.

"Who would have known one of the best assassins in the world would protect a *demon*."

My teeth grind hard enough to make my jaw hurt. "Don't get used to it. Clearly I didn't want some part of our agreement to be ruined by an attempt on your life."

He ignores my poor excuse, but the mirth in his voice is evident. "Why not?"

"Because after this two-day pact is up, I'm first in line to bury a knife into your throat."

"Yet you'd stop others from doing the job for you?" His taunt bleeds into curiosity, and I keep sweeping the crowd as we pass the entrance of the building.

I'd be lying if I said the question hadn't come to mind through all of this—as if I don't have enough to think about.

"If anyone gets the pleasure of ending your eternal life, demon, it'll be me."

That's the best and only answer I give him as he releases a low chuckle.

"Marked by Scarlett Ashford herself. What an honor." His voice is laced with sarcasm as we slow to a stop, and I want nothing more than to strangle him.

The valet takes his ticket and hurries away, leaving us amidst the bustle of people arriving late.

"You act surprised, like I'm not supposed to kill you for what you are." I murmur as he leans in close.

"I suppose you do have a history." He muses. "Still makes it that much more exciting."

That's it. The moment we get in that car he's a dead demon.

"You act like I murder indiscriminately, demon prince." I seethe under my breath, and his lips twitch.

"Oh, but you do."

The engine purrs as the valet pulls around front, hurrying over to hand Orobas the keys and I struggle to make sense of his accusation.

Of course a target given to me by command is just that, but the way he says it is like I don't know who my mission is going to rid the earth of.

My steps are borderline stomps as I pull the door open and throw myself into the passenger seat with a huff.

Orobas slowly saunters around the front of the vehicle, and I'm entirely certain he knows how much those four words are circling my brain.

Because of-fucking-course I murder demons without interrogation on what they do or who they are. It comes with the territory of being an assassin. You don't ask questions.

You just receive details, prepare, and carry it out.

Asking questions gets people killed.

Mako and Grizz come to mind as Orobas pulls the door open, and my limbs twitch on reflex with the need for action. When he slides into the driver's seat, his crimson eyes find my hands gripping my thighs and flick to meet mine. His mouth drops open, but the words flow from my tongue before I can stop myself.

"I don't owe you an explanation or anyone else, demon. Your kind have wreaked havoc on this earth, and I'm the one who takes out the imminent demonic threat."

He shifts the car into drive and pulls away from the building, maneuvering around other cars. "Not just demonic, Viper."

My brows pull together. "What?"

A moment of silence stretches between us as he turns onto the main road. "What were demons before they became demons?"

I scoff. "If you're trying to manipulate me into being on your side, it's not working."

He smiles, and his tongue glides along his teeth. "Have you ever considered that I'm simply showing you the truth of the side you've been on this whole time?"

"The hell does that mean?" I snap, feeling like I'm on the verge of losing control.

For whatever reason, Orobas pushes my buttons, perhaps without even trying, and it's taking every ounce of restraint not to terminate this agreement.

Not knowing the consequences of breaking it is the only thing keeping me from saying fuck it.

Orobas shakes his head. "It means that demons were once angels, Scarlett." His tone isn't condescending or rude, but matter-of-fact, and that gives me pause more than anything.

"And I was once a homeless kid eating garbage to survive." I toss back. "Change is inevitable, demon."

"And Servilians?" He asks, but he doesn't wait for me to respond before he strikes another jab. "I doubt you were trained to remove them from the world too, no?"

I scoff and glare at him. "Nice try."

"I'm serious, Scarlett. You don't need to change your mind about what you've done, but you deserve to know that a third of your targets have been Servilians."

He's lying to get under my skin.

Just another demon tactic to sway my loyalties.

Still, as much as I'm determined to not let him get to me, his words bounce around my skull. They crawled into my ears and buried themselves under my skin to multiply and fester.

"Just give it some thought. I may not be many things, but I am quite patient."

Casting him a sidelong glance, he shrugs, but the barely restrained humor in his expression is arguably as insufferable as he is.

"Demon prince and patience don't sound like they go together." I grumble, smoothing my dress along my thigh.

"Living eternally sort of makes one patient by default, though I'm sure Druv and Thal would say otherwise." When I raise a brow at him, he laughs. "I'm not perfect, Viper, even if I might look it."

The comment earns him an eye roll, and I stare out the window at the houses we pass by.

"Why even bother helping Dennis?" I ask, not troubling myself to look over at him as the silence extends.

"When I met Dennis, he was trying to push legislation through that would make healthcare more affordable, but he was running into some bumps along the way."

My chest flutters as he tiptoes around a topic that could expose him and how he's manipulated politics.

"He felt like his approach was too stilted to work—his views too progressive to gain traction. So he sought me out."

My head snaps toward the demon prince, and I stare at him with wide eyes. "How?"

"There are ways to summon me or any of my brothers—somehow he'd figured out mine, and prophecies happen to be my specialty."

I file that information away for later.

"Needless to say, I simply told him whether the path he's on would give him the desired results to affirm his direction or not, and he'd adjust accordingly."

Thinking back to the past few years, I can't remember any health-care law that was passed or amended, and Orobas must see the confusion on my face because he laughs quietly.

"The bill was throttled and voted out by a majority of the Senate, but it was close. Either way, it put his name out there as one of the most progressive candidates, and his funding was cut shortly after."

That makes no sense. Why cut funding when he's doing what he's supposed to?

If anything, you'd think that they'd solve for the reason the Senate voted it out.

"Why?"

"Because he was a threat to the status quo. Before the war in Kharidia was televised internationally, most of the world was in the dark about what people in power were perpetuating. It wasn't hard for senators to tell their constituents that the legislation and amendments were bad without going deeper. But now, everything has changed."

Something akin to butterflies twist in my core, and I take a steadying breath. As much as I want to find the lies in his words, he shows no sign of deception.

No increased tempo to his respiration, or change in the pitch of his voice. He's not fidgeting or stumbling over his words.

Just steady, level relaying of information.

Even knowing it's likely the truth, reconciling what blatantly counters my knowledge sends a throbbing pang through my skull.

"When the reality Kharidians faced came into international view, that was when Dennis' progressive beliefs became the center of attention. Only a few politicians haven't been corrupted, and he is one of them."

"How is it he's kept up with those who have funding, though?"

Orobas huffs a quiet laugh. "For a while, he wasn't. Millions were spent campaigning against him, manufacturing scandals or leaking secrets that furthered the agenda of those corrupt individuals. Some of them worked to his advantage in the end—funding the rebellion in Kharidia being one. Once the perception of the war changed, suddenly his transgressions became the highlight of his career, and he embraced it."

Again, not a single hint of deception in his voice, and the seed of doubt in the recesses of my mind grows.

"How did this war suddenly change things?" It doesn't make sense for there to be an acute shift in perception of something so large, not to mention foreign.

Orobas merges onto another highway, using one hand to turn the wheel, the other rubbing the stubble along his chin thoughtfully.

"Media and news outlets had reported one narrative for years. The half-century old genocide started long ago when the corruption within our governments really took root. It wasn't until the age of technology that they created reports that would allow them to remain under the radar, but slowly social media exposed holes in their stories. It wasn't enough for change, but it was a good start."

Half-century?

I don't get time to fully absorb everything as the deep tenor of his voice fills the surrounding space again.

"My brother joined the rebellion early on, creating safe houses and destroying ritual sites—really anything he could do that wouldn't tip the scales of justice too much."

"Ritual sites?"

Crimson irises slide to me, and I see that uncertainty from earlier in them, simmering beneath the surface.

"I'll answer that question another time, Viper. Remind me tomorrow."

My brows pull together. "Why?"

"Because, as curious as you may be, too much information at once is a risk. Some things you have to learn firsthand to truly comprehend. Knowledge without experience is simply letters on a page. You will have to see it."

I let out a long sigh. "You speak in riddles, demon."

He smirks, flashing sharp canines as he clicks his tongue. "Comes with being a prophetic demon—there are pros and cons to seeing glimpses of what's to come."

The blood drains from my face, and a shiver runs down my spine. "Does that mean you knew I was going to try to steal the dagger?"

Or that I was posing as a housekeeper? That I'll kill him when it's all over?

As horror builds with each unspoken question, he shakes his head. "No. I did not foresee your arrival or intent."

Oh, thank god.

I guess that means killing him is still on the table after tomorrow night.

Even with everything he's told me, even if it's the truth, it doesn't change the fact that he's a demon, and a rather important one at that.

Taking him out would save hundreds of thousands of lives.

A pit forms in my stomach as he turns onto the long driveway, creeping toward the entrance with guards positioned around it. When I don't see Druv or Thal there, something close to dread makes the pit impossibly bigger.

The gothic architecture takes on a more ominous aura, and for once, an odd note of fear makes the hair on the back of my neck stand on end.

I have to remind myself that they wouldn't ambush me inside when their own leader has promised to keep me alive, but even still...

"This doesn't change anything, you know." I whisper as Orobas brings the car to a stop. "As soon as these two days are done, you and I will be enemies again."

The engine cuts, and I see him adjust his grip on the wheel. "Then so we shall, Viper. Just don't forget that venom when you bite, I'd hate for you to lose your head."

"Careful, demon. Saying words like that might make one think you're going soft."

We both climb out of the car as the guard, Mennon, walks over, taking the keys from Orobas. He turns to me, smirking enough that it makes me want to hurl the nearest object at his face.

"And yet here you are warning me." Orobas tosses back, not waiting for my reaction. "I wonder which of us is going soft first."

My teeth grit together, and I reluctantly follow him up the stairs.

I may not make it another 24 hours without trying to kill him.

God, help me.

Chapter 17

Scarlett

"I'm not sleeping in your room again."

Crossing my arms, I glare at the door he's holding open with barely restrained humor.

"You're not sleeping in a room alone." He tosses back as Thal and Druv turn the corner to my right. Their footsteps slow to a stop when they see the showdown between us.

Druv rests his hands on his hips, tilting his head with a cautious grin. "Glad to see there are no visible knife wounds yet, Oro."

"Emphasis on yet—she looks like she might be close to it." Thal adds, crossing his arms over his chest.

Orobas glances between the demons, and I see the decision in his crimson eyes before he says it out loud.

"Absolutely not." I say, shaking my head. "I'm not sleeping in a room with these two."

Orobas shrugs as Thal rears back, his eyes wide. "Oro, that would be a death sentence for us."

"What will it be, Viper? My room or theirs?" He muses, and I glare between the three.

There's no way I'd be able to slip from a room with two demons, but one I might. Even though something tells me it will be impossible either way.

Thal and Druv seem less inclined to let their guard down for the simple fact of letting Orobas down. Meanwhile, Orobas could be overconfident and make that mistake.

Either way, I'll be in the company of demons, and one is better than two.

"Tick tock, Viper," Orobas says, and my eyes narrow on him.

"Fine. I'll sleep in your room." I huff, seeing the other two demons exhale a breath of relief.

"Have Ishari bring in a change of clothes." Orobas says, and Thal nods curtly. Seconds later, he's turned on his heel and disappears down the hallway.

Orobas' crimson eyes flick to Druv, leveling him with a seriousness I've yet to see from the demon prince. "I want you and Ishari to pull another team together to watch Tildman's daughter. Constant surveillance with minimal downtime."

My eyebrows twitch upward.

I'd forgotten about Tildman's request to protect his daughter after receiving death threats. Hearing Orobas not only make good on his promise, but Druv and Thal are clearly his most trusted circle...

It's surprising, to say the least.

"On it." Druv gives a lazy salute, takes a long step backward, and chuckles as his gaze bounces between us. "Don't stay up too late, kids."

This time it's Orobas' turn to roll his eyes. He gestures through the doorway, and I exhale a long breath, taking full strides into the minimalistic room.

I scrunch up my nose and spin in a circle. "Have you ever considered hiring an interior designer?"

Orobas lets out a genuine laugh, and I can't help but grin with the demon.

"It hasn't been on my list of priorities." He says, loosening his tie and unbuttoning the top of his dress shirt. Inked skin peers out from the collar, and he shoves his hands in his pockets.

"Clearly." I murmur, walking toward the washroom, leaning on the wall once I'm there. "At least get a lounge chair or something."

"Why would I need a chair?" He asks, genuine confusion etched across his face.

Gesturing to the space around us and then myself, I blink at him. "You know, in case you have company? It's hosting 101 to make your guests comfortable."

He lets out a dark chuckle. "In hundreds of years, I've yet to have **company** in my private room, Viper, and once you're released, I don't plan to have any. I do not need a chair."

I just shrug as a knock sounds at the door before it opens, and Ishari paces in with a bundle of clothes in her arms.

"Thal said you need a change of clothes." She eyes us nervously and walks over, holding the small pile between us.

Regardless of being a demon, I don't shy away from her, reaching over to take the pile from her hands. "Thank you, Ishari."

She blinks before a soft smile graces her features. "Right. Let me know if you need me." Her gaze flicks to Orobas for a moment. "Or if you need a break from mister broody."

I snort a laugh, and she joins in as Orobas shakes his head. The tentative humor in his expression tells me he didn't mind the jab as she exits the room with a wave over her head.

"Could it be that Viper has made friends with a **demon**?" He muses as I slip off my heels.

"Don't get excited." I say, reaching around to unzip the back of my dress. "The moment our deal is done, all heads are on the table as long as they're demon in nature."

Orobas is silent for a minute, his eyes simmering with the same uncertainty I caught earlier, and I sigh. "What is it, prince?"

"Can I show you something?"

Why he's asking when he has full control of my life right now, I'm not sure, but I shrug and slide my heels back on. "Be my guest."

He walks to the doorway and holds it open again, but he says nothing, so I place the stack of pajamas on top of the dresser and follow him into the hallway.

"Where are we going?" I ask, my heels clicking against the quiet of the evening, with the halls absent of any other demons.

Orobas' tall form at my side no longer has me in a constant state of unease, thankfully. But the uncertainty I've caught not once, not twice but three times is the sole contributor to the note of dread in the back of my mind.

Something about the demon prince being concerned like this just doesn't sit right with me.

"Tell me about one of your missions."

I snort. "That's classified, even for you, demon prince."

He clicks his tongue in disapproval. "You say that like the information won't die with me in a little over twenty-four hours."

Even though he doesn't really know my plans for when our treaty is up, I swallow against the lump in my throat all the same.

Still, he has a point.

"Two years ago, I was assigned to a solo mission in Alaska to take out a cell of demons in a remote town called Nuiqsut. Demons had moved there to set up a base of operations, and I was tasked to eliminate all targets."

Orobas' jaw feathers, but I push on, following him as he guides us to the end of the hallway and up the familiar staircase. "When I arrived, the population of Nuiqsut was not very high, but these demons had settled into a secluded area of town. It took thirty-six hours, but the sixteen demons listed were neutralized and disposed of without incident."

Orobas is quiet for another long moment, climbing the final stairs before entering the room where he'd summoned a portal to see Dennis the first time.

My stomach flips nervously at the thought.

Does he plan to teleport me to some barren space and leave me there? It would be an effective way to get rid of the immediate threat to his life.

"Sixteen demons?" He asks, his head tilted to the side as he picks up the amulet.

When I incline my head once, he says nothing in response, but holds the amulet to his mouth, his knuckles turning a shade pale as he murmurs an incantation.

Once more, the air before us shimmers, at first like a mirage of heat from an unknown source, but then the space in front of us fades into white and green.

"Is this where you push me through a portal and laugh victoriously?"

My attempt at a joke doesn't land, and Orobas remains silent as ever—the tension in his jaw the only sign that he heard me as he steps toward the portal.

"Ladies first." He says in a low tone, and my gaze flicks between him and the shimmering visage of a coastal town.

"Here goes nothing." I sigh, stepping through the apparition.

Chapter 18

Scarlett

As my foot touches solid ground, the first thing that registers is the cold air biting into my bare skin.

Next are all the icy flakes that have crumbled on top of my foot in the knee-deep snow.

I really should have mentioned a mission in a warmer climate.

Orobas' towering form steps alongside me, seemingly unbothered by the frigid air as he smooths the sleeves of his suit.

"Well," I murmur as a shiver runs through me. "Where to now?"

Orobas does the same motion to shield me from being seen by people before he gestures behind me, and I turn to an open field with snow-covered headstones. Some topped with crosses, others with a broad slab of stone.

"Recognize any?" he asks quietly, and I step closer to one.

The snow melts into my shoe, soaking my foot as my toes freeze. The name on the headstone is hardly legible, but from what I can tell, it doesn't match any I know.

So I move on to the next.

And then the next.

By the time I'm three rows and twelve headstones in, I'm losing hope of recognizing any, with my feet nothing more than ice blocks attached to my legs.

Putting one foot in front of the other, I make it to the next headstone, and my entire body stills.

Harriet Gentry

Beloved mother, sister and wife.

I frown.

How the heck would they have buried her when I was so cautious in disposing of the bodies?

Only a handful were thrown to the bottom of the ocean, dragged down by eighty-pound stones to ensure they wouldn't reappear. The others were plunged into a ravine nearby or rolled in a deep cavern in the ice that drops so far that no one has dared to scale it.

"What is it?" Orobas asks, his gaze curious as he looks between me and the headstone.

"I don't know how they would have found the body to bury." I murmur through chattering teeth, moving to the next one.

Norrant Eldrin

Dearest husband and son, taken too soon.

His name stands out, just like the last, and I cross my arms thoughtfully.

These were unattached targets without families, yet for whatever reason, their graves paint an entirely different story.

I move to the next headstone, and the next, and before long, horror and denial rage against one another. Because how in the world did this slip past me?

The files said they were mercenaries without families, paid to insert themselves into everyday life in Nuiqsut to gain control of a prominent trade location.

If they didn't have any, how the hell can I explain this?

When I turn to look at Orobas' tense gaze, emotion clogs my throat, and I swallow hard against it. "They had families?"

He doesn't answer, but brings the talisman to his mouth again and murmurs. The shimmering image shows the same snow-covered town as before, but I don't question it when I step through.

When my frozen feet sink into another deep snowbank, my teeth chatter uncontrollably, but I pay it no mind. I can't when something so basic has counteracted what I knew.

My dress absorbs more and more of the melted snow, weighing me down as much as the growing seed of doubt in the back of my mind.

Orobas steps in beside me, and I watch as a young girl throws herself into the fluff of snow in her backyard. Her thick winter jacket swishes as she extends her arms to make the shape of an angel.

"Who is this?"

I almost regret asking as Orobas leans in, his voice barely audible over the giggling teenager mere feet away.

"This is Penelope Gentry, Harriet's daughter."

My mouth drops open to call him a liar, but the words die on my lips when I see the seriousness in his expression.

Penelope's eyes light up as the back door of the small house opens, and she clambers onto all fours, shrieking loudly in excitement as she hurries away.

"Oh, no you don't!" A male voice chimes out, which only makes Penelope run faster through the snow toward a bank twice her height.

A sudden gust of wind rips past us, exposing my bare legs which have long become numb from the cold. The burst of air sends Penelope four feet in the air, twists her onto her back and drops her into the fluffy bank of snow.

She shrieks louder and laughs; the sound muffled by the insulation of the snowbank.

Servilians are in league with demons?

My attention turns to Orobas, but his crimson gaze is locked on the two oblivious to our presence.

I had always been told my targets were solely demonic. Even though I'd known about their existence, I'd never been tasked with eliminating a Servilian threat.

So the only logical assumption I can make is that Harriet was a demon... or I'd been lied to.

The latter couldn't be possible.

No.

None of these targets used any magic when I'd eliminated them, so there's no way they'd have been Servilian.

That has to be it.

"So, Servilians and demons are working together now?" I ask, meeting Orobas' gaze.

He shakes his head. "Servilians know we exist, but they stay out of our affairs—besides, they already have issues reproducing; they can't afford to water down their gene pool further by doing so with angels or demons."

I scoff, tucking my hands under my armpits for warmth. "Clearly you're wrong, because we see evidence of it here."

"You're damn stubborn, Viper."

A heady dose of warmth surges through me, rising to my cheeks as I whirl on him. "Stubborn?! I'm not stubborn, I just refuse to be manipulated by a prince of hell. I should gut you here and leave you to die with the rest of your kind."

My chest heaves as I glare up at him, but instead of responding, he slides his foot behind mine and in a fraction of a second, shoves me backward.

I don't know what I'd expected, but clearly I'd let my guard down around him, because my numb arms flail for a moment before I fall into thick, fluffy snow.

Gasping, it crunches beneath my weight, and my eyes widen as it melts against my skin, soaking into the back of my dress. My hands, long since sluggish, clumsily move to prop myself up, and my teeth chatter loudly.

"Y-y-you a-a-assho-o-ole." I chew out, glaring at the demon prince who's grinning from ear to ear.

There's nothing I want more than to smack it off his face right now.

Even with how numb they are, I wrap my fingers around a handful of snow, and quickly hurl them with surprising accuracy.

He must not have been expecting retaliation of any kind, because even as he flinches his face to the side, both snowballs slam into his cheek. They explode upon impact, with a small tuft sliding down to his stubble from where they hit.

Crimson eyes flash in warning, and I hardly get a second before he bends down and grabs a handful of snow, forming a ball and taking aim.

I roll to the side just in time, but the cold makes my motions lag, even through the sudden rush of adrenaline. The ball hits my hip and explodes as I huff a frustrated laugh, forming two in each hand from where I brace myself. The balls are half-assed with how sloppily I've shaped them, but they still hit Orobas in the chest, casting his black suit with flakes of white.

His nostrils flare, and the challenge in his expression sends a fresh wave of energy through me, so I scramble to my feet and run. My heart thunders as I struggle to sprint in the knee-high snow in open-toe heels, with each step more arduous than the last.

When I don't hear him behind me, I glance back, only to see his hand near his mouth, murmuring with a mischievous grin tugging at his lips.

My brows pull together, and I look forward as the shimmering portal comes into view. Air suspends in my lungs, but my momentum is too fast to stop myself as I hurtle through.

My first foot in doesn't connect with anything, and butterflies explode in my core. My gut twists as the ground disappears, replaced with treetops covered with snow.

When I see the snowbank ten feet below me, it's already too late, and I'm free-falling. A gasp of air fills my lungs just in time for me to plunge face-first into the cloud of snow that absorbs my impact with a soft thump. Icy particles fill my nose and mouth, and every inch of my skin's beyond frozen as I struggle to twist upright. There's no ground for me to gain purchase, and each move I make has more snow falling to replace it.

One eternal minute turns into two, then three, and the electric pain in my limbs has long since disappeared, with numbness a welcome reprieve. My body shakes violently, the crumbling snow pieces around me the only sign of my involuntary movement.

I'm going to die here.

Against my will, tears spill from my eyes only to freeze on my cheeks, but I don't have the strength left in my limbs to wipe them away.

He's trying to kill me.

A sudden rush of wind bites at the top of my head before I'm hoisted into the air by invisible hands, and a shrill, strangled noise escapes me as I'm hauled from the snow.

The deep bank of white disappears before the treetops come into view once more. When I'm turned in the other direction, I spot Orobas standing beside a man and Penelope, the two of them giggling as the wind suspends me in the air, slowly descending me to the ground before them.

My wet dress clings to my body like a sheet of ice, and my teeth chatter with my limbs frozen to the bone. When my feet find purchase on the ground in front of the others, my knees buckle under my weight.

Large hands on either side of me help me to my feet, but I can't bring myself to look at them even if I wanted to.

"She's going into shock." The male voice says hurriedly as the demon prince curses.

"We should bring her inside." Orobas murmurs, mirroring the other's concern.

It's odd to hear considering *he's* the reason for it.

"F-f-f-uck-k y-y-ou-u-u." I chatter almost inaudibly, and the male to my left chuckles.

"Quite the mouth she has." The male muses as Penelope opens the door a few feet ahead, holding it ajar with wide eyes.

"Always a viper." Orobas murmurs in agreement, and they haul me into the log house. "Do you have any spare blankets or clothes by chance?"

Warm air washes over me as we cross the kitchen, and the male helps us toward the couch. When they bring me just in front of it, there's a moment of silence before the male nods in my periphery.

"My late wife... I still have some of her clothes..." The pain in his voice is thinly veiled, and beyond any reason, my chest tightens. "Penelope, come help me find some."

The man hands a wide blanket to Orobas before he and Penelope disappear into another room. My teeth chatter as they leave me and the demon prince alone, surrounded by photos of the small family.

Harriet's petite visage appears in each one, smiling as she poses with Penelope or her husband. She seems genuinely happy.

Who knew demons had the capacity to love?

Orobas leans over my shoulder and unzips my dress as I recoil.

"T-the hell a-a-re y-you d-doing, demon?" I manage the say between the chattering, but he doesn't seem to care about my discomfort.

"Your dress is going to give you pneumonia if you keep it on." He says matter-of-factly, hooking his fingers under the sides to slide it down. "Admittedly, I didn't know daevari aren't able to withstand the cold."

I swat at his arms weakly, my limbs still fully numb, making my attempts frustratingly unsuccessful. "It-t-t's ind-d-decen-n-t-t-t."

He huffs a laugh, his crimson gaze burning into mine as he uses my dress as leverage to keep my attention on him, as if emphasizing that I'm not the one in control right now.

And I hate it.

"I'd rather not have you die before our deal is up." He whispers, but the concern swirling behind his eyes says there's more he's not telling me.

I have half a mind to think it's because he might actually care, but then I remember the unknown consequences of our deal, and it makes more sense.

Good to know that there is some assurance that he can't end my life either.

He tugs the frigid material down my chest and over my hips before it falls loose to the wooden floor with a wet thunk. Crimson irises flick to the scars that litter my skin, some still healing, but he says nothing. Unbuttoning his frozen suit jacket and shrugging it off, it falls to the floor behind him, and he reaches over to wrap the blanket around my back.

What I'm not expecting is for him to pull me flush to his body, his arms encircling my back as his delicious heat bleeds into me. I stiffen as he squeezes me to him, and gaze to the only item in my line of sight beyond the white of his dress shirt—a photo of Harriet, Penelope and her husband.

My skin burns at the warmth, and I can't help but wonder if it's because my body itself is rebelling against the touch of a demon, or if it was just that frozen.

When a shiver wracks through me, and my fingers tremble, I have to assume it's the latter.

"I brought some clothes—" The male's voice cuts off as he comes in the room, and I move to withdraw from Orobas' embrace, but he just clutches me tighter.

Still too weak to fight, I grit my teeth and lean into his chest. If I'm going to use his body heat, I might as well absorb it faster.

The sooner I can function properly, the sooner I can get away from the demon.

"Penny, go play in your room."

She groans, but her footsteps recede further away, and a door clicks shut.

"I'll leave these here." The male voice says, sounding a few feet closer to my right. "And put some tea on."

Quiet footsteps fade before cupboards open and shut, and my eyelids grow heavy. Orobas' scent is as warm as his body, and even though I want to find the nearest sharp object to ram it into his jugular, for a breath of a moment, I feel...

Calm.

My eyes snap open, and I swallow hard, taking a shaky step back.

What the fuck is happening to me?

Thankfully, Orobas loosens his grip to wrap the blanket around my body in his absence. He leans over to grab the fresh set of clothes from the table beside us. Sweatpants are the first thing he hands me, and I clumsily bend to slide them up my body, nearly losing my balance before he passes a thick sweatshirt to me.

"Thanks, demon." I murmur, tugging the sweater overhead, and his eyebrows twitch upward.

A grin creeps across his face, and I regret saying anything.

"Warm drink, anyone?" The male asks, carrying in a kettle with steam rising from the top.

He pauses in the corner of my eye, and Orobas nods. "Please, and apologies for intruding."

"Ah, we don't get guests much around these parts, so it's our pleasure."

Something in me twists uncomfortably as the male pours us each a mug of tea, stepping closer to hand them over. His gaze lingers on Harriet's sweater before he gestures to the couch, and we ease into our seats with cups in hand.

"This doesn't seem to be a typical place for a Servilian family." Orobas says, tilting his head with feigned curiosity. "Oh, where are my manners? I'm Orobas, and this is Scarlett."

The way he says my name burns my cheeks for a whole new reason, reminding me of the way he easily exposed it during the banquet.

At least this time he used his own.

The male gives us a warm smile. "Nice to meet you both, name's Garrett, and you've met my Penny. Our history here is... complicated. We lived on the southern coast for forty years, but after magic returned and tensions grew, my wife became paranoid that we were being watched."

My pulse picks up its tempo, and I bring the tea to my lips, gently blowing on it to cool it off.

"We'd decided on Nuiqsut because it's coastal, and she loved the water." Garrett falls quiet, and I take a slow sip.

"How did the two of you meet?" Orobas asks, leaning back comfortably with his mug.

It doesn't take a rocket scientist to see why he's asking this line of questioning, but I'm curious where he's trying to lead with it, so I remain silent.

Garrett's attention flicks to the picture of the family to our right, and his expression turns somber. "We grew up together. Our parents knew one another on Servilia—they raised us as a community. We were visiting Earth when our magic disappeared and the portals were no longer functioning. When we were older, and it returned, everything was great until her paranoia grew. I thought maybe her pregnancy caused it, but even after Penelope was born, it just got worse. By the time we moved here, she was constantly looking over her shoulder, and we were arguing about it every day."

Air suspends in my lungs, and it takes everything I have not to react.

Chapter 19

Scarlett

This can't be real.

They grew up together. They're both Servilian.

She *was Servilian.*

Nausea roils my stomach as my mouth waters, and I take the smallest sip of tea, not caring when it burns my tongue.

Garrett winces, like the memory brings him pain. "When we settled in, she'd told me she was going to do everything she could to relax. She'd promised that she would be more present for me, for our family... but she disappeared and never came back. I've kept her stuff just in case, but we had to assume the worst."

This is my fault.

I tore their family apart.

"I apologize for dampening the mood." Garrett says, swiping the tear from his cheek. "What brought you both to Nuiqsut?"

The lump in my throat grows, and thankfully Orobas answers. "She'd said she wanted to see snow for the first time, and who was I to deny her?" He muses, his crimson gaze meeting mine, but there's no humor in them.

There's only a quiet knowing, as if he knew that this revelation would devastate me more than any injury could.

Because I tore an innocent family apart without questioning ***any-thing***.

I might be a weapon, but damn it if that is not all I am, and I used it as an excuse not to doubt any of command's orders.

"Ah, well, by the looks of it, you saw your fair share of snow, Scarlett."

My eyes snap to Garrett's, seeing only warmth and sadness in his chestnut irises.

If I didn't know any better, I'd say there were several knives buried in my chest, each twisting left and right as I struggle to maintain a modicum of composure.

The urge to come clean, to confess my sins to him is strong, so much so that I seriously consider whether it would help or harm him.

His wounds would become fresh, but he'd know exactly what happened to her. But it wasn't pleasant.

My mouth drops open, but Orobas speaks first. "This was kind of you, and we appreciate your hospitality, Garrett, but we should be going. We have a busy day tomorrow, and Scarlett needs her beauty sleep."

Garrett chuckles, and we all rise to our feet, but I can't help feeling as if I'm a stranger in my own body now.

Because if they lied to me about these sixteen so-called demons, what else did they lie to me about?

Orobas already proved they lied to me about the warehouse.

Were Grizz and Mako even killed by demons?

Was I nearly killed by demons?

Who have I been targeting all this time?

... You think me to be your enemy, Scarlett, yet you've been raised by the very wolves you were taught to kill...

I give Garrett a weak wave goodbye in my half-dazed state, and Orobas slides his hand into mine, guiding me out the front door of the house.

Frigid air bites into my skin, but I pay it no mind. I'm hardly aware as Orobas murmurs to his palm, and the shimmering portal appears once more, the visage of his property a mirage against the snowy backdrop.

"Do you want to talk about it?" He whispers, but with the way his words carry in the air, he might as well have shouted it at the top of his lungs.

Truth is, I don't know what there is to talk about.

There's no telling how many of my targets were innocent people. Sure, there might have been a handful where I'd seen their transgressions firsthand, but of hundreds of missions, the comparison is...

My teeth grind, and I shake my head. "I'm fine, demon." I whisper and step through the portal with Orobas following closely, his fingers still intertwined with mine.

It's the only solace I offer myself, and it's likely more kindness than I deserve.

When the empty tower room comes into view, I exhale a tense breath and release Orobas' hand. If he notices, he doesn't show it when he smooths the material at his thighs, wiping away any snow from them.

Desperate to distract myself, I wrap my arms around my torso. "This fundraiser tomorrow—what's my purpose for being there?"

He sets the amulet on the dresser and slowly paces to the stairs, so I follow his strides.

"While it's a fundraiser for Dennis' campaign, in politics, even those you know well can turn against you. You're there to observe only. My brother and significant other are special guests as Kharidia's guardian, which means there's a good chance some prominent adversaries of Dennis will be there as well."

I frown. The descent down the tower steps somehow makes me more dizzy than normal, so I hold on to the railing. "Is he a prince of hell, too?"

The question rolls off my tongue, but oddly enough, I've asked it without the usual malice or disdain, and I don't even want to know why.

Perhaps some part of me knows I'm just as bad as he is.

"He is. It's been centuries since we last saw one another. In fact, the last time I'd seen him was when I'd warned him not to tip the scales of war in our favor too much. There was some variation of the future where he'd destroyed every living being within five hundred miles of the country's border, though I'm not sure what would have triggered such a reaction."

I swallow at the mental image of such raw power.

If his brother is capable of that, what kind of destruction can Orobas bring?

Finally, at the base of the tower, Orobas leads us to his room at a snail's pace.

"So I'm there to be a fly on the wall?" I ask, leaning into the topic to keep my mind from wandering to my world-shattering revelation.

Orobas inclines his head as we approach his room, and he moves to hold the door open. "I'm sure something interesting will happen. At the very least, if we stay late enough, you may snag one of those handy steak knives from dinner, and do what you've wanted to since we met."

My teeth grind, and I force a laugh. "Are you that eager to die, demon prince?"

When his lips curve into a smile, it only makes me more irritated. "Eager, perhaps. Or curious if it will finally be my time."

He reaches over to the door, tugging it open for me, and I stride toward the dresser where the pair of pajamas still rest from earlier.

Thank goodness for Ishari.

If I had to go to bed in the clothes of the woman I'd tortured, maimed and murdered, I'm not sure how sleep would find me.

Hell, I'm not certain how much I'll be able to even with a fresh set of pajamas.

Orobas paces to the other room, and I hear running water before he reappears with a towel in hand. "Believe it or not, Viper. I don't blame you for your actions." He offers it between us. "To wash up."

I gingerly take it from his hands, my gaze meeting crimson irises that might very well see right through to my soul. "You should."

Not bothering to explain further, I walk past him, peeling off Harriet's clothes and tossing them aside. The shower door clicks behind me, and I ease under the hot water, letting it pelt the top of my head, saturating curls of hair that straighten beneath the weight.

Everything bends when carrying something heavy.

The question is, when do I break?

For years, they had tortured, trained, and molded me into the perfect weapon.

Brainwashed not to ask and to trust a corrupt system.

Trained to kill demons, yet somehow a prince of hell is the one opening my eyes. Perhaps this is some form of insanity, and I've simply lost my mind.

But the truth is, they all died at my hands. Innocent or not.

Water pours from my skin as I stare down at my upturned palms, as if looking for the blood that I know stains them.

Here I am, a manufactured weapon with a mission to retrieve an even deadlier blade from a prince of hell, who somehow cracked through whatever blindfold was held over my eyes.

My mind wanders to Evelyn and Omen, and I can't help but wonder how they'd react if they'd seen the warehouse.

How many lies did we fall for?

How many injuries did we get for no reason?

Am I willing to accept that Grizz and Mako died for nothing?

Bash comes to the forefront of my mind, and my hand curls into a fist as I brace against the wall.

A heady mix of embarrassment and guilt creates a toxic concoction in my head, and the mental image of Grizz being pulverized has me recoiling my fist and slamming my knuckles into the wall.

They were broken.

The walls shake as my fist hammers tile that cracks on impact, creating a web of hairline fractures.

They were ***murdered***.

Another strike against the tile sends pieces to the ground with a clatter, and the next splits the skin covering my knuckles. Grout and dust fall in chunks to the floor as I repeat the action over and over.

They died for nothing.

I don't recognize the guttural shriek that escapes me as the walls shake, and a hand wraps around my bicep, pausing my assault as my lungs run out of air.

"Scarlett, that's enough." Orobas' voice fills the air as he whirls me around.

When I recoil my other fist, I choke on water with my next ragged breath. He must see it coming because he quickly snatches my wrist and forces me back to the tile wall, pinning me with the length of his body.

"Let me go, demon." I growl and cough, writhing in his bruising grip that only serves to heighten the anger rifling through my veins.

Blood runs down the back of my right hand as he holds it up against the wall, and I glare into his crimson eyes that seem to mirror the shade.

"You do not scare me, Viper."

My jaw tenses, and I fall still. Rage simmers under my skin, amplifying all the hatred I've felt for his kind over the years, and the vitriol held toward him, urging me forward like a rat trapped in a hot bucket.

The only way out of this is through him, and damn if I won't do it.

"Then you're an idiot." I whisper, and that's the only warning before I move.

With several areas exposed, I use the water to my advantage and slip to the side where he has the least amount of leverage, twisting my wrists to break his grip.

His reaction is fast, turning with me and anticipating where I'll move, but I did not get my nickname from my poison preference alone.

My elbow juts into his rib cage, the hardest impact slamming against the soft spot between two bones near his diaphragm. Within a fraction of a second, I've spun, using the momentum to hammer my shin into the back of his knee.

My arm shoves at his chest and the water from the shower does the rest of the work, sending him tumbling backward. The scalding liquid sluices down my body, as I stand over him.

His crimson eyes widen as he hits the floor, but I'm not done.

"I'll call Dennis to give him the news of your absence from the fundraiser." I say in a low tone, my vision turning as red as the blood streaming from my knuckles.

I lunge forward, and he deters my next two strikes aimed for his face that slam into the hard floor before my enraged state fully takes over. Another shriek escapes my throat as I straighten, but he catches my ankle and flips me onto my back.

The white dress shirt he'd worn in Nuiqsut is transparent from the onslaught of water, his tattoos fully visible through the saturated material as he climbs on top of me. His actions are slow from his soaked clothes, and I slip away, rolling toward the wall and pushing onto my hands and knees.

"If you're going to kill me, Viper, you'll have to be faster than that." He taunts, and it hits the exact nerve he intends to as he rises to his feet.

Whirling around, I slide down to trip him, forcing him onto his back with a wet thud, the shower pelting his chest for a mere moment until I'm on him.

My knees slam to the tile on either side of his body as my hands encircle his neck, squeezing the veins supplying oxygen to his brain. I'm hardly aware of his fist in my hair, and he constricts it tight, forcing my head to tilt.

His free hand flattens to the tile, and he flips us, crashing my back against the ground as air escapes my lungs in a whoosh. My ankles lock around his waist to keep distance between us, and I tighten my grip on his neck as he inches closer.

The way his eyelids flutter tells me he's losing oxygen, but nowhere near the rate needed to subdue him, so I squeeze harder.

He smirks in response.

"What happens if I kill you?" I whisper, feeling more and more like a caged animal trapped in a corner.

"I think you should ask yourself what happens if you don't, Viper." He challenges, and my chest heaves.

Orobas is an immovable object, towering in my vision as water cascades off his shoulders, and streams down the longer locks of his hair falling forward as he gazes at me.

His hard body tenses as my bare thighs tighten around his waist with my effort to cut off blood flow to his head, but there's no sign that it's working.

"I hate you." My voice cracks, and he yanks my hair back slightly, as if to prove that he could have access to my throat if he wanted to.

He tilts his head, his crimson eyes searching my face for a moment, and the rage I'd felt mixes with frustration.

"Prove it." He whispers, and when the ghost of a smirk graces his face, I yank him close, crashing my lips to his. He kisses me in return without missing a beat, leaning in with all his weight, my legs tightening around him for a whole other reason.

My nails bite into the sides of his neck where I'd been squeezing, and I break our kiss long enough for my teeth to catch his lip—a metallic taste exploding on my tongue before my lips find his again.

There's a desperation growing in my veins to feel him like this—to feel him everywhere—and fuck if it doesn't piss me off even more.

The hand at the back of my head still tightens, but this time it's to gain access to more of my mouth. His tongue finds mine, fighting for dominance as my fingers curl between the buttons of his shirt.

With one quick yank, the material tears apart, but he doesn't bother to shrug it off; instead, he digs his fingers deeper into my hip as I suck in a breath.

Using my legs as leverage, I shove him back and recoil my left fist, driving into his cheek as his head snaps to the side.

His expression darkens when his crimson eyes meet mine, and he lifts me into the air in one swift motion, slamming me back against the tile wall.

A soft grunt barely escapes me before his lips are on mine again.

Orobas doesn't shy away from my aggression; he drinks it in. Consuming everything I offer out of anger, frustration and need.

When he breaks our kiss, I half expect him to pull back, but he pins my hips with more weight, and I moan as he sinks his teeth into my shoulder.

My eyes flutter open, and I gasp.

The rage in my body dissipates as Orobas raises his head. Droplets of water fall from his hair to my breasts, and his nose brushes my cheek. His shadowed gaze meets mine as we breathe each other's air.

"If that's what you do to people you hate, Viper, I'd love to see what you do to those you like."

My ankles unlock, and I slide them down to bear my weight, desire pulsing in my core as I glare daggers at him. "Maybe if you live beyond tomorrow night, you'll find out."

He lets out a dark chuckle. "Enjoy your shower, Viper."

My heart thrums steadily as he backs away and exits the room, leaving me alone with my thoughts and the unrelenting desire raging through my body.

I'm going to kill him.

Chapter 20

Scarlett

By the time I'm finished showering and in the center of Orobas' room, I'm pleasantly surprised to find it empty.

His minimalistic decor leaves the bed as the only comfortable place to rest, so I sigh and slide under the plush covers. It wouldn't be hard to fall asleep here with how my body melts into the mattress, and the soft, silken sheets caressing my skin...

Yet as I lie in his darkened room, with nothing to do but relax, sleep is as evasive as ever.

I have half a mind to suspect it's because of what happened earlier, but it meant nothing—simply a natural reaction for me to expel whatever frustrations had been building since I'd met him.

Besides, it's not like he's hard to look at.

The more I consider it all, the more I convince myself that what happened was a symptom of circumstance.

It takes quite a lot of convincing.

Footsteps pass the door, with Orobas' voice muffled, and I frown. Sure, he might not have to spend every waking moment with me, but to leave me alone to my own devices like this?

It seems out of character, even for him.

Within a fraction of a heartbeat, I'm slipping out from under the sheets, and tip-toeing to the door. The silk nightshift Ishari had provided swishes with my quiet steps, and I press my ear to the wood.

Orobas' voice is hardly audible, so I cautiously turn the handle, keeping it from clicking or creaking as it eases open. The vacant hallway is a sight for sore eyes, and I hug the wall, inching closer to the next room where the murmurs are coming from.

... "think you should reconsider." Thal's voice carries, and I frown, taking another step closer.

"I'm not changing my mind." Orobas bites out, and a long moment passes.

Whatever it is, he sounds thoroughly annoyed.

"She could kill you, Oro." Druv's voice is next to ring out, making me feel like the whole gang might be there.

"Azrael could reap my soul any second, and none of this would matter—"

"Oro, you can't seriously be considering this," Thal says in a low tone. "There has to be some other way."

The sound of something slamming down onto a hard surface nearly makes me jump.

"Enough. Whether I die at the hands of Azrael or Scarlett, none of it matters. We are at the point of no return. If we don't *act*, we will lose this war."

Silence falls over the room, and I swallow.

Could they be talking about using the dagger?

How many will die?

Someone sighs loudly, and Druv speaks up. "How long do we have?"

"From what I can tell, it's a matter of weeks."

"Weeks?!" Ishari squeaks as Thal curses loudly.

"I thought we had more time, but Samael has gone quiet, and the number of their charges has tripled over the last few months. They're ramping up for something—I just don't know what."

"What do you mean?" Thal asks, his voice plagued with concern.

"You can't see it?" Ishari interjects.

My heart's in my throat as I wait for Orobas' response, like hanging on by a thread.

"It's rude to eavesdrop, you know." A voice whispers to my left, and I jolt, my head snapping to the side.

Pai, the dark-haired man I'd run into with Orobas, flashes a grin and brings his finger to his lips in a hush. He straightens to his full height and shoves his hands into his pockets.

"I didn't hear anything." I whisper, almost inaudibly as the others continue to chatter in the room.

His blue eyes are bright as he gives me a knowing look. "I have no clue what you're talking about. Now, you have roughly one minute before everyone leaves that room, Oro included."

Hearing his warning loud and clear, I swallow and hurry to the room, leaving Pai behind without a second thought.

For once, butterflies dance in my core—it's an unusual feeling considering my line of work.

Early on in my training, before they'd broken me down to nothing, it used to happen all the time. In fact, I'd be so nervous that even talking to command was enough to give me a panic attack.

I slip into the room, easing the door shut silently before hurrying to the bed. A long-repressed memory of walking the hallway to the small conference room with hidden cameras and a single speaker comes to mind as I tuck myself into the plush covers.

The anxiety I'd had that day going to receive my first assignment was unlike anything I'd ever felt.

My palms were slick, my pulse raged in my ears, and I was out of breath without exerting myself at all.

Perhaps even back then, I had suspected something was off.

The door creaks open, and my heart skips a beat when I see Orobas come into view.

His crimson eyes seem to carry a heavier weight than before.

Or am I imagining things?

He crosses the room, unbuckling his belt with his mind distant, dropping it onto the dresser with a clatter. Whatever happened in that room has clearly affected him, and I'm viciously curious about what it could have been.

But I also strangely dislike seeing the demon this distracted.

He skillfully unbuttons the dark shirt that he must have exchanged for the one I'd torn open, tossing it to the floor before moving to the waist of his pants.

I chew my lip, and my eyes avert to the ceiling, hearing the soft thud of his clothes hitting the floor. There's no chance in hell he'll be open to telling me what happened, and I shouldn't have overheard their conversation, so it's not like I can ask.

Orobas eases himself to sit at the edge of the bed, and my attention slides to his tattoo-covered back on full display. Low light from the single lamp on his bedside illuminates the ink just enough for me to see a scroll on fire. I can't make out much else as he drags his hand over his face.

"Rough night, demon?" I ask, and his head tilts to the side to glance at me.

His gaze lingers for a moment until he releases a low chuckle and slides under the covers. "In more ways than one, Viper."

Hopefully, he's not referring to our little dalliance. I might be inclined to ram sharp objects into his jugular, but it couldn't have been *that* unpleasant for him.

A jolt of unease courses through me that feels dangerously close to insecurity. "Want to talk about it?" Offering an olive branch between us seems weird. "It's not like I'm going anywhere."

He releases a low huff, but there's no humor in it. "You say that as if you won't assume I'm lying or trying to manipulate you."

I shrug and glance over to see him staring at the ceiling. "Once upon a time, someone told me you don't have the ability to manipulate people."

Crimson eyes study me in the dim light before he rolls onto his side.

I'd be lying if I said the view wasn't a glorious one, even considering that he's a demon prince. Ink covers every visible inch of him above the duvet up to his neck, and the artistry doesn't hide his corded muscles, which would make anyone with a pulse's mouth water.

He eyes me for a long moment. "And you believe that?"

The short answer is yes, even if some tiny nagging voice is shouting that he's a demon and can't be trusted. He didn't have to show me any of the contradictions from my missions, nor did he have to go through the whole exercise of introducing himself as different personas to Dennis' team.

If he truly could manipulate people, he would have done it, but I haven't seen any evidence of it.

Instead, he's acted rather human.

Minus his strength, and some of the more obvious indicators of being a demon.

"I believe you use the same methods of manipulation that humans do, which is not what was stated in your file."

He tries and fails to suppress a grin. "Things would be much easier if I had the capability." I watch him roll onto his back and stare at the ceiling. "Do you have any idea why they assigned you to eliminate Servilians?" The question comes out gently, but it might-as-well have slapped me across the face.

It's a topic I have avoided, but after everything I've seen, and realizing that I've been a weapon to kill innocent people—I owe it to them to face the truths that I had been blind to. Willingly or not.

I shake my head. "It could be to reduce their numbers, take out those considered a threat by command, or clear the way for some rhetoric they'd use in the future."

"Or all of the above."

A lump forms in my throat, and guilt is an unbearably heavy weight on my chest. "Looks like we both have much to atone for then, demon."

"Do you think the others in your unit would make amends for theirs?"

The question strikes me as odd, and though alarm bells go off in my mind, warning me not to give out information to my enemy, I take a moment to really consider it.

Omen might be a dutiful soldier, but she's not one to doubt command. She takes her missions seriously and executes them flawlessly.

Evelyn, on the other hand... She would be the first to atone, but she would do so leaving a trail of blood and bone in her wake.

"The one remaining Wraith would require much more convincing than me to show she was in the wrong, and even then, I'm not entirely certain she would regret it."

Crimson irises meet mine. "But the Harbinger—"

"She would be command's reckoning, and would die trying to atone for our sins."

"Sins?" He looks at me curiously.

"What else would you call frivolously murdering hundreds—if not thousands—of innocent people?" I mutter, knowing that I'm speaking of myself as much as I am the other Revenants.

There's so much blood on my hands, I'll never be clean of it.

I'm not sure that I want to be. It's evidence of how easily everything can change, or how quickly one can find themselves on the wrong side of the fence.

"Those are not your sins to bear or receive judgment for."

My brow raises. "Was it not our blades that ran them through?"

He shrugs. "If a plane malfunctions and crashes into a building, is it the pilot's sin for killing the people in the building, or the manufacturer's for cutting corners on safety and quality?"

I snort. "Apples to oranges, demon."

Still, the thought that the puppeteer strings tugging at me for years were to blame settles deep into the back of my mind.

Could I really be so easily absolved of my own accountability?

Does that not make me just as bad as them?

"Apples and oranges are still fruit, Viper. The fact remains that you were all forged into weapons, but it's he who wields who bears the responsibility."

"Careful, demon." I warn. "You're close to convincing me I did no wrong." The invisible stain of blood on my hands says otherwise, but I push that thought from my head.

Because if I'm not responsible, it leaves a long to-do list for me.

Orobas chuckles. "Heaven forbid."

My eyes widen, and he just grins even wider.

I still don't understand why all of this death and destruction would be worth it. Why take so many people out of the picture? What purpose did my actions serve, if not to make things better?

I know I need to ask him now—I may not have a chance tomorrow.

"Are those who pulled me off the streets really that evil?" My voice comes out softer than expected, and equally uncertain. I hate it.

His face turns contemplative, and I see his brows pull together in the shadows. "If not evil, misguided perhaps. Some maybe more than others. One misled soul can cause a chain reaction and influence many. It does not mean they're evil, nor more than you or I."

I roll onto my side, sliding my eyes shut. "Smooth way to imply you're not, demon prince."

A huff of laughter reaches my ears. "Someone has to."

I fight back the smile threatening to tug at the corners of my lips. "Goodnight, demon."

"Goodnight, Scarlett."

Chapter 21

Scarlett

Druv and Thal spend the next morning hovering around me like overprotective bodyguards as Ishari takes me through her closet.

As if a girl would betray the woman lending her clothes.

Who do they think I am?

Ishari's shoulders brush mine in the small space as she reaches in front of me, shoving clothes aside and lifting a dress off the rack.

"I think this one is nice and classy!" She grins, and I make a face.

The neckline is high over the collarbone, with no shape to it, so I shake my head. "I'd rather wear a cardboard box."

Snatching it from her hands, I toss it behind us at the looming security guards.

"Ow!" Druv says, and I bite the inside of my cheek to keep myself from smiling.

They've been insufferable for the past two hours as Ishari did my hair and makeup, fussing over her leaning too close to me or for putting sharp objects in my line of view.

If I wanted to kill her, I would have.

Clearly, they don't understand that.

Ishari files through dresses until I see one, and my heart skips a beat.

"There!" I say, snatching the hanger and lifting it off the rack. "This one is perfect."

It's a little short, and not the classy 'below-the-knee' length that most would expect, but why not add some flare to the evening?

Add the deep-set neckline, thick straps and a material that looks like it will hug the bodice in the **best** places?

We have a winner.

"It's a fundraiser, not a bar." Thal grumbles, but Ishari cuts him a glare.

"I think it's perfect." She beams, and I have to admit, it's growing harder not to like her.

There's a very good chance I'll let her live after this.

Especially considering everything Orobas has shown me—my biggest hang-up on fully believing him now is one burning question.

Why?

I have yet to find an answer, and I'm starting to wonder if I ever will. There has to be one.

Endless murder, death and destruction has to have a reason behind it. If not, I'll have a hard time believing this isn't an intricate series of lies and illusions of some sort.

Unlikely, but there's still a chance.

Ishari ushers me from the closet as I chew the inside of my cheek, my eyes narrowing on Thal and Druv as they both step aside.

"Over by the mirror, please." She chimes, and I brush past the two demon bodyguards, sliding onto the stool in front of the dresser.

With my hair half up, the rest curled elegantly to frame my face, the little hairs exposed at my shoulders stand on end and I shiver.

Everything Ishari has done to prepare me has exceeded my expectations, from the sharp cat-eye, the natural-yet-beautiful smokey eye and bold red lipstick.

"Alright, you two, out." She gestures to the door, and I watch the two men share a glance. After everything they've seen, I couldn't care less if they stayed in the room, but I appreciate her desire to give me privacy all the same.

I'll take it where I can.

Thal shoots me a warning look in the mirror, and I stick my tongue out at him.

Even animals know not to bite the hand that feeds them.

When they're both out of the room, she sighs loudly. "Thank God." She mutters, tugging the dress from the hanger. "Let's see how well this fits."

It's a whole thirty seconds to slide into the smooth velvet material. My hands glide over the fabric as I turn from side to side, and I sigh in contentment.

It hugs my body in all the right places, with a small slit along the thigh, giving my legs more freedom to move. The neckline plunges between my breasts, and I adjust the thick straps on each shoulder.

"Ugh, it looks incredible on you." She says with longing in her expression. "You're going to have to keep it. I'll never make it look this good."

I chuckle and shake my head. "I'm sure you wore it well too."

It's not a lie. Ishari has a similar build and stature to me, minus being slightly taller than I am, so I'm sure she filled it out better than I can.

She shakes her head but hurries to the closet, returning with a pair of heels that match the color. "These should do!"

When she bends to place them on the ground before me, I feel more like a princess than a government assassin sliding my feet into them.

"I guess I shouldn't be home past midnight, huh?" I say, raising an eyebrow at her, and she just throws her head back, releasing a cackle.

"Orobas will keep you out as long as he wants." She muses, just as a knock at the door rings out.

"Come in!"

Her voice quiets down as both males return, but I'm not expecting the third demon between them striding into the center of the room.

Crimson eyes meet mine before they drop, devouring every inch of me as he takes in Ishari's handiwork. If I didn't already know what he tastes like or how he feels against my body, I'd sure as hell be wondering now with the way he's looking at me.

Heat rises to my cheeks as Druv clears his throat, catching Orobas' attention.

Thank God for it, too.

My body's visceral reaction to the demon prince has me worried, to say the least, because unless I can uncover the big picture and who is to blame for this shitstorm, the target on Orobas' head is still clear.

Not to mention retrieving the damn dagger from him.

The one I haven't seen since that day.

"The car's out front. Are you ready?" The way he says it feels like a double entendre, and my pulse thrums steadily as he offers me his arm.

I can't help but feel like my path has split in two, and I'm tip-toeing toward the fork in the road. There's going to be a point of no return.

I know it.

The question is, what the fuck am I going to do?

"As long as there's drinks and food, I'm more than ready."

Orobas chuckles, and the sound sends heat through me as we lock arms. I don't miss the flagrant concern etched into Druv and Thal's expressions as we pass by them, but I can't bring myself to care when I'm inching closer to my freedom.

Whatever they're worried about is not my problem in the slightest.

My only concern is what the hell I'm going to do once I'm free.

Just a few more hours left.

Chapter 22

Scarlett

I've been to a number of extravagant parties and events in my life, but this one takes the cake.

The moment we walked into the enormous building the size of a football stadium, the number of people here makes it feel like we were heading into a sold-out convention. Gigantic vases filled with roses line the hallway to the grand hall, with the constant hum of chatter all around as people make their way inside.

Round tables line the room draped in deep burgundy linens, with occasional camera flashes flickering as journalists or guests take photos with others. Some arrived in tailored suits and others in evening gowns. They form circles, chatting amongst themselves, with a handful of them glancing at the podium on the opposite side of the room. The microphone illuminated by a single spotlight reflects off the polished wood lectern.

It's elegant, and I'm almost overwhelmed by the number of people. If it weren't for Orobas' tall form at my side, his arm still gently hooked with mine, I'd have probably faltered once or twice just walking inside the building.

For someone like me to say this is too many people—that's saying something.

He guides us with the flow of incoming traffic toward the tables, and my eyes adjust to the dimly lit room. A subtle mix of expensive cologne and perfume fills the air, and I snag a glass of champagne from one of the waitstaff passing by.

Orobas' gaze slides to the drink, and I shrug. "I'd have grabbed you one, but I only have one free hand."

His lips twitch, but something straight ahead catches his attention, turning it into a full grin. It's not until I follow his gaze that I understand the change in his demeanor.

At a beautifully set round table sits a couple, with two empty seats in front of them. The woman's long hair shifts against her collarbone as she surveys the room. She's slender, and doesn't look out of place, but there's a tension in her shoulders that tells me she's on edge.

The man next to her in a well-tailored suit drapes his arm around her waist with his gaze set on Orobas and a broad smile etched into his expression. His dark hair and stature is the only similarity to the demon prince at my side, but the giveaway that this is his brother is his eyes.

They're pale gold but bright even in the dim light of the room, like two small suns locked on the man guiding me in their direction.

The woman notices her partner stand, and she looks at us approaching before rising to her feet. She doesn't show any recognition when she sees us, so it's not hard to tell that she's meeting Orobas for the first time.

Somehow, that makes me feel moderately better.

"Brother." The demon prince says fondly with a smile, striding over toward Orobas as I release his arm. The two hug, and I watch the exchange with quiet curiosity.

I've seen people greet one another over the years, whether they be family, friends or lovers, but there's an unspoken sincerity in the way these two demons embrace.

It reminds me of a movie where two soldiers reunite after a war they almost didn't win.

"It's good to see you again." Orobas smiles broadly. "And with such an excellent taste in company."

The golden-eyed prince of hell snakes his arm around his companion's waist, bringing her front and center with pride etched into his handsome features. "This is Maris Sylvara. She is..." He pauses, his gaze lingering on me for a moment. "She is everything to me."

Well, fuck.

Why did he look at me like he was worried about saying it in my presence?

Does he know who I am?

Even if so, why would he think me to be some bloodthirsty psychopath wanting to kill his woman?

I might hate demons, but not enough to murder an innocent person.

Harriet comes to mind, and a lump forms in my throat.

Well... I wouldn't do so knowingly.

"So good to meet you, Maris. I'm Orobas." Orobas embraces the woman for a moment, stepping back to allow me to do the same.

"This is my brother, Sitri. Sitri, Maris, I'd like to introduce you to Scarlett Ashford," Orobas says with a grin, gesturing to the man with suns for eyes then to me.

A wave of panic washes over me hearing my full government name, but I shove it away before it's written on my face. They're demons—if they wanted to cause me pain, it wouldn't be by exposing who I am.

"Hello, it's so nice to meet you both." I say, the words coming out more awkward than intended.

"Come, we have much to discuss." Sitri says, gesturing to the table on his right. The possessive arm he keeps around Maris' waist hardly moves as he escorts her to her seat. When he adjusts, his hand slides to the small of her back.

"We do. It appears my baby brother won an entire war without me knowing." Orobas muses, and I think back to what he'd said about his brother destroying a country.

Sitri chuckles. His amused smirk is a stark contrast to the reddish hue of Maris' cheeks. "I have Maris to thank for that. If it weren't for her, I'd still be playing cat and mouse."

Orobas nods thoughtfully. "I figured as much since you have lived to tell the story." His crimson gaze turns to Maris. "Which means I owe you a debt of gratitude."

She shakes her head. "No debts needed. I simply did what I had to do to get Sitri back."

"You did more than that." Sunlight eyes grumbles beside her and Orobas laughs.

"How did you win the war?" I ask Maris, and three pairs of eyes land on me. I want to retract my question and slink back into my chair.

Sitri's attention turns to Orobas, and I see the prince of hell nod in my peripheral. Is he asking permission to tell me?

What the hell is going on?

"It was nothing—"

Sitri huffs a laugh and shakes his head. "You mean other than taking out every base of operations and overtaking national media coverage?"

My eyes widen.

Suddenly, this slender, bashful woman beside him seems so much more interesting. Just looking at her, you wouldn't guess that kind of history.

Never judge a book by its cover, I suppose.

"Technically, according to official reports, the bases were lost due to severely inclement weather in the region." Maris muses, tossing me a wink. "An odd series of naturally occurring phenomena."

"All at once. An impressive feat for mother nature." I murmur, and Maris' lips twitch up into a grin.

"Countless years of battle ended in mere weeks at her hands." When Sitri notices my brows pulling together, he adds more context. "Kharidia had been a war zone for far longer than I care to admit."

"Why couldn't you stop it?" The question comes out of me before I can help myself, but I don't regret asking.

It makes no sense that a prince of hell capable of destruction would be unable to stop a war, but Maris somehow swooped in and saved the day.

Maris glances between the two demons, and Orobas nods once, giving her the go-ahead for something.

Didn't they *just* meet? Why do I feel like I'm missing something important?

"How much do you know about the conflict in Kharidia?"

I shrug. "Not a lot. I knew of it, but I was involved in other affairs."

She nods thoughtfully. "It's a land without strategic resources, with smaller, less advanced neighboring nations that don't hold stake in what happens there. It was a lone country surrounded by smaller fish, with a dense population that most of the world paid less attention to. That's why for years, the real demons plaguing this Earth manufactured conflict in Kharidia."

I frown. Clearly she isn't referring to Sitri or Orobas, and I instinctively have half a mind to laugh at the fact that she's implying they're not bad at all, but I let her continue.

A member of the waitstaff walks past, and the princes both grab two glasses of champagne, placing them on the table as if we're going to need it.

She takes a small sip from her drink, keeping her voice low. "They set up ritual sites in five locations throughout the country, and would lure civilians there before—" She cuts off, her gaze grows distant for a moment, and I know she's reliving some trauma, so I can imagine what happened from there.

Bile rises in my throat.

"Who are 'they' in all of this?" As much as I don't want to consider the parallels to my own experiences—my command chain—somewhere in the recesses of my mind, I already am.

"It could be anyone." Sitri growls, but Maris places her hand on his, and he grows quiet. Strange that she's the one to speak when it seems both princes have the knowledge, but I file that away for later.

"I don't know how much Oro has told you, but I'll tell you who it was for me. It was my boyfriend and co-journalist, my media director, the general in Kharidia who oversaw all the moves our military made, high-ranking officials and much of the population of soldiers there."

My lips part, but all I can do is look at her.

All these people were demons, and yet she was the one to take them down?

"Why did it take you so long to win the war?"

Sitri's gaze drops, but again, Maris is the one who answers, her voice low. "The princes are bound by rules to keep the balance—rules that the real demons of this world don't care to follow, nor seem to apply to them."

Confusion must be clear on my face, because she gives me an apologetic look as Orobas speaks up.

"Azrael is duty-bound to reap the souls of any angels who upset the balance on Earth. It is why they must be cautious about giving too much information, or making too great of action."

That makes sense for angels, but these two princes are demons.

Maris huffs a laugh. "Thankfully, Azrael didn't seem to care when Sitri filled me in—that, or he was too busy to act on his duty."

"It was a risk all the same." Sitri interjects solemnly. "I'm glad for his inaction, but it needed to be done."

"Why would Azrael's duty apply to demons?"

The table falls silent, but it's Maris who answers. "All the princes and their legions were once angels, Scarlett."

Oh. Right. I should have known that.

"So that's why you're the one telling me all of this?" I ask Maris, and she nods.

"We are not bound by the same rules as they are, hence why I was not reprimanded in the slightest for my actions. If Sitri would have done it, I don't think he would be here today." She shudders, and he rubs circles on her back in a soothing manner.

"So, are you a demon too?"

Orobas stiffens beside me, but Maris shakes her head. "I'm not."

If she's not, how did she do so much to win the war?

My mind goes back to Garrett and his ability to control the wind. "Servilian?"

Her lips twitch, and she shakes her head again. Her gaze flicks to both men before settling on me. "Sitri shared his powers with me before they took him captive."

My eyes widen, and I look over at Orobas. "Demons can do that?"

His lips twitch, but there's still an undercurrent of tension in his expression. "Very few have abilities, but yes, some can share or impart slivers to others."

Yet more information stored away for later.

"How do I know this isn't some elaborate ploy to gain my trust?"

Maris' gaze softens, and she moves to rest her hand on Sitri's thigh. "At some point, you just have to look at what's in front of you and make a decision based on instinct. Everyone had told me about the feared magic user and his transgressions before I'd met him. The thing is, once I met him, I realized almost everything I'd been told was a lie."

My heart thuds loudly in my ears as more parallels to my own experience when meeting Orobas form.

Truth is, if I were in his place, and an assassin walked into my home to kill me, I would have eliminated him out without a question.

Orobas, however, did not take that route.

No. He took steps to contain me and convince me of reality—his truth.

The question is, with all this information pointing in one direction, do I believe it?

"Have you spoken to the others?" Sitri asks, his inhuman eyes fixed on his brother, who nods.

"Seir mostly. He's working with Vassago and Stolas to counter influence along the east and west coasts."

Sitri's eyes widen. "Stolas, you say?" His lips twitch as his shock turns into amusement. "How in the world did they enlist his help? He has refused for millennia."

Orobas chuckles. "Let's just say he's had a change of heart." Crimson eyes land on me, and I fight the urge to grab a fork from the table.

I might be starting to realize that command lied to me and used me all these years, but there's nothing to say that Orobas isn't just as bad.

I refuse to trade one handler for another.

Understanding flashes across Sitri's face, but the conversation is stunted when someone walked onto the podium, positioning themselves at the lectern.

"Thank you everyone, for coming to our annual fundraiser to support our progressive campaign, aimed at delivering lasting changes to improve the quality of life for our constituents. First, I'd like to thank our donors for helping fund our efforts, ensuring that we can continue to do meaningful work."

The speaker drones on, listing a handful of donors who have contributed to give them a special highlight, and I notice a shadow moving in the corner of my eye again.

"In recent days, Dennis Tildman's team has proudly established a widespread grassroots movement, organizing protests and raising awareness about dishonesty on our national stage. For too long, politicians have been bought out, resulting in the flagrant display of corruption of power that we see today."

The shadow hasn't moved from my peripheral, and my heart thrums steadily in my chest as I wait.

Could it be the same one from the banquet?

... "and today, in honor of combating corruption in the media, as leaders in doing what is right, even when it's hard, it's my pleasure to announce that Maris Sylvara is here with us."

She stands at the table as applause erupts from all around the room. The spotlight swings to her, and she waves awkwardly for a moment, but when it returns to the front stage, the clapping continues.

It continues long after she's sat down, her cheeks flushed bright red.

"Maris Sylvara is a shining example of integrity, having captured the attention of our nation, exposing the truth about our military's purpose in a foreign conflict."

"If only they knew." Maris murmurs, and both princes nod their heads solemnly.

The burning why question I've had simmering at the back of my mind surfaces again, and I completely tune out the speaker.

"Why are they doing all this?"

Even though I whispered the words, three heads turn in my direction. But I don't have to look at them to know Maris is the one who plans to respond.

"She really doesn't know *anything*, does she?" Maris asks Orobas, and he inclines his head in agreement.

"There's been some setbacks, and we've had to handle it delicately."

"It would help if someone told me." I growl, but that only earns a chuckle from the demon prince beside me.

Asshole.

Maris' expression turns more serious, and my stomach twists uncomfortably. "They're harvesting human souls, Scarlett."

Chapter 23

Scarlett

I'd say this is a prank, but the look on their faces tells me that laughing right now would be in poor taste.

Which means the words she just spoke were the truth.

"I don't—I don't think I heard that right." I whisper.

She laughs under her breath, but there's no humor in it. "You *heard* just fine—it's the answer that's bizarre, even if it's the truth. They set up ritual sites, lure groups of people near them and the souls are claimed for their army."

Her words are hushed now, her gaze sweeping the area around us. It's then that I realize the shadow is missing, and I tense, leaning forward to place my hands on the table.

My right palm covers the knife, the pad at the base of my thumb squeezing the handle.

Whoever this shadow is, I'll be ready for them.

Taking my momentary distraction as me absorbing the information, Maris sighs. "I know it sounds crazy, Scarlett, but I saw it with my own eyes."

I frown. "How?"

She looks around nervously, but Sitri leans back, resting his hand on the top of her chair. Even if she's not sure about eavesdroppers, Orobas and Sitri should be able to spot any.

"I saw the ritual sites with my own two eyes. At one point we were separated, and they herded an entire group of people, myself included, into the general vicinity of one before opening fire on us all. Men, women... and children."

My eyes widen as she shudders, her gaze going distant as Sitri brushes her cheek with his knuckles, tucking a lock of hair behind her ear.

The action is so beautifully intimate that I feel a twinge in my chest. Sitri might be a demon prince, but the way he's silently supporting Maris without words brings my loneliness front and center.

After seeing this and how Thal treats Ishari, I'm seriously starting to wonder just how wrong I've had it all along.

I remain silent with my thoughts as the fundraiser goes on, but I'm distracted. My world was flipped upside down when Orobas exposed the warehouse, but I chalked it up to his manipulation. It wasn't until he brought me to see Harriet's family that I really questioned things.

And now?

Now I can't help but feel that, out of everyone at this table, the real demon is me.

I don't know how I feel about that, but the nausea twisting in my gut tells me it's not favorable.

Fuck.

I'm so distracted that I don't notice the shadow moving along the edges of my vision as the speaker continues their speech. I'm not paying attention when Dennis Tildman gets up on stage and delivers his own.

My thoughts are a jumbled mess, running through each mission I'd been assigned, trying to decide where I could have done something different.

I don't snap out of it until Maris and Sitri rise to their feet, giving us warm smiles.

"I'm going to run to the ladies' room," Maris says with a sigh. "That drink ran through me."

I look at my own untouched glass, feeling more and more tempted to down the contents to cope with each world-shattering revelation.

Maris and Sitri disappear behind me, and I reach over to grab the champagne. Before my fingers brush the smooth glass stem, Orobas' tattooed hand slides over mine, halting me in place.

"No one likes a warm drink." He murmurs, flagging a server down and taking two from his tray. He hands one to me, bubbles streaming from the bottom.

"Thank you." It's all I can muster through the cloud of uncertainty fogging my brain. Somehow, from the time I posed as a housekeeper until now, everything has changed.

I don't know what my purpose is anymore, or who to blame, and it's like there was a layer of mist clouding my judgement. Day by day, hour by hour, it's been slowly dissipating, but nowhere near fast enough.

Bringing the rim of the glass to my lips, I tilt my head and down the contents. Orobas offers me his, and it's seconds before that one is empty too.

"Is it the event or what Maris said that's driving you to throw back drinks like you just hit legal age?"

I snort, placing the glass onto the table. "Why not both?"

"Can't say I blame you." He murmurs, and snags two more from a server. "At least we only have another thirty minutes to endure."

My lips twitch. "I've been tortured many times, but sitting through these two events might take the cake."

"Who?"

I turn to him as his jaw feathers. "Who, what?"

"Who tortured you?" The look on his face is the same calm demeanor he always has, yet I can't help but feel like there's an underlying tension that's about to snap.

I shrug. "Who hasn't at this point—the list is long." I consider him for a moment and grin. "Probably nearly as long as the people who want your head."

With how discombobulated my mind is, the tentative peace between us feels right. I don't think twice about his motives or what he is as he hands me a fresh glass of champagne.

The first speaker steps up to the lectern, his voice grating on my nerves so much that I tune him out as he reiterates Dennis' position on key issues.

So much posturing.

Still, if Orobas thinks he can do well, I guess all I can do is hope for the best for him.

"Ten o'clock." Orobas murmurs, and my gaze snaps to the man weaving through the crowd toward Dennis. The politician stands twenty-five feet away, talking to Maris and Sitri with a broad grin.

While I'm sure some of it isn't forced, I have no doubt he's ensuring his appearance with her because of the public's scrutiny of lawmakers that supported the conflict.

When I get a better view of the man creeping closer to the politician, it takes a second before I recognize Tyler Hall, Dennis' legal director. It's when he scowls at Maris that everything clicks into place.

"That's our guy." I murmur, and Orobas nods in agreement, using his cell to send a quick text.

Tyler inches closer to the group as Dennis pulls his phone from his pocket. He hardly looks at his screen for more than a second before sliding it back into his pants.

I fight the urge to stand up, which proves difficult until Dennis' attention turns in the direction Tyler approaches.

Orobas sends another text, and I watch Dennis intently, but he never reaches for his phone. This time, it's Sitri pulling out his cell and sliding it back into his pocket.

He leans over to Maris, whispering in her ear as she nods.

"What did you tell him?" I ask, but Orobas shakes his head.

Right. He probably doesn't want to voice it just in case.

Maris grasps her glass in hand and excuses herself from the table for a moment, heading in Tyler's direction.

Watching this unfold is like a movie, except I know the actors, and I have no idea what's going to happen next. I'd expected Dennis or Sitri to intervene, but for whatever reason, Maris is the one taking the lead.

That's when it all clicks into place.

They're unable to take affirmative action for fear of repercussions, so Maris is the one doing it.

My gaze tracks her as she gracefully weaves through the crowd, and when she's close enough, she bumps his shoulder. Shock covers her features, and she places her hand on his arm, leaning in to say what I assume is an apology.

Tyler's back stiffens almost imperceptibly, and his eyes glaze over. He nods before walking straight to the lectern, and Maris' lips curve into a smile as she returns to Sitri and Dennis.

"Orobas?" I say, as Tyler climbs the steps to stand behind the microphone.

"Hmm?"

"What are Sitri's abilities?"

"He summons fire." We watch Tyler approach the stand and lean forward. "And he can coerce or command others to do his will." Orobas' voice is pure amusement as a high-pitched whine from the microphone fills the hall.

"Hi everyone." Tyler's gait is awkward as he stands hovered above the lectern, his mouth an inch from the microphone. "My name is Tyler Hall, and I am Dennis Tildman's legal director."

My heart thunders, and I'm so caught up in what's happening, I don't notice the shadow to my right disappearing from view again.

"I'd like to announce my formal resignation. I can no longer work for Dennis' campaign because I disagree with his policies. Kharidians and Servilians, both godless people, must be eradicated in His name."

My eyebrows shoot up, and I look over at Orobas, who's laughing under his breath.

The fact that I was terrified of Orobas because I thought he could do exactly what his brother *can* doesn't escape me.

I still can't believe that Maris was given those abilities and literally just used them in front of us—and everyone else, for that matter.

"The CIA hired me to infiltrate Dennis' campaign and report whether he was threatening the status quo. I believe this to be true; therefore, I am unable to work with him any longer."

What the hell.

It's so quiet you could hear a pin drop, but Tyler just moves the microphone in place and steps off the stage, disappearing into the crowd.

People boo, and soon the enormous room is a chorus of various pitched discontent.

"Well, Viper," Orobas says with a sigh. "I believe that's all the entertainment for us this evening—shall we leave?"

"Thought you'd never ask." I down the rest of my drink and slide the glass further onto the table. My head swims a little, but I don't mind.

Not when it's dulling the chaos threatening to consume my thoughts at any moment.

I know I'm inching closer to the fork in the road between me and the demon prince, though I can't help but wonder if he'll make good on his promise to let me go free.

The question is, do I even return to my old life?

I know too much now not to ask questions, and with Evelyn and Omen still wrapped up in it, I might find myself at odds with them.

They won't take kindly to my pestering them with doubts when that's not our job. It's not a weapon's duty to concern itself with morality.

And then there's Orobas' existence. I'm painfully aware that his presence means a great deal, namely that the war between demons and humans is ongoing.

Yet somehow, in 48 hours I've gone from repeatedly wanting to stab a sharp object into a major artery and let him bleed out—to being uncertain that he's the devil command painted him to be.

It's enough to make my head spin without the help of alcohol.

And I'm running out of time to decide.

Each step alongside Orobas feels like I'm tearing my mind in two. On one hand, everything I've been told, everything I am, is in opposition to Orobas.

I was trained to kill him and those he cares about, taught to despise everything he does, and to exterminate his kind.

Yet, in this very moment, the thought of it gives me pause.

The murmurs and chatter of the crowd fade behind us as we exit the building. The crisp evening air blows against my cheek, shifting my hair as one of the valet staff approaches.

Orobas passes the man his ticket. "I'll have that over in one second—" The man's mouth snaps shut as the demon prince shakes his head.

"No need; we can retrieve it ourselves."

He looks like he's going to protest until Orobas slips a hundred-dollar tip into his palm. The valet worker blinks.

"Are you sure?"

The demon slides his wallet into his suit pocket and nods. "Enjoy your evening. Come on, Scarlett."

I fall into step alongside him, leaving the valet behind as we follow the sidewalk to the back of the building. With the banquet still in full swing, with no patrons coming or going, the dimly lit walkway takes on an eerie edge.

Well-trimmed bushes to my left cast shadows along the path, blocking the scarce light from the windows of the building. Orobas' arm brushes my shoulder with each step, but it's the sudden silence that has me coming to a stop.

Another breeze makes the hair at the nape of my neck stand on end. Orobas turns to look at me with a frown as the shadow in my peripheral jerks to my right. He cocks his head and I hear the softest swish of motion.

That's when I act.

Twisting, I throw my body toward the demon prince, and his eyes widen. But I can't bring myself to focus on him as everything slows, adrenaline surging through me.

By the time my back is to him, surprise coats my veins as Omen's body collides into mine. The dagger in her hand that would have aimed for Orobas' neck now swipes toward my face.

Flinching away on instinct, I know it's too late. There's no way for me to move in time.

The thought is fleeting, but I'm not expecting it when a weight around my waist tugs me backward just as the blade slices into my cheek.

Omen's face is pure rage and steeled determination as she bares her teeth at me. As if suddenly realizing that I've protected the demon.

A hollow pit forms in my stomach as I stare at her.

I did it without a splinter of hesitation.

Noticing I'm distracted, Omen lunges again as a shadow in my peripheral darts out from the cover of the bushes, knocking Omen off her feet.

She tumbles, arms flailing wildly as the shadow solidifies. A mess of dark hair and tactical gear forms first, before the demon's sharp features, his bright blue eyes as prominent as his smug grin.

Orobas chuckles behind me, his arm still wrapped around my waist, securing me to him. "Looks like I owe you one, Caass."

The shadow demon's hand elongates as he pins a snarling Omen to the ground. What once would have been a gloved index finger is now a talon pressed into the column of Omen's throat.

"Been tracking this one for two full days." The blue-eyed man says, his piercing gaze flicking to me and Oro before returning to the assassin beneath him. "I was wondering when she'd make her move. Surprised it wasn't a hit on Sylvara, though."

The shadow was this Caass demon?

Which means Omen had been tailing us all along.

Does this mean Eve is too?

"Scarlett." Omen growls a half plea, and I freeze, looking at her as she bares her teeth at Caass.

The blue-eyed demon keeps her restrained with one arm and reaches for her dagger as an icy wave of terror washes over me.

No.

He can't kill her.

When his hand wraps around it, I finally find my voice.

"Stop."

Caass freezes, his gaze flicks from Orobas to me.

"Don't hurt her." Not a plea. Not a command either.

My whispered words reach the demon, who instead sheaths her dagger.

"I won't, but I'm not releasing her." He says with a deadpan look, gesturing to Omen squirming between his thighs from where he pins her. "Besides, she's kinda fun."

His taunt only makes Omen angrier, and she grunts with effort, trying to launch him off her. When she slams her thigh into his ass, the fucking demon just smiles wider.

"Get the fuck off me—" Omen thrashes, still easily held by the blue-eyed demon. "Scarlett, *do something*."

I swallow hard as Orobas' arm slips away from my hips, his warmth at my back disappearing as he approaches my side.

When she sees me unrestrained but not moving to help her, she stills.

Her brows pinch together, and she shakes her head in denial. "After everything we've been through?"

Orobas steps closer to her as terror twists her expression, and she angles herself as far away from him. He kneels beside Caass and places his hands on either side of her head.

She squeezes her eyes shut, as if bracing for death. A long moment passes between the three of them, and Orobas retracts his hands slowly.

"Bring her to the southern safe house." The crimson-eyed demon prince murmurs, pushing to his feet. "It will take time, but perhaps she can be saved."

"You fucking asshole—"

Caass uses his free hand to give Orobas a lazy salute. "This should be fun."

The lump in my throat becomes larger as he turns Omen onto her stomach, securing her arms behind her back. Her expression grows distant, and I already know where her mind is.

It's the same place mine goes.

And I fucking hate that for her.

Chapter 24

Evelyn

It's been an hour since I caught sight of the demon prince and Scarlett through the tinted windows of his car, leaving the property.

The guns and knives strapped to my body are a familiar comfort in all of this, and I bring the binoculars to my eyes as movement catches my attention.

The two male demons that had just finished their rounds scale down the front steps, filing into a car that one of the guards had brought around.

The engine rumbles loudly from here, and a tremor of excitement works through me.

This is it. With the leaders gone, they won't know what to do when they're attacked.

My heart thrums steadily, and I scale cautiously down the tree. With any luck, Omen will have tracked Orobas and Scarlett. Her orders are not to engage, so I don't bother worrying about her well-being.

Then again, Grant *did* state not to go in guns blazing...

But *he* is not the leader of the Revenants.

My feet hit the hard ground with a crunch, and I hide behind the trunk as the two demons pass by in their car. Counting each second, I'm at twenty before surging forward from the shadows.

Who knows how long this window of opportunity will be open.

Unsheathing a dagger and removing a gun from its holster, I stalk toward the guards at the open gate. My hand clutches the handgun resting atop my other wrist as I take aim.

Two shots land on their marks, the sound of each muffled by the silencer attached to the front of the barrel. Blood splatters from the exit wounds before they each collapse, and I hurry past the gate.

One, two, three more demons drop like stones, crimson pooling beneath their lifeless bodies. It takes seconds for me to cross the front yard and slip inside, firing two more shots at males in my immediate line of sight.

After clearing the first level and reloading multiple times, I scale the stairs to the second floor, locking another clip of bullets into place.

The dagger that command had assigned Scarlett to locate is nowhere to be found, and with that, I pray it's on the second floor. Or else I've made Scarlett's situation that much worse, for no reason.

I will have no bargaining chips to secure the exchange.

With another shot aimed, I pull the trigger and the gun jams, making my heart stutter before I hurl the dagger in the demon's direction. The blade buries in his throat, and I close the distance between us, holstering the jammed handgun.

It would take longer to fix the jam, and I have plenty of daggers at my disposal.

Besides, getting my hands a little dirty is no issue.

The next five demons I run into don't stand a chance, and with crimson splattered across my chest, I open the door to another room. It swings wide, and I see the female with her back to me.

"Back already, Thal—?" She turns, and her eyes land on me before they widen, finally registering as I recoil my arm.

"Don't scream." I warn in a low tone, and she freezes with her hands raised.

Chapter 25

Scarlett

Caass hauls Omen off the ground, keeping her arms behind her back as he secures her over his shoulder. The way he adjusts her is cautious, and something tells me he's not inclined to hurt her.

The next breath from my lungs comes easier with that observation in mind.

Crickets sing as Caass carries Omen to a black SUV, and an odd note of guilt snakes down my spine.

"He won't hurt her." Orobas says carefully. "But she will have to be contained until she can accept reality, Viper."

My tongue clicks once on the inside of my teeth before I shake my head, my arms wrapping around my body. "I can't help but feel like I've let her down."

The words feel raw and vulnerable to voice, but to his credit, Orobas doesn't balk or reject it. He just nods thoughtfully, sliding his hands in his pockets as he takes a step closer.

"Any inaction to clear her mind or feed into their lies would do her more of a disservice."

I frown, letting his words sink in.

"There's a fine line between whether a human can be saved from their influence, or if it is a mercy to end their lives, Viper. I'm certain you understand this maybe more than anyone else would. Like an animal bleeding out, do you let them suffer, or could they survive?"

He turns toward the parking lot and gestures for me to follow.

"So you'd play God?" I ask, willing my steps to be more certain as I fall into line beside him.

"If you think Father decides who lives or dies, I have news for you." My eyes widen, and he laughs under his breath. "He may pull some strings here or there, but to control everything? Impossible."

"He wouldn't... smite someone?"

Orobas laughs harder and shakes his head. "Especially now, not at all. Though over the years humans have assumed he would. They'd blame odd events or catastrophes done in His name, as if persecuting some entities for someone's benefit."

"So when people talk about His wrath—"

"A fallacy." Orobas clicks the button on his keys and moves to hold the passenger door open. "Father wouldn't have the time or power to spare. Contrary to what people may think, there's a reason angels delivered messages and why miracles were rare.

"Divine intervention was done entirely by archangels. Father has spent most of his energy keeping heaven intact. There's no way he'd have the power to exert a flagrant influence on humans on such a large scale."

My eyes widen, and I stare at him for a breath of a moment before sliding into the seat. The door clicks shut, and I absorb his words as he walks around the front of the vehicle.

If God doesn't have that kind of influence, were all the texts and teachings wrong?

Who the hell would have lied about that?

The demon prince slides into the driver's seat and turns the engine on, pulling out of the parking spot with ease. Droplets of rain patter against the windshield, the sound melding into the hum of the engine.

"Why would so many texts say it was His divine will, then?"

Orobas grimaces, rubbing his hand along his jawline. "A script translated multiple times and written by humankind can hardly be trusted. They've all twisted over the years. Recounts of events thrice separated from the person who originally observed it, then translated into another language multiple times. Each transcription deviated further and further from the truth.

"Humans, especially those corrupt and full of greed, with an agenda to manipulate as many as possible, use fear as their binder. Adhesion to religion based in terror will always take root. Father taught us all to love and protect each other—to accept our differences and lift one another up. To preserve what is good. But humans, angels, and demons alike have forgotten his philosophies."

He maneuvers the vehicle onto the long road leading to his property, and my thoughts war against each other.

Command had drilled the fear of hell into my head from the time they took me off the streets.

Sure, it might have been slow at first, but it was there.

They tied it all in to eliminating demons, giving me a wicked and cruel way to bring about manufactured justice.

I suck in a ragged breath. "When command found me as a child, I was skin and bones, fending for myself in the back alley behind a restaurant on the streets of New York. A man in tactical gear approached me to offer me a roof over my head in exchange for training and some undercover missions. The nearby businesses had called the cops twice when they found me digging through their garbage, so I hadn't eaten more than a slice of bread that week. I was desperate.

"That week was one of the hardest of my life. They might have fed me and given me a bed to sleep on instead of the ground, but on the first day with them, they introduced me to the enemy."

I shudder at the memory.

Normally I refuse to sink back into those experiences, but if Orobas really wants to understand me, he will have to hear this.

No matter how much it hurts.

"They told me I was going to see a demon—an *actual* demon. They'd warned me he would not have horns or a forked tongue—no tail to whip back and forth. But when they threw me into that room with a man who looked entirely human, I thought there was a mistake.

"It wasn't until I realized there was a single camera in the ceiling and the door locked shut behind me that I knew I was truly in danger. They left me in that room for a full twenty-four hours before men in tactical gear came in, pulled him off me, and I was taken to the hospital for my injuries."

Orobas' hand tightens on the steering wheel until it groans. "Scarlett—"

"Four broken ribs, a fractured pelvis, a broken nose, a broken wrist and a concussion in addition to hours of sexual assault is all it took to turn me into someone who feared and hated demons."

Orobas curses under his breath, and the car jerks to the side of the road close to the long driveway to his property. We both lurch forward as he slams on his brakes, his chest heaving deep lungfuls.

But he doesn't interrupt or stop me. His crimson irises burning with an intensity of anger that sends a chill down my spine.

"They sent me for counselling shortly after, claiming to care about my mental state and that the demon hadn't broken my spirit, just my body. I was sent to a priest and kept in therapy for weeks to teach me to overcome my fear of demons. They channeled that terror into anger and used it to reinforce my physical training.

"It only took them days to bring me into a room with a subdued demon and ordered me to kill him. They claimed it would help me overcome my fear knowing I—a divine survivor as they called me—could kill them. So I did. But that wasn't the end. They pushed me harder, exposed me to different methods of torture to ensure I knew how to survive it. Days turned into weeks, then months... It didn't take them long to rebuild me as their demon-killing weapon."

A moment passes, and I look over at Orobas, his tongue grazing the sharp edge of his canine with a blazing vengeance in his eyes.

He exhales a breath. "Get out of the car, Scarlett."

His seatbelt clicks and whirs as he surges from the vehicle, rain pelting the car harder with each passing second. I'm in a nervous state of disbelief and confusion as I watch his suit become drenched with each step he takes around the car.

When he tugs my door open, my heart lurches into my throat, and my blood rages.

Is this where he slices my neck open and discards me to the side of the road?

A broken, damaged assassin who's too much of a threat to him and his company.

He leans in to unbuckle my belt, gently tugging me to my feet, the droplets quickly saturating my hair as it sticks to my skin and clothes. Rain splatters my bare shoulders, streaming down my collar and into the thin material of my dress.

"I don't—"

The words catch in my throat as he pulls a dagger from the back of his suit. I'm stuck between my confusion about how the hell he'd hidden a blade and the innate fear of what he plans to do with it. But he doesn't give me long to wonder as he thrusts the weapon's hilt in my palm.

Rain streams into my eyes, and I blink it away, glancing between him and the dagger.

"The deal we made is up. You've held up your end of it, attending both events with me, and we uncovered the rat within Tildman's staff. You're free to do what you came to do, Viper. I'm giving you back your fangs."

The look in his eyes is fierce, and I shake my head. When I retreat a step, he walks me backward, towering over me as my ass hits the door of the car.

I should be ready to kill him.

My fingers twitch against the hilt of the dagger.

This is what I spent my life training to do.

Seeing my hesitation, he holds my gaze and reaches down to grab my hand still clutching the dagger. When he presses the blade to his own throat, the sharp edge biting into his skin, my heart thrashes in my chest.

"This is the part where you're supposed to kill me, Viper."

His body blocks most of the rain, but it still streams from his hair onto me as I search his face. There's not an ounce of indecision in his expression, only rage.

But it's not directed toward me.

I try to angle the edge of the blade away from his skin, but he tightens his grip and digs it in further into his throat.

"Key word is **supposed**, demon prince." I rasp, my breathing ragged as I fight the anxiety pumping through my veins. Whether due to him giving me an opening to end his life or the fact that I'm not taking it, I don't know.

"Then why haven't you?" He asks, and I shake my head.

The urge to pull back—to let go—it's lightning in my veins, rebelling against everything I've been taught.

He squeezes my hand tighter, pressing the edge to his skin as crimson pools under it. It bleeds into the onslaught of rain sluicing down his skin, and I raise my eyes to meet his.

"Because," I whisper, the word drowned out by the rumble of thunder in the distance. "For the first time, I don't want to."

He lets me pull the blade away by an inch before tugging it from my grasp, tossing it to the ground beside us. The rage in his expression vanishes as he searches my eyes, replaced by relief and something else I can't quite place.

With my heart beating out of my chest, I fall still as Orobas' hands cup either side of my face. He leans in slowly, holding my gaze until he presses his lips to mine.

The stubble of his beard tickles my skin, and I melt into his touch. That's when he kisses me in earnest, slanting his mouth over mine, his tongue placing a silent request against the seam of my lips.

I'm squeezed between the length of his body and the side of the car, my mind blissfully empty as I let myself exist at this moment with him.

A loud crack of thunder breaks us apart, but he still holds me close, searching my face as if waiting for me to suddenly change my mind.

I know I won't.

My hand moves to cover the superficial wound on his neck, and his warmth seeps into my skin. The same warmth that bled into me when I nearly froze to death. The very heat at my back after I'd saved him from Omen, and he'd kept me from having my cheek sliced open.

It's a warmth that I could hide in, and yet I'm unsure I deserve it.

My body trembles, and my eyelids shutter. "I don't know what to do—" I confess into the space between us, as if the rain itself could clean the blood from my hands. "Or where I belong."

His palm glides up to cover mine, the other cupping my face with a tenderness I'd never expect from a prince of hell. His thumb brushes my skin, catching the rain on my cheek, and my eyes slide shut.

I selfishly lean into his touch, giving in to temptation even if some part of me reminds me of all the terrible deeds demons have done. More and more, that voice sounds like command's instead of mine.

The one that instilled all my prejudices and judgments.

The same voice that has kept me from believing the prince of hell, who was doing everything he could to show me the truth.

True demons exist in this world. I know that to be a fact.

But they aren't **him**.

"If you return to them, they will kill you, Scarlett." His words are agonizingly soft, a sharp contrast to the harsh implications behind them.

But he's right.

"Come back to the house, stay the night. We'll figure the rest out together."

Together.

One word that I never expected him to say, but I'd be lying if I said it didn't mean everything.

Crimson eyes burn bright into mine with a certainty that snuffs out any doubts of my own as I nod. "Druv and Thal won't be happy."

He laughs under his breath and straightens, turning to look thoughtfully into the yard of his enormous property. Even from here, the towers aren't visible over the treeline.

Orobas stills, his gaze fixed on something in the distance.

"What is it?" I ask as his hand slips from my cheek, and within seconds he's sprinted to the fence overlooking his the long driveway.

"Oro?" I take two steps toward him, only to hear him curse and run to the driver's side of the door.

"Get in the car, Scarlett." The urgency in his voice throws me into motion. I slide in the passenger seat as his tires squeal, and my heart's in my throat.

"What's going on?" My words fall on deaf ears as he slams on the brakes, and we lurch to a stop. That's when I see it for myself.

Each guard within eye-shot of the front door lies motionless on the ground. The singular bullet wound to their necks or heads with a pool of crimson around them sends bile into my throat.

Even this downpour of rain has done nothing to wash away the blood staining the ground.

These were familiar faces, but thankfully none are Druv and Thal. It's a conscious effort to ignore the part of me that balks at my reaction to the murdered demons, but a fresh wave of terror fills me when the door to the house is ajar.

Within seconds of stopping, Orobas is out of the car and halfway up the front steps, with me trailing close behind. It's a conscious effort to avoid the rain and blood-soaked stairs for fear of losing my footing, but Orobas' horror keeps me focused.

"Druv!" My heart clenches as his shout echoes in the eerie silence of the house. "Thal! Ishari!" His voice cracks, and he spots bloody footprints making their way up the stairs to the second floor. He follows them up, two steps for each one of mine, and he hurries down the hall.

I barely catch up when he bursts into his office, only to find it empty with bloody fingerprints stamped all over his laptop. My heart skips a beat when he flips it open and pulls out a piece of paper that was wedged between the screen and the keyboard.

Bring Scarlett to the abandoned warehouse on 53rd street, near museum. Don't bother with traps. One wrong move and the demon bitch dies. You have 24 hours.

- Evelyn

With everything I know now, Evelyn's actions feel especially heinous. These demons were kind to me, even when they had no reason to be.

Orobas blows out a breath, his fist crumpling the note before he hurls it to the side.

"She took Ishari?"

Orobas' gaze meets mine, and he nods as heavy footsteps thud against the hardwood floors downstairs.

We both freeze.

"Ishari?"

"Oro?"

Druv and Thal's voices fill the air, both thick with concern as I sprint to the doorway. "Up here."

Thunderous footsteps grow louder until both demons are in view, jogging into the entrance to the office. When they see the tension in Orobas' expression they both fall still.

"Where's Ishari?" Thal asks, his eyes wide as he glances between us. "Where is my soulmate?"

His soulmate.

A fracture webs through my heart, splintering pieces off as my chest tightens.

"She was taken hostage."

"Where is my Ishari?!" Thal bellows, and I flinch at how the walls reverberate.

"Enough." Orobas snaps. Even though the demon in front of him has wide eyes and palpable rage in his expression, he falls silent. "The Harbinger believes Scarlett has been taken hostage. She wants to trade for Ishari."

"You did this," Thal says in a low tone, his index finger pointed at the demon prince. "You brought this snake into our home, and now we're all paying the price."

"Thal." Druv warns, but Thal points his finger at me.

"You should never have been here. Oro should have put you down like the rabid dog you are."

"Druv, take Thal to his room. Make sure he stays there tonight." Orobas' voice is cold. Distant.

The demon nods once, putting his hand on Thal's shoulder as he shrugs it off. When they're both out of the room, Orobas slides into his chair looking more stressed than ever before.

"Demons have soulmates?" I whisper, afraid to broach the topic, but love and demons are two things I never thought could co-exist.

Orobas releases a tense breath. "On Earth, humans marry for love. It's a legally binding contract, but has no implications on any other part of one's being. With demons—and angels, technically—their form of marriage is to bind two souls. It is where humans got the term soulmate from. The ritual is eternal and cannot be undone. Both must truly desire the union, or else it will fail. It means that they will be tied to each other in this life and the next, and every one that follows. They will seek no others' warmth. They won't have eyes for the flesh of anyone but the one they're bound to. Their souls will wander restlessly until they find their other half."

Tears prick the corners of my eyes.

"If Evelyn kills Ishari, I'm certain Thal will decide to forfeit his life. This will make them return to essence as one and be reborn into their next lives at the same time. If he does not forfeit his life, he will have to search for her for eternity while mourning her absence and yearning for her return."

My throat constricts. "Will they still be demons?"

Orobas shakes his head. "As humans. They will have to regress in the cycle. It will take over a century for them to return here, and hope they find each other. To be soulmates is to accept the trial of locating one another in each lifetime. It is no easy feat, Scarlett."

"Shit."

He lets out a wry laugh, but nods in agreement.

My concern about Ishari being in Evelyn's grasp grows with each passing second as I consider his words.

I've broken up enough families.

Exhaling a long breath, I step in close to where he sits. "I'll go to Evelyn by myself."

Guarded crimson irises flick to where I stand, and I know he's worried about command taking me.

"She thinks I'm being held hostage. What if I can convince her I'm not?"

His eyes widen. "And if you can't?"

"Can't say I haven't thought of that." I breathe. "I'll have to fight her if I'm not able to convince her."

"I don't like this, Scarlett."

The lump in my throat grows, and I swallow hard against it. "Neither do I, but we don't have a choice if we want to get Ishari back."

Chapter 26

Evelyn

"Let go of me!"

The female demon twists over my shoulder, her legs and wrists both bound as I haul her into the middle of the warehouse. The blood covering my hands crusts against my skin.

"Put. Me. Down!" she shrieks, and I release a tense sigh.

"You asked for it." I shrug her off my shoulder, letting her body drop to the hard, unforgiving ground with a loud thunk. The air rushes from her lungs in a whoosh, and she gasps, her eyes wide as she stares at me.

"What?" I say expectantly. "You wanted me to put you down."

It takes a second and some coughing before she can collect herself enough to glare at me. "What did you do to the others?"

I raise an eyebrow, studying her for a moment. It's not every day that they ask about other demons.

In fact, usually they're too selfish to.

"There were plenty of others. You'll have to be more specific." I say, dragging her by her wrists over to a pole that's secured into the ground.

I can tell by the rise and fall of her chest that she's panicking and trying hard not to show it. I can almost see her pulse hammering in her neck from here, and I bind her hands to the pole.

"There was..." She swallows and licks her lips. "My mate, h-he went to get food for me with his friend."

"Ah, yes. The taller one with long black hair, right?" I whisper, watching to see her face light up with terror. The sight makes me think twice about telling her he's dead just for the fuck of it. "I'll let you know happened to him, but you need to tell me where the dagger is."

I don't really expect her to tell me. My only goal here is to get Scarlett out of these demon's hands, but if I can retrieve the blade, too...

"I don't know." She says, tears pooling in her eyes. "Orobas moved it—none of us know where it is."

Figures.

"Well then, I suppose you'll have to wait to know whether your mate lives and breathes." I say with a smile, dragging a chair closer to where she's bound. The demon sobs, her body shaking as I roll my eyes. "No one likes a blubbering mess." I grumble, not bothering to sweep the area yet.

I have to admit—I didn't think it was possible for a demon to have such feelings. In all the missions we've had, most have been cold, callous assholes who fit the stereotype.

This mess of a demon isn't even in the same league as them.

My leg swings over the chair, and I straddle the seat, bracing my arms on the back. Tears pour down her flushed cheeks as her breath hitches.

Odd.

Such a human reaction.

"Are you going to kill me?" She chokes out after I unsheathe a dagger, twirling it in my fingers mindlessly.

The question shouldn't have taken me by surprise, but it did. I hadn't considered what was next for her once I got what I wanted. For a long moment, I study her, ignoring the terror in her expression.

"The answer to that depends on whether I get what I want." I offer, tilting my head to the side, my long ponytail shifting down my collar to my chest with the motion.

"W-w-what do you w-want?" She stammers out between nervous hiccups.

I'm feeling bad for a demon. For God's sake.

"Your boss has someone I hold dear to me. He's keeping her captive, and he has the dagger we need."

Her eyes widen. "Scarlett?"

I can't help the surprise I feel at her familiar use of Viper's name. She must notice as she backtracks.

"I mean, she was a hostage, yeah, but that was just at first—"

"Listen, demon-girl, I don't mean to interrupt, but you need to offer new information or make yourself useful before I get bored." I let out a long sigh, flicking the blade in my hand toward the female.

She yelps when it slams tip-first into the wooden planks near her foot, and she scoots back as far as possible with her eyes wide. "W-what the hell?!"

I push off the chair and step in close to retrieve the blade. When she notices that I'm bracing to do it again, desperation takes over. My wrist flicks as the dagger whistles through the air, slamming into the wood beside her leg. She shrieks and moves to jerk herself back, but the blade is halfway buried into the ground, her pants pinned with it.

"Okay! Okay. She's changed since she became a hostage, okay? She's different, and she's not under their control anymore! And the dagger was never supposed to be in their hands, anyway! It belongs to Azrael!"

I roll my eyes because now I know she's lying. "You really think I'm about to believe that?"

She sobs, but some quiet voice in the back of my mind tells me that there's a chance she's being truthful.

Chapter 27

Scarlett

"It might help if I can breathe when I face her." I grumble, wincing as Orobas snaps the leather strap around my thigh tightly.

His large hand grips the tender spot on the inside of my thigh, sliding a thick finger between the leather and the bodysuit as if emphasizing that there is room.

I suck in a sharp breath. "On second thought, I'll be fine."

Standing in the center of his bedroom, with Thal still under Druv's supervision, Orobas wasted no time finding me protective gear with special straps for weapons.

Leather strips pin the sheaths against the bodysuit of tightly woven Kevlar that surprisingly fits well. The material's thickest around my vital organs, thinning near my joints and allowing flexibility.

It's reminiscent of the gear command provided to us, and while I'm curious how he obtained a fitting pair so quickly, I set my questions aside.

In this ocean of problems we have, I couldn't care less about where or how he got it.

He yanks the leather toward him, leaning in until our chests brush. "When she realizes you're not on her side, no matter what happens, do not let your guard down."

My lips twitch. "Yee of little faith, demon prince."

He looks around the room with a cautious expression. "Having a snarky Viper at my side hasn't been all that bad. Do you blame me for hoping you'll come back in one piece?"

My heart stutters when his crimson gaze lands on me. It's one thing to not hate him, and another to admit that my feelings for this demon run deeper than I could ever acknowledge out loud.

And to know after everything I've done, he wants me to return...

He must realize the same, because the guarded look fades as his palm cups my face, thumb gliding along my cheek. The action is so tender that I fall still, uncertain how to react.

Every instinct pulls me into his touch, to be closer or want more, but years of violence make me expect him to lash out.

His thumb trails from my cheek to tease my lower lip. "*Will* you return?"

Each breath feels starved of oxygen. "I don't know."

It's the only answer I can offer when I'm beyond lost in what my next steps should be. Once I retrieve Ishari, who knows if I'll be in any shape to come back.

Evelyn could kill me in the process of all this.

Orobas' free hand moves to my collar, curving along the base of my neck. His palm flattens against my skin, the tip of his thumb brushing the center column of my throat.

"I don't know whether you're about to strangle or kiss me, demon prince." I whisper, and his lips twitch.

"I've considered both."

"Yet you do neither. Are you afraid?"

His gaze darkens at my challenge, and he leans in to slant his mouth over mine. His tongue grazes the seam of my lip, and my mind empties of all rational thought. The hand against my cheek moves to fist my hair, tightening to angle my head back further, gaining full access to my mouth.

Tasting Orobas on my tongue is an experience I never want to recover from. Breathing his air sends heat coursing through me, and even with our bodies melded together, I can't seem to get close enough to him.

The hand at my throat slides down my breast, and I moan into his mouth when he digs his fingers at my hip. My body presses against the hard, muscular plane of his chest as he breaks apart, searching my face.

"You can bite me, Viper, but your venom has only made me crave more than you can give." Pressing his forehead to mine, our breaths mingle between us. "Others might fear you, with every right to, but I will gladly tangle myself in you, come whatever consequences may."

His admission makes my heart tumble over itself, and I'm at a loss for words.

Because there's a chance I won't be in any shape to return to him after I see Evelyn. Not if she realizes that I've gone AWOL.

"And if those consequences mean death?"

I don't bother specifying his or mine, because truthfully it could be either. The end comes for us all someday.

He studies me for a long moment, soaking in my question as he reaches over the bed. Grabbing the last dagger, he spins it in his palm once before sliding it into the sheath at my hip.

"You will not die today, Scarlett." He says, his thumb gliding across my bottom lip. "No one else dies today."

Chapter 28

Evelyn

A loud thud sounds off to my right before her voice fills the air, bringing relief with it.

"Do I look like a hostage to you?"

I whirl at the sound, halfway surprised that the young Wraith snuck up on me like that. She steps out from the shadows of a tall stack of large wooden crates, her black bodysuit helping her blend into the darkness. Thick leather straps at her thighs, waist and arms secure curved daggers to her limbs, though, there's no sign of her poisons.

I'd have to assume they're back on base.

Or she coated the blades with them.

"How did you get away?" I ask, and the demon girl just laughs deliriously.

Scarlett, however, remains cautious as she takes another step closer. Her eyes slide to the bound demon, lingering where she's tied to the pole.

Clearing my throat, her attention snaps to me again. "Who said I had to get away at all?"

My eyes narrow at her. "He just let you go?"

Throwing her hip to the side, she crosses her arms. "Well, you *did* kidnap Ishari, so, yeah. Oro brought me here to get her."

So, he blackmailed her then.

Whatever he has on her must be huge if she's willing to come to retrieve demons from his own legion.

"Right. Well, let's slit her throat and get out of here then." I murmur, taking a step toward the female. When Scarlett mirrors me defensively, I fall still.

The apprehension on her face is clear as she keeps an arm outstretched between me and my hostage.

But this doesn't make any sense.

"What are you doing, Viper?" I say, my voice dropping low.

For years, I'd watched command build her up and tear her down, but for her to act like this after a mere week of this solo mission?

Something is **very** wrong.

"I told you, I'm here to retrieve Ishari." Scarlett takes another step, placing herself fully between me and the female—the very same demon that's trembling behind her, staring at her like she's the world's greatest gift.

"Right. And now you're freed from that prince's influence, so let's gut the bitch and leave."

Scarlett shakes her head, and I want to pinch myself. Or punch her. Is this real life?

"You have it all wrong, Eve. We both did."

"Don't—" I glare at her in warning. "Don't you dare say what I think you're going to say."

She swallows, dropping her hands to her sides. "You haven't seen the whole truth. There is evil in this world, Eve, but we've been the ones doing its bidding."

"Scarlett," I whisper, feeling out of breath as I stare at her. "They will kill you for this. This is treason."

"This is humanity." She offers as a correction. "This is about having morals and having a say—it's knowing right from wrong."

My hand tightens on my dagger, and she glances at it hesitantly. She knows as well as I do that I have patience with my team, but treason? To stare command in the face and flirt with their wrath is not the decision she should be making.

Me, maybe. But not **her**.

"Besides," she says, licking her lips. "They've been killing us for years."

"You know as well as I do that I have no love for them, but they've given us a life, and we've made a difference, Scarlett."

"Have we?"

I rear back, staring at her with wide eyes. *Has she lost her mind?*

"You can't tell me you haven't noticed, Eve. There's a reason you protected us from command's judgment. Don't pretend you haven't."

My teeth grind together. "And yet here you are, throwing all of my hard fucking work in my face. Do you want to return home in a body bag, Scarlett? Cause that's what it looks like to me."

My anger rising, fueled by her blatant disregard for the status quo—for everything I've done for her—it reaches its boiling point, and I act before I know what's happening.

My arm snaps to the side, my wrist flicking with it, and the dagger I'd been fidgeting with hurtles through the air, aimed for Scarlett's right jugular.

She must have seen the attack coming, because she leans to the side half an inch, not bothering to break eye contact with me as the dagger slams into the wooden crate behind her.

"You missed." She says in a bored tone with a raised brow, but I can see the way her breathing has picked up.

"I won't miss twice." I whisper, and we both unsheathe a dagger. First to move with my jaw clenched, I surge from my chair toward her, slicing my blade through the air.

My actions are fluid. Practiced.

But so are hers.

Again, and again, and again, we clash. I catch one blow—she deflects a strike with my weapon. I slash at her—she evades my follow-up.

It's only been weeks since the last time we sparred, and while our back and forth is familiar, at any moment we could pass the point of no return.

So I toe the line between subduing her and bringing her down, taunting her and warding her off. But after minutes of twisting limbs, deflected blows and countered attacks, I've realized that Scarlett has kept herself positioned between me and the demon.

Like she's **protecting** her.

For whatever reason, that enrages me more than all else.

Because after everything we've been through—all I've done for her and the others—she's defending one of **them**?!

Scarlett twists to the side to swipe her blade at my ribs, but I've already decided where my next strike is going, keeping me far from her attack.

Her gaze tracks my movement, and her eyes widen.

With two blades at my hips still, I hurl the small dagger at the demon with as much force as I can muster. By the time my heart's beaten once, it's spinning toward the female whose face has only begun to register her shock.

But faster than I ever thought possible, Scarlett throws herself in front of it and my lungs seize.

I shouldn't care.

This shouldn't send this much panic through me.

She uses her own blade to knock the tip aside, but it still slices the back of her forearm open and clatters to the side. With a loud thud, she falls overtop the demon, who tugs against her restraints.

"Scarlett!"

The worry on the female's face only pisses me off more, and I lunge forward. An acrid taste blooms on my tongue when my fist collides with Scarlett's cheek, her head snapping to the side from the force.

Frustratingly, she doesn't move away from the demon, instead using the strength of her legs to shove me back.

Blood streams down her arm, dripping to the floor as my lip curls. "I should have figured that you'd take their side after what happened with Grizz and Mako."

"Stop." Scarlett warns, the hand of her good arm flexing into a fist.

My rage is a living, breathing beast, and it's aiming for her fresh emotional wounds. "You think I don't know what the fuck went down or why we got caught?"

"Shut up!" She snaps, her teeth bared. *There's the vicious little Wraith I know.*

"How does it *feel*?" I whisper, ready to pour salt directly into her wounds. "To know that Grizz and Mako would still be alive if it weren't for your stupid fucking reckless decisions."

Right now, it doesn't matter that I've blamed myself since it happened, or that I still consider Scarlett like my little sister. I want blood, and violence is the only outlet the two of us have ever known.

"I said, shut the fuck up!" She screams and throws herself forward.

Her emotions clear on her sleeve make her strikes obvious as she swings for me in wide motions. The blade clutched in her fist whistling through the air as I dodge each one.

With a jab here, and an elbow there, I wear the Wraith down. Her labored breathing a clear sign as every strike she makes contorts her face into a grimace.

My blows are harder than they need to be, enough to break a rib or fracture a bone, but somehow Scarlett has kept her head above water against me.

Which only pisses me off more.

Her fist's an inch from my face when I catch it, snatching her wrist tight. I lean in with a cruel smile, fully aimed at taunting her.

"Does Omen know yet?" I whisper, and her face flushes in anger as I feign a gasp. "Oh, she does?"

"These demons are better to me than command has *ever* been. Better than *you've* ever been!" She screams, and I see red as the words register.

I land an unexpected blow to the side of her head, knocking her onto her back before I'm on her. Straddling her chest, I recoil my fist and land another blow. Her hands raise to protect her head, but it's no use.

Crack. Crack. Crack.

The sound of my knuckles colliding with her cheek fills the air, mixing with the demon's shrieks for help mere feet away. But I can't seem to find it in me to stop.

Not when she's so blatantly wrong.

She's my enemy.

My Scarlett.

Arms hook around my torso, dragging me backward as my eyes widen. The female looks shocked, and maybe terrified, so I twist to the side to find Grant's pained expression.

The only concern in my mind as a sliver of panic works down my spine is that now I'll really have to kill Scarlett for treason.

Some part of my bloodied, stone heart fractures at the thought of it.

Chapter 29

Scarlett

I should have known better than to trigger her anger like that.

The taste of copper fills my mouth, and I spit a wad of crimson saliva to the ground. Pai's dressed in a military uniform as he drags her backward, her face distant, like she's lost in her own head.

"Scarlett," Ishari hisses, tugging her arms. "Untie me."

I groan and drag myself over to her as Evelyn struggles against Pai's grip.

"Let me go, Grant!"

I freeze, my gaze sliding to where Pai holds her to him with an apologetic look on his face.

Of all the times I'd gotten a device to be cracked into, Evelyn had always offered to bring it to Grant in order for me to rest sooner.

So if she's saying *this* is him...

Holy fucking shit.

"Eve, it's just Scarlett." He whispers into her ear, and her brown eyes lock with mine. When her gaze drops to the rest of my body, her face crumples.

She shudders, and the fight in her gives out. Her knees buckle, but Pai supports her weight.

"I'm so sorry, Scarlett." She says, her voice cracking, but I shake my head.

It hurts too much to talk, so I do the only thing I can do—I work on freeing Ishari.

With my right hand clumsy, between the half-inch deep incision in my forearm and the blood that's coating my fingers, I can't seem to get a good grip.

A clatter echoes into the warehouse before footsteps grow closer, and I reach for my blade. When I see Oro's tall form appear from the shadows with Druv and Thal in tow, relief washes over me.

I drop to my knees, hearing someone suck in a breath. Within seconds, Druv and Thal are beside us, Thal untying his soulmate as she sobs.

"What the fuck, Grant," Evelyn hisses. "Why are you acting like they're not—" Her words cut off abruptly, her eyes widen, and she glances between all of us.

I know that look. It's the same one she gets when everything clicks into place.

"You look like shit, Viper." Druv grimaces, easing me into the chair Evelyn had been sitting in earlier. Oro steps in close and kneels at my side, pulling a cloth from his suit and pressing it to the top of my forearm.

"I'd say you should see the other girl, but..." I chew out, the insides of my cheeks cut up and swollen. I've had the shit kicked out of me before, but damn Eve's punches hurt like a bitch.

"I'm glad we came when we did." Oro murmurs, brushing a lock of hair from my face.

The urge to lean into his touch is strong, but I focus my attention on Evelyn as Pai holds her still—her expression murderous.

This can't be good.

"Eve," I say, and her eyes flick to meet mine. "Command lied to us."

She grits her teeth, and Oro gestures for her to come closer. "Pai, bring her here, please."

Her eyes widen, but she hardly appears shocked as he escorts her to us. The wild look she has is like that of a caged animal, and I watch with rapt attention as Oro stands, placing both hands on either side of her head.

Before he does anything, their eyes lock.

"I'm not going to hurt you, even if you suspect I will. Pai will take you somewhere safe, but I need to make sure you understand. What I'm about to do now is necessary."

Within seconds his face turns into steely determination, and Evelyn's body goes taut, like she's tripped a live wire with electricity pumping through her limbs.

She writhes, her face contorting in agony as Pai watches her nervously.

"Oro, is she supposed to look like she's in that much pain?"

I think back to when the demon prince had used his magic on me to shield me from manipulations—or *freed the viper* as he called it—but there had been no pain to accompany it.

He retracts his hands from her head and kneels to continue putting pressure on my wound. "She's much stronger than I expected, but their influence on her has deep roots. The next twenty-four hours will be the hardest." When he sees the concern in my eyes, his expression softens. "Imagine having your free will—your decision-making—contained within an iron cast for over a decade. What they did to control her was not typical, because it was like removing barbed wire from her mind all at once. She will need to recover, and even more time to return to who she was without their influence."

I swallow and try to avoid mentally picturing barbed wire in her head as Pai tightens his hold on her thrashing body. Sweat beads down her neck, her ponytail sticking to her skin as she gasps for breath.

"Take her to the safe-house, Pai. We won't make a move without you." Oro says in a low voice, his wary gaze trained on the Harbinger as Pai nods.

He hauls her out the door, and my eyes slide shut—the tense breath I'd held finally escaping me.

"Are you alright?"

I don't bother opening my eyes as I shake my head. To see Eve like this, as her enemy, has been one of the hardest face-offs of my life. That's not to mention the emotional dagger she buried in my chest by bringing up Mako and Grizz.

Truth be told, I'd be lying if I said I was anything but broken right now.

My face hurts, throbbing like I'd gone ten rounds with a heavyweight champion without protecting my head. I'm pretty sure I have a concussion, and judging by the faces the others are making, it looks as bad as it feels.

Thal removes Ishari's bindings, and she sobs, throwing herself into his arms. The way he embraces her back makes my chest tighten to the point of pain.

Self-deprecation quickly overwhelms the pang of jealousy that hits me, because I know without a doubt that I'm the last person who deserves to find something like that.

"Come on, let's get you home," Thal murmurs, pressing a kiss to the top of her head as he helps her up.

I have to look away as my throat constricts. With how many innocents I've likely killed, I wouldn't be surprised if I'm merely greeted with an agonizingly painful death instead.

Or perhaps even that is too much of a mercy.

Orobas' touch is gentle as he wraps some cloth around my arm, securing it in place before his gaze meets mine. "She'll be safe with Paimon." He says cautiously, as if trying to see into my mind as he rises to his feet, holding his hand out for me.

I don't have the words to tell him I know she is, and that I'm not worried about her safety right now, not when I just want to curl up into myself and sleep for an eternity, so I nod.

Sliding my good hand in his, he helps pull me to my feet, and I sway.

His arm snakes around my waist in support, and I lean into him even more, grateful for his strength when mine feels like it could give at any second.

Chapter 30

Scarlett

Someone cleared the bodies from the house in the time it took for Evelyn to hand my ass to me three ways from Sunday.

Only faint splatters of blood show any evidence that a crime happened at all. Ishari had walked through the doors with her hand covering her mouth, sobbing the entire way until she and Thal disappeared down the hall together.

Druv didn't linger for long after they left either, murmuring something about needing to gather supplies as he vanished out the doorway. The haunted look in his expression tells me he's more affected by the deaths of the others than he lets on.

But I couldn't care less about all of it right now.

Not when the hollow feeling in my chest threatens to swallow me whole, chew me up and then spit me out in fragments of who I once was.

Our footsteps shatter the tense silence in the hallway as Orobas leads me by the hand to his bedroom. But the quiet is a prison of its own, leaving me to my torturous thoughts.

I tell myself it wouldn't be so bad if Eve hadn't said what she did, but the reality is I've been silently chastising myself in the same manner since they died. Her words are no different from the ones I'd been hurling around internally.

It just hurt more to hear her say it out loud.

The rage in her expression when I told her that Oro and the others had been better to me still leaves a pang of regret because it was mostly a lie. Evelyn might not have treated us like daughters, taking care of us as one would, but to her, we were family.

Even if command told us not to become attached.

It was one of the few rules we'd quickly broken, even if we used the excuse that we had trauma bonded over the torture training.

Orobas is silent at my side as we ascend the stairs and make the journey down the long hallway to his bedroom. Each second seems to last an eternity. Every echo of our footsteps is thunder to my ears.

I can't deny that a part of me feels that the demons have treated me well. Perhaps the shock that they weren't going to rip toenails from my body or waterboard information had paved the way for them to sneak into a soft spot in my closed-off heart.

Maybe Ishari chipped ice from my soul so that Orobas could thaw what remained.

Either way, I don't know where this leaves me anymore.

The demon prince steps forward a few paces to pull the door open. The look on his face tells me he's just as lost in thought as I have been, and something twists in my gut.

I can't help but wonder if he's realizing how dangerous it is for me to stay here. We don't even know if command assigned Evelyn to retrieve me or if she did so of her own volition.

If command suspects anything, we're beyond fucked.

It won't matter how many legions Orobas has if he's unable to fight back enough to make a difference.

"Fresh towels are in the washroom. I'll be back soon." He says in a low tone, and my heart slinks into my stomach.

After everything that has happened, he still wants me to be this close to him? He'd risk inviting more assassins to his house—to his room—and for what? Just to make sure I'm not stealing his damn dagger.

I don't even want the damn blade anymore.

"You want me to stay in your room?" I ask, crossing my arms over my chest. "Our deal is done." I add, as if needing to clarify that I don't think he simply enjoys my presence.

Crimson irises fixate on me, and I choke down the sudden urge to squirm.

"I could offer you another room, and you might be more comfortable without my presence, Viper, but I cannot say the feeling is mutual."

So that's it then. Keep your friends close, keep your enemies closer.

"Fine. Keep the assassin within arm's reach." I chew out, and head for the shower. I'm only a few steps away before Orobas is in front of me, his brows furrowed.

"You think that's what it is?" He asks, searching my face. "You believe that you're simply the assassin once more? That's what you want to be—the enemy?" I suck in a breath, but my lips remain tightly shut. "Is that what you want to be to me?"

"I—"

He steps forward, crowding my space, and my head tilts to look at him, but even with how close he is, he doesn't touch me.

"After everything, you think I've reduced you to a weapon?" He lifts a tangled lock of my hair and brushes it behind my shoulder, sending a shiver through me. "Or is that what you'd *like* for me to see in you?"

My eyes widen. "Why would I want that?" I ask, my voice low, caught between warning and confusion.

His jaw works, and his tongue glides along his teeth. "Because it would make this easier. Because if you were simply an assassin—a weapon to be used—I could keep my distance. I wouldn't—" He cuts himself off, his crimson irises burning. "But you're not, Scarlett—and even if you see yourself that way, I'll be here to remind you that you are so much more than that."

"What if more people get hurt because of me?" My voice is hardly audible between us—as if, if I say it too loud, it might become reality.

"Then whoever dares try will have to contend with me." The backs of his fingers trail along my cheek, like he can't help but touch me. "Shower, but stay here with me, Scarlett."

A long moment passes where I weigh my options, balancing the scales of justice in my mind between what I'm willing to risk for selfish reasons, and I let out a soft sigh.

"Okay." I whisper, giving him a slight nod. "I'll stay."

I don't tell him that the jury is still out beyond tonight, and will change as I gather more information. I can't just remain here and hide away forever in his home, with people he cares about.

He might have some grand plan, or maybe he doesn't, but I know command will come for us. They won't let their curated team of assassins go free without a fight.

Orobas searches my face for a moment, like he's deliberating on something before he steps aside, gesturing toward the washroom. "See you in a bit, Scarlett."

He doesn't wait for me to respond as he heads to the other room to shower, his footsteps fading into the hall opposite of me. I'm too exhausted to mull over everything he's said, so I let out a sigh, and walk mindlessly to my own shower.

Chapter 31

Scarlett

After towel drying my hair, I glance around for my pajamas and silently curse myself for not grabbing them before showering. My skin's still damp, so I wrap the towel around my body, cautious not to strain my injured arm in the process.

My footsteps are quiet as I leave the washroom and pad toward the dresser. Orobas has to have a t-shirt I can snag if there's no actual pajamas in here.

The first drawer rolls open loudly, and I rifle between countless pairs of socks and underwear before moving to the next. A moment of triumph surges through me when I see stacks of t-shirts, and I search for one that's more casual.

My thumb hits a piece of wood sticking out from the rest as a tiny door snaps open. Inside, I see the wooden box with the lid already ajar, revealing the ruby-inlaid dagger.

I blink at it for a moment, fully expecting my eyes to be deceiving me, but when the blade doesn't disappear, I swallow.

Before all of this happened, I would have taken the dagger and run, but now?

I gently close the door with a click and grab the casual grey t-shirt.

"Looking for something?"

I nearly jump out of my skin. "Holy shit, you scared me."

Orobas chuckles, and I feel his warmth against my back as he steps in close. "Do you feel any better?" His breath cascades over the shell of my ear, and I shiver, sliding the drawer shut.

"Much." I whisper as he pulls my hair from my shoulder.

The cool air makes goosebumps break out over my skin as his lips brush the tender spot behind my ear. Another kiss placed lower follows, and another.

"Your arm?" He asks, pressing a kiss to my shoulder, and his hand snakes around my waist.

"No longer bleeding." I whisper, the air trapped in my lungs as he spins me to face him.

His bare, inked chest fills my vision, with damp locks of hair hanging over his forehead. Piercing crimson irises search my face, and the towel wrapped around my body suddenly feels like it's all too much.

"Good. I'd hate to replace this bed when it holds so many of our memories." He murmurs before leaning down to capture my lips with his.

I'm not sure who leaned in first, but our bodies press together as my good arm hooks around his neck. The woodsy cinnamon scent of his cologne invades my senses, and I surrender myself to it, to the taste of him on my tongue.

Our future is so uncertain that I know how I want to spend each moment I can afford.

He must feel the same, because he reaches down and lifts me into his arms to carry me onto the bed without breaking our kiss. His hard body tenses until he lays me in the center.

That's when he pulls back to look at me.

His gaze itself caresses my skin as it travels down the length of my body, and his eyes flutter. "Your violence has a certain beauty to it, Scarlett, but seeing you beneath me like this is my own personal bliss."

My heart thunders, and I drag the towel away from my body. It might feel cliché to offer myself to him in such a way, but I know without a doubt if I handed him my soul on a silver platter, he would never harm it.

Heat flashes through me when his expression darkens. He tosses the towel aside onto the floor before leaning over me to tug his own underwear down, pressing kisses along the length of my body as he does.

His lips brush against every scar covering my skin as his hands roam freely. When his fingers inch closer to my core, my breathing picks up in anticipation.

"I want you undone for me tonight, Scarlett." He groans, gliding his finger along my soaked entrance, and my lungs seize. When he repeats the action, I'm not expecting the way his thumb circles my clit, and he eases his finger in slowly.

"How?" I breathe, but he answers by sliding a second in deep, earning a moan from me.

For a demon with self-proclaimed patience, he doesn't wait long to be everywhere at once. His mouth claims mine, tongues dancing between each breath, every whimper that escapes us both as he continues to coax pleasure from me.

My core throbs, and I grind against him, my hips chasing the euphoria he offers, but it's not enough.

I need him.

My hand snakes between us to wrap around his length, and he hisses at the contact. When I glide my palm from base to tip, he groans with his forehead pressed to my stomach.

The sounds he makes at my touch sends my desire into a tailspin, and the orgasm he'd slowly brought to the surface crashes over me suddenly. My pussy clamps down on his fingers as I cry out, grinding into his hand as we both breathe heavily.

When I've finally come down, he's still pressing kisses to my shoulder, his heavy body over mine, and I wonder for a moment if I died in that warehouse.

Because this has to be heaven.

I suppose for Orobas, he probably knew what heaven was like once.

My heart squeezes in my chest, and I hook my arms around his neck to claim his lips with mine.

The need to feel him closer becomes too great to ignore, and I dig my heels into him when he throbs against me. He doesn't break our kiss, but I know he understood when he reaches between us to settle himself at my entrance.

My heart skips a beat, but he kisses me harder and eases in. The stretch is borderline painful, and my mouth drops open as he pushes me further.

But I won't complain.

Not when being with him feels like this.

He breaks our kiss when he's fully seated, leaning back to move my hair from my face as he withdraws. Gathering my dark locks at the back of my head in one fist, his expression is filled with as much reverence as it is need. His thrusts are long and languid as I roll my hips with each one.

Crimson eyes hold mine as he moves inside me, and I know that what I feel for this demon transcends all reason.

Because Orobas isn't just any prince of hell. He's *my* demon prince, and I will spend my life proving it to him that I might have been a lost assassin when we met, but I know exactly who I am now.

He snaps his hips to mine, and I cry out as my orgasm crests once more, like a taut thread in my body fraying at the edges. His hand reaches for my uninjured arm, and he laces our fingers together, holding them overhead as he repeats the action.

And again.

When I find euphoria once more, Oro follows with me, and I know neither of us will be the same.

I never want to be.

Chapter 32

Evelyn

All my body knows is pain.

Every inch of my skin, each muscle, and nerve ending—even my blood itself—is like an infinite number of live-wires being tripped, exploding in sequence, with the ripples of each blast ricocheting off one another.

I'm not sure how long it's been, or where I am anymore.

The moment that demon put his hands to my head, I should have known that would be it for me—his words were warning enough.

Not that I could have stopped him with Grant—*Pai*—holding me still.

Beyond the pain coating every orifice of my being, I build walls up in my mind to block it out. Despite that, a shudder runs through me.

How could I have been so blind?

To have a demon within arm's reach for years and not figure it out? How the hell did command not notice?

The thought is sobering, so much so that the agony causing tremors in my body lets up just long enough for me to pry my eyes open.

Slivers of the room are a blur of grey, the light burning my eyes as they water. Within seconds everything dims, and my heart sinks.

I'm not alone.

Ignoring the way my body feels like it's being ripped into a million shards, I force my eyes open more.

The room isn't terribly cramped—just large enough to pace myself into madness given time. A small desk to my right along the wall holds a pitcher of water and two glasses. Two doors on my left mark what I have to assume is a washroom and the only exit. A chair positioned near the bed seats one uniformed, and hesitant-looking Major Grant Allen—or whoever the fuck he is.

Our eyes meet for a long moment.

"You lied to me." I whisper, sitting up with a wince. A metallic clatter echoes into the room from the chains restraining me to the bed. My hair sticks to my skin, still slick from sweat even with the chill in the air.

An acrid scent burns my nose—judging by the pail on the floor and the tang at the back of my throat—I've spent a good amount of time vomiting, even if I don't remember it. When I sit up, ripples of pain are still ever-present, pressing against the walls I'd erected in my mind.

"Lying and not offering information are not the same."

My teeth grind together. "Semantics. You still lied." I snap, wincing when a pang hits my skull.

Grant gets up and moves to the table, pouring water from the pitcher into the glass. The vein in his hand is more pronounced as he steps over, offering the cup between us.

I stare at it. The way my tongue feels like sandpaper in my mouth makes the temptation grow, but I don't move to take it from him.

"How do I know it's not poisoned?"

The look on his face is grave, and I almost feel guilty as he shakes his head. "I may be many things, Eve, but I'm not an absolute monster."

"I'll be the judge of that." I murmur, taking the glass from him and leaning forward to put it to my lips. The moment the liquid hits my tongue, my mind empties.

It's so refreshing that I wonder for a heartbeat if it was tampered with. But by the time the cup is drained, I let it go, and pass it back to him with a clatter from my chains as he returns it to the table.

If he had wanted to murder me, he would have already.

"Where are we?"

He glances around, and I fully expect him to string me along.

"A safe house about an hour from where we left Oro and Scarlett."

At the sound of her name, a thick layer of shame washes over me. I'd thrown something in her face that wasn't her fault, and I'd done so knowing it was going to inflict the same hurt that I'd been experiencing.

The walls I'd erected against the pain suddenly give way, my head feeling like it's being split into two. The room spins, and I grip the bed, chains rattling as I groan.

Whatever Orobas did to me is borderline torture.

"Easy." Grant—*Pai*—murmurs, hurrying over to my side.

I want to bat his hands away as he helps lean me back onto the bed, but my body doesn't cooperate. Muscles spasm, and the way my mouth salivates, mixing with the taste of bile, tells me I'll be needing that bucket again sooner than later.

"It's alright." He whispers, reaching over to the table to my right. Water sloshes for a moment before something cool touches my forehead.

My eyes roll back. *God, that's nice.*

It's easier to focus on that instead of the temptation to throw up everywhere, and I cling to the feeling as I reinforce the walls in my mind.

He moves a lock of hair stuck to my collarbone, and my hand twitches with the urge to knock his away. The restraints clatter quietly, but I'm too exhausted to try.

Another wave of pain slams against my mental barriers, and I wince, my breath hitching.

"It's alright, Eve. I'm here." He whispers, and while that should be a relief to hear, there's a small voice in the back of my mind reminding me he said that before he betrayed me too.

Because the man I'd trusted so willingly—the person I'd given so much to—was the enemy all along.

I should have known.

There were so many signs that I had ignored.

The dam breaks, and my walls crumble against the onslaught of pain radiating from every cell in my body.

"I'm right here." He says in a hurry, and the last thing I hear is the scream tearing from my lungs before darkness claims me.

Chapter 33

Scarlett

"I miss Mennon already." Ishari murmurs, watching the demon's replacement lumber around the house.

When new members of Oro's legion arrived most of them understandably had a healthy dislike or distaste of the Revenants. Once word spread that Orobas is housing one, the looks I've received since are that of fear or disgust. I prefer the former.

"Well, he's dead," Thal retorts flatly. "So unless you have a magic wand to summon him back into a fully healed body, we'll have to get used to having Seph around."

I track the demon's movement as he hangs his jacket beside the front door and rolls his shoulders. Seph is one of the few I hadn't met since the change in staff happened.

He's a tall, bulky demon. His blonde hair buzzed short at the sides, melting into his pale skin that's such a contrast to the others. Where their sun-kissed skin is rich in color, Seph's seems void of it.

He'd play a great vampire. Just a really beefy one.

He stalks over, giving a nod to Druv before addressing Thal. "Everyone is in place for the night." His eyes flick to Ishari and then lands on me. "Any word if we expect trouble tonight?"

My eyes widen. "Me?"

He stares at me. "I'd think a Revenant would be able to tell us whether we're about to be under attack again."

My heart sinks into my stomach as Ishari scowls at him. "Fuck off, Seph. She knows as much as we do."

He holds my gaze, his hard expression not giving way to any humor. "Well?"

I scoff and shake my head. "If you're relying on me to for your intel on government missions, we're all fucked."

He sneers. "We were fucked the moment Oro let you—"

"Enough!" Thal barks, and I flinch at the sound—not for any fear of him, but because of the surprise of him being the one to interrupt Seph's blatant display of distaste for me.

"Don't tell me you approve of her being here." Seph asks incredulously, as if expecting Thal to see his point.

"If it weren't for her, Ishari would be dead or wish she were." Thal snarls, baring his teeth as he stands, his face an inch from Seph's. "And when the time comes when they send reinforcements here, I hope to God that she has her back then, too."

The morsel of pride I'd felt at Thal's sudden defense shrivels into ash. It shouldn't be surprising that he would want me to protect his soul mate, but seeing it this clearly... Can't say it doesn't sting.

Seph glances between us, and his lip curls. "When the Viper poisons you all in your sleep, don't come crying to me."

The demon stalks to the front door and slams it shut behind him, making the house rattle. A tense silence falls over us before Ishari blows out a breath.

"I want Mennon back." She murmurs again, and both men shake their heads.

"He'll come around." Druv says wistfully. "And if not, you always have us." He offers with a smirk.

I can't return the sentiment.

Not when I still feel like I'm just a weapon with a different wielder to some of them.

Ishari sighs and pulls out her phone. "That's it. I'm ordering dinner, and we're having a movie night."

Druv groans.

"Stop pretending it's such a drag. You enjoyed the last one we'd had."

"Did not." He corrects, shaking his head—but the other two demons just give him a deadpan stare.

"Here, pick the movie we'll watch, Scarlett." Ishari shoves her phone into my lap, and I blink, glancing between her and the cellphone for a moment. *They really want to include me in this?*

My eyes find Ishari's, and she looks so encouraging that I nod. "Alright. Fair warning, I don't watch movies, so—"

"What?" all three demons ask in unison, each as wide-eyed as the other.

"You don't get much downtime between missions." I offer, clicking on the first movie and reading the description.

It's a movie about a giant worm terrorizing a town. The second is a horror film that seems more comedic. Third is a superhero movie that looks action-packed, so I pick that one and hand her phone back.

Druv peers over her shoulder and grins. "Good choice, Viper."

Thal just rolls his eyes, but doesn't argue against my selection.

"Right. Well, we're fixing that today. No wonder you're so uptight sometimes—you never got to relax."

She has no idea.

"So you didn't do **anything** for fun?" Druv asks as Ishari scrolls something on her phone, but I see her hesitate as she waits for my answer.

It takes a long second of reflection, thinking back on every moment between assignments or what I'd do during travel. Most of it was preparation for the mission, resting or training to keep up my strength.

When I shake my head, Druv blinks, as if still expecting an answer.

"The missions were close together. Sometimes I was injured, so all I could do was rest. Other times, I would prepare for the assignment or spar to keep my skills honed."

Thal curses under his breath, but it's Druv that speaks up. "They didn't let you do **anything** else?"

The words are on the tip of my tongue. It would be so easy to tell them the thing I enjoy most is music, that I'd listen to it, immerse myself in it... but I don't.

It's the one secret me and Evelyn shared, even if she had no idea.

Perhaps that's why even though the three demons look disappointed as I shake my head, I stay quiet—keeping that close to my chest.

Ishari stands to her full height and stretches, her joints popping loudly in response. "Well, I'll grab some snacks from the kitchen. Wanna come with me, Scarlett? I could use an extra set of hands."

Thal huffs a quiet laugh. "Make sure the snacks actually make it to the entertainment room this time."

I hear Druv snicker behind me, and her eyes widen. "That was one time, and I hadn't eaten in like ten hours! I was hungry!"

Druv finally appears in my periphery, but from the corner of my eye, I can see his shit-eating grin. "That was one time? But what about the chicken wings we had delivered that you ate before we got back from getting drinks?"

"Or the pizza you scarfed down in the time it took me to use the washroom before starting the movie?"

She shoots him a glare, motioning for me to follow her. "That was different, and you know it. I waited forty-five minutes for you to use the washroom, and the pizza was getting cold. I hate lukewarm pizza." She gags for emphasis, and I can't help the smile tugging at my lips.

In another life, maybe, the Revenants will have camaraderie like this. Perhaps we could build our own family without trauma, blood, sweat, and tears.

Ishari waves her hand in front of my face, bringing me back to the present once more. "Earth to Scarlett." She says with a giggle. "Let's go before they change their minds about leaving us alone."

It takes a conscious effort to keep pace with her, her long legs making each stride equal to two of mine.

Good thing I'm in shape.

"Do you prefer sweet or savory?" She asks, casting me a sidelong glance. Her pace slows, whether because she's wanting to talk more or noticed how quickly I need to walk to keep up, I'm not sure.

Can't say I'm not grateful for it though.

I shrug. "I'm not sure. The only time I got to indulge was if I was undercover, but that's a steak here or a lobster tail there."

"Do you prefer dinner to dessert? Or would you eat dessert first if it were socially acceptable?"

"Hmm." I shove my hands into the pockets of the sweatpants Orobas had offered to me last night. "I can't say that I'd ever given it serious thought. I don't usually look forward to dessert as much as the main course, so I guess that's your answer."

"Then it's settled—savory snacks it is." Our footsteps echo down the hall. It's been eerily quiet since Eve's attack, and I find myself once again wondering how she's doing.

Not that long ago, Eve had been knocking at my door, making sure I wasn't isolating myself after Grizz and Mako died. My chest squeezes painfully at the memory, and I can't help but wonder if she did it more for me or herself.

Because why else would she bother?

"Alright," Ishari breathes as we walk into the kitchen. "Let's make popcorn and grab a couple of other things." She gets to work bustling around like she owns the place, and I watch her, still fully lost in my thoughts.

If she notices, she says nothing.

Instead, she hands me two large bowls full of popcorn, muttering something about one being for the guys to share because they're dirty and gross. She stuffs various drinks into another bowl of ice that she tucks between her chest and arm, carrying a variety of other snacks in her hands.

"That should do it," she beams. "Movie night, here we come!"

Her enthusiasm sends a pang of guilt through me, because if I hadn't been here, all the demons she'd known at Oro's would still be alive.

It's an odd experience—to go from despising them to feeling guilty that I was the reason for their deaths.

We're greeted at the entrance to the entertainment center by a scowling Thal. At the sight of his mate, his frown lightens, but not enough that Ishari doesn't take notice of it.

"Did Druv do something?" She asks as Thal hauls some snacks from her arms.

His gaze flicks between us, and I don't need him to explain.

No matter what truce we might have had earlier, he still doesn't fully trust that Ishari wasn't going to be hurt in his absence.

I think the logical side of me knows it's a rational concern after he was so close to losing her. But I'd be kidding myself if I ignored the voice in my head whispering that it was all my fault, and I'm to blame for it.

"Took you two long enough," Thal grumbles, gesturing into the room as we walk past him. "Druv and I thought maybe Seph had stepped out of line with how long it took."

"I told you not to let them get snacks while hungry." Druv grins, his attention focused on the armfuls of food and drinks we hauled back.

"It's her first movie night, we're not skimping on treats." Ishari says, narrowing her eyes at the demons. She sits down in the middle of the long couch that lines the wall, and Thal perches himself next to her.

My eyes gravitate to the single-seat recliner to the right of the couch, but Druv's already on route to it, so I settle for sitting on the other end of the couch closest to him.

Ishari turns the movie on and grabs a bag of candies, offering one to Thal. The warmth in his gaze as he leans forward to take it from her fingertips, his teeth grazing her fingers before she smothers a heated smirk.

I have to force my attention to the opening credits of the movie, listing a handful of names of actors and actresses that star in it. Druv leans forward to my right and grabs a drink from the table, but I'm not expecting when he offers the popcorn toward me.

When I don't move to take it, he shakes the bowl slightly. "You're going to want this." Grabbing a bottle of soda, he extends it between us and adds. "And you'll want to wash it down with this."

It takes a few minutes, but I readjust on the couch, crossing my legs with the popcorn cradled in my lap. The position is oddly com-fortable, and as the movie continues, I'm fully enveloped in it.

I'm not sure if it's because the movie began packed with action, risk and the superhero being the underdog, but I'm so glued to the screen, I gasp when there's a twist in the plot or the villain shows up.

It goes on forever, and I'm fully invested with my undivided attention, nodding along to Ishari's random commentary.

The superhero spent the first half of the movie struggling, fighting himself and his enemies as he tried to save the city when he ran into the villain again. The two banter about the superhero joining his side before the villain grins at him.

*"My condolences for your loss, but remember, I **tried** to give you an option."* The villain snaps his fingers as chaos breaks out. The superhero whirls around to see armed men gunning people down.

I'm shoveling popcorn into my mouth as the superhero fights to save everyone, and that's when he sees the woman he's been pining after the whole movie.

Time slows to a stop. My eyes widen when I'm least expecting a sudden bang of gunfire and something explodes on screen.

The superhero saves the girl, and my shoulders sag.

I didn't realize I'd been that tense.

Another three pops go off, but the superhero doesn't react.

Then three more, sounding closer than before and the walls shudder.

That's when I realize the gunfire isn't from the movie.

"Shit!" Thal throws his bag of candy aside and hurls himself over Ishari, whose eyes are wide.

The gunfire grows closer, and my heart's in my throat as Druv crosses the room. "Scarlett, stay here with her."

My mouth drops open to argue, but Thal's words earlier catch them in my throat, and I slide over to her.

"Come on." I say, tugging her toward the back of the couch. She fights against my grip, clearly torn between going with Thal and Druv.

"Scarlett, I can't." She whimpers, and my heart hurts, but I yank her harder into me. "Please, we need to help them."

I grab the sides of her head and search her eyes. "If you get hurt, Thal will **never** forgive me, and I'm not about to be the reason he loses his soulmate. Let's go."

I'm aware my tone is colder than it needs to be, but judging the way her tear-filled eyes harden, it works. Her breath hitches, but she helps me pull the couch to the side, angling it away from the door.

"Stay here." I whisper, and she looks terrified, but nods.

Good.

Fear will make her obedient, which is better than her being flighty.

Rapid pops sound out, and I can tell whoever this is has gotten through the front doors now. Seph's question rings around my head again, and I swallow against the lump in my throat.

I shouldn't be here, and because I am, more of these demons are going to die.

Chapter 34

Evelyn

The room stinks of bile and sweat, but thankfully my blurred vision clears. The bucket of vomit next to the bed has disappeared, and Grant—*Pai*—along with it.

I don't know whether I'm relieved or disappointed.

My limbs tremble, muscles straining to bear my weight as I push myself upright. The chains at my wrists clatter with my movement, and my heart sinks with each metallic pang that shatters the stillness.

Yet the door into the room doesn't open.

My hands pull toward my lap, but stop halfway, the chains not long enough to allow them to be close. Probably for security measures and to make sure I can't pry them from my wrists.

Smart move.

I am not surprised that a demon who works at the same facility as the Revenants knows the escape methods we were taught. That will make things much harder.

Leaning over, I lift the sheet where the chain links to the bed only to see a soldered connection where the joint had once been opened, with the metal bed frame in the center.

I release a tense sigh. Looks like breaking free from this is out of the question.

As much as I want to hate Grant—*Pai*—for chaining me up like a fucking animal, I can't say I'd have done any differently. Not after what I did to Scarlett.

I'm not sure which betrayal hurt more in the end. Scarlett always had a rebellious streak in her, but I'd opened myself up to who I thought Grant was in a way that I'd never done before.

I'd trusted him. I'd given him that freely.

My chest squeezes to the point of pain, and my throat burns.

A small voice somewhere in the recesses of my mind quietly whispers that trust only brings regret, but I shove that reminder away with force.

Command taught me many tactics, but if I plan to get out of this, I'm going to have to take a different approach than anything they instilled in me. Or at least try to.

Even so, what Scarlett said in the heat of everything wasn't entirely false. She knew somehow that I'd tried to shield the Wraiths from command at every turn, and it's true.

Why that comment hit me the hardest, and seems to have stuck like a thorn in my side, I'm not sure. Perhaps because it was her way of trying to convince me that command's been lying, or that we've been pawns to a greater enemy.

Either way, it's obvious that it struck a chord, and the note's been buzzing around my mind since I woke up.

The realization that Grant has been the enemy this whole time, and that Scarlett's gone AWOL was a little too much to handle in the beginning, but now I've got an actual minute to think about it.

I guess I should have seen the signs from Grant—*Pai*.

My teeth grind together at how many times I've had to correct myself. That's something I'll have to get used to if they don't plan to kill me.

Judging from the fact that I'm not dead yet, nor being tortured, it's unlikely that they are going to.

The memory of Scarlett's battered face sends a shiver down my spine, and I swallow audibly.

Right.

Maybe her betrayal hit harder than I suspected.

I know the way she protected that demon with her body shouldn't have sent me overboard, but it did. I haven't seen her do that before for anyone. Not even Grizz, Mako or Omen.

So, to see her body block a dagger for a ***demon***?

It makes me seriously consider the validity of her words.

She might be reckless, but she wouldn't end her own life for someone else's without a ***really*** good reason.

That's what is giving me the most pause in this whole situation.

Then to have both her and ***Pai*** on the same side now...

I blow out a breath just as the door swings open, and Pai's tall form steps through the doorway. For whatever reason, the sudden clarity I'd seen the room with has extended to him, making the light grey of his suit more regal.

Can't say it's not weird to see him in this instead of his gear. Not that I'm complaining.

"Glad to see you're awake." He murmurs, extending his hand between us. That's when I notice the full glass of water he's offering, and against all rational thought, I accept it.

I have to lean down and hold the cup with one hand to drink it, but it doesn't take long to empty the contents, only losing a small droplet that runs down my chin.

"Thank you." I freeze, feeling overly uncomfortable that I can't seem to reconcile who Pai is versus the man I thought I'd trusted—but if I'm being honest with myself, I'd already been wary of command for a long time.

It makes sense that, given everything Pai showed me of who he was, I'd have aligned myself with him.

The question is—how much of that was really him?

Pai drags a chair over, his expression remaining more curious than anything else.

"How are you feeling?" Tilting his head, his dark hair shifts to the side. The blue in his eyes seems brighter than usual, but then again, everything appears so much more vibrant.

"Physically, mentally, or emotionally?" I say sarcastically, but he genuinely considers my response.

"How about all three?"

I lift my hands suggestively; my restraints clattering loudly. "Physically, I think you can imagine how I feel." He grimaces. "Mentally and emotionally—I'm still processing."

My chest aches at the glimmer of hope in his eyes. I desperately and foolishly pray my Grant is in there somewhere.

"I owe you an apology, Eve." He hesitates, as if unsure how to continue. "I can't change how everything happened, but you know I had no choice."

"That's bullshit." I whisper, even though I know he's right, I still hate that he is. "You could have told me."

"You wouldn't be in this room if you'd known who I was all that time. You know as well as I do that you would have exposed me to command, and we'd still be at odds."

I nearly snort a laugh and lift my chained wrists up again. "You couldn't possibly know that for certain."

He pulls the chair in front of where I sit, and eases into it, bracing his forearms against his knees. "You mean to tell me if I unchained you right now, you'd be a good little Harbinger and play nice?"

The scent of his cologne hits my senses, and the fracture in my heart grows. I want nothing more than to keep trusting him, but for him to hold this big of a secret for this long?

For a moment, I play the scenario out—I walk into his office; he tells me he's a demon. I spend the night reeling because the man I've given my heart to is the enemy, then when I see the Wraiths, I know I can't go against them, so I turn him in.

Now it's no different, except that somehow my right-hand Wraith is on *his* side and I beat the ever-living shit out of her.

"It's safer if you keep me restrained." I whisper, and his blue eyes search mine for a long moment.

"Because you could try to escape?"

"I might try to kill you." I correct him, my eyes widening when he chuckles.

A bitter note of horror trails down my spine when he pulls a key from his pocket and goes to unlock the cuffs around my wrists.

"Stop." I jerk away, and he stills but doesn't withdraw his hands. "What if—"

"You won't hurt me, Eve." My brow twitches upward, and he chuckles. "Besides, you can fight me all you want, but I'm not keeping you chained. Think what you may, but I'm not like them."

I want to laugh in his face—or scream—but it's all I can do to hold his gaze. "I don't trust you." My voice is soft, knowing I'm entirely out of my element right now. "Not anymore."

The Revenants were forged with blood, sweat and tears, but my relationship with Grant—*Pai*—was always an exception. He was my safety net when life was too heavy. My escape. Communication between us was so easy, it was like breathing.

It doesn't appear as if he wants that to change, but God help us all if the demons convince all the Revenants to switch sides.

I'm terrified that I'm already inclined to hear him out.

Pai nods. "I'd accuse you of lying if you said any different." The humor in his expression lightens the mood around us, and I couldn't be more grateful for it.

"So is this the part where you recruit me to the other side?" I ask wryly, and the look he gives me makes the lump in my throat grow.

Pai just eases the key into the lock of the cuff and twists it. The metal falls free, and we both stay still for a moment before he moves to the other.

"I want you to be free of them. Is that so wrong of me?"

"Why?" The question comes out before I can stop it, but I don't dare correct myself as he frees my other arm.

"Contrary to what you might think, what we had wasn't a means to an end, Eve. I meant every word I said. I'm with you no matter what—I just want *you* to make your own decisions."

"And if my decision is to return to command? To tell them everything about you?"

He holds my gaze for a long moment. "Something tells me you won't, but if you did, I'd be right there beside you."

My eyes widen. "Bull-fucking-shit."

He leans in until his face is mere inches from mine, and I don't dare breathe. "You could drive a blade through my heart right now, and I wouldn't stop you. Torture me if that makes you happy. Bring me with you wherever you go or not, you'll never rid yourself of me. I will remain in your shadow at every turn, whether or not you wish for me to be there."

"You're insane." I whisper, and his lips twitch upward.

"I may be, but that changes nothing." He straightens and rises to his feet, towering over where I sit. "You deserve to make your own decisions, Eve, and know the truth about everything command has had the Revenants doing."

My heart sinks into my stomach. "The hell does that mean?"

For the first time, Pai seems uncertain, and he crosses the room to grab some clothes from the table. "I can show you, but I'm sure you'll want to clean up and get changed."

"Why do I feel like you fear how I'll react?" I ask cautiously as he crosses the room to hand me the clothes.

"It is not your reaction I fear, Eve."

"Then what is it?"

His gaze drops to the floor. "Showing you the truth won't be pleasant."

Something about the way he says it makes me believe him—not that I'm going to admit that out loud—but I dread what's coming.

"I'm not afraid to do the hard things, Pai." Saying his name was a mistake, because his eyes flash and my heart thunders in response. "Where do I go to shower?"

My less-than-subtle change of topic doesn't go unnoticed, and he gestures to the door on his right. "Everything you need should be in there, but I'll be outside the room should you require anything else."

His gaze roves along my hair and face like a gentle caress, his expression so soft that it makes my chest tighten. But he doesn't linger, rocking onto his heel and heading for the door.

I look back at the bed; the sweat-stained sheets splattered with what I can only assume is bile or long-dried remnants of vomit. Whatever Orobas did to me seems to have cleared my mind in ways I'd never expected, but at least the cost wasn't too great.

Who knows how long it took his magic to work, though.

My stomach growls angrily, and I rub at it. Asking Pai to stop for a snack before he upends my world couldn't be too much, right?

I turn around and head to the door, catching a whiff of my own body odor as I twist the knob.

Yeah, I can't wait to shower.

Chapter 35

Evelyn

It feels like an eternity has passed by the time I'm done and changed into the fresh clothes Pai gave me. Unsurprisingly, everything fits well, though it's hard to fuck up a pair of baggy sweatpants and a t-shirt.

Still, I feel a million times better leaving the washroom than I did going into it, making the unsettled nerves in my gut just a little easier to handle.

I open the door to see Pai lounging on a chair a few feet away. The hallway isn't cramped by any means, but Pai's tall form can make any large space claustrophobic.

"I don't think I need to ask if you feel better, judging by the look on your face." He murmurs, pushing to his feet with a grin.

"And what look is that?"

His lips twitch. "The one where your eyes seem brighter, you stand taller, and your shoulders are relaxed. It's the same look you'd have whenever you were leaving my office."

All of a sudden, the walls feel like they're a little too close for comfort, and I swallow. "Quite the observer, aren't you?"

His smile grows, and he laughs under his breath as if the answer is an inside joke with himself. "Must be my thing."

I don't bother asking him to explain, so I cross my arms over my chest. "Where to first?"

My confidence is entirely fake, but he doesn't need to know that.

"You'll see." He holds his palm to his mouth and murmurs something too low for me to hear.

The air in front of us shimmers, and I take a wary step back. "How do I know you're not just luring me to a long, torturous death?"

I'm mostly joking, but I can't deny that it could be possible.

Pai casts a sidelong glance at me and shakes his head. "I would sooner throw myself into the mouth of a volcano, Eve."

The shimmering space has formed a mirage of shipping containers, but it's the blurred visage of a staircase that holds an air of familiarity.

He can't mean to bring me to the warehouse where Mako and Grizz died...

Before I can ask, he's grabbed my arm and dragged me through behind him. The surface passes over me like water, but only for a moment until Pai's hand slides into mine.

My eyes snap open as he squeezes gently. "Recognize where we are?"

From here, the staircase to the main building is clearly visible across the room. Even though it's as if I had just been here yesterday, the absence of any blood, bodies or sign of police presence is unsettling. I might not know much about what happened to our targets, but I know enough about crime scene investigations to expect some signs left over.

A sudden loud bang to our right catches both our attention, and I sidestep to Pai next to a wooden shelf full of boxes. More clattering echoes closer along with indiscernible voices.

Footsteps grow louder until six men come into view, stopping in front of some crates stacked on top of one another. They lift a lid for a heartbeat, and a soft glow emanates from it.

Calmness washes over me, which is odd considering our current circumstances.

The sight of it is warm, like the first rays of sun on an overcast day, when the bitter chill of night still nips at your skin.

One of them murmurs to the rest, and they split up—three climb up the stairs and the others head back outside. I keep my gaze fixed on the last person to disappear from view, but whatever is in that crate keeps me preoccupied.

So much so that I'm still staring at the door long after they've vanished.

"Say something, Eve." He whispers, squeezing my hand that, somehow, he never let go of.

That snaps me out of my daze.

"Why isn't this warehouse closed off?" I ask, tearing my gaze from the crate to look at him.

It doesn't take a genius to know the answer, but I want him to say it. I need to hear it out loud.

He must understand, because even through his pained expression, he still answers. "Your mission here was a test from command, Evelyn."

The dread in my gut turns to rot, and I shake my head. "There's no way, I—"

"Grizz and Mako didn't pass the test—do you not remember where they went after Viper separated from the group?"

My eyes are wide, and I stare at him with a newfound sense of horror. "They searched the warehouse while I backtracked to look for her. But I gave them specific orders—"

"Orders they did not obey." He says softly, but his words may as well be a punch to my gut.

They didn't listen. I told them not to touch **anything**, and they died for not fucking listening. But it makes no sense. How could command have known?

"It's not possible." I whisper, but deep down I know each of the Revenants has a rebellious streak. Viper would take her missions too far if she knew or could prove the target's maliciousness to innocents. Mako was paranoid, and even though she never asked questions, they were clear on her face. Grizz refused to take no for an answer and often received compliance training because of it. Omen, on the other hand, was a vault.

She kept her cards close and only showed her hand when she knew for a fact there was a favorable way out.

"They saw what was being moved in this warehouse, Eve."

The thought that I could have kept all this from happening if I'd prepped like every other mission crosses my mind, and I have the sudden urge to vomit.

"I could have saved them." I whisper, unable to stop the words before they come out. "If I had scouted the facility first, like always, I would have been able to save them."

Pai shakes his head. "Remember what happened the night before the mission when you came to see me?"

I frown, but my mind is going a mile per minute as I run through the events of that day.

"I woke up, had training with the others, and command briefed us on the details." I offer, and he looks at me expectantly.

When I don't continue, he grimaces. "You received the mission sent to your quarters, along with your favorite candy—"

My heart sinks into my stomach. "That I told you about when I came to see you, and I offered you some, but you said you wouldn't eat anything command gives you..."

No, it can't be.

Because of that candy, everything I had planned went sideways.

"You knew?" I whisper, but the apologetic look in his expression tells me all I need to know.

"I was acutely aware of everything they did to you, Eve. The candy was no exception, but I was in no place to intervene while they held such influence over your mind."

I can't even begin to comprehend everything he's said, not when the entire reason I'd blamed myself for their death. And they died for what—searching the fucking warehouse?

"What is in the crate?" I ask, my low voice flat.

"Eve..."

"What is in the god-damn crate, Pai?" I need to know. If they died after seeing what's in them, there's no way in hell I'm letting their deaths be in vain.

Pai's expression is torn, like he wants to tell me but something's keeping him from doing it.

I *need* to know.

My breaths come in quick, and I rip my hand from his, my feet hurriedly carrying me to the crates.

"Eve!" he hisses from the shadows, his footsteps quickly following mine. "Eve, stop!"

It doesn't take me long to get to them, and I pry the lid off the one I'd seen the glow coming from.

Light pulses from it in waves, with rows of thin pieces of bark stacked beside small vials of substance. They look oddly familiar, but I can't seem to place where I'd seen them before.

The aura emanating from the bark inside of the crate makes my eyes water, but it's all I can do to frown at it.

The hell is this? Gold wood?

"Eve," Pai says in a low tone. "We shouldn't be out in the open like this."

Ignoring his commentary, I gesture at the contents of the crate. "What is all of this, Pai?"

He glances at the door nervously. "It's wood from the tree of the gods, and—" His throat bobs. "The vials are tinctures made with the blood of daevari."

My heart falters, and I stare at him—but in some distant place in my mind, I know the vials look remarkably similar to those that the nurses keep in their cabinets.

This can't be possible.

"You're lying." I whisper, but when he says nothing, I shake my head, eyeing the vials more cautiously than before. "What are they?"

Pai glances around and eases the lid from my grip, gently setting it back down. "Eve, I will tell you what you want to know, but not here."

"You **brought** me here."

"I did."

"If you didn't want me asking questions, then why show me this?"

"Because if I told you without you seeing it for yourself, you wouldn't have believed me."

"Who's to say that I believe you now?"

His brow twitches up, as if daring me to say that I don't. And I can't.

"I have questions, Pai." I whisper, and he nods, bringing his hand to his mouth and murmuring into it.

"I promise to answer all of them, no matter what the cost." The way he says it leaves an unspoken dire chance of death hanging in the air.

The shimmering portal he'd summoned to bring us here solidifies, and his hand encircles mine. When I don't move to step through—the unfamiliar conjured mirage giving me pause—he walks forward, tugging me behind him.

My eyes squeeze shut as the barrier washes over me, like a line of silk feathering along my skin, and I hesitantly peek at my surroundings.

The decor of the room matches that of the hallway we'd left, with the dark wood beautifully carved along the ceiling, mirroring the hardwood floors. A long oak table lined with chairs in the middle of the room seems to be the centerpiece, with tall ornate vases marking each corner of the space.

With the portal no longer in sight, I release Pai's hand to curl mine into fists at my side. "Why bring me there, Pai? Why show me that?"

He releases a long breath before his blue gaze settles on me. "Because I cannot live another day without you knowing the truth. It's been years, Eve. I refuse to wait any longer."

My heart picks up its pace, and I nod along with his words. "But why? You have to understand what this means for the Revenants—-for Mako and Grizz."

His face falls. "We had tracked each of you for years, and followed your assignments. Mako and Grizz had multiple instances where they'd exhibited signs of empathy on their missions."

"How the hell could you possibly know all of this?" I stare at him, too afraid to even blink.

"Do you forget what my job was on base?" he muses dryly. "There's a reason I risked everything to be close to them. It was the only way we could stay ahead of their movements. They'd orchestrate covert operations wherever beneficial, taking out Servilians and demons alike."

I rear back. "What did they want with Servilians?"

"They've spent years capturing hundreds of them, pushing humans and Servilians to the brink of war. A young researcher named Kilian Sterling, however, recently uncovered that Servilian blood was how they have obscured their operations from us."

When I give him a confused look, he clarifies. "Seir, Orobas, Vassago, Balam... many demons have the ability of foresight or omniscience. When they could not see the future or the past, we thought the war was taking a turn for the worst, but evidently, our enemy was just resourceful. They'd carve symbols in Servilian blood around the bases of their operations and use the same blood in magics used to conceal themselves."

"What does all this have to do with Grizz and Mako, Pai?"

His gaze lingers on mine for a long moment. "They saw too much, Eve. They became a liability, and they were human—that made them expendable. Why would they use resources to bring them in line when they had two daevari assassins at their disposal?"

"So the vials in the crate—"

"They used the same liquid to keep you in line. Remember the intravenous hydration they'd give you both once a week? Remember how sick you'd become if your missions made you miss a dose?"

My heart skips a beat. "And the golden wood?"

His voice is painfully soft, like he knows all this knowledge risks shattering every illusion they'd ever cast. "They manipulate it, using the wood to bolster their magic, allowing them to harvest larger numbers."

I frown, and I almost don't want to ask, but I know I have to. "Harvest **what**, Pai?"

A long moment passes, and he leans forward, the wooden edge of the chair groaning in his grip. "They have manipulated the space that transcends life and death —the transition from the living to the dead. Their rituals require multiple participants, but using the tree of the gods, they need none. By simply marking an area with symbols and lighting the candle infused with its magic, they can harvest all recently disembodied souls, forcing them to transition into the after-life and be recruited for their army."

I have no words.

If I thought command was corrupt before, even if only a fraction, there's not a single doubt in my mind now.

Not after this.

Chapter 36

Scarlett

Whoever command sent isn't dead yet, and Ishari's nearly vibrating with terror.

Whether it's for herself or her mate, I don't know. But, by God, if it isn't making me antsy. She jumps at each pop, and it's taking everything in me not to throw her into an enclosed space and run headfirst toward the sound.

Shouting echoes down the hallway before more loud bangs, and Ishari grabs my arm with so much force that I wince. "Scarlett, please. *Please*, we need to do something."

I'm torn in indecision, searching her face as I contemplate breaking my commitment to Thal.

She must see it written in my expression because her grip tightens. "I'll stay here and hide. Please. I can't stand the thought of him out there." Tears stream down her cheeks now, and my hands squeeze into fists.

"Ishari—" I grind out, but she grabs me by the shoulders as more gunfire echoes through the house.

"Scarlett, please!"

The terror on her face breaks my willpower, and I nod. "Okay. Stay low to the ground here." I say, hauling the coffee table on top of her body and hurtling over the back of the couch toward the door.

It takes half a minute before I spot Druv by the stairs. He's splattered with blood, pistol in his hand and a gunshot to his thigh. When he spots me, he winces, readjusting to fire a shot down the steps as I hurry across the opening to where he is.

The answering pops have me ducking even more into the wall. "Where is everyone? Where is Thal?" I pull the dagger from my waistband, using it to cut my sweats into strips long enough to wrap around his thigh.

Druv says nothing but gestures to his left. Between that and the gunfire outside, I've gathered the ambush isn't going well for him.

"Where is Ishari?"

"Safe. How many are there?"

He just shakes his head. "Too damn many. They won't come inside, but Seph and Korra are out there still."

My teeth grind together, and I cover his gunshot wound with one scrap of cloth, wrapping another around it and securing it tight. "Stay here." I murmur, and he snorts a laugh.

"Not much of a problem there."

More gunfire pops outside, and I don't bother looking back as I head the way he said Thal went, gripping my blade in my right hand.

I have one dagger, but that's enough.

Better than none.

As long as I can tell Thal to hang back, to distract them while I head around behind them, we can take them out. I just need to find him first.

Each crack that echoes into the house rattles the windows with short tremors, and I arrive at the side exit a full minute after leaving Druv behind.

Ishari's pleading circles my thoughts, and I feel her urgency as if it were my own. It makes my heart thunder harder and sends adrenaline through me that's entirely different from what a fight like this brings.

Because what they have is precious. I knew that before, but seeing them together on that couch, I felt it in my bones.

And even if I may never deserve that kind of love, Ishari does, so I will do everything I can to keep it alive.

The side exit is empty, with the door cracked open an inch, so I crouch down to peer out, spotting Thal behind a pillar that supports the towers.

Shots whiz past the door where I've cracked it open another few inches. There's a quick break when he leans out to return fire, but that's when I see it.

Movement near the corner of the house to my left as someone takes aim, holding their fire for him to expose himself, and my heart skips a beat. I move on instinct, rushing from my hiding spot just as he inches from his position.

Everything's slowed as my feet dig deep to gain momentum, but I fear it isn't enough. I'm terrified with every fraction of a second that I'll be too late.

Ishari's pure terror is seared into my mind as I urge my limbs to move faster. The gunman to my left takes aim just as he's in view, his eyes widening as he spots me.

I hear the shot go off a fraction of a second before my body collides with his, and we tumble back behind the pillar. My torso covers his as we hit the ground, and I brace to feel the pain of the shot.

But nothing comes.

Another shot rings out as Thal coughs, but I'm only half paying attention to him as I drag him fully out of the line of vision from the shooters on the other side of the pillar.

"The hell were you thinking, Thal?" I hiss, but my anger shrivels into shock when I see the crimson pouring from between his fingers pressed to his throat. "No."

The word flows from my tongue as I hold my hand over his. "Shit. No. This isn't—"

Bullets whiz past us, but Thal holds my gaze, his mouth opens, and I want to tell him to save his breath—to conserve his energy—but with the amount of blood pouring from him, I know it's pointless.

I hold my hand to his jugular all the same.

"Take," he mouths, "care—" He winces, and I swallow down the way my heart is shattering for him and his soulmate at the same time. "Of Ish—"

He doesn't get her full name out before his eyes flutter, and the blood streaming from his mouth bubbles with a strangled exhale. I stare at him for a long moment, denial thick in my veins as I wait for some miraculous recovery.

But his eyes don't open again, and his chest doesn't move.

That's when the sob I'd choked down crawls out of my throat, and the tears that had stung my eyes flow freely.

This is my fault.

I distracted them. I brought command to their door.

It's *my* fault that Ishari's soul mate is dead.

Another round of shots hit the pillar, sounding as if they're closer than before. My breaths come in deep, and the scream that tears from my throat seems to shake the very ground beneath me, and the house itself shudders in response.

Or maybe it's me shuddering.

My body's too numb to tell.

The gunfire pauses, and I reach my bloodied hand down to grasp Thal's pistol. Tucking it into my waistband, I slide the blade of my dagger between my teeth.

Channeling the anguish that threatens to overtake my mind, I move to the pillar, using my bare feet to climb. It takes only a minute to scale to the top, keeping to the shadows along the ledge. I spot three hostiles with their guns trained on the space I'd dragged Thal for cover.

The fourth is inching closer to it with his weapon drawn, but I already know I'm going to save him for last.

His death will be Ishari's to claim if I can help it.

Slinking along the edge of the roof, I spot a tree branch thick enough that it should be able to support my weight, with the trunk a mere five feet from two of the three assailants.

It's only half a minute as I silently descend the length of the tree, careful not to disturb any branches, using the chaos of gunfire around the rest of the building to cover any noise I might make.

My feet quietly hit the soil, and I creep closer to the first soldier. When I'm a foot away, I strike fast. Dagger firmly in my hand, I cover his mouth and slice deep across his throat, severing his major arteries and trachea in one quick motion.

The strike helps build momentum for my recoil, and I flick my wrist forward at the peak, letting my dagger fly into the second soldier's throat.

It buries into his body with a sickening crunch, and I quickly grab the first soldier's pistol. Aiming without a thought, my finger tugs the trigger. The recoil punches back as the pop signals the bullet's flight, and within seconds the third assailant is down.

The fourth whirls around at the sound, his eyes wide when he sees me, and his weapon jerks in my direction. But I'm already a step ahead.

I pull the trigger again, and before the man can do anything, his weapon drops to the ground. He gasps, clutching his hand where a gaping wound seeps blood.

"You bitch!" He spits, but I couldn't care less what he has to say, so I fire another shot at his uninjured hand for good measure.

He screams, and as much as the sound is music to my ears, I know there's a good chance that he wasn't the last assailant to come after us tonight.

The side door swings open with a harsh groan, as if someone burst through it with such force that the hinges fell apart.

"Thal!" Ishari's shrill voice cracks, but it's her sudden ear-piercing scream that bleeds into a pained wail that breaks my heart all over again.

I take a handful of strides to get to the man, and even less to drag him to where Ishari hovers above Thal, tears streaming down her cheeks.

She gazes up at me, and her expression is as haunted as it is broken. Whatever she sees in my face, it seems to register when she looks at the man I've grasped by the collar, clutching his bloodied hands and groaning in pain.

Even if there was something I could say, I'm not sure if I'd be able to muster the strength as I release him with force, thrusting him into the ground before her with a thud.

I don't wait to see what she'll do with him as the faint sound of footsteps from the front grows closer. Every cell in my body vibrates with the need for more blood, and I am happy to oblige.

It's half a heartbeat to pull the pistol from my waistband, and another half to surge from behind the pillar. At first glance, I mark at least six new hostiles, with two more coming around the corner of the wide-open gate near the front.

The world narrows in as my mind goes silent and I welcome it—the familiar embodiment of a living weapon.

Exhale. Aim. Squeeze the trigger.

Inhale. Move.

Exhale again. Aim. Squeeze the trigger. Aim again. Squeeze the trigger.

I move with practiced precision, putting distance between myself and the pillar where Ishari is exacting her revenge. At least I hope she is.

I would be.

By the time I've rounded the corner to the driveway, three more hostiles enter the front gate and I fire two shots into the closest pair of assailants before diving behind the nearest car. Pops fill the air that hit the metal body of the vehicle, and I inch further from the gas tank.

While it's only been mere seconds that I've used it as cover, the gunfire seems to erupt from a variety of areas on the other side. Judging by the number of shots and where they come from, the five I took out hasn't diminished the sheer numbers.

A shot whistles past the top of the car, and I drop to the ground. I chance a look under the car—seeing the three pairs of shoes a few yards away on the other side.

It takes two full seconds to send three bullets out, aimed directly at each foot. I don't wait to see the results—there's no time.

The still-healing wound in my forearm screams as I force myself from the ground, aiming over the top of the hood when a bullet hits the barrel of my pistol.

Everything happens so fast, yet all too slowly at the same time. I flinch away ever so slightly as the metal barrel explodes, shards slicing into my skin. I'm too slow to drop the handle as pieces fly in all directions.

On instinct, I throw myself to the side—desperate to make any attempt to get further away from the explosion. But the move costs me.

I'm free-falling to the left and away from the hood of the car, into the open as at least seven barrels aim in my direction. My body hits the ground with a thud, the air escaping my lungs as I wait for someone to do it—to pull the trigger and end it all.

I should have known this is how it would end.

Revenants don't go out any other way. To think otherwise would be a pipe dream.

When one soldier reaches into his pocket and tosses his phone to the ground between us, I grind my teeth.

So that's what this is, then.

The screen lights up, and I roll onto my side to pick it up, still assessing my odds of fighting my way out—they aren't good.

Keeping my attention on the soldiers in front of me, I put the phone to my ear.

"You look well enough, Viper."

Even though I'd only seen images of those who make up command's small unit of leadership, I can picture the smug grin on their faces as I hear some chuckles in the background.

"Are you ready to come home yet?"

My teeth grind together. There's no way they would let me return and keep me alive. I'm as good as dead right now, and the only thing they want is information.

I won't give them that.

"I think we both know the answer to that question."

A long sigh comes through the speaker, and my arm throbs painfully. "I was afraid it might come to this before you were ready."

The blank stares of the men pointing their weapons at me make bile rise in my throat. Is this what I was all those years? A mindless killer?

The soldiers don't seem antsy as I adjust my position and brace myself on my knees. "You'd better hope these soldiers have better aim than the others." My voice is low, but I might as well be shouting it with how their grips adjust on their weapons.

"If you think you're making it out of this alive, Viper, you're delusional." Command threatens sharply. "Don't force our hand faster than we need to."

I nearly laugh, but the thought of Thal's motionless body nearby buries the humor. Bringing the phone in front of my face, I tense my muscles, keeping them coiled.

"I'll be seeing you soon." I hit the end button and thrust myself aside as shots go off, pelting the ground where I was moments ago. My hearts in my throat, but I don't stop to think; I just move. One step, three, five, and I'm at the nearest soldier.

Either I'm moving faster than usual, or they're slower than I expected, because another shot goes off, still missing my side by an inch. It's all the opening I need.

Two quick strikes and a firm grip has one soldier in my arms like a living meat-shield. The cool metal of his handgun in my palm as I whirl toward the first group of hostiles.

Exhale. Aim.

My finger squeezes, but nothing happens as the bullet gets jammed. Shit.

A shot fires off to my left, and I hear it whiz past, pulling the man in close as bullets hit his armored chest. The reverberations jerk him back into me, and I dig my heels into the ground.

The shots stop, and the body's suddenly knocked aside, nearly taking me with it as I gasp. The barrel aimed at my head sends a wave of terror through me, and my mind turns to Orobas once more.

Will he risk his life in vengeance when he knows I'm gone?

The soldier's lip curls, his hand flexes and his knuckles turn white as he goes to pull the trigger.

My eyes slide shut.

The resigned terror in my gut tells me that even though I knew this is how it would always end, I think I secretly hoped it would have ended differently.

Sure, I never pictured myself as the white picket fence kind of gal, but maybe, just maybe, there would have been more than death. Maybe that's why I was so intrigued by Orobas and what he offered to me.

It wasn't salvation he tempted me with, or riches.

No, he provided me with understanding and the truth, no matter how much it hurt.

And fuck, did it hurt.

Peering beneath my lashes, my eyes flutter open just as the soldier sucks in a breath and tightens his grip. My eyes widen, staring at the barrel, counting each fraction of a second to my inevitable end.

One heartbeat passes, and I've accepted my fate, but another thrums in my chest as shadows come alive. Everything seems to happen too fast as dark tendrils coil around the weapons. The soldiers gasp and gargle, their mouths opening and closing.

The guns are thrown aside as some stagger, clutching their throats, and others pull at their balaclavas.

It's only then that I notice the blood pouring from deep incisions, and even though only three men expose their wounds this clearly, it's not hard to tell they're all sharing the same fate.

"I regret killing them so quickly." Orobas' voice is jarring, and I jerk my head in his direction. I'm as angry to see him as I am relieved—because if he had come sooner, Thal might still be here.

"There are plenty more where they came from." I meet his gaze, and the weight of Maris' words becomes infinitely heavier.

The princes can't take meaningful action without forfeiting their own lives.

"Will Azrael—" The words catch in my throat, but he seems to understand what I'm trying to say as he surveys the bodies that line the yard.

"I don't know." He steps in close, offering his hand between us. "We've pushed limits before, but not like this."

"Maybe things are changing?" I ask, using his strength to steady myself on two feet with a wince.

"Or the scales are tipping faster than we realize." He whispers.

It's a sobering thought—especially knowing how many came after us tonight. If they can throw away this many lives without a second thought, they must be getting bold.

I mean, sure, they'd killed people before, but that was for top-secret assignments where one to five would be sent, not fifty.

Well, not counting Eve's kill count.

The sound of Ishari's sobs in the distance brings my attention front and center.

"Oro," I whisper, "Thal—"

"I know." He says, his voice wavering as he gazes in Ishari's direction. "Thal was bound to me—I felt it the moment he died and came as quickly as I could."

My heart sinks into my stomach. So many connections, so many bonds, all shattered, for this?

I need to come up with a plan, and fast, or else it will be impossible to stop command. And I can't let any more people die at their hands. I won't.

Chapter 37

Evelyn

"Then this means that—" My voice cracks and I swallow. "How many did we—"

"Don't," Pai whispers. "Don't do that to yourself, Eve."

"How can I not?" I step closer to him and search his face. "We spent years killing innocent people, Pai. I have so much to atone for."

His expression hardens. "Don't take the blame that rightfully belongs to the assholes in command. You weren't the one who assigned the missions."

"But I pulled the trigger. You said it yourself. Grizz and Mako were eliminated for questioning command and learning the truth. I should be right there with them."

"But you aren't!" he snaps, cupping my cheeks between his palms. "And thank God that you're not. I wouldn't be able to live in a world without you in it, Eve."

My heart skips a beat, and he brushes my lower lip with the pad of his thumb. "One day you'll have to, Pai. My line of work doesn't have a long life expectancy."

His expression darkens. "You are not the actions they forced you to take, Eve. That wasn't you."

"You don't know that." He's so close that his breath skates over my skin.

"I do." He whispers, his gaze dropping to my lips. "I know you like I know myself. I know the *real* you, Eve. The one who hums to herself when she thinks no one's listening. The Evelyn that took the worst punishments so that the others wouldn't get theirs as bad. The same Harbinger who killed hundreds of people when she knew those she cared for were in danger. And the very same woman who burst into my office with enraged, tear-filled eyes because she suspected her Wraith was being held hostage."

My heart squeezes almost to the point of pain. I didn't know he'd seen *all* of that.

"Do I need to go on?" He whispers, but he doesn't wait for a response. "To remind you I know the Eve who keeps snacks in her room to bring to the others if they're being denied meals? What about every time you'd threaten the armory to make sure they had Scarlett's poisons replenished? Or Mako's medications?"

He presses his lips to mine, and tears sting the corners of my eyes when he pulls back to look into them. "I have seen you, Eve. I've watched every act of kindness that slipped through command's control over you, and waited for the day when I could remind you that you're more than what they made you."

Tears slip down my cheek, and he kisses me again, but this time he doesn't stop.

~

"She's not going to want to see me after what happened, Pai." I remind him as he turns the vehicle off the road, pulling into Orobas' driveway.

"You don't know Viper as well as you thought, then." He muses, bringing the car to a stop, and a man approaches the door.

It's still odd to see so many demons and not feel repulsed immediately. The fact that I initially saw them as people, not demons, and was confused by my positive response shows how brainwashed I was.

My visceral reactions before were rage-inducing if I thought someone was a demon. I'd sink into the calm of impending violence because that's where I was told I thrived.

I can't believe just how wrong I was.

My door swings open, and I notice the fresh bullet holes lining the exterior walls of the house as Pai offers his hand between us. At first, I wonder if I'd just blocked out memory of so much gunfire, but with each step closer to the property, it's more and more clear that they've been attacked.

"Pai—"

"I know." His jaw's tight as we walk through the front doors. More bullet holes decorate the walls. Even though it looks as if there's been some effort to clean up, reparations don't appear anywhere close to happening.

The damage makes it clear that command didn't just send one or two mercenaries. No, this was the job of multiple fucking units.

Judging from the returning gunfire, it looks like they were out-manned. "What if they got her?"

Pai leads me up the flight of stairs that creak beneath each step we take. "We would have heard from Oro if that were the case."

"How can you be certain?" My heart thrums hard in my chest as we follow a hallway to the boardroom where I'd found the female demon last time.

The door is half ajar, with low voices carrying from inside. Air suspends in my lungs as he pushes the door open wider. When I spot her familiar slender frame, my shoulders sag slightly, but it's the cold, calculated anger that gives me pause.

That's when I notice the female demon on the other side of the table, her face red, her eyes swollen. My gaze flicks to Orobas, the red-eyed demon beside Scarlett, before landing on the male leaning back against the wall.

Memory of that night when she'd come to the warehouse is fuzzy toward the end, but I vaguely remember the demons who had shown up, and it's not hard to tell one is clearly missing.

Shit.

All but the female demon look in our direction. When Scarlett's expression warms slightly, relief washes over me in earnest.

"Pai." Oro says with a nod of his head. "Glad to see you're both safe."

"The hell happened here, Oro?"

The red-eyed demon's lip curls. "There were no signs of an attack coming. Not even the slightest hint."

Pai's expression is grave. "So you were unprepared."

Oro's attention flicks to me for a moment before he nods. "The legionnaires who replaced the others didn't know the area as well, and we were flying blind."

That's when his words sink in, and a thick layer of guilt weighs on my shoulders. I'd taken out all his guards and workers before kidnapping the female.

This is my fault.

"I'll kill them all." My eyes widen as I look at Scarlett. Her expression is murderous, and she calmly straightens, her gaze pinning me in place.

"I think before we go on a lethal rampage, I owe you all an apology."

"Damn straight you do." The male near the wall murmurs, but the female demon just stares at the table—a fresh wave of tears streaming down her cheeks.

"Enough, Druv," Orobas says in a low voice. "If we fight amongst ourselves, we will lose more than we already have."

Scarlett stares at me, her eyes red at the brim even though I see the bloodlust simmering beneath them, and I nod. She doesn't need to tell me what she wants to do—I feel it in my bones.

The urge to find every last one of them and feel the essence of their lives seep from their bodies —it's a summoning to the most vicious parts of me. Of us.

Whatever she has in mind, I'll hear her out and see it through, but I have a score to settle with command that grows by the second. What they did to us, what they did to so many others, demands justice.

"Before you arrived, we were discussing our next move." Orobas offers to Pai, crossing his arms over his chest. "We can't keep waiting for them to come to us. Our defensive strategy is failing because they mask their actions. If we were to hit them, it could bring each member of command out from hiding, and we could cut the head off the snake."

"They're never seen in person." I murmur, drawing everyone's attention. "Catching them out in the open will be impossible."

"Not quite." Pai responds, rubbing his jawline. "The main base might be composed of several sections, but there's a top-secret wing only accessible with maximum security clearance."

"That has to be it." Scarlett's hands tighten on the edge of the table. "So that's where we strike."

"And how do you plan to get inside?" I offer, earning me a glare from the young Wraith. "You think they're just going to let you walk in after everything?"

"Well, no, but—"

"Then it's settled. I will escort you on base since they don't know that I'm no longer under their control. You can keep our exit clear while I hunt them down."

"Fuck that." Scarlett snarls, storming up to me. "You think you're the only one who deserves to draw blood? I watched Grizz and Mako *die*, Eve. For what? For them to have been pulling the strings the whole goddamn time?"

"And you want to run in headfirst, guns blazing, just to fucking join them?" I toss back, and her cheeks flush.

"If I may," Orobas says cautiously, "I don't think we need to do this in an overly complicated way."

Both of us turn our heads to the demon, and he crosses his arms over his chest.

"Does the infamous Viper not have tools in her arsenal?" He grins, and she nearly snorts a laugh.

"So you want me to what—poison them all?"

"Evelyn will go inside and investigate this wing first. They likely believe she's under their control, so while she does that, you will make your way through to the water source and poison it. I imagine you might have one in mind?"

Scarlett grins. "Several, actually."

"I'd expect nothing less." He says, turning his attention to me. "I assume you're willing to re-enter the lion's den?"

"Willing?" I laugh under my breath and ruffle the hair at the top of Scarlett's head. "You'd have to chain me in a room to stop me. Again." I add, tossing a wink in Pai's direction, and his lips twitch.

The female demon—Ishari—sniffles and wipes her eyes in my peripherals. Whoever the other male was to her, clearly she cared deeply for him.

My attention drags to where Pai stands with his hands tucked into the pockets of his coat and the lump in my throat grows.

Perhaps I understand her more than I'd like to admit.

The exhaustion on her face, the dark circles around her sunken eyes—it all makes my heart want to thrash free from my chest.

"Let's get some dinner. We'll prepare and strike tomorrow." Orobas nods as Pai steps in close, hooking his arm around my waist.

Druv walks over to Ishari, but instead of trying to convince her to move, he just slides into the seat beside her.

I'll deliver her pain unto them. For all they've done, they deserve nothing less.

Chapter 38

Evelyn

"Will you let me come with you?"

I pace across the room, toweling my hair dry. Pai's enormous shirt hangs midway down my thighs, just long enough to obscure most of my body from view.

Not that I'd mind it being shorter.

Tossing the damp towel across the room, it lands in the laundry basket by the washroom door, and I cast a sidelong glance at the demon. "I'll consider it."

The lie sours on my tongue, but I ignore it and shut the light off. A gentle glow from the lamp on my side of the bed illuminates my path, and I crawl under the blankets with a contented sigh.

"Tell me you'll be careful." He whispers, gathering me into his chest. "I've spent years watching them do things to you that most people couldn't dream of, and nearly snapped more times than I can count. If something happens—"

I interrupt him, squeezing him against me as the lump in my throat grows. "I promise I'll be careful."

"I mean it, Eve. I haven't felt like this since they sent Gunner to your room."

The memory I'd repressed threatens to send bile into my mouth, and I shake my head. "That was a long time ago."

"A year, actually—a year and fourteen days."

My heart skips a beat. "I was fine, Pai."

"Bullshit. That was the first time you looked truly scared for as long as I've known you." His arms tighten around me. "You know how close I was to going into that wing myself that day?"

"Why didn't you?"

"Because everything I had worked toward would have been thrown away if they knew who I was or if I went through with it just for Azrael to show up."

For a moment I wonder what it would have been like to know what Pai was back then, but with their hold on me so concrete and all-consuming, I know it wouldn't have worked.

It's like this is how things had to be.

But to what end?

"What's on your mind?" he asks, searching my face, and my cheeks warm.

"I was just," I pause. "Well, I was contemplating how things could have been if I'd known who you were the whole time."

Pai presses his lips to my forehead, cupping my cheek with his free hand. "That's easy enough. You would have had my severed head mounted as a trophy."

A quiet laugh escapes me, and he uses his thumb to angle my face to him. His bright eyes burn into mine, and even though I know the truth, I can't help but wish I'd had more time.

More time to know him without secrets.

"Is it odd?" He brushes a lock of my long hair over my shoulder, exposing my skin to the cool air. "Knowing what I am now, does it change things?"

My lips twitch slightly. "I wouldn't be lying in bed with you if it did."

He laughs under his breath before leaning down to press his lips to mine, and my eyes flutter shut. One thing about being freed from their control was how vibrant the world around me was, but it doesn't stop at colors.

Once I'd gotten past the jarring revelation that Grant was a demon, and command's hold on me ceased, it was surprisingly much easier to accept.

I'm not sure if it's the daevari in me rejecting the indoctrination, but it wasn't overly hard once he'd shown me the truth.

"I think coming to terms with everything would have been much more challenging if you hadn't been here." My lips brush his as I whisper my truth. "I think your strength helped me through my hardest days, and that even though I was their puppet in actions, your presence cut through to the core of me."

He presses his forehead to mine and tightens his grip on me.

"You're still the man I gave everything to." I whisper, tears pricking the corners of my eyes. "And I don't regret it for one second."

Pai releases a ragged breath, and his head drops, his mouth claiming mine as goosebumps break out over my body. The air around us hums to life.

The heat in his touch, the way he kisses me, as if trying to memorize every part of me, the shape of each breath, the taste of each heartbeat thrumming in my chest.

Pai's hand disappears from my neck and glides along the length of my thigh as I groan.

I missed this.

I missed **him**.

Thunder above the house rattles the windows, and the wind blows harder, making the unrelenting rain pelt the roof in waves.

Pai was mine before I knew what he really was, and if I'm being honest with myself, I was his, too.

He rolls me onto my back, his weight pressing me further into the bed with his hips pinned against mine. My legs hook around his, and I clutch him close, desperate to feel him everywhere.

I should be more angry about his deception, but was it really a betrayal if I was the villain all along?

The truth is, I can't be mad at him for it when I'm more disappointed in myself for taking so long to wake up.

Pai's hard length throbs between us, pressing against my clit, and my eyes roll back. He might be a demon, and suffering from the same need for me as I am for him, but there's a reverence in his kiss that makes my chest squeeze to the point of pain.

Corded muscles flex under my palms as he pulls his boxers down, not breaking our kiss until he's tugging his shirt over my head and tossing it aside.

Feeling him everywhere will never be enough. His touch itself is transcendent, a ritual of offering his body, his soul at my altar.

His arm hooks under my back and cups the nape of my neck as we move in sync. I don't know where my longing for him ends and my desire begins, but every thrust of his hips against mine sends little bolts of pleasure up my spine.

It's not enough.

It will never be enough.

I squeeze my legs around him, digging my heels into his muscular thighs in a silent request for more. Desire pulses through me like a starved beast, and my fingertips bite into his back as he groans.

The sound makes my mind go blank, and I reach between us, wrapping my fingers around him. His breath hitches, and I glide my palm up and down the length of his shaft, the bulging veins making my mouth water.

"Everything I am, Eve," Pai breathes as I angle the head of his dick. "Everything I am bends to you, and will eternally."

His blue eyes search mine, and I know in the depths of my soul that we were always meant to be here. We were always meant to experience this moment, and no matter what comes tomorrow, he will always be my Pai.

Tears sting the corners of my eyes, and I lean in to capture his lips, because words would never express enough of what I feel.

His hips pin forward, and I moan into his mouth at each delicious inch stretching my body to accommodate his size. My arousal only goes so far for providing lubrication, and he withdraws before pushing in with more force until he's fully seated. The veins feeding his dick massage my walls as he moves in earnest, making my eyes roll back.

His arms encircling my shoulders hold me in place as he sinks in deep, my body consumed with the euphoria building in my core.

My breathing picks up, but he doesn't stop or slow. My hips meet his, chasing the feeling that threatens to tip me over the edge.

Our foreheads press together, our breaths mingling between us as urgency takes over. My nails dig into his skin, fighting the urge to let it all go now.

Whatever illusion of control I thought I had breaks when he slams into me, hitting a spot that has me crying out with the first wave of my climax. He keeps grinding deep into me, and I ride out my orgasm, panting between mumbled and incoherent pleas.

When my mind finally clears, he pulls back to look at me, searching my face with a heated expression. "My ruination." He whispers, leaning in to capture my lips once more.

He withdraws, only to slam in again, and my overstimulated nerves tremor, making my legs twitch.

Ruination to salvation.

That's what we are to one another, and I plan to spend tonight showing him just how much he saved me.

~

Dark brown hair falls forward onto his pillow, and bright blue eyes gaze back at me from where Pai lies as he gently runs his fingers through my hair.

"Have you decided what we're going to do?"

I nod.

In the end, it wasn't even a question. Deciding to do the right thing came to me as easily as breathing, but going against the people I've trusted my whole life—that was the hard part.

"I'll need to do this alone, Pai." His eyes flash, and his mouth drops open, but I put my finger to his lips. "Please."

Tears fill his eyes, and he fists my hair behind my head as he presses his forehead to mine. "You are my weakness in all ways, and I hate that I must concede this because I will lose you."

Red brims his eyes, and he swipes at the wet stains on my cheeks as my own fall to the pillow.

"You will not lose me."

His breath hitches, and his hand squeezes at the nape of my neck, tugging my hair slightly. "Promise me."

My voice is hardly more than a whisper as my heart feels like it's shattering, and I know that I'm about to lie to a man who sees me like no other. "I promise."

Pai's phone vibrates on the side table, and we both know we've run out of time to hide in our own world away from everything else.

He reaches over and glances at the screen before releasing a long sigh. "They're ready for us."

For the first time in a long time, a wave of nausea from nerves twists in my gut.

I don't want to leave this room, but we have to.

There's no choice here.

My mind wanders to last night, and I replay Orobas' words over and over again from when he pulled me aside before we'd left his house.

"Well," I sigh, sitting upright and swinging my legs over the edge of the bed. "I guess we couldn't hide away forever."

A long moment passes before he stands up, pulling his jeans on slowly. "As much as I want to."

I swallow hard and reach over to grab my suit from the dresser. "You and me both, Pai."

The drive to Orobas' house feels shorter than usual, even though each minute felt like an eternity in itself.

Our footsteps echo in the halls as we close the distance to his office, and I fight the urge to disassociate. Today could very well be our last day if something goes wrong, so I force myself to remain present.

Because I have to believe we were brought together for a reason.

I have to be positive that we'll make it through this, even if the odds are against us.

Pai holds the door to the room open, and I walk inside, my mouth watering at the nausea roiling in my gut.

Orobas' crimson gaze feels like it's laser-locked onto me as we approach, and my pulse picks up.

"Hope you both got some rest last night." He says, but the knowing look he gives us, and the bags under the others' eyes tell me we weren't the only ones savoring every moment.

"As much as we dared to." Pai says beside me.

"Are you ready?" Orobas asks me and Scarlett, and we both nod once.

He steps forward, handing me a small black dagger with an inscription etched into the side of the blade. "I don't think I need to explain to you what will happen if you fail."

I shake my head. He doesn't.

"If I fail, I die."

Orobas nods. "You will die, but they will resurrect you into their army. I will make your soul insusceptible to their manipulation if that should happen, and this dagger has been inscribed with the same magic, though I hope it's not necessary."

I nod, clinging to my positive thoughts with everything that I am. "I won't need it."

He inclines his head and gestures over my chest, murmuring an incantation as Druv steps up beside us. "It's time, Oro."

The crimson-eyed demon nods before glancing between us. "Evelyn, Pai will bring you on base. He is only to retrieve his equipment from his office and return here in order to hack surveillance cameras without putting himself at risk. While he does that, Scarlett will sneak into the water treatment facility, and poison it. The facility provides clean water for drinking, cooking and bathing, so we should see an impact over the next few days."

"Evelyn will investigate the hidden wing using Pai's instructions and take out any members of command she runs into." His blood-red eyes fixate on me and nod.

"Let's fuck some shit up." Scarlett grins, and sheaths a dagger at my hip.

If there's one positive to all of this, it's that I have the unique opportunity to send command back to the hellhole they crawled out of.

And that's exactly what I plan to do.

Chapter 39

Scarlett

Somehow the guards keeping watch within the exterior of the compound are even worse than I'd thought.

Not that I'm complaining.

I slip along the shadowed edge of the roof, making my way across the series of buildings toward the water treatment facility. This mission would have been much shorter, but unfortunately they'd discovered years and years ago that a pollutant contaminated the water, and built a treatment plant as a solution.

Or at least that's what they told us. Who knows what the truth really is.

Either way, it's the best place for me to do this.

The bag strapped around my body is a comfortable weight; the liquid sloshing quietly inside as I near the edge of the roof. Three buildings from here stand between me and the treatment facility, and I head for the piping that runs down the edge.

Descending takes half a mind, even with my injuries from my encounter with Evelyn still healing. My feet find purchase on each rung of metal holding the piping in place until I'm on solid ground.

Cameras angled away from my position give me a clear line of sight to the next building, and I hurry to the other side. There's still the odd patrolling soldier or unit that I hear in the distance, far enough away that I don't have to be too concerned about them.

Nevertheless, I keep my ascent slow and controlled until I'm on the roof once more. For whatever reason, command never bothered putting cameras up here, so I pick up the pace.

Sand and debris crunch under my feet with each step, and I gaze two buildings over to the water treatment facility with a tense exhale.

Halfway there.

My path is more time-consuming than dangerous, and I don't know if I'm relieved or annoyed. On one hand, anyone I take out here might help ease the pressure on Eve as she infiltrates command. Yet, on the other hand, it could raise the alarm pre-emptively, and she could be caught off guard.

So I keep to the shadows and rooftops, then.

By the time I've gotten to the facility, it's been oddly quiet. So much so that I spend an extra minute waiting in the darkness before crossing the roof in the open.

No one's in sight as I reach the only entrance to the building, and slide through. Each near-silent footstep shatters the stillness of the tall, winding staircase. Metal groans under my weight as I continue down for what feels like an eternity.

The stairwell gives way to a large room filled with tubes big enough to fit my entire body. They span from one side of the space to the other, connecting to one pipe that's double their width and runs along the side of the room.

A low hum fills the area from the water being pumped from one section to the next. I won't pretend that I have any idea what much of this machinery does, but I have a pretty good understanding of what I want to do.

It takes a few minutes of careful navigation through the facility that's much larger than I'd originally expected, but I finally track where the 'treated' flow of water exits the building. With that identified, I trace the piping backward to another room. Two tanks dominate the space, the tops sitting over three feet above my head.

The poison around my torso seems to gain a pound with each passing minute, and I'm eager to get this over with.

The sooner I can finish my part of this, the sooner I'll be able to join Evelyn.

Sure, she ordered me not to, but there's not a chance in hell that I'll miss out on this.

The tanks are the center point storage space from the filters on the other side of the room, and I circle one to look for a way up. The thin metal steps ascend opposite to the entrance, with a sealed panel at the very top.

The latches pop open one at a time, but it's when I lift the lid, and an oddly familiar scent hits me like a bag of bricks. It's metallic with a tang that I don't think I'd forget in a million lifetimes.

The same vials I'd seen in the warehouse lie empty at the bottom of the tanks as my heart drops—I should have known it was in the water.

No wonder they establish complete control of large populations so fucking quickly.

My pulse skips as I wrestle the container of poison front and center, unscrewing the lid loudly, not caring if anyone notices I'm here. At this point, I welcome the confrontation.

Flicking the top off, it plops into the liquid below before I dump the poison in. By the time it's empty, I drop the container in with the lid, and close the panel once more.

I'm not sure how long it'll take for that shit to circulate to each building, but it won't be fast enough for my liking.

With that done, I don't bother waiting around or worrying if someone catches me. In fact, I'm so unconcerned that instead of heading to the staircase, I aim for the front door.

The modest amount of security just shows command's hubris, and how they probably never imagined their plot to take over could ever be undermined—nor that their own creations would be the ones to take them down.

My footsteps echo, the sound fading into the constant hum of the machines pumping water through the pipes. I'm only halfway in the room when my phone vibrates.

Ishari: Scarlett, there's people outside the property. Are you okay?

My heart sinks into my stomach.

Scarlett: How many? Where are the others?

Ishari: They're aware. Druv is securing the entrances, and Oro is on his way back.

Ishari: Scarlett... I can't lose anyone else.

Her words sink in and take root as I picture Oro facing them alone. The thought that they waited for us to retaliate for their final move on him makes my blood boil.

As much as I'd wanted to find Evelyn and help her tear the entire place down, Oro will be in serious trouble if they struck knowing we'd be gone.

I don't even want to think about the possibility of him being hurt.

Scarlett: I'm coming.

Sliding the phone into my pocket, I hurry to the door with renewed urgency.

Hang in there, Ishari.

Chapter 40

Evelyn

My footsteps are hardly audible on the smooth tile floor. Years of reinforced training making each movement like fluid; the air conditioning blowing from the vents covers what little sound I create.

Not that it seems to matter. For whatever reason, there's almost no one wandering the hallways—it's unsettling.

I tell myself that it's not the first time command has kept most staff members on missions, and that it makes sense with them losing Scarlett that they'd be using all available resources, but still.

Something about it twists my gut.

I try not to picture the young Wraith by herself outside the complex of buildings. There's enough on my plate for me to focus on.

After passing a handful of soldiers without being accosted, and still getting the wide berth they so often provide me, my shoulders relax. My stride becomes more natural—each lungful isn't a manual effort.

It's not until I near the end of the long walk to the hidden wing, and I glance behind me before approaching the false storage closet door. Easing it open, I step inside—my gaze darting around for any sign of cameras. To my pleasant surprise, I find none.

The bare wall to my left is unassuming, but with what I know now, it's the gateway to hell. I guess considering what these assholes do regularly, that might be more accurate than anything else.

Still, my fingers trail the side of a broad cabinet searching for the button to open the door. Nothing has ever stopped them from having cameras hidden, so I waste no time. It takes less than a minute to find the small circular metallic release that could easily be mistaken for a loosened screw.

The moment I press it, a whoosh of air rushes from my left. The wall jerks inward by an inch, and then slowly rises into the ceiling. Seconds pass and the pathway to this secret wing comes into view—the pristine linoleum flooring reflecting the white LED lights above.

Footsteps in the hallway send me into action, and I head deeper into the secret wing. A mechanical whirring signals the door sliding shut behind me, leaving me alone in the long, curving hall.

I walk for what feels like forever until I reach a dead end, with only a stairwell and elevator left as my options. And while I'd rather not take the elevator, the sooner I'm done with this, the better.

Orobas' words flit through my mind as I press the singular button, and the doors let out a quiet hum as it ascends.

The enchanted dagger Orobas gave me weighs heavy at my hip, so I unsheathe it, stepping to the side as a low chime signals the doors to open.

My heart thrums steadily as I peer inside to find it empty. I know they'll likely have a camera within, but I don't plan to make this a quiet strike.

Besides, I doubt they normally see strangers venturing in here, and I've been itching to get a little blood on my hands. I just need to make sure it's the right blood, this time.

A singular image inside the panel sits above the normal open or close door button—the center of it is some sort of fractured cross topped with a droplet-shaped loop. A serpent coils around the base, with thorn-ridden vines encircling the entire symbol.

The sight of it makes my stomach churn uncomfortably, but I press it anyway, chalking the sensation up to nerves.

It's common for cults and secret societies to have their own symbolism with hidden meanings—I can't imagine these demons to be any different. Despite that, there's a small seed of dread in my gut that I can't seem to shake as the doors slide shut.

Seconds pass in my descent like an eternity, and when the low chime rings, I move to the side of the elevator, waiting for the doors to open. Without a blueprint of the area ahead of time, I'm really flying blind here.

But this is how I earned my accolades as Harbinger of the Revenants. Sure, my combat skills were stellar, and I was a good assassin as much as I was a decent leader—but I did better under pressure when everything was going south.

Somehow even in a pit of despair, when all appeared to be lost, I always found the light and reflected it in the darkness.

I inch to the side, peering into what looks to be an empty common area before taking a step out of the elevator. The room is minimalistic, with floor to ceiling porcelain tile walls and chairs set around various white tables that line the room. Enormous stone vases mark each seating area, filled with some kind of ash.

Spotting a door to my left, I slowly ease along the wall, keeping the elevator in my peripheral for any movement. Even though I'd known there was a chance firepower here would be light, something still feels off.

I creep past the doorway, and down an empty hall that continues for what seems like forever, but I'm not alone for long.

Voices carry on the air as I venture further, and my heart picks up its pace. The light's become increasingly dim, with shadows forming in the corners of the hall.

From here it's impossible to understand the voices, so I hurry forward to where the hallway intersects with another. One heartbeat passes, then two. By the third, I'm glancing between three doorless entryways.

The halls to my left and right are identical, with the one straight ahead appearing far more grand. Intricately sculpted pillars mark either side of the entry, mirroring the symbol from the elevator.

The direction of the voices I'd heard is hard to pinpoint, but since they seem to be louder to my left, I decide to take that doorway first. The distance to the next room is thankfully shorter, and by the time I'm nearing the entrance to it, I know I'm close to contact.

... "take a miracle at this point."

I slide in near to the wall by the corner to listen.

"I just don't understand how the fuck they *lost* a Wraith."

"Too focused on the bullshit that damn archangel is spewing about the war."

Someone scoffs. "As if it matters. By the time they realize the scales have tipped too far in our favor, it'll be too late for them to course correct, and we'll finally have the numbers to wipe out these demons once and for all."

"That's assuming the rumors about Lucie are true." The other man says grimly. "Just because no one has seen him in millennia doesn't mean he's dead."

"Either way, they stand no chance. The ritual tonight just secures our victory even further."

"I still think we're getting ahead of ourselves. Just because we'll have the numbers this time next year, that doesn't solidify our victory tonight. We can't force students to learn the rituals in religious studies anymore. Blackwell's operation left us vulnerable to litigation across the fucking country. The medications being prescribed for cancer are off the table since it's been cured, setting us back a third of souls harvested per year. Kharidia's no longer operational, and now we have resistance groups watching our every move across the globe. What part of that seems like we're ahead?"

The voices grow slightly closer, and the footsteps stop.

"You say that as if we don't have three more operations like Kharidia. Besides, you know as well as I do the Vatican gives us our strongest charges. Half the shit soldiers we get from these other areas die before they get their wings, anyway. With the wards and our sheer numbers, they stand no chance."

Footsteps continue to grow closer, and I crouch down as they near the wall I'm hiding behind.

"You and I both know that Arkhaios will want—"

They round the corner, come to an abrupt halt. Recognition flashes across their features and I launch forward, my blade slicing through the first man's neck. I don't stop long enough to take in his features as my left hand juts out, gripping the second man by his throat.

He struggles against my grip, gasping for breath as I drag him in close and drive the blade deep between his ribs, puncturing his lung. When I withdraw the dagger to flip it in my palm, it's mere seconds before I slice the metal edge across his throat too.

Blood spurts from his severed artery onto my face, streaming down my chest and seeping into the thin material hugging my body. Within seconds, he drops to the ground like a stone.

The rest of the room is filled with computers, all of them locked except for a handful of security feeds. This has to be some sort of command center, by the looks of it. Thankfully, they hadn't noticed my arrival, or if they did, they didn't realize my intent.

With crimson painted across my body, I circle the room once, looking for any other doorways and find none, so I head back the way I came. By the time I'm at the cross point again, I hear faint murmuring coming from the direction of the elevators, so I hurry across the room to the other entrance.

If I can clear this section before anyone notices, I'll feel much better knowing my six is free of hostiles.

I don't bother keeping to the wall as I sprint to the end, my breathing even as I listen for any sign of people up ahead. Having already taken care of their poor excuse for a security command center, I don't have to worry about any blaring alarms for now.

The room at the end of the long hallway opens into a triangular shape. A table in the middle with eight chairs surrounding it, a screen in the center, and more ash-filled vases line the room.

The pit of dread in my gut grows as I near the first corner of the room, passing by one of the enormous jars. Deep engravings in the ash form the same symbol on the button down the elevator, and my pulse picks up. The hairs at the nape of my neck stand on end as I move to the other vase, only to see the same.

"Well, I'll be damned." I fall still at the familiar voice grating against my ears. "Scarlett's betrayal we expected, but this? This is a surprise."

The thought that they might have intercepted Scarlett during her mission to poison the water supply flits through my mind, but I shove that away with force.

I need to focus and not let them throw me off. I'll figure the rest out later.

My hand tightens around the grip of Orobas' dagger, and I turn slowly to see three men in the entryway. The relaxed visage of Commander Vale in the center is the first thing I notice, and my heart skips a beat.

He's hardly taller than I am, and for whatever reason, the notion is laughable to me. Some part of me had always pictured Vale as a towering behemoth of a man. I'm disappointed.

The two beside him look a little more antsy to his right, and even though I don't recognize them, I commit their faces to memory.

"Why do you do all of this? What do you want?" Vale looks amused at my line of questioning, and I tighten my grip on Orobas' dagger.

"Why? Isn't it obvious?" He steps to the vase closest to him and caresses the edge reverently. "A new order is coming, Evelyn. For longer than any of us can count, our influence has grown, but now? We're close to changing this weak, messy, chaotic world into one where humans serve *our* purpose. But to do that, we must eliminate those in our way first."

"You plan to create a new world order and take over the human race?"

A cruel smile creeps across his face. "Humans and whatever Servilians stand in our way. I doubt they'll keep their portals to Earth open for long once we destroy heaven."

My entire body goes numb, and it's all I can do to stare at him. "You're insane. You all are."

He shrugs as the other two chuckle. "Once our control is global, the gods will tremble at the thought of Arkhaios and his followers."

Footsteps down the hallway grow closer, and several soldiers file into the room. They've donned the same uniform I've worn for years, and my fingers tighten around the hilt of my dagger.

Without knowing these men, I'm not sure how easy it'll be to fight my way through. Only time will tell, I guess.

"So the Revenants served what purpose, then? A test run?" I ask, sidestepping slightly to gain an inch of distance from the six men in front of me.

"A test would be putting it lightly. You and yours were the archetype, paving the way for us. You see, for so long we could only use single-influence magic—whispering in one ear at a time to corrupt or infect a soul into doing our bidding. This method was long, tedious, and easily countered by the abominations that used to call themselves angels. So we sought a new way to gain control, by tainting the blood of those most resistant to our influence.

"Millennia passed before we found the first daevari on Earth: a young girl named Oriana Sharpe, who was admitted for a mental health break. For days, we harvested her blood, and experimented. Using tainted essence of the daevari, we extended the reach of our influence over the military, lawmakers, politicians and the like.

The head of command turns his attention to the vase beside him and sighs wistfully. "And now that you've returned to us, we secure our hold on this world in His name. You will be His champion."

My molars grind, and I sneer at him. "Over my dead body, asshole."

Any hint of amusement in his expression bleeds away as his gaze burns into mine. "So be it."

The soldiers in front of him launch to action, and within seconds, my vision is a blur of calculated strikes. Dodge left, swipe right, drop low, jab up, swipe to follow.

I take three out before they land a hit that knocks me off kilter. A fist slams into the side of my head, and my vision turns black for a breath of a moment, clearing as I struggle to gather myself.

What was I doing? Where am I?

The answers to both questions come back just in time for me to miss a strike aimed at my head. A hand encircles my bicep, and I react on instinct, twisting away but not fast enough. When another hand grips my right arm, it stalls my next move.

My mind's still shaken, my reactions lagged, and by the time I'm dropping to break their hold, a hard body collides with mine from behind.

Shit. There was three.

Vale and his two cronies step closer, and I struggle in the others' grip. The soldier to my right twists my arm suddenly in an unnatural position, and I inhale a sharp breath.

One man recoils his fist, and I'm not fast enough to erect walls in my mind against the pain before it makes contact. My head snaps to the side, and a metallic tang fills my mouth.

"What a good feeling it is," Vale muses, stepping closer slowly as blood pours from my lips. "To secure our victory for all eternity."

Chapter 41

Scarlett

This fucking bike isn't fast enough.

Engine humming beneath me as I weave through traffic, hurtling me toward the house at breakneck speeds.

My cell vibrates in my pocket as I yield off the main highway and onto the road to Oro's property, the turn taking an eternity. Each breath comes and goes like a lifetime, but I can't spare a second to look at my phone when I'm nearly there.

The roaring engine will give me away, but I couldn't care less as I speed past the open gates. I brake hard, my bike turning with the sudden maneuver, tilting onto its side as the body skids across the concrete driveway.

Not a single body scatters the lawn, but I don't bother inspecting further as I launch myself off the bike and toward the front door. The building doesn't seem to have any bullet holes in it, but that means nothing if they're inside already.

Throwing the door open and hurling myself into the main entry, I'm hardly more than ten feet when Druv and Ishari freeze in the middle of the hallway with wide eyes.

"Scarlett? Everything okay?" Ishari whispers, alarm clear in her expression as she glances behind me.

Druv takes a step toward me. "Did something happen, Viper? Spit it out?"

My mouth opens and closes as I shake my head. This can't be real. She texted me.

I'm going insane.

Did I hallucinate it?

"Scarlett?" Ishari whispers, sounding closer than before.

My body's numb, and my fingers tremble as I fight with my own clothes to pull my phone from my pocket. Each lungful brings a wave of denial mixed with dread, because I know what I saw.

And yet—

My phone unlocks to the conversation with Ishari, and I see the bottom half of a picture. I don't need to scroll up to recognize Eve's figure, but it's the two texts under it that truly make me see red.

Ishari: We will always get what we want, Scarlett. You should know better than to let your unit venture deep into enemy territory alone.

Ishari: Any last words for your Harbinger?

No.

I stare at it in disbelief for a long moment, but I'm moving before I know it.

They want war? I'll give them a fucking war.

Door by door, I storm past each room until I see Oro's and burst through the entry, coming to a stop for a breath.

Where is it?

Where the fuck did I see it?

I turn in a full circle until I spot the dresser.

Phone still in my hand, I cross the room and dig for the wooden button at the bottom. The door clicks open, and I don't linger or admire the gem-adorned weapon nestled in the center. The moment my free hand wraps around the cool metal, it hums against my skin as if it can sense the violence promised to it.

It takes a second to swap it for one dagger at my hip before striding from the room and descending the stairs to the front entryway where Druv and Ishari are still standing.

I don't say a word as I walk past Ishari, but her arms shoot out on either side of her as she steps directly into my path.

"Where are you going?" She asks, her voice wavering as she shuffles to the side, placing herself between me and the doorway.

"Move out of the way." I whisper, and though I'm staring into her eyes, I'm not really looking at her. Not when Eve's bloodied image is seared into my mind.

"Scarlett, tell us. We can help." She pleads, glancing toward Druv just as his hand wraps around my bicep.

That's when I snap.

My body moves of its own volition, and within the blink of an eye, I've slipped from his grasp. The lamp to my right is the nearest non-lethal object I can throw, so I pick it up and hurl it toward Ishari.

She screams and dives out of the way as the lamp crashes against the far wall, the ceramic base shattering from the impact.

"What the fuck, Scarlett?" Druv growls, taking a healthy step away, but all I can think of is getting past them and finding Eve.

When footsteps come up the front stairs, my mind empties, and a tall figure fills the doorway. "What was all that noise?"

Pai.

My chest heaves as I raise my eyes to his. He looks between all of us with his brows pinched. It's all I can do to reach into my pocket, unlock my phone and throw it to him.

He catches it midair and turns the screen to him, looking at it for hardly a second. When his face snaps toward Ishari, I know he's just as fucking surprised by this as I am.

"Ishari, where the fuck is your phone?"

She rears back; her face paling. "I—"

"She lost it when Eve kidnapped her." Druv says darkly, and Pai curses. "Why?"

"I'm going after them." I growl, my body vibrating with the rage simmering in my veins. If I don't find an outlet soon, I'm just as likely to snap on them as I am command.

"Not alone, you're not." Pai retorts as I head toward the door, but I'm not looking at him.

"Suit yourself." I murmur, descending the stairs. "Just don't slow me the fuck down, demon."

"Wouldn't dream of it, Viper." He says, striding past me with ease. "Just let me drive."

I don't argue as he lifts the motorcycle with ease and turns the engine on. As much as I want to be in control, the adrenaline pumping through me mixed with how my limbs tremble would make driving a liability right now.

The bottom half of the photo's imprinted in my brain, the crimson running down her abdomen, darkening her already black gear.

I'll kill them all.

Pai doesn't spare a second after I've climbed on before he peels out, kicking dirt and rocks up behind us.

I don't know what the demon has planned, but it can't be anything small. Not with the way he's speeding right now.

Wind whips past us as I lock my arms around him, keeping balance as we pass by cars that might as well be crawling on the road.

"What are you going to do?" I ask loudly, competing with the wind as he hurls us down the highway.

"I'll kill them all." He says, not loud enough to be yelling, but just enough to be heard against the roaring in my ears.

"What about Azrael?"

"Fuck Azrael." He growls, turning onto the main road. "If anything happens to her, I'll find Samael myself and make him bring her back."

My chest tightens. At least we're aligned there.

"He'll answer to both of us, then."

The ride to command passes like a lifetime, and I spend the entirety of it with one arm hooked around Pai's waist, but my mind replays every moment that led up to this.

It doesn't escape me that Eve went in alone knowing it could be a trap. She spent years protecting us by surveying our missions in advance—not that I ever told her I knew about it.

I'd track her leaving base the night before or the morning of, likely to scout out ahead. But that's who she was. She was a worrier, who over-thought every outcome, and weighed the options that came from it.

Of course she would have done this alone.

The chances of her being caught in a trap or taken prisoner were too high, and she knew that.

My teeth grind together until my jaw cramps. Eve was there for us whenever we needed her, even when the odds were against us.

Yet when the tables are turned, I'm fooled by a fucking fake text message.

I should have known it wasn't Ishari. She doesn't text like that.

Even if she was scared, it clearly wasn't her.

My pulse picks up as Pai turns onto a side road that leads to the main gates.

I hope he wasn't lying about killing them all. Judging by the path he's taking into base, it looks like he wants to make a loud entrance.

I unsheathe the dagger on my hip, feeling the gem-inlaid weapon of destruction humming against my other.

Soon.

I'll satisfy its thirst soon.

First, I need to draw blood to satisfy my own.

Chapter 42

Evelyn

"Bring her to the auditorium."

Commander Vale and his cronies walk ahead of us as the other three drag my bound body down the hall. It took all of them to keep me still as they tied both my arms and legs, but having me fully restrained didn't stop their blows from coming.

After several strikes without being able to block them, I reinforced the walls in my mind, building them as high as they are thick to separate myself from the pain.

It still seeps through, though. The ache and throb find their way between the cracks.

So as they drag me along, my mind wanders and I wonder if Scarlett has poisoned the water yet. I doubt they would have had time to ingest it, which means in all likelihood I won't be lucid or even alive to see them all die.

The men drag me to the right, through the large double doors, and into an enormous room. Thick lines cover the floor in some kind of odd symbol, and they drag me to the crimson-stained center.

Walling my mind off once more, I try but cannot keep my focus elsewhere as they chain me to a metal object erected from the ground. It strikes me that the shape matches the symbol in the vases and the elevator, as well as the layout of this entire damned wing.

With my bound arms hauled in front of me, they secure my neck to a hook on the rounded top, and Orobas' words from last night fill my mind.

"The others cannot know Evelyn, or else we will lose this war for good." Orobas' crimson eyes search my face. The demon, who normally looks so determined and certain, suddenly shows the weariness of a man with far too much weight on his shoulders. "Thousands of possibilities, infinite threads of fate, and yet only one illuminates with hope for a better future."

"What are you trying to say, Oro?"

The pained expression he wears tells me all I need to know, but he offers an explanation still. "You will not return from this mission, Evelyn. Every path that I, Vassago, and Seir have combed through... we cannot see it because of the magic obscuring their actions, but the only truth we know is that you will not leave that base alive."

The two others walk away, lighting candles all around me. The three who dragged me over to the center of the room move to the entrance of the auditorium, and the pit of dread in my stomach solidifies.

"Evelyn, Evelyn, Evelyn..." Vale tuts absently as he grabs the black dagger Orobas gave me. "In light of our reserves being depleted, your fresh blood will help fuel our supremacy." He steps closer, and I struggle against my restraints, but not enough to make a difference.

That's when I notice commanders Redd, Knox, Holt, Kell, and Ward lining the room, lighting candles along the outskirts.

The sharp edge of the blade bites into the tender flesh of my wrist, stinging as he slices deep. With the walls erected in my mind, the pain slams against them, but instead of letting shock take root, I focus on my breathing, and he makes an incision across the other.

Inhale. Exhale.

My thoughts wander to Pai, and my chest tightens.

Inhale. Exhale.

My head spins, and my heart picks up its pace. I might not be able to keep my promise to him in any literal sense, but at least they will not control me. My mind will be my own until my last breath.

The voices around me grow louder, but it's only then that I realize they've been chanting, with Vale standing proudly in front of me. His cruel smile grows wider, and he slices a deep cut across his palm, his voice joining the others as he holds his hand out. Crimson drips to the ground, mixing with mine in a steady stream.

"Our combined essences will power this magic, solidifying our control over every soul in this country. Tomorrow will be a new day, and with a new day, a new age will begin. This marks the end for humanity, and the era of Arkhaios." His voice grows louder and louder with each word—overtaking my own thoughts as the edges of my vision grow dim.

His words bleed together as he joins the chant, and I slant forward, the bindings around my neck constricting against my weight. The pooled blood on the ground under my wrists smokes as the world narrows in, my vision tunneling with each labored breath.

A frustrated shout catches my attention, and I slowly look up at the head of command. His expression is taut as he glares at me. Each breath is a negotiation, and it takes a conscious effort to make out his words.

"Why isn't it working?!" If I had enough energy to laugh, I would have done so at the sight of his reddened face. The veins in his forehead look like they could explode, and his lip curls as he spews some vitriol in my direction.

Orobas' magic shielding me from them must extend to whatever they're trying to accomplish, and I silently thank God for his intervention.

Knowing why they can't use my blood makes me want to laugh even more.

But I can't.

Not now.

My heart rate slows as I fight losing consciousness—*fight letting go*—some part of me clinging to the desperate hope that Pai could come storming in to save me.

Vale's lip curls in disgust, and he murmurs something I can't make out. But when he steps forward, thrusting me back into the metal object with one hand, and Orobas' dagger held high in the other, it's clear what he intends to do.

Seconds stretch into an eternity as I picture Pai's kind eyes, his mischievous grin when he was up to something, and the softness in his face when the world faded away.

That's how I hope he remembers me.

Not the bloodthirsty assassin. Not the terrifying Harbinger.

Just Evelyn—the Evelyn who loved music and her team, but above all else, the Evelyn who loved *him*.

A dull, bitter pang of regret squeezes my chest when I think through how long I'd spent under their control, and oblivious to who or what he was.

Above all else, Pai was special. He cared far more than anyone ever should, and in the end, I can only pray that he finds some peace in all of this.

He was my—

He thrusts the dagger downward, and I don't register the pain as he buries the blade in my chest. My lungs seize, and I gasp short, jagged breaths as he glares into my eyes.

But I don't notice his hatred or vitriol when my vision is filled with the visage of the man who was willing to throw it all aside for me.

Pai.

Chapter 43

Scarlett

Pai's rage and desperation very well could match my own.

The tires skid to a stop as he pulls up to the security gate, lurching both of us forward. The soldier guarding the entrance steps closer, and before he can ask him to present his ID, Pai's hand snatches the man's neck.

I don't flinch when he snaps it suddenly, the crunch of vertebrae as his spinal cord severs. Neither the sound nor the sight bother me. In fact, if anything, I was more disappointed at the lack of blood spilled.

I'll get my fill soon enough.

It's only mere seconds later, as the body collapses to the ground that he's reaching over to hit the button and open the gate. The engine hums louder as the tires squeal before we're off once more, speeding toward the main building.

When we ascend the stairs to the entrance, the gem-inlaid dagger at my hip zaps my skin through the thin bodysuit, and I quickly move to unsheathe it.

The metal hums up my arm, and I grow increasingly restless—like the blade's thirst for death feeds into me at the contact. But what's more than that—as we walk through the entrance, with not a single soldier in sight yet—I can *feel* the presence of life nearby.

"Scarlett." My attention snaps to Pai, and he gestures past me down the hall. "I'll hit the barracks first to look for her, but you should head to the medical bay for supplies, then we'll hit the hidden wing."

I nod once. My grip tightens on the dagger as the nearby lives fade away slightly.

"Let's go, demon." I whisper and break into a jog, unsheathing a second dagger.

I don't bother to look back to see if Pai's behind me as I propel myself forward faster.

We're coming, Eve.

I can't deny the pit of dread in my gut at the thought of her, but I refuse to give in to despair. Because if something happened to the Harbinger, I plan to make them all pay.

We pass through open doors of offices as we head for the main administrative hall, but after the first couple that were empty, my trust in whatever power this dagger holds grew.

Now, I find myself solely focused on the tiny flickers of life in the main hall—the center point between the barracks and med bay. In fact, I'm so fixated on it as my legs pump hard beneath me, I don't notice the soldier at the end of the hallway, taking his gun out of his holster.

A thundering pop erupts first, and I drop instinctively as the shot goes wide. But it's the sudden crash behind me that jolts me in place, and I look back to see Pai with his fist against the sundered ground.

Flame curls around his head like a crown, illuminating his features as his gaze flicks to me. The power emanating from him, radiating in waves, is beyond suffocating.

That's when I realize Pai is an entirely different level of a demon than Oro or the others, and the dagger clutched in my grasp sings in my palm.

I felt the life force of the soldier as it disintegrated, and it doesn't take a rocket scientist to put two and two together.

"Any other fancy magic tricks up your sleeve, demon?" I ask, looking at the pool of crimson where the soldier once was. There's no body remaining. Just a giant puddle of blood in his place.

Pai stands to his full height, and I push to my feet with him.

"This isn't a game, Viper. Meet me at the wing. You have ten minutes."

Biting back my sarcastic retort, I nod. Arguing won't do us any good right now, and we both want the same thing.

"Ten minutes." I reaffirm before launching into a sprint again, the normal dagger in my left hand ready to fly as I head further down the hallway.

The entrance to the administrative hall is nearly empty, with two soldiers to my right that I dispatch with relative ease, only stopping to retrieve my dagger from one.

It takes two and a half minutes to get to the medical center, and another to fill a bag with supplies. With the strap across my chest, I'm about to head out of the room when I freeze.

My gaze slides to the lab on the other side of the hall—to the bottles behind the protective glass cabinet that hold the newest poisons they had been creating for me.

I spend a split second making my decision, and before I know it, I'm hauling open the doors, putting the pin into the access pad for my poisons.

For whatever reason, my pin still works, and I spend another minute distributing it to each of my sheaths, exchanging two of my blades for specially made ones that hold the poison along the edge.

By the time I'm done, and turning toward the hallway, I fall still. Without the gem-inlaid dagger in my hand, I'd lost sight of where any flickers of life had been.

Now, staring at four barrels pointed at me, I'm regretting not paying closer attention and letting my guard down. But I don't have time to curse myself for relying too much on the dagger when I notice one soldier growing antsy.

His eyes dart from me to my hands, his grip tightens, and I drop like a stone. Halfway to the ground, the first deafening shot goes off, then another, and I roll to the side, using a cabinet for cover.

I scramble to the opposite end as gunfire continues to ring out, glass chattering as debris flies into the air. With how many soldiers I'd seen, I try to count the shots as they ring out, but it's almost impossible.

It's not until they stop to reload that I jerk to the side and hurl a dagger at the closest target. While it's in flight, I grab another blade and hurl it at the next as a bullet whizzes past me.

The cracks of gunfire ring out before I realize one grazed me, and I duck back down as the sharp snap burns against my skin.

I've been shot enough to know that it's superficial, but still too close for comfort.

Grabbing the stool next to me, I lift it high for a split second as more shots slam into it. Even with the chair raised for a heartbeat, they hit it twice as the legs vibrate in my hands, and I drop it to cover my head.

I'm in real trouble here.

There's a reason the saying exists about bringing a knife to a gun-fight.

I'm near certain that I took two of the four out, so I grab the stool and slide to the edge. Tossing it where the gunshots came from, I dive out from my hiding place. My free hand snatches a shard of glass on the ground, hurling it at the first target I see.

I'm three steps out when I realize more had joined them, and I just make it to the closest soldier as the others raise their weapons.

My heart thrashes, and every second lasts an eternity and the air in front of me shimmers. Flashes of light from the barrels flare out as my eyes squeeze shut, and shots ring in the air.

This is it. The moment I knew would always come.

Something slams into me, forcing me back, and my eyes snap open again. A tattooed neck and dark hair fill my vision as more gunfire erupts.

Orobas.

I'm not sure when his arms had encircled my shoulders, but he hugs me tighter to him as each bullet hits his body.

No, not him too.

We already lost Thal, and might lose Eve.

But **Oro**? I won't let these demons take him too.

The gem-inlaid dagger in my hand burns hot as its power extends all directions like life-seeking missiles. Two more shots go off as it reaches each soul, and a surge of energy bursts from where we stand. Chairs, beakers, and everything in between are thrown from us and into the walls. The dagger's power shatters glass all around—the room shudders as various items fall from nearby ledges.

Tucked tightly into his chest, I peer over his shoulder, but see no one left standing behind him.

And instead of gunfire, all around us is silence.

"Oro? Are you okay?" I whisper, my heart in my throat as I look for wounds.

"I'm fine, Scarlett." He says in a low voice, but he doesn't release me from his grip. "The hell were you thinking?"

My eyes widen. "They have Evelyn. They'll kill her."

He says nothing, his jaw tightening as I fall still.

For a moment I wonder if he could have known all along, but there's no way.

Right?

"We need to stop them, Oro." I whisper. "I'll patch you up, but we have to find her."

"I'm fine, Scarlett."

"But you were shot—"

"I am not injured."

"I don't... I don't understand." I murmur, my fingers finding the countless holes and tatters at the back of his suit.

He steps aside and looks at the bloody heap of soldiers a few feet away, surrounded by bullet casings. "It appears the dagger has more than one use. When you reaped their souls, the blade answered your will as you satiated its blood thirst."

I look down at the weapon in my palm—the rubies seeming to shine more brightly than before.

The effortless way it took these lives, and the sheer force of power it showed...

The lump in my throat grows, and I slide the dagger into its sheath.

"I'll figure out a way to thank it later, but we need to find Eve." I whisper.

He nods cautiously in response. "And if we're already too late?" He asks softly, and my chest squeezes to the point of pain.

"We won't be." I say, snagging two daggers from fallen soldiers and sheathing them.

We can't be too late.

Chapter 44

Scarlett

It's been more than 10 minutes.

By the time we found the utility closet, Pai was nowhere to be seen, but when we saw a single pair of bloody footsteps that disappeared beyond the bare wall, we knew he'd gone in alone.

The door whirs shut behind us, and I break out into a sprint, following the footprints down the long hallway. After seeing Pai use his abilities earlier, I shouldn't be concerned about him walking into what could be a trap.

But I am.

Truth be told, there's been a cloud of impending doom hanging over me all night.

I dread what this means for us.

For Eve.

The hallway continues for what feels like a lifetime until we get to a dead end. Crimson covers the elevator button, and I press it hurriedly before looking at Oro.

"Can't you just teleport us or something?" I ask impatiently, but he shakes his head.

"Teleporting to you used the last of the minerals in the amulet. Even if I wanted to, I couldn't summon another portal." He says grimly. "Besides, they have this entire wing warded against teleportation, it seems." He adds, his gaze distant as if he can feel them.

"Do you think they're okay?" I ask. The words left my lips faster than I could stop them, but I can't take them back now, so I just hold my breath and wait.

Oro's crimson gaze falls to the ground, and he shakes his head. "I hope so, Scarlett..."

I hear the words he leaves unspoken. They carry in the air between us and hang like daggers, ready to fall and run me through at any moment.

A low chime signals the doors opening, and my eyes widen at the blood-soaked tile beyond.

Clearly, Pai met resistance, but by the looks of it, it didn't last long against him.

My feet slip as I step inside, grimacing at the sheer amount of it.

"Pai couldn't have had a cleaner power?" I mumble, pressing the button as Oro moves to stand beside me.

"This is tame, actually." He sighs. "But I worry that he's going to catch Azrael's attention if he continues this way. Eve would never forgive him if he died in all of this."

I know he's right, but I can't help but commend his viciousness all the same.

Another low chime brings my attention front and center as the doors open, but before I can leave, Oro grabs hold of my arm.

"If he's still fighting—"

"I'll take over." My hand brushes his, and I search his concerned crimson gaze. "I won't let him die, Oro."

His eyes flutter, and he leans down to press a kiss to my lips. "Strike fast, little Viper."

And with that, I launch down the hall with more urgency than ever.

Blood covers the ground, with a single set of footprints trailing through it, but judging by the shouting up ahead, I'm clearly not too late.

I've just crossed a four-entrance intersection when I see Pai up ahead. Shots erupt, bullets pelt the wall in front of me before I see a handful of soldiers fall to the floor, exploding into a splatter of blood.

Within seconds, I've unsheathed the dagger, and it burns hot as Oro's words rattle against every corner of my mind. There's nothing to say that the way I'm about to use this weapon right, but it seems like it might very well understand intention.

So I bring my arm across my body and snap it toward the closest soldier. The vibrations from the dagger hum as it hurtles through the air at them. I'm not ready when the blade buries into the militant's throat, and the same shockwave I'd felt in the labratory tremors all the way to entrance of a pavilion of some sort. As the man sputters, every other body in my sight drops like a stone.

From the room beyond, more soldiers hurry toward us as Oro grabs Pai and throws him to the ground.

"They have her, Oro!" Pai bellows, but I'm still sprinting for the dagger as the new hostiles raise their weapons.

Each long stride to the corpse is an eternity, and with every lungful I wonder if I'll make it as barrels take aim. I dive and grab the fallen soldier's arm, my free hand on the hilt of the dagger as I haul the body over me. Bullets rain down just as another swell of power radiates from the hilt up the length of my arm.

That's when I feel it.

The dagger sings as it pinpoints each living body nearby. Blood soaks into my bodysuit, clinging to my hair and skin as the dead soldier absorbs two shots.

"Feed me your blood."

The voice hums in tune with the dagger's vibrations, and an ounce of trepidation hits me when I realize what it's requesting.

"The meat shield won't last long. Bind us or die."

Another two shots hit the body, with one bullet exiting the other side and cracking against the floor.

Shit.

I know this could be a bad idea. Hearing a dagger's voice in my mind is one thing, but listening to it is probably not what I should be doing. But Orobas didn't stop me when he knew I had it.

Another bullet hits the floor beside me, and I quickly slice the bloodied blade across my right palm. When I grab the handle with my newly cut hand, the world around me falls still.

The hallway pulses, and my ears ring. Vibrations that had once echoed from my palm to my shoulder have stretched through my limbs. The energy pulsating into me is restless, hungry and endless. The dagger might have cut me open, but now raw power bleeds from the handle.

"Now, we hunt."

I feel the dagger's presence. Its power. Its **thirst**.

Throwing the body aside, it goes further than expected, and each second stretches as the militia take a single step back.

But I'm already on my feet. Crimson covers my body from head to toe as I skid to a stop in front of the first one. As I slam the blade into the soldier's chest, their reactions are delayed as gazes start to follow my movement.

Each life between me and the auditorium winks out, and I focus on the seven in the center of the giant room.

The thought that one of them could be Eve sends a dangerous surge of hope through me.

That thrusts me into action.

My strides are long and purposeful until I breach the main tunnel opening, seeing Commander Vale standing shoulder to shoulder with the others. They scowl in my direction, but I know the moment they see me.

The flicker of fear, terror or horror is clear in their expressions as I step out from the dark. I know what I look like to them, and every part of me relishes it.

Blood sticks to my skin, coating it and my hair that's fallen on either side of my face. My lightweight bodysuit has gained a few pounds from the essence that's seeped into it, squelching with each step.

Right now, I look all too much like the Wraith they created.

A true demon.

"You think this changes anything?" Commander Vale spits. "There are thousands more where they came from!"

I tilt my head to the side. Even with how loud his voice projects, there's an edge to it that's deliciously satisfying.

"Where is she?" I growl, glaring at the commander who gave us all those orders—sent us on all those missions.

He's the one responsible for Grizz and Mako.

He made us murder all those innocents.

"You mean the Harbinger?" He sneers and steps to the side.

I fall still at the sight of a bloodied and bruised Evelyn behind him. Her glazed-over eyes stare at nothing, with a pool of blood under her.

The blade buried in her chest isn't what sends me over the edge.

No, it's the dagger's power that reaches her, and finds nothing that makes my vision turn red.

Can you heal her? Bring her back? Whether because of the binding between us or my doubt, I already know the answer when it responds.

"Death is irreversible."

Something inside of me fractures. Even though I knew it, it doesn't sting any less.

"Well?" Commander Vale smirks cruelly, and I stalk forward until we're chest to chest.

The others don't move, but I feel their fear, smell it on the air. It's a pungent scent that I would gladly cause for the rest of eternity.

But I know Oro is holding Pai back, and he won't be able to forever. The last thing Eve would want is for Pai to die because of his rage.

Oro was right about that.

Placing my hand on Commander Vale's chest, his eyes roll back, and I feel his life flow into me. The others fall to the ground as the dagger tears the soul from their bodies, but I drain Vale slowly.

His skin wrinkles, his eyes become sunken, and he gasps for air. Within seconds he collapses to his knees, and I hear footsteps come to an abrupt stop behind me.

"Eve!"

Pai's voice cracks, and I withdraw my hand from the commander's chest, keeping him an inch from death. I see Pai take Eve's head in his hands as he sobs.

His shoulders shake, and he presses his forehead to hers, whispering things I can't quite make out. But I don't need to.

The love he held for her—I know it.

I know it because not only did I hold love for her, but I know how I would feel if it were Oro with a knife buried in his chest.

Pai's shuddering slows, and he turns to look at the head of command. The violence in his expression makes me glad I halted bringing the Vale past the point of no return.

As if intrigued by the promise of suffering, the dagger pulsates, stirring the dirt and dust around us as the commander suddenly ages backward.

Wrinkles fill out, his normal pallor returns, and the dark bags under his eyes lighten.

*"**Death** is irreversible."*

Pai slowly rises to his feet, standing tall, and as the Vale gargles, the voice reverberates in every corner of my mind. The dagger sings in approval as blood vessels in his eyes burst. The whites of his irises turn red, blue and purple, bruising blooms across his skin, and his nose bleeds.

The dagger hums against my palm, working to undo the harm Pai caused the asshole, if only to extend his suffering.

"You will not live to regret the day you took her from me," Pai says in a low voice, and I feel Orobas at my back, his arm snaking around my waist.

The commander chokes and sputters blood as it streams from his mouth.

"I promise you, I will find her someday, but not before I bleed every one of you dry." He wraps his hand around the Vale's throat, and squeezes. "Bring that message to your false god and tell him I'm coming for him."

Pai's lip curls, and the flames in his crown burn brighter as the body in front of him explodes. Crimson flies outward, coating Pai and splattering me where I stand.

"I was wondering when you'd finally grow a spine." A deep voice catches my attention, and our heads snap toward the sound.

A man draped in robes of darkness stands near the wall, his bright blue eyes almost white as he glances between us. When he steps closer, the shadows at his back billow out, creating what could only be broad wings of smoke.

Like an angelic specter made of night itself.

The dagger pulsates, its power extending toward the newcomer tentatively. The moment it reaches him, his eyes flick to mine.

"Aetheris chose well." He says softly, his dark hair shifting as he turns to look at Orobas. "Another daevari?"

"Yes. Any idea why six daevari have been born within twenty years of one another?"

Six?

The newcomer shakes his head. "Too many are missing to know the answer."

"Bring her back, Az."

He doesn't mean Az as in Azrael, does he?

The demand makes my eyes widen, and I watch Pai push to his feet to glare at the newcomer. "Bring her back."

Azrael shakes his head. "You know I cannot, brother."

Pai lunges forward, but Azrael's shadows dissipate into nothing only to reappear a few feet further back.

"I cannot remain here." He says, his attention turning to Orobas. "They seek my power, so my presence is nothing more than a visage until it is safe to return."

"Is that the reason for your absence, then?" Oro asks, and Azrael's gaze drops.

"Stolas put us all at risk summoning me for his not-so-mortal woman. They have a power that I've never seen before in the years of my creation. It is dark, **dark** magic, Oro—unlike anything we've seen. And if they were to catch the angel of death..."

Pai curses loudly. "So what, we wait for them to destroy every-thing?"

"Not quite." Oro says, his grip tightening on me. "Seir and Vas-sago suspect that Eve's transition was necessary. Like our own Tro-jan horse."

My eyes widen, and my blood freezes in my veins.

He knew.

"Death is irreversible, daevari." The voice reminds me, and I'm about to snap back at it when it adds onto its previous statement. *"Fate is inevitable."*

I want to tell it that fate can fuck off, but Pai catches me off guard as he storms toward us.

"You **knew** she'd die this whole time?" The rage and pain in his expression is a punch to the gut, and nausea roils my stomach.

"No," Oro says, his warmth at my back an odd reassurance. "But I had to consider the possibility, and what the future would hold if she did. We took every precaution, Pai. She's not transitioning blind. She will remember everything, all her training, us, the reason she passed on and the events that led up to it."

"She better fucking not be going in blind." He snarls, and Azrael's shadows flicker. "Or else it will be *your* head on a fucking pike."

My body pulses at his threat, but it's Azrael that interrupts us. "I need to return, but I'm thankful to see Aetheris in good hands." He says with a nod. "She will serve you well."

Chapter 45

Scarlett

Ten months later...

"Are you certain you want to do this?"

Orobas' crimson eyes darken, and he chuckles. "I'm going to pretend you didn't just ask such a ridiculous question."

To me, it doesn't seem outlandish. I mean, sure, I'd find him in every lifetime, but to know this demon feels this way about me?

Well, I'd say pinch me if I weren't sure he'd actually do it.

He must realize I'm not convinced, because he steps in close, invading my space as he searches my eyes. "Your heart doesn't scare me away, Viper. And I see your violence for what it is. I do not wish to be in a world without you and your fangs in it. Allow me this honor."

His conviction makes my chest squeeze painfully, and I nod. "Okay."

He reaches over to Aetheris and places the blade in our palms. The metal hums quietly between us as he wraps a loose cloth around our joined hands. When his voice fills the air, murmuring in a language I can't understand, Aetheris pulsates. He squeezes, and I follow suit, feeling the blade bite into my skin.

Our blood mixes, and power swells between us in waves until crimson soaks the cloth wrapped around our hands. When Oro finishes chanting, his expression is soft, and my heart clenches in my chest.

"So that's it, then? It's done?"

His lips twitch, and he nods. "It is not a difficult binding spell, but it is one that has much more significance than anyone thinks."

Considering everything we've been through, it means even more.

In the past ten months, Oro helped pull strings to appoint the right heads of command to the base we'd taken out, and he's spent most of his time making sure no actual demons slip through.

Last I'd heard, Omen was giving Caass a run for his money, and he's still trying to domesticate her to this day. Being human, the manipulation she'd endured was nearly impossible to undo, but he's been very consistent with his efforts.

No one has seen Pai since Eve died. He said he was going to find Samael and begin his search for her before leaving the auditorium.

Beyond the ritual we'd just done, Aetheris was quiet once Azrael left. I guess the battle satiated her bloodlust as much as it did mine.

Orobas presses a kiss to my forehead before pacing to the door. "I'll get Ishari for your movie night." The way he says it is mocking, so I stick my tongue out at him.

He just laughs and leaves down the hallway, his footsteps fading as he gains distance. Wind howls outside the window, and I release a long sigh as I walk over to look at the lawn below.

My gaze lands on a man in a dark suit standing by the treeline. His hands sit comfortably in his pockets and even from here I can see his light grey eyes that pin me in place.

On instinct, I tap into Aetheris' power, feeling each life form within the building and surrounding it. But when it extends close to the stranger, it bounces off an invisible shield and my heart stutters.

The longer I stare at him, the more my eyes burn, and when I finally blink, he's gone.

Something tells me this war is far from over.

Evelyn

I never thought dying would be so comfortable.

At least, I think I died.

The darkness surrounding me is suffocating, like at any moment it could encircle my limbs and drag me into its depths. Only the faint light in the distance keeps my focus, and I slowly make my way toward it.

At first, my feet dragged along the invisible ground, but each step feels easier than the last, like I'm shedding some unseen weight, and I pause.

How did I even get here?

My shadowed palms still look normal, if not slightly pale. The soft white material hugging my bodice flows to the ground, without a thread out of place. The silken robe is hardly noticeable with each step as it brushes against my skin.

*Wait, how **did** I get here?!*

I come to a stop, wracking my brain for a memory—any memory—but nothing comes.

Panic wells in my chest as my hands tremor.

Okay, breathe.

Start basic.

What's my name?

Why can't I remember my name?!

.... Find out what happens to Evelyn, in Wings of Doubt, book one of the Eclipsed Souls serries, coming soon.

Acknowledgements

Once again, a huge thank you to Amanda Dumky for the gorgeous cover. I will forever appreciate your immense talent more than you will ever possibly know.

A huge thank you to my husband, who supports all my chaotic hobbies, endeavors and passions without a second thought. I love you to the moon and back. In all the romances I write, there's always so many layers of the devotion and undying love that you surround me with that inspires these connections, and I will never take that for granted.

Thank you to my street team for being so supportive, hyping me up even when I was lost in the sauce, and always bringing excitement to my life. You are all beautiful humans and I cannot tell you how thankful I am to have you all in my life.

Lastly, much like with my Unbroken series, thank you to all the readers who decided to give this new series a chance. I can't promise it's the most well written, or well written at all... but I, as with many authors, put a piece of myself into my work, and taking the time to read it... well that may be the best gift of all.

It's just my hope that you enjoyed it, even if only for a moment before you move on to your next adventure.

Other Works by Aella C Grey

The Unbroken Series

Shadows of Dusk (Unbroken Book 1)

Light of Dawn (Unbroken Book 2)

Prince of Hell Series

Summoned (Prince of Hell Book 1)

Barred (Prince of Hell Book 2)

Convalesced (Prince of Hell Book 3)

Syndicated (Prince of Hell Book 4)

Classified (Prince of Hell Book 5)

Eclipsed Souls Series

Wings of Doubt (Eclipsed Souls Book 1)

Obsidian Flames (Eclipsed Souls Book 2)

Ascent of the Fallen (Eclipsed Souls Book 3)